The Other Side of the Clouds

by j. l. virtanen

© 2016 j. l. virtanen

For Lisa and Liliana

Prologue

Jacy Morgan never did forget the day she died. She never dwelt on the minor statistics like the exact time of day, or the actual date of her demise. Jacy instead preferred to focus on the unseasonably warm March weather, the wisps of clouds that streaked the spring sky, and the pain, oh Buddha, the pain. Not the pain of her death, mind you. That pain either was so quick it was an incidental experience or maybe it didn't even exist at all.

No, the pain Jacy recollected stemmed from the fact that she, a happy, 33-year-old Canadian lady, was *extremely* pregnant. At 11:34 AM PST, March 29, 2013, after an early morning of waddling around doing basic chores, tidying, dusting, and for Christ's sake why can't Beau hit the goddamned laundry hamper, her morning became one of brutal contractions. She and her husband, Beau with the errant laundry basket shot, exited their cute rancher that Jacy adored and Beau tolerated and hustled down the cement walkway to the purple Toyota that Beau loved and Jacy loathed.

"It's all good, baby. The hospital knows we're coming," Beau spoke in what he thought was a soothing voice but in reality Jacy found it annoying.

Jacy admonished herself as Beau raced around to the driver's side. She loved Beau with all her heart and he was doing everything right, but *Jesus God Almighty* did she ever hurt. Her pain rose to a volcanic level as Beau backed out of their driveway and onto the road. He reached over and gave Jacy's knee a reassuring squeeze before driving off.

Jacy attempted some rhythmic breathing, staring out the passenger side's window at what would've been a welcome and wonderful spring day in any other season of her life. Today, though, wasn't like any other season, year, decade, whatever. It was *"Holy motherfucker, is that kind of pain even legal?!"* kind of time.

"You're doing wonderful, baby, keep breathing slow and deep," Beau continued in that aggravating voice.

For a moment Jacy wondered if she had screamed her last thoughts aloud, but then realized she didn't really care if she had or not. She just wanted this baby, this beautiful, spectacular baby whom she already loved with every ounce of her being out of her. Jacy sighed and tried to banish negative thoughts from her pregnant brain as they passed the always busy Tim Horton's, which, for some reason, totally pissed her off.

Mercifully, Tim's faded from her view as they glided to a stop at the lit intersection of the Vancouver Island highway and 1st Avenue.

Jacy and Beau lived in the idyllic town of Ladysmith, British Columbia. Unfortunately, though, because of ever popular government cutbacks, Jacy couldn't give birth at the town hospital. They either had to go 25 minutes south to Duncan or 25 minutes north to Nanaimo to deposit their little bundle of joy.

For no particular reason, Jacy chose Nanaimo and Beau went along with her choice. It was a decision that Jacy never gave much thought to, even after her untimely demise. At the time it was an innocuous decision but one that would later tear Beau apart at the seams.

After an interminable red light that Jacy mostly thought happy thoughts, the light finally changed to green. They turned left onto the highway and kept a steady 10 clicks over the speed limit. Losing her battle in trying to be positive and ignore the excruciating convulsions of agonizing torture that were becoming more frequent, Jacy tried a new plan of attack.

Ahhh, that's it. Jacy tried focussing on the song the radio station was playing. Jacy thought of herself as a bit of a connoisseur when it came to music. She never played music herself, not really, anyways. She could strum a few three chord songs on her battered acoustic guitar around a campfire and would finger plunk on her electric piano now and then, but mostly she just loved and appreciated good music. Never one to follow Top 40 or opera, she had a pretty wide palate of musical tastes for most other genres. Beau used to razz her about her IPod that would have her personal favourite Steve Earle followed by an Eminem track trailed by Hank Williams III chased by KISS. Jacy would tease him back that he never listened to anything newer than 80's hair metal bands.

On this day, though, with Beau continuing to coo, Jacy cursing herself for ever discovering sex, and the pretty Vancouver Island landscape passing by, Jacy listened to the song crooning from the radio.

"This girl is on fiiiiirrreee….."

She was pretty sure it was an Alicia Keys or Rihanna song, and apparently the song's subject was about a girl being on fire, which seemed apropos as that's exactly how her groin felt. Jacy liked the song, though, so she leaned her head back into the head rest and tried to focus on the lyrics before another *Oh my God that freaking hurts* contraction came on.

Clenching her body tight as if this would ward off the pain, Jacy ground her teeth a second too late as a moan escaped her lips. Beau tightened his squeeze on her knee.

"Just breathe baby, nice and deep, just…." Jacy tuned him out and did her utmost not to squeal like a pig.

Jacy's head lolled to the left and she saw they were about halfway to Nanaimo. They made their way through Cassidy, a rural area that squatted between Ladysmith and Nanaimo. It would always burn Jacy later on that of all the places she had to die, it was in Cassidy. When she was growing up, Jacy's friends and she joked that if Canada was a body, Nanaimo was the shoulder, Ladysmith the elbow, so consequently Cassidy was the stinky armpit.

At this point of her journey to the hospital, of course, Jacy had zero idea she was about to perish. All's she knew was that she was never going to have sex again and *why wouldn't Beau drive goddamned faster so she could put an end to this lancinating experience?!*

By now the song had ended and an oldie by the Backstreet Boys came on. That was enough for Jacy. She was *not* going to go through this physical pain while "I want it, thaaaaaattt waaaaayyy" assaulted her ears.

Jacy leaned forward to change the station. This is just how these things go sometimes. Some people have a deep, almost religious moment. Others recall loved ones or treasured childhood memories. Some will have a natural inclination that something; it could be either good or bad, but they knew *something* profound was about to happen.

Others, like Jacy Morgan, a pregnant 33-year-old pretty Canadian woman, never ever did see or think or feel what was about to happen.

It was just BAM!!!!

Jacy was no more.

PART I

REBIRTH

Death is no more than passing from one room into another. But there's a difference for me, you know, because in that room I shall be able to see.

—Helen Keller

1

Maise Elantina rushed down the darkened pathway, muttering to herself. "Jesus fucking Christ, Flair, I can't believe what you've done this time."

Though she could barely see a few feet in front of her, Maise didn't worry of tripping, slipping, or plummeting off the pathway. This trail, one member of a numerous trail family meandering throughout the powerful redwoods and gallant Douglas Firs towering overtop her, was one of her favourite walking spots. She'd trekked and thought and pondered and travelled this trail for, well, forever.

Maise sighed. Why couldn't tonight's jaunt be like one of her normal ambles through the woods?

'Because of freaking Flair!' a voice bellowed from within her over-filled brain.

Maise sighed again, but this time it was more to shush the voice within her head than it was out of exasperation. While there was more than a good chance Flair was behind that day's cluster-fuck, she still didn't know that was 100% true. It may have been 99.99% true, but Maise did not get where she was by ignoring even a hundredth of a per cent on anything.

Hell, Maise didn't even know for sure where Flair was right now, but she had a pretty good idea. Rounding a soft bend in the trail, she headed off the trail and waded through the thicket running alongside her. Pushing, ducking, stepping over, belly crawling, she finally made it to the opening where she deducted Flair would be.

And there he was, sitting on a gnarled log, head hung low, navel gazing. Maise allowed herself a simple smile. This was *definitely* not what Flair was usually up to in the clearing.

Shaking her head, she approached him. Flair knew she was there. They had been partners for so long that they knew each inside out and upside down. But tonight, Maise recognized, was one of the many reasons she had broken off their partnership. Not that she relished these reminders. Flair's mistakes more often than not had a calamitous effect not just on her, but countless others, as well.

Flair barely raised his dishevelled, blond haired head. "Maise…"

"No," she interrupted him. "My turn first."

Flair shrugged one shoulder and returned his gaze downwards.

"Do you have *any* idea what this will cause, Flair? Gravigo is going to blow his fucking top, and you remember what happened the last time something like this happened. Jesus fuck, Flair…."

Maise restrained herself, for two reasons mostly. One, she hated raising her voice, even to a motherfucker like Flair. And two….

"But *nothing* like this has ever happened, right?"

Maise looked at Flair. "Hmmm?"

Flair looked at her with ice blue eyes. "That's what you were about to say, weren't you? First you got upset with yourself for raising your voice, and then you realized we are now in entirely uncharted new waters here. I mean, shit, we've had some heavy storms to deal with before, but they'll all seem like a spring shower compared to what this fucking hurricane will cause."

Flair stood and slowly moved towards her. Maise shook her head.

"Why'd you do it Flair? Why? Especially to her? You *know* what she meant to Grav…."

"I didn't do it," Flair hissed.

"Oh, come on, Flair, do you really think I'm that…"

Flair had now closed the distance half-way to her. "Stupid? Of course not."

Maise felt a twang of vexation inside her. At one time she supposed it might have been cute how she and Flair could finish each other's sentences, but those days were long, long, long gone.

Flair was now within ten feet of her. "I swear, Maise, I did not have anything to do with tonight. Hell, why do you think I'm here?"

Maise nodded inwardly, now understanding what that one hundredth per cent of a doubt was. If Flair was behind what happened, he wouldn't be here, that's for sure. He'd probably be in The Lair with his partying henchmen and big titted strippers celebrating this moment while putting the next stages of their plan into motion. Today's fiasco wouldn't, by its solitary self, be much cause for catastrophe. Put it together with a wild and intricate web of deceit, concoction, counter-punches and vengeance; well, the result could and probably would be nothing short of calamitous.

"I mean, hell, I don't relish what the aftershocks of this will be, but I could give two shits about Gravigo and his little bitch. I'm concerned about how this went down without me knowing a thing about it."

Now this was ringing more true to Maise's intellect and hunch. This is the Flair she knew, hated, and well, respected.

"Do you know who it was?" she asked.

Flair gave her that one shouldered shrug again. "Maybe."

Maise decided not to push it. The answer would be known soon enough. Her concern was if this thing erupted like a volcano. Shit, up until now, even with all that had gone right and wrong, the waters remained relatively calm. But with this? Flair was right about one thing. They were definitely in unknown territory now. There was only one thing she could do.

"How can I help?"

Flair was now directly in front of her. "You need to be the bridge between Gravigo and me until we sort this out."

"We?" Maise hesitated here, unsure how deep she wanted to wade into this cesspool. She and her group had nothing to do with this; they were free and clear.

Flair smirked, as only Flair could smirk. "Well, until *I* sort out my end of things. But make no mistake, Maise. We all need to be in this together, or all this?" Flair swept his arm at their surroundings.

"All this will be scorched to the ground. And I'm not talking about this clearing or your favourite thinking trails. I'm talking about *everything*."

Maise didn't argue. She knew Flair wasn't exaggerating. "Okay, I'll do my best. We need to get on this now, though."

Flair nodded, turning his attention to the sound of someone traipsing through the underbrush. Maise followed his gaze and noticed The Bam Slicer step into the clearing. If he was surprised Maise was here with Flair, he did a great job in hiding it.

"Well, what did you find out?" Flair was never one for small talk.

The Bam Slicer raised his eyebrows. "I'm afraid I've got some bad news, Boss."

2

When Jacy died, an odd thing happened. She didn't hear any harps, see any great light, or any other stuff that she perceived may happen when one dies.

What Jacy did do was swim. Not swimming in the conventional sense of the word, but swim was the best word she could find to describe what she did. Jacy drifted in an amazing substance that was clearer than glass and lighter than air. She floated, dove, did clumsy somersaults. She could give one tiny flutter kick and float for what seemed like a billion miles, or she could paddle with all her strength and not travel an inch. Distance and time ceased to be linear or relevant. Jacy was in that most elusive place of all—she was allowed to simply be.

So as Jacy swam, she remembered and lived any part of her 33 years she lived on Earth that she wanted to. The good, the bad, the happy, the sad, as a good folk song may say. Jacy swam and remembered. She remembered and swam. She relived her first date with Beau at Alexandra's restaurant in Nanaimo and the fumbling make-out session in the back of his car after dessert. She touched on the day her mother drove down the driveway when she was 7 years old, abandoning her to her grandparent's care. She laughed happily at the Saturdays her and her grandfather spent at Sandown Raceway, betting on the horses.

Jacy swam and swam and swam and remembered and remembered and remembered.

Her first of five times seeing Steve Earle play live. Scoring the winning basket on her School District #68 Champs Grade 6 basketball team. Missing the tag at the plate in the B.C. Championship game in her last year of competitive softball.

Jacy smelled her grandma's oh-so-tasty country style ribs. She touched here and there on her high school years, but there weren't a whole lot of great memories to re-hash there. Her grandfather walking her down the aisle and shaking hands with Beau.

As Jacy swam and relived all parts of her life, she could hear sounds; beautiful celestial sounds she never knew existed. Sometimes the sounds were clear as mountain air and other times grimier than tar sands, but they were always there and they were always beautiful.

Somewhere on this transcendental journey she was on, Jacy felt her spirit expand. There was no other way to explain it. It was like she was an anomalous puzzle, and she felt the incongruous pieces click together seamlessly.

As she swam, she distanced herself from the events of her own life to…to…to where? She felt the fear of a small child playing in the sewers of Mumbai. She understood the odium of captives at Guantanamo Bay. She discerned the hopelessness of lost souls in the innumerable ghettos of the world's cities. Warsaw. Detroit. Vancouver.

Jacy swam and swam and swam and felt and felt and felt.

Hookers strolling through the streets of Buenos Aires. Children swinging on swings in the warm spring of Helsinki. CEOs of multinational companies seated at boardroom tables.

Click. One more piece. Click. Another. On and on and on and more and more and more.

Jacy sensed the peculiar mosaic take shape. She felt the wonderful, beautifully ugly tapestry meld into an intricate fresco more breathtaking than anything she had ever seen. She understood the significance of what she was experiencing. Everything, everybody, from the enslaved to the free to the newborns to the elderly, *all* was connected.

But it was so much more than that, she realized as she felt every glow of love, every barb of hatred. It was so much wonderfully more than that.

A blossoming hydrangea in Canada shared roots with giant Amazon trees. Swirly, white Virginian clouds were sisters of London's fog. A poodle in Seattle was akin to a naked mole rat in Jakarta.

This curious journey led Jacy to the realization of something that she and every single other habitant in the history of Mother Earth instinctively knew from birth but had allowed to be buried.

We are all linked, one way or another. I am you and you are me and we, we are one. All is connected.

And then, all of a sudden, after all the swimming and remembering and feeling and knowing and unawareness of what was up or down or sideways, Jacy felt herself rising, rising, rising. The angelic noise rose in volume with her, then BOOM!

Nothing was the same for Jacy ever again.

3

Flair burst out the doors, then spun around. "Fuck that, and fuck you, Gravigo, you fat piece of scum-shit. You've gone *way* too fucking far this time!"

A few people were straggling around the lobby, rubbernecking at Flair. Flair glowered back.

"What the fuck are you looking at?" he snarled, causing the bystanders to scurry away. Flair shook his head in disgust, at them and at Gravigo's request.

Fucking Gravigo. Fuck him. Flair walked over to the floor to ceiling window and looked outside, but he wasn't really seeing anything. Trying to calm his raging thoughts, he practiced autogenic breathing, something Neva taught him that at first he thought was a bunch of bullshit but came to find it did help him sometimes. He breathed in for a four count, held it for a four count, and then exhaled for a four count.

Nope. Didn't help this time. He whirled to storm back into the room but was met by Maise Elantina who waited patiently for him outside the doors with The Bam Slicer.

"Your tantrums aren't helping, Flair," Maise raised her eyebrows as she spoke.

Flair rolled his eyes. "It's Gravi-fucking-go's unreal requests that are not helping here. Does he really think I'd agree to all of that shit?"

Maise shrugged. "Is what he's asking for that out of line? Consider the alternatives to what will happen if you don't give him what he wants."

Flair narrowed his eyes. "Maybe I don't want to consider the alternatives. Maybe I think we should just let the chips fall where they may."

"Are you really willing to gamble that uncertainty over this?" Maise Elantina half smiled at him. She would refresh Flair's memory that Flair recently asked for and received the exact same thing that Gravigo was requesting if she needed to, but for now, she would hold her tongue.

Flair sighed, returning his gaze out the window. Maise strode over and stood beside him. They remained in their own thoughts for a bit, before Flair finally broke the silence.

"Do you really think this is as far as he's willing to negotiate? Do I have any more wiggle-room?"

Maise shook her head. "I don't think so. I agree what he's asking for is a little unusual, but it kind of makes sense if you think about it."

Flair did think about that. "Jesus Christ, Maise, we had only one of them here since all this began, and now we have two more in such a short time? And look what happened to the first two. What a complete waste of energy that was."

"Don't go connecting dots that shouldn't be connected, Flair. Baz is Baz. He did what he did and he's paying for it. Lita has nothing to do with Jacy, you know that."

"And lucky for her. Lita's a fucking bitch."

Maise chuckled. "Actually, Lita is not a bitch whatsoever, but I'm not going to sit here and argue with you about that."

Maise turned so she was facing Flair. "Look, Flair, you asked me for help and this is the best I can do. Please try and think of this rationally. Gravigo is not asking for too much. You guys broke the rules."

"Buzzed Rottid broke the rules, and he's paying for it. I didn't do anything."

"Buzzed was one of your guys, Flair. You know how this works."

"But….ahhhh, fuck it. You're right, Maise. This isn't worth the hassle. Tell Chubby Wubby that since he doesn't give a shit about diluting the gene pool around this place, he gets the deal. But same rules for her as there was for Baz and Lita. We all get a chance at her."

Maise nodded. "Fair enough, Gravigo wasn't asking for the process to be changed. He'll go meet her today, and then you will get your opportunity to meet with her. Then me."

Flair looked deep into Maise's eyes. "I think this is a huge fucking mistake, Maise, I want you to know that."

"No," Maise said, "the blunder is what happened to Jacy. This decision is our best available attempt to rectify that."

Maise returned to Gravigo to tell him the news.

4

Jacy broke the surface to a crescendo of lights and sounds. Attempting to gather her wits and bearings, Jacy treaded safely in the substance she was in. She gazed at the crystal walls that seemed to touch the sky.

What the hell?

Meandering in a lazy circle, Jacy was awed by the azures, teals, and violets that flickered through the amazing walls. As each colour sparkled, an exquisite, unknown musical note accompanied it.

Jacy treaded and listened and looked. A deep, surreal feeling threatened to blanket her. When she looked down the bottom had no end, and when she looked up the walls seemed to stretch forever. She was in the middle of everything and nothing. She wondered if she should go back the way she came.

She never got the opportunity to try, though. The curious voice of an eight-year-old boy caught her attention.

"Hey, Lady? Up here."

"Huh?" His voice startled Jacy. "Who's there?"

"I'm Dougie. And I'm way up here. Behind you."

Jacy treaded a slow 180 degrees, squinting upwards at his voice. She couldn't see anybody. "Dougie? I…I can't…"

"Swim straight to the wall," Dougie interrupted her. "You'll see the stairway when you get closer."

Jacy looked hard at the wall fifteen feet in front of her. She could see nothing but sheer crystal wall. "Dougie, I don't see…"

"Trust me, Lady, it's there. Please. You've *got* to come see this."

Shrugging and raising her eyebrows, Jacy followed Dougie's instructions. It wasn't until she was inches from the wall that she could decipher the stairway. She reached out and touched the smooth first step. Taking a deep breath, Jacy hoisted herself out of the water and into a sitting position.

"Dougie…" she began to call out but her breath caught in her throat. Her hands rested on her stomach. On her *flat* stomach. Jacy was no longer pregnant.

Jacy raised a hand to stifle the wailing cry that tickled the top of her throat. My baby! Where the fuck is my baby?!

"Lady? You okay?"

Jacy barely won the battle with her escaping cries. She took a few deep breaths to try and keep her world from spinning from its axis.

"Lady, are you…"

"Where are we, Dougie?"

Jacy could almost hear the shrug of his shoulders in Dougie's voice. "I don't know, but you really need to come up here and see this."

Jacy rose on shaky knees. Strangely, an old Hunter S. Thompson quote sprang to her muddled mind.

Buy the ticket, take the ride.

Jacy stared at the spiralling stairs that led up, up, up. A vague sense of clarity began to break through the jungle vines of her mind. *Find out where you are first. That'll help you find your baby.* Jacy nodded in agreement with this thought and began to ascend the crystal stairs, running her hands along the sheer walls as she rose higher. Around and around she went, on and on and on. Finally, the stairs stopped spiralling. She now looked up a straight flight of stairs. And there, for the first time, she laid her eyes upon Dougie.

He was an ordinary, average eight-year-old boy who wore cut-off jeans and a Dropkick Murphy's t-shirt. His blond hair was mussed and he wore a goofy, crooked grin.

"Pretty cool, huh?" Dougie was vibrating with excitement.

"Pretty cool," Jacy answered as she started up the final stretch of stairs. "Not as cool as your t-shirt, though."

Dougie looked puzzled for a moment, and then looked down to see what he was wearing. He nodded in agreement. "Come on. You need to check this out."

Jacy lost sight of Dougie for a while but he soon came back into view. Dougie faced away from her, a terrific blue sky framing him.

"Dougie, where are we? What is this…"

Dougie looked at her from over his shoulder. "Just come up and see. You won't believe…hey, what's your name, anyways?"

"It's Jacy."

"Hurry, Jacy," Dougie looked away from her again. "You've got to come see this."

Jacy sighed and picked up her pace a bit. She had been wrong in her original estimation of how many steps there were in this final climb. She first thought there were thirty or forty, but now realized there were a few hundred. She was making progress, though, slowly getting closer to Dougie.

Jacy scaled the final dozen steps or so. "Dougie, maybe you should step back from that…"

Dougie turned his head and smiled that crooked smile of his.

"Bye, Jacy." Dougie stepped off the ledge.

5

Flair lazily watched a 38DD stripper work the stage in front of the many hooting members of The Skulls.

The Skulls. The *Skulls*. Just the name of his group, no, not just his group, the name of his *people*. The name never failed to give Flair a biting pang of joy. Every single member of The Skulls was a brother, sister, aunt, and cousin in spirit. And he was their leader. The head of the family. The Godfather.

In short, some would say Flair was the *man*, but in reality he was all that and more. A legend among men, a God and his underlings, take every cliché in the book and wrap them together in a larger than life package, and Flair would be the one standing there.

Smirking, he watched Sultana Yelp, a female Skull whom he knew quite personally, stand and bury her face between the dancer's massive breasts, causing even louder cheers. Flair took a long swig of his beer and tipped his bottle in toast and appreciation of Sultana's actions.

His eyes roamed over the rowdy room to his house band, the Ten Hep Kings, as they plowed through a swaggering version of Flair's favourite My Darkest Days song.

"She wraps her hands around that pole
She licks her lips and off we go
She takes it off nice and slow
That's porn star dancing…."

Flair's two table companions, Bait Tambit and Chainsaw Helms, sang gleefully along with the last line of the chorus before shooting shots of Don Julio Real. Normally Flair would be singing along with them, or he'd be joining Sultana in sampling the dancer's wares, but tonight Flair wasn't feeling quite up to his exuberant self.

"Gentlemen," he addressed his two cohorts. Chainsaw and Bait immediately gave Flair their full attention, as did any Skull Flair gave his attention to.

"Yeah, Boss?" they said in unison.

"The perfect vagina. Go discuss."

Chainsaw Helms and Bait Tambit stood, making their way to a table closer to the stage, animatedly discussing their thoughts on the shape, size, and design of their preferred female genitalia. Flair drained his bottle and gestured towards The Bam Slicer, who was standing by the bar. Bam approached.

Flair nodded at him when he got to the table. "Please, sit."

Flair waved over a naked waitress. "A beer for me, and…" he raised his eyebrows at The Bam Slicer.

"Same for me." The Bam Slicer's voice carried the rumble of a logging truck.

Flair looked at The Bam Slicer once the waitress departed to fetch their order. Normally, Flair never needed to start a discussion.

Most people, especially fellow Skulls, would be jabbering like old hens when in Flair's presence. He was unsure why this was, but it worked for him. Information was power, and here, well, power was everything.

"How have things been going for you?" Flair broke the silence.

"Busy, but nothing I can't handle," Bam shrugged.

Flair eyed Bam for a moment, then two, then longer. None of this ever worked with Bam, but Flair always tried.

"Buzzed?" Flair spoke the name that had given them fits the past while.

"Buzzed Rottid is ancient history. Fuck him."

The waitress arrived with their beers. Flair slowly ran his hand up the back of the waitress' legs and up and over her naked ass. She placed the beers on the table and stood patiently while Flair fondled her.

"Nice work," he nodded. "Your calves are a little muscular for my taste, though. Can you do something about that?"

"Of course, I can," their waitress smiled at him as she stood taller, thrusting her salacious breasts out. "I'll do it right after my shift. How do you like these?"

"Nice, very nice," Flair concurred. The Bam Slicer drank his beer in reticence. Flair waved the waitress off and looked at Bam for another long moment. Bam looked back.

"Well put. About Buzzed, I mean."

Flair cracked a smile at his own joke. Bam merely nodded.

Flair shrugged, sneaking a peek at the stage again. Sultana Yelp had now climbed the stage and sat down on the stripper's face. Flair watched for a moment before he moved his gaze back to Bam.

"Would you like Buzzed's former position?"

Flair almost saw the beginning of a smile on The Bam Slicer's face which would've been a foreign land for that grin. Bam regained his composure before that could happen, though.

"I would like that very much."

Flair smiled and raised his beer bottle to Bam's. Bam clicked his against Flair's. Flair immediately felt better. Not that he was concerned Bam was going to turn his offer down, far from it. Anybody in the Skulls would've chewed their own foot off to be offered Bam's recent promotion. The Bam Slicer was now the number two most powerful person in the Skulls.

Flair took a long swig of his beer. "Fantastic. Meet me here tomorrow at O-Nine hundred. We've got a lot of household business to attend to. Ever since Buzzed's fucking disaster movie I've been dealing with nothing else. Let's get caught up on things."

"I'll be here," The Bam Slicer stood.

"Before you go, go tell Sultana Yelp and that ripper who's eating her out to meet me in the clearing in a half hour."

"Sure thing," Bam departed.

Flair watched Bam approach the stage. He smiled. He knew he made the correct choice, but at one time Buzzed Rottid was the correct choice, too. Flair wasn't going to get torched a second time. He trusted Bam, but he'd keep a much closer eye on him than he'd done with Buzzed. The future of the Skulls, hell, the future of *everything*, depended on it.

6

"DOUGIE!" Jacy screamed as the little boy stepped off the ledge. Jacy had no idea how far from the ground they were, but she did know they were higher than Steven Tyler had ever been. Jacy scrambled towards the ledge, one hand still holding her non-pregnant tummy.

"Dougie?!" she called out, hoping against hope she'd find him sitting on another niche like she'd seen on countless Saturday morning cartoons. She could almost picture him, lying on his side while munching a carrot. "Eh, what's up, Jacy?"

As she made it closer to the edge, Jacy's breath hitched in her throat. They weren't as high as she had originally surmised they were. They were *higher*.

"Jesus, Dougie," she whispered as she peered over the edge. Nope. No secondary cartoon ledge with a carrot gnawing Dougie on it, either.

Movement on the faraway ground caught her eye. Jacy had to squint to see that far down. When she saw what she saw, she squinted even harder. There stood little Dougie, waving his arms wackily at her. She had no way of knowing for sure, but she was pretty sure he was grinning that crooked smile of his, too.

"Jesus, Dougie," she repeated, though not with the fear and alarm her voice held earlier. Now she spoke it out of awe.

Dougie continued to wave at her as he backed away from the cliff face. Jacy waved back enthusiastically. As she took in more of her surroundings, her breath caught in her throat for a second time.

"Wow," she whispered, standing to full height, her hand resuming the rubbing of her empty belly. Jacy stared at the sky, a brilliant blue.

Jacy pulled her gaze from the sky, soaking in the desert like terrain that was such a deep brown, it almost looked red. The burnt umber ground reached the horizon and beyond.

This is when Jacy first noticed the lines of people and other beings snaking along the ground. There were hundreds, no, thousands, maybe even millions of these lines. Some ran straight and true, others diagonal, some in crazy S shapes. What really caught Jacy's attention was the orderly chaos it seemed to possess. No matter how scattered or off course a line seemed to be, each single line seemed to move with a single minded determination.

"What the hell?" Jacy spoke to herself as she returned her attention to Dougie. He had made it to one of the lines. He stood there for a moment or two, then moved on to another one. He repeated this process forty-seven more times. On the forty eighth attempt, Dougie stood studying the line and in a blink of an eye he was gone, another link in a massive, marching chain.

Jacy was about to call out his name when she heard a splash from down below. Tearing away from the ledge, she returned to the top of the stairs and looked down at the pool she had recently surfaced from. She watched an elderly lady tread gentle water.

"Hello?" the lady called out. "Is anybody there?"

"Hi," Jacy startled the heck out of the poor lady.

"Who...who's there?"

"My name's Jacy, what's yours?"

"My name? It's...." the lady chuckled. "It's Margaret. My name is Margaret."

Jacy nodded at the lady's name. Did she know her name was Margaret? Jacy didn't know how she would know that, but somehow she thought she did.

"It's nice to meet you, Margaret. Come on up here. You really need to see this."

Jacy watched Margaret do the same treading circle she herself had done, what, 5 minutes ago? 16 hours ago? 297 days? Jacy shrugged, knowing somehow that not only did time not matter anymore, it didn't even exist.

"How do I get up there?"

Jacy smiled, jostled from her thoughts by the same query she asked Dougie. Jacy easily scouted out the stairs. "Go to the wall, 90 degrees to your right."

Jacy watched Margaret turn and strain to find the stairs. "Go on, the stairs are there. I'll see you up here."

Jacy left the puzzled Margaret and returned to the ledge. She stood tall and proud, one hand on her vacant stomach as she breathed the sweet air deep into her lungs and admired the beauty and grandeur around her. She watched the endless marching beings make their way to wherever it is they were going. She briefly wondered where Dougie was.

She heard Margaret making her way up the stairs. "Jacy?"

Jacy turned and smiled at the approaching Margaret. "What do you think, Margaret? Isn't this the most beautiful sight you've ever seen?"

Margaret's eyebrows drew in. "Where are we, Jacy? I'm so confused."

Jacy smile grew wider. "Don't be confused, Margaret. You'll figure it out."

Jacy turned and took in the majestic view once again. Breathing deep, she soon felt a wonderful feeling envelope her with arms of doubtless grace. Jacy knew what she was supposed to do.

"Can you help me understand where we are, Jacy? I'm…"

"Sorry, Margaret," Jacy murmured to the wind. There was somewhere she needed to go. It was her turn to step from the ledge.

And that was exactly what she did.

Jacy never knew what made her think it was a good idea to step off a cliff a billion feet in the air, and to be honest, she never put much thought into it later. It was just one of those things, like thinking of someone and that same someone phones a couple minutes later. It was something that merely happened. When she took that initial and fateful step, Jacy had no idea whether she'd plummet like a one ton safe or magically float like a duck's feather and touch light to the ground.

Neither happened.

Instead, Jacy's first step produced a gorgeous, long sprawl of glass stairs. The stairs were magnificent, so clear, and so fragile that if she'd thought about it, she may have been concerned whether they'd be able to hold her weight or not. She didn't think about that at the time, though, as she gracefully floated down the stairs like a goddess descending to her followers. Okay, maybe that's a bit of a stretch, but she did stride pretty confidently, still absentmindedly rubbing her empty stomach.

Just over halfway down, she stopped to look behind her. To her shock, no stairs were there. Not understanding, Jacy bent down and reached back to touch the stair she'd just stepped from.

Her hand swept through the warm air. There was nothing there.

Jacy moved quicker now, glancing back to notice the stairs disappeared underneath her feet. She had no idea if this crazy staircase was on time constraints or what, but she was betting with the house and hustled her ass to the bottom. Once her feet hit terra firma, she backed away from the cliff's face just in time to see Margaret's head poke over the edge.

"It's okay, Margaret," she said, knowing full well Margaret couldn't hear her. Jacy walked backwards, waving to her, her words probably dying a quarter of the way up. She did this until she finally saw Margaret return a feeble wave.

Satisfied, Jacy spun on the red ground and faced the crowds of wandering lanes. She noticed her hand was still doing small circles on her stomach. She stopped the circles, leaving her hand on her stomach. She took a deep breath.

"Okay, Jace, buy the ticket, take the ride," she gave herself a small pep talk, while asking herself one thing.

What the fuck was she supposed to do now?

7

Maise Elantina found her usual peace of mind as she wandered down her fourth favourite walking trail. She didn't understand why or what the criteria she used when she ranked her top 10 trails, much like she didn't comprehend the how's and why's of many things around here. This would come as a shocking surprise to many who knew her, and all who didn't.

This was because Maise Elantina was The Wise One, The One Who Knows All, The Princess of Perception. Maise had heard and laughed quietly to herself at all these titles. To be truthful, she found amusement in any and all labels.

Yes, while Maise Elantina may have found the sentimentality of denominations goofy, she sensed the enjoyment and an almost necessity others felt in all of it, so she kept her thoughts to herself.

This wasn't too difficult as she used words as economical as a cheap boss giving out pay raises. Not that she was as mute as The Bam Slicer, not even close. Maise just had that innate ability to project her words with an intuition that was as strong if not more powerful than the most eloquent spoken word. Most everyone knew what Maise Elantina desired before she had the chance to express it verbally.

She sighed, enjoying the solitude and the faraway birds whistling their lilting songs to all who took the time to listen. Maise embraced the hush in her surroundings; she felt she had talked more since Buzzed Rottid's already legendary stunt than she had since she'd first set step one in this place.

Buzzed Rottid. No matter what Buzzed did, Maise was unsure how she felt about his punishment. Maise Elantina disliked *any* type of punishment, but she understood the need for some type of penalty in this case. She was just unsure if this particular punishment was just or not. Maise had long struggled with the difference between justice and punishment, how close yet so very far away from one another the two often were.

But as in most things of this nature and others, Maise pontificated then let it go. What is, is. Things really were as simple as that. As she wound her way through the somber Dogwoods surrounding her, Maise Elantina noticed someone who was galaxies away from simple.

Hammer Coolie.

He was twenty yards or so in front of her and had just rounded a bend in the trail. Maise got but a glimpse of him, though she didn't even need that. She had that *feeling* since she began her solitary stroll.

Maise slowed for a moment, unsure if she wanted to disrupt her peaceful trek with a conversation with Hammer Coolie. It wasn't as if she didn't care for him. She liked him. Hell, she liked him more than she probably ought to. Maise was far from the only one who felt this way, that's for sure.

So that wasn't the reason she slowed her step just a tiny bit. Maise sensed Hammer Coolie a few times almost approaching her since the whole Buzzed Rottid fiasco, but he had yet to do it. Did she really want to get into this now?

Maise Elantina, without a mean feeling in her being, decided she didn't want to. It wasn't *him* she was avoiding; it was contact with anybody she was circumventing. That was enough for Maise to not feel remorseful and to turn and walk back the way she came.

Of course, it was no surprise to her who she bumped into when she rounded the bend.

"Hi Maise," Hammer Coolie smiled that wickedly attractive smile of his. "If I didn't know any better, I'd think you were avoiding me."

Maise Elantina grinned at Hammer. There once was a time where fresh faced lies would've slithered their way through her lavender lips as smooth as Motown jazz, but that time had long ago passed.

"I guess you don't know any better then, because yes, I was avoiding you."

Hammer Coolie took this honest retort on the chin. "Fair enough, Miss Elantina. My apologies for intruding. I will leave you to your stroll and your dodging of me."

Hammer Coolie, in all his unconventional handsomeness, passed by her. Maise watched him walk away and sighed. Maise Elantina would never, ever, *ever* rue the simple honesty she never hesitated to use, but she was fully aware that sometimes her delivery overshadowed her message.

Not that she worried about offending Mr. Coolie. She knew him well enough by now that Hammer was not the type to be insulted by something as unadorned as the truth. In fact, Hammer Coolie was no typical type at all, at least as far as Maise could ever find.

When she looked at it more intricately, Maise realized Hammer Coolie was not all that dissimilar than herself. On many more than one occasion, she mused whether their two groups should merge, but for one reason or another, no action was ever taken.

So Maise Elantina continued to be Maise and her Bones, Flair was Flair and his Skulls, Gravigo was Gravigo and his Hats, and Hammer Coolie was Hammer and his…his…his what? Hammer and his rag tag bunch of misfits/free agents? His hoodlums with true intentions but questionable actions? His loosely linked group of rebels with a cause? Maise Elantina knew full well most referred to them as free agents or rebels and the free agents called themselves the free ones, but Maise had yet to find a title that caught their essence in an adequate manner.

Maise sighed again, and began to follow Hammer down the path. Maybe she'd speed up and catch Mr. Coolie. Or maybe she wouldn't.

Either way, Maise Elantina knew she'd be talking to Hammer Coolie soon enough. Today was the day Gravigo was making contact with Jacy Morgan. And while she didn't share Flair's opinion of a scorched earth prophecy, she did recognize that nothing was going to be the same again.

8

Jacy stared at the gorgeous brown woman passing by, her face as serene as an early summer breeze. The woman's face, lit with an ethereal smile that should be envied and vied for, carried on, replaced by the harmonious and wizened face of an older white gentleman, his shaggy beard flowing behind him. The entire line of wandering people was a wonderful mixture of males and females from any and all ethnicities. The line moved purposefully, not rushed, not laggard, just an easy speed used where you know where you are going but are in no particular hurry to get there.

Jacy stood alone and watched the line pass by, without a clue of what she was expected to do, though she figured Dougie had no idea what he was meant to do, either. She recalled watching him approach several lines before he joined one. Maybe he did this until he had the same feeling Jacy felt when she stepped from the cliff.

Or maybe not. It didn't matter to Jacy, though; as she didn't see she had many options. Buy the ticket, take the ride, right?

So with that theory in her hip pocket, Jacy, with one hand idly rubbing her absent tummy, began to approach different lines. One, two, three, five, eighteen, thirty-eight, ninety-one, one hundred and nineteen. The lines didn't cease, they just carried on and carried on. At each new rise in the burnt umber floor, a new group of lines emerged.

The lines stretched as far as Jacy's patience, which was pretty incredulous as patience was never one of Jacy's strong points. She would merely stop near each line for a moment or two, and feeling nothing out of the ordinary, she would move on.

Like everything else, though, all things must come to an end, and Jacy's tolerance finally fractured. After scouting out 784 of them, she attempted to barge into one of the lines.

BAM! It was like walking into a 200,000 volt force field. Jacy ended up on her ass.

"What the fuck?" she muttered, picking herself up off the sandy ground. Once back to her feet, she eyed the passing line. Nobody tossed her a glance.

Jacy's spirit sagged a little. None of the eternal lines invoked even a glimmer of intuition on how to proceed so far. What if none of them did? What was she supposed to do? Try every single damn one of....

Jacy shook her head to clear it, still eyeing the line that rejected her. Jesus, the line Dougie chose absorbed him like some magical shammy and this one would have nothing to do with her? What, she wasn't good enough for their precious fucking line?

Jacy's anger boiled over and she was about to try a second disastrous attempt, when a male's voice startled her from behind.

"Hello, Jacy."

Jacy turned, and for the first time, she laid her eyes upon Gravigo. She would later learn Gravigo was the one most credited with being the creator of life on Earth. Technically speaking, Gravigo was the lead supervisor of a team of six whom gave life to the planet, but Gravigo got most of the credit. He never corrected anybody about their assumptions, either.

Jacy had no idea about any of this at the time, though. All she saw was a portly, curly haired guy who resembled Newman from Seinfeld.

"Who are you?" she asked.

"I'm Gravigo," he answered, staring at her with an almost paternal look.

"How do you know my name?"

Gravigo didn't answer, he merely stared at her with that father/daughter look and an incredibly gentle smile upon his face.

"Hello?" Jacy waved her hand in front of Gravigo's face. "Anybody home? And while we're at it, where's my baby, where the hell are we, why…"

"Sorry," Gravigo interrupted her flurry of queries. "I've known you forever, Jacy, but to finally meet you…"

Gravigo eased out a wistful sigh. "It's a little disconcerting, that's all."

Jacy grunted and waved her arm at the static lines that stretched on for infinity and were completely ignoring the two of them. "Well, join the fucking club, Gravigo. All this is a little disconcerting for me, as well."

Gravigo chuckled.

"I always loved your feisty sarcasm. I'm glad you brought it with you." He gestured towards her stomach. "I'm sure you've noticed something didn't come along with you, though, but please don't worry. She's doing fine."

Gravigo's words hit Jacy with all the subtlety of a sledge hammer to the pinkie toe.

"What…how…who…what…she?" Jacy spoke all these words in a single syllable blurt.

Gravigo held his hands up between them. "I'll explain everything, but you need to give me some time to do it."

Jacy shut her mouth, and let out a long, laborious breath. Her baby was fine. Her baby was safe. Her baby was…her baby was a she?

"Okay," Jacy replied, "but I need to know one thing. Why did you call my baby a she?"

Gravigo's smile grew three times in dimension.

"Because that's what *she* is. Your baby is a healthy girl. They managed to save her after your unfortunate accident." A dark cloud briefly touched Gravigo's eyes, but evaporated just as quickly. "She was seven pounds, 4 ounces. Beau named her Derian."

Jacy closed her eyes, a gazillion tons of weight lifting from her heart.

"I loved that name, Beau didn't," she whispered.

Gravigo nodded.

"Beau named her that in your honour. And her middle name is Jace. Beau wanted to use Jacy, but his mom felt Jace went better with Derian. Personally, I love it, especially since that's what…"

"…my grandpa always called me," Jacy whispered, finishing his sentence.

"Jace with the pretty face," he quoted her Grandfather's oft-used line.

Jacy and Gravigo stared at each other for several long moments.

"Who *are* you?" Jacy studied Gravigo intently.

"I told you, I'm Grav…"

"No, who *are* you? You tell me my baby…I mean, my daughter, my daughter Derian, is safe, you know Beau, you know my grandpa, you…" Jacy's voice trailed off.

"Jacy…"

"No," Jacy whispered, holding a finger up to hold him quiet, letting her gaze stray from his as she attempted to sort things out. She felt pieces slowly clicking into place. Her eyes imperceptibly returned to Gravigo.

"You said 'they managed to save her'," "Jacy's eyebrows furrowed slightly in thought. "What did you mean by…"

Before she could finish her sentence, everything hit her like a bull moose. Gravigo noticed the reaction on Jacy's face.

"Jacy…"

"No," she put her hands up. "No, don't. Am…Am…Am I dead?"

Gravigo sighed and tried again. "Jacy…"

"Gravigo! Answer me. Am I dead? Am I fucking dead?!!"

Gravigo looked away from her, a troubled look growing on his chubby face.

"Gravigo?! Answer my question, you mother…"

Gravigo silenced Jacy with a look that was both blazing and soothing the same. "Yes, Jacy," his voice was polite but firm. "As you think you know it to be, you are dead."

9

Lita sat on the stony edge of the magnificent fountain, seeing many people wander around, but not particularly paying them any attention. Today she wandered in her own thoughts.

Her contemplation held no true focus, though, she just ran through a wide-ranging array of recent happenings. She ruminated about the new girl who would soon be here, of course. People were chattering about nothing else lately. Even though Lita was just a relative rookie and held no real standing whatsoever, she knew the story of Jacy well enough and knew she'd be talking to her soon. Gravigo would see to that.

Besides, who else would be better for this Jacy woman to meet with? Baz wouldn't be of any help. This left Lita, and well, while she was intrigued about the soon-to-be arrival, Lita had bigger fish to deal with at the moment.

And one of those sharks walked towards her, now.

"Well, if it isn't Lita, sitting all by her smuttily dressed self," Flair snarled.

"Fuck off, Flair," Lita sighed. She was getting awfully tired of dealing with him, but quickly checked her attire, which pissed her off even more.

"Wow," Flair plunked himself down beside her on the fountain's edge. "That's not the quip-filled Lita I know and dislike. Where did you learn that original retort?"

Lita noticed The Bam Slicer, lurking not too far off. Lita would never admit it, but The Bam Slicer frightened her. Flair, well, he was capable of things that made her uneasy, too, but Lita wasn't scared of him.

The Bam Slicer, though? He made Lita weak in the knees, and *not* in a good way.

"I think Mr. Talky-Pants there taught me," she nodded towards Bam.

"Now, now, you should be nicer to Bam, Lita," Flair scolded her. "I don't think you'd be so lippy if I choose to let him…"

"Don't you ever get tired of being such a dick, Flair?" a new voice entered the conversation, and the owner of this voice was someone else who made Lita weak in the knees. In this case, though, it was the exact opposite way that The Bam Slicer did.

Flair rolled his eyes.

"Don't you ever get tired of being such a god-damned cement-head?" Flair stood to face Hammer Coolie eye to eye. The Bam Slicer had quietly moved and now stood behind Flair, looking over his boss' left shoulder. Hammer looked at him and smirked.

"Congrats on your promotion to number two bum-fucker, Bam," Hammer spoke in his familiar rasp. "Just come back from the clearing and some dictation?"

The Bam Slicer tensed but didn't say a word. Flair put his hands up.

"Easy, Bam," Flair didn't take his eyes from Hammer. "We'll deal with Mr. Coolie here when the time is right."

Flair's eyes flared. "Especially after that cute little job you recently pulled in Wisconsin. I mean it, Hammer, you're fucking with the wrong man."

Lita watched this exchange. Well, truthfully she couldn't take her eyes off of the amazingly sexy Hammer Coolie. Up until this moment, Hammer Coolie had basically ignored her.

"We'll see," Hammer returned his attention to Flair. "Or maybe Wisconsin is just an appetizer."

Flair shrugged. "Have it your way, Hammer. I'll leave you to this little harlot."

Flair began to walk away. The Bam Slicer remained rooted for a moment, his eyes blazing a hole into Hammer. "Heads up, eyes open, asshole. We're going to come at you hard."

Not a muscle in Hammer's face flinched. "I look forward to it."

"Bam!" Flair barked. The Bam Slicer allowed himself a mere suggestion of a smile.

"See you *really* soon, fuckshit," The Bam Slicer half jogged to catch up to his boss. Hammer Coolie watched them depart before turning his attention to an awed Lita.

"Fuckshit?" Hammer repeated. "The guy's a regular Shakespeare, isn't he? Mind if I sit?"

Lita nodded, not daring to speak in case her voice squeaked like a baby mouse. Lita both loved and hated the way she felt the few times she was in Hammer Coolie's presence, but had come to find she was powerless in this area.

"How are things going with you, Lita?" Hammer asked as he stretched out his legs and lolled his head back to accept the sun in his face.

Oh my freaking God, the response inside her head cried out. I can't believe that you, Hammer Coolie, are *sitting beside me right this second*!!! *I could come just smelling you*!!!

"S'alright," was what she said aloud, though.

Hammer looked at her through half closed eyelids and raised his eyebrows, which constricted her throat even tighter. "Really? From the reports I hear, you're doing much better than alright."

Lita's mind ran on a tilt-a-whirl. Hammer Coolie? Hammer fucking Coolie heard reports about me?! *What* was going on here?!

"I had...I had some good training, I guess," she managed to stammer.

"You happy in the Bones?" Hammer quickly sat up straight and looked deep into her eyes. Lita's heart, knees, and groin all melted simultaneously, which, for some strange reason, totally pissed her off.

'Get your ass together, bitch,' she recalled a friend from long ago saying whenever Lita screwed up.

"What's happy?" Lita began to find her true voice. "I like Maise. She's a good spirit. I might have issues with the politics and shit, but I bet all the groups have the same problems. I'd rather be a Bone than a Skull or a Hat, that's for fucking sure."

"Better to be a Bone than a Skull or a Hat," Hammer made little air quotation marks as he spoke. "I can't really argue with that, but is it better to be a Bone than be with the free ones?"

Okay, Lita thought, now even my toes are freaking weak. But Hammer Coolie or not, Lita would not...ok, who was she kidding? She'd swallow broken glass just to feel his breath on the back of her neck.

Instead of verbally expressing this, Lita leaned forward, looking out over the fields of rich grass. "What are you trying to say, Hammer?"

Hammer thought for a moment, then stood. Lita felt a brief moment of panic. Jesus Buddha, she thought, did I go too...

"I'm not *trying* to say anything," Hammer fished out a pair of sunglasses from the pocket of the ripped jean jacket that hugged him to perfection and put the shades on. "I'm just throwing out a fishing line. If you don't want to bite, then don't."

He began to walk away, then stopped and looked back at her. "Are you curious about the new girl coming?"

Lita's eyebrows turned inwards in confusion. This was all too much for her brain to take. "Sure. Why do you ask?"

"Well," Hammer shrugged, "I figured since Baz is where Baz is, you're the only one of her kind here. You seem a natural ally for someone like her."

Lita's mind raced a zillion miles a second, almost on the verge of overload, but not quite. Despite her lovesickness of Hammer Coolie, Lita *was* still Lita, after all. "Is this what this is, Hammer? Just a ruse because you think I'll be a link to her?"

Lita couldn't see Hammer's eyes because of the recently adorned sunglasses, but she thought she heard a tinge of disappointment in his voice. "If that's how you feel, Lita, then maybe you are better off being a Bone."

With that, Hammer Coolie walked away. Lita didn't hide her interest in watching his ass and wondering what it looked like under those tight jeans. Lita sighed, but not entirely out of exasperation, as there was a faint note of hope that Hammer was interested in her. Lita allowed herself a soft smile, and stretched her long legs out, bending her neck back to greet the sun.

Okay, new girl, she thought. Let's see who you are and what you got. Either way, as long as you get me close to Hammer Coolie, you'll be worth my time.

10

Jacy stared at Gravigo with Pyrrhic eyes, as she rubbed the side of her face, trying to comprehend Gravigo's words. She was a fantastic failure at this.

"Jacy…"

"No," Jacy stopped rubbing her face and held up a hand to emphasize her word.

Gravigo silently harrumphed, but acquiesced to her request. Jacy eyed Gravigo warily, allowing her anger and frustration to melt away as his fatal words sunk in. Well, the words didn't actually sink in as Jacy was now more confused than ever, but she did *hear* what he had just said. Breathing deeply, Jacy wandered a few steps away to assemble her thoughts.

"Okay," Jacy started after a few moments of musing. "Let's see how well I follow you so far."

Gravigo nodded.

"One, Derian is alive. My daughter is okay."

"Yes."

"Two, Beau is alive. He's okay, too, right?"

"He was injured, but he's recuperated physically. Beau is alive, too," Gravigo spoke after a minor hesitation. Jacy stared at him, waiting for Gravigo to elaborate. Gravigo shrugged.

"What? Do you want me to tell you he's fine? Well, I won't, because he's not. He's mourning the death of his beloved wife, he's trying to raise a daughter on his own, and his left leg will trouble him for the rest of his life due to injuries in the accident. He's alive, Jacy, and he's doing the best he can to adapt to his new situation. That's all I can say."

Jacy nodded and began to pace, hoping she'd get more information out of him later. That was many steps down the path from where she was right now, though.

"Okay, so Derian's alive, Beau is alive," Jacy counted off her fingers. She stopped pacing. "But I'm not alive. Is that what you're telling me?"

Gravigo sighed. "Jacy, I know this is hard for you to…"

Jacy held her hands up. "Gravigo, please answer my question. You told me I'm dead, but here I am, standing and chatting with you. Excuse my fucking confusion, okay?"

Gravigo sighed. "I wish you wouldn't use so many profanities."

Jacy almost blew her top, but she re-started her pacing to contain her burn. She heard Gravigo harrumph again, a sound she would in the future realize how much she enjoyed.

"Yes, Jacy. Your life on Earth is dead. But if you would let me..."

Jacy held her hands up again. "Please stop, Gravigo. I need to do this at my own speed here."

Jacy ceased pacing, but wandered a few steps away. Under the circumstances, she was amazed at the relative calmness she was feeling since she had just been told she was dead. She couldn't wrap her head around why; if she was lifeless, how the hell was her corpse having a somewhat intelligent conversation with some funny named dude called Gravigo?

Jacy looked at Gravigo for a moment, a faint light peeking through the fog. "You said 'my life on earth' is dead. Are you telling me we're not on Earth right now?"

Gravigo looked like he was about to say something, but restrained himself. "Right."

Jacy looked around at their surroundings. "Are we in heaven, then?"

Gravigo chuckled. "No, we *definitely* are not in heaven."

His response kicked Jacy in the guts. Gravigo noticed her wince.

"Jacy...."

Jacy put one hand up to silence him while her other held her stomach as if she had been physically hit there. She was dead but wasn't in heaven? Where the fuck did that leave her?

The answer came, causing an inaudible squeak to escape her lips. She began to pace again. Hell. That's what it left. If she wasn't in heaven, then she was in Hell, and goddamn it, that just didn't seem fair to her. Jacy would never argue that she was a pure-as-snow angel, but wow! She wasn't bad enough to reserve a seat in Hell, was she?

Jacy's pacing became more frantic. What had she done to warrant a position in Hell? Her mind raced through a montage of all her less than perfect deeds that qualified her for *maybe* deserving residence in Hell. And if she could recall some particularly nefarious deed, could she plead her case? Was that who this Gravigo guy was? Would she be able to convince him that her good *far* outweighed her bad?

In short, was her entry into Hell negotiable?

Jacy halted her pacing, surprised to see how far from Gravigo she roamed. He hadn't followed her; he seemed to be studying the lines of people passing by. Jacy sighed, sitting down on a rock, or whatever the fuck a rock was called in this place; whatever this place she was in was called.

"Argggh!" Jacy grunted, confused more than ever. She punched the top of her legs. She needed to concentrate, as all the other addle headed thoughts weren't helping. She pondered for a few minutes, a plan slowly taking seed in her brain. It wasn't perfect, but it was all she had at the moment. She stood, ready to face Gravigo again.

Jacy was going to show Gravigo that every shitty thing she had done in her life was answered with three, no five, no fifteen, yeah that was it, *fifteen* really good things that she did. She'd recite every door she held open for a stranger, every quarter she tossed a homeless person's way, every single nice comment that ever escaped her lips.

She'd be like Tom Cruise in that movie where he hammered the shit out of Jack Nicholson's character on the witness stand. She started to formulate her case in her mind as she took the first step back towards Gravigo. After Jacy was finished with him, she could almost picture him screaming, "I can't handle the truth!" and he'd have to let Jacy go.

And then, as quickly as her confidence rose, it evaporated. What if Gravigo wasn't a negotiator or whatever she hoped he would be? What if Gravigo was Lucifer himself?

She felt a frozen pit blister in her stomach and her knees wavered a little. Jacy could still see Gravigo studying the lines of passing people. She had to admit that at first blush, he didn't really look like Beelzebub, but then nothing else around this place made sense to her.

Jacy could see he was paying her no attention whatsoever. And there was about 100 yards of desert earth between them.

Jacy made a split decision. She spun in the opposite direction and ran like the devil.

11

Lita took one last look in the mirror before that evening's duties. She couldn't help the smile that crept over her face. In a previous life, she would've been mortified by her appearance, but in this place, she got a mild kick out of it. Halloween was always a favourite holiday of hers back in that erstwhile life, so she saw no reason why she couldn't enjoy playing dress-up here every now and then, too.

Satisfied with her gothic, bondage queen attire, she did one last pirouette. She caught a glimpse of the purple G-string that fit perfectly underneath her sheer stockings. She sighed, wishing the ass she had now belonged to her back on Earth.

Shrugging, she reminded herself that now was now. Now was never going to come again. Allowing herself one grope of her perfectly sculpted gluteus muscles and an adoring gaze at her knee length, high heel boots, she exited the room to meet her partners.

Strolling down the empty hallway, her mind travelled back to her earlier impromptu meeting with Hammer Coolie, which made her a little giddy, and the run-in with Flair, which did the opposite. She wished she had a chance to talk with Maise Elantina about it, but didn't pursue a meeting with her. It seemed too trivial to bother her about. Maise was swamped enough with the recent Buzzed Rottid happenings to deal with much else.

Lita shook her head to focus on that evening's job. She passed through the main entrance doors and spied Walleye Disdain and Jinnion Crust waiting for her by the same fountain she was at earlier in the day when Hammer Coolie flustered the crap out of her.

Walleye whistled in appreciation of what he saw. "Jesus, Lita, you are smoking hot."

Lita spun seductively around, pushing her ass up, looking over her shoulder at her two colleagues. "This ole rag?" she drawled. "You ain't seen nothin' yet, boys." Walleye laughed and clapped in appreciation. Jinnion Crust looked uncomfortable.

"Nice boots," he said. "You two perverts ready?"

Lita laughed, falling between the two Skull imposters, taking their arms as they began to leave the fountain area. "Really, Jinnion? Nice boots? How could you even notice them with my perfect 10 ass shaking in your face?"

"You have a face?" Walleye cracked, which made Jinnion smile.

"Yeah, yeah, I may have noticed it for split second," Jinnion admitted. "We have to focus, though. We have a job to do."

"Sir, yes Sir!" Lita and Walleye called out in unison. Walleye saluted with his free hand. Lita would've, but she had no free hands as they looped down and groped her escorts' asses.

"Lita!" Jinnion moved away.

"Sorry," she smiled innocently. "I just couldn't help myself. You boys look so, I don't know, so dangerous, tonight. It's very, *very* sexy."

"I went with my Izzy Straddlin circa 1989 look," Walleye Disdain said proudly. "One of the coolest looking mother fuckers in rock."

"Very nice," Lita purred. "And you, Monsieur Crust?"

Jinnion Crust smiled. He was the unofficial leader of these bi-monthly trysts and he tried to keep it as official as he could. With cohorts such as Lita and Walleye with him, though, he was not always as successful as he hoped.

"I went with the Scandinavian Viking look," Jinnion moved closer so Lita could crook her arm within his again.

"That's a very chic cod piece," Lita chided.

"I could impale you with what's underneath there, Lita. You have no idea how big that thing is."

All three laughed as they made their way through the darkness to their destination. Walleye was the first to return to the task at hand.

"Are we expecting any surprises tonight?"

"It's a general group meeting of the Skulls," Jinnion shrugged.

"Aren't there always surprises?"

Lita and Walleye Disdain nodded in agreement. All three were members of the Bones and were part of the Skulls Recon committee. Their job was to attend the Skulls general meetings. The meetings themselves weren't too difficult to infiltrate, as it was well known that all groups spied on the other groups' general meetings.

One still had to be vigilant, though. Once in a while, just to shake things up, the Skulls would make an example of spies at their meetings. Jinnion's current committee had yet to go through that ordeal, and they all wanted to keep it that way.

"Besides the usual, what are we looking for?" Lita asked, her business tone taking over her earlier playful one.

"Same as usual, but Maise wants a goddamned full report on this one."

Walleye snorted. A full report meant a ton of extra work for him. Usually the committee would just give her a verbal summary of what went on.

"Because of the recent happenings?" Lita asked.

"Of course," Jinnion Crust nodded. "From what I hear through the grapevine and from Maise, the stupid Skulls have no idea how close they came to causing a full out war."

Lita raised her eyebrows at this, but didn't say anything. Flair and his Skulls were dangerous and reckless, but unaware and foolish they were not. Not by a longshot.

"Looking forward to meeting the new one?" Walleye Disdain looked at Lita.

"I guess so, but it's not on the top of my mind at the moment."

"Good," Jinnion Crust nodded his approval. "Let's focus all our attention on tonight. This is the first general meeting since all the shit went down. We'll need to keep on our toes."

All jocularity evaporated as the three marched towards their duty.

12

As Jacy raced faster than Usain Bolt could ever dream of, crazy images exploded through her mind. Jacy pictured Gravigo the Demon, once he realized she escaped, turn into some grotesque, eighty-foot beast with teeth the size of elephant tusks. At any second she expected to hear a mighty roar escape his anaconda size lips which would shake the very ground she was galloping for her dear life on.

No mighty roar came, though. Jacy ran and ran and ran, tossing numerous glances over her shoulder as she was positive Gravigo was so close he could lick the back of her neck. Without any idea how far she had run to actually escape his clutches, Jacy slowed to a brisk walk. Zero sign of Satan/Gravigo. Maybe he had bigger fish to fry?

The thought ignited a miniscule flicker of hope inside her. After all, that line of reasoning was *somewhat* plausible. The more she contemplated this idea, the larger the flame grew inside her. Shit, there were murderers, rapists, and Wall Street criminals who deserved the devil's attention *much* more than she, the simple Jacy Morgan, should receive. Maybe Gravigo just lurched for the low hung fruit, and missing his chance with her, moved on to more bountiful spoils.

Feeling a little bit more confident, but not enough that she didn't check over her shoulder every three seconds, Jacy faced her next hurdle. How would she actually get accepted into one of those lines? She still didn't have a clue on how to do this.

Jacy pursued her earlier theory; check each line and see if she felt some kind of divine intuition. This time, though, she knew she didn't have the luxury of spending all day doing this. After checking out six lines, she stood in front of the seventh one. Bingo! This time she was pretty sure she felt something. While yes, the feeling wasn't anywhere near as profound as the feeling that swallowed her whole when she took flight from the edge of the cliff earlier, she definitely felt something.

Holding her chin high and pushing her breasts out, Jacy stepped confidently into the line of happy people.

WHAM! Same result. Jacy tumbled to the dirty ground, cursing.

"What is *wrong* with you goddamned people?!" she shouted at the blur of joy-filled faces that passed her by. "You all fucking suck, you know that?!"

Jacy stood, wiping the sand from her ass. No one even acknowledged her. Jacy shut her mouth, staring defiantly at the line, silently daring someone to toss a glance in her direction. Nobody did.

"Jesus," she whispered out of exasperation, trying to come up with a next course of action. Maybe she would...

"Hi, Jacy," Gravigo stood twenty feet or so away from her, looking more than a little uncertain of himself.

Jacy's shoulder sagged, defeated. She looked at him. At least he wasn't that 80-foot-tall ogre she imagined earlier. Jacy's resolve melted as the answer hit her. There *was* no getting away from Gravigo. He was uneludable, and Jacy could give two shits if that was an actual word or not.

She sighed, realizing her two options were to fight Gravigo physically or to convince him she wasn't worthy of a place in Hell. She tried the latter, first.

"Okay, okay," Jacy put her hands up in surrender mode. "Just give me a chance first, though, okay?"

"A chance?" Gravigo's quizzical look gave Jacy a momentary boost of confidence.

"Yeah," she said in a cheery voice, slowly walking towards him. "I mean, come on Grav, why do you want me in hell? I wasn't *that* bad back on Earth, was I?"

"Oh, Jacy..." Gravigo rolled his eyes.

Jacy's confidence plummeted. She began to babble.

"Come *on*, Gravigo," she pleaded. "What did I do that was so horrible? Cheat on some high school tests? Nip a few bucks from my Grandpa's wallet?"

"Jacy...."

"No, no, give me an opportunity here, at least," she interrupted him. "What else? Is this about the time I let Joey sneak into my room when I was a teenager? Puh-leeeze. I didn't even let him fuck me. Christ, I barely even gave him a blowjo..."

Gravigo lost his patience. While his anger didn't cause the ground to tremor, it was still pretty forceful.

"Enough!" he barked, doing some weird movement with his hands. The ground where they stood was now vacant. Jacy and Gravigo disappeared.

13

The stadium where all Skulls General Meetings were held was a pulsing thump of humanity. Tonight, the crowd was on the topside of 400,000 Skulls, nearly half of their full roster size.

The atmosphere rivalled that of a heavy metal festival. Strobe lights boogied across the nighttime sky with its' swathing glow. The Ten Hep Kings blasted through a blazing version of Motley Crue's 'Kickstart My Heart' from the main stage. The energy of the place touched every fiber of Lita's being.

"I have to admit; the atmosphere here is pretty damn cool. Better than ours, anyways," Walleye Disdain remarked, or rather shouted, to his two partners before departing. Lita nodded in agreement while Jinnion Crust took an awkward look around to make sure nobody overheard what Walleye said. Lita gave him a playful nudge with her elbow.

"Don't worry about our cover. Nobody gives a shit," she leaned in and spoke close to Jinnion's left ear. Lita jutted her chin at a Skull grouping about 20 feet in front and a little to the right of them.

"Think they care?" she asked.

Jinnion's eyes followed Lita's directional nod. Inside the group of circled Skulls, two female Skulls were having sex with a male Skull. One of the women, an incredibly sexy woman with a brush cut was straddling the prone guy, riding him reverse cowgirl style. The other female, a fiery Latino wearing only a leather bra and a strap-on dildo, stroked her fake penis.

"Probably not," Jinnion agreed, shaking his head. "That doesn't give us the right to be unprofessional, though."

Lita nodded, conceding that point. Even though it was pretty damn easy to get caught up in the wild atmosphere of a Skulls' general meeting, they were there for a reason and they would do what was expected of them. To do their duties proper, though, they had to blend in; hence their theatrical get-ups this evening.

Walleye returned, noticing the group sex Lita and Jinnion had been spectating.

"Hmmm. That's oddly erotic. Here." He watched the action as he handed two cold beers to Lita She passed one of them to Jinnion, who screwed his face up at the sight of it.

"Sorry, Jinnion," Walleye leaned across Lita to be heard, "but they didn't have any Krug Clos d`Ambonnay for you."

Lita laughed. Jinnion smiled.

"Unfortunate, but fine," Jinnion relaxed a little, taking a small swig of his beer. "There's no accounting for sophistication in this place, though."

The group sex spectacle forgotten, well, maybe not truly forgotten as Lita did sneak the odd glance when she noticed the threesome changed positions. The male Skull now fucked the short haired girl doggy style while she licked and sucked the fake phallus the Latin girl wore. This was apparently a popular move, as the spectators surrounding them began to cheer loudly.

Reminding herself not to get too caught up in the surroundings, Lita watched as the Ten Hep Kings finished their tune. As the last powerful note echoed on and on, the lights cut out, leaving one lone spotlight shining down on the empty stage. The crowd began to roar and chant.

"Flair! Flair! Flair!"

To further blend in, the three of them raised their left arms and punched the air to each growing chant of Flair! It was so loud nobody would guess they merely lip-synched the chant. All three of them hated Flair; Walleye Disdain more than most.

"Douche! Douche! Douche!" Walleye yelled his version into Lita's left ear.

Just then the chant dissolved into an unholy roar. Flair stepped into the spotlight. Lita pretended to be cheering, too, but the sight of Flair made her skin crawl.

With one hand gripping a half-filled bottle of Ketel One vodka, he brought his outstretched arms down to waist level and the volume of the cheering diminished. Flair smiled, levitating his arms to nipple height. The noise grew with his arm movements. Flair played this out for a bit, raising and lowering his arms until he finally kept raising, raising, raising them until they were outstretched above his head. The noise was incredible, and only grew when Flair tilted his head to the sky and started pouring the vodka into his mouth.

The place went bonkers, even more so than before. Walleye leaned in to Lita's ear.

"The guy's a hack!"

Lita laughed, but couldn't disagree with his words more. Flair was many things, but a hack was not one of them. When Flair emptied the bottle, he reared back and hurled the bottle in a high arc that would make Derek Carr proud. The bottle ended up deep into the ocean of Skulls in front of the stage.

"Somebody use that as a sex toy tonight, please!" Flair's words caused the chaotic frenzy of the Stadium to erupt even more. He smiled and bathed in the euphoria for a few moments before raising one hand in front of him and lowered it slowly. The crowd obeyed his wordless command.

Flair cocked his head as if looking out to all those in the cheap seats. "Finally," he growled. "I am BACK where I belong!"

The crowd cheered again. Flair pointed out people in the crowd before him. "I'm back where I belong with you, and you, and you, and…."

Flair stopped, moving closer to the front of the stage. He leered at someone in the crowd. "And *definitely* you, sweetheart. Hey," he yelled overhead," get her on the screen!"

Lita looked to the giant screen that was instantly filled with a beautiful, raven-haired female Skull with breasts threatening to burst through her Die Antwoord tour shirt. The crowd began to chant again.

"Tits! Tits! Tits!"

The girl on the screen smiled and played the role perfectly, pretending to pull her top up, then stopping. The chant grew in volume.

"The classiness of this place is killing me," Jinnion Crust had to shout into Lita's ear to be heard.

Finally, the Die Antwoord fan whipped off her top and exposed her breasts to the crowd. She twirled the shirt over her head as the place went nuts again.

"Very nice, and very mountainous, too," Flair noted his appreciation before he resumed control of the crowd's attention. "Let's get down to business."

Lita, Walleye, and Jinnion focussed intently, as Flair's speech was the reason they were here for. With practiced experience, each of them had certain parts of "the business" they were in charge of remembering. After the meeting was done, they would re-hash the evening together which Walleye would then put into an official report.

Lita was surprised Flair didn't talk more of the Buzzed Rottid fiasco.

"With the artist formerly known as Buzzed Rottid finished," he said to his worshipping followers, "The Bam Slicer is now my right hand man. Which is good, because I need my left hand free to fondle all the lovely lady Skulls!"

The female Skulls went bananas, offering all kinds of sordid requests that Flair could bequeath upon them. Jinnion rolled his eyes. Walleye didn't crack a smile. Lita, as always, marvelled at the power of Flair while being disgusted with him at the same time. After 45 minutes of business, Flair began to wind up for his big finale.

"Now, more than ever, I need all of you to stand tall and be a Skull to be proud of. I need each and every one of you to remember that you are a Skull. You are the Nina…"

The crowd picked up and began to chant, exactly in time how Zach De la Rocha sang it.

"…the Pinta! The Santa Maria!"

"Again?!" Flair cupped his right ear and leaned towards the crowd.

"The Nina! The Pinta! The Santa Maria!" The volume was more thunderous now.

"…yes yes yes, you are the Nina! The Pinta! The Santa Maria! You are also the noose…"

"…and the rapist! The fields' overseer!"

"What?!"

"The noose! And the rapist! The fields' overseer!"

Flair worked himself into a lather. He pumped his left arm madly.

"The agents…" he led the crowd.

"…of orange! The Priests of Hiroshima!" The crowd responded.

"One more?!"

"The agents! Of Orange! The Priests of Hiroshima!"

"Oh Gawwwd, yes, yes, YES! You are all those and SO much more. You are the vessel that carries our mantle forward, and I can only do what I do with you, every single one of you, having my back and having each other's! I can't...."

Walleye nudged Lita who in turn nudged Jinnion. They had all heard the finale before. Time to go. Walleye led the other two single file through the bulk of the crowd. When the crowd began to thin, they began to walk three abreast again, each male flanking Lita who played the Skull girl act to perfection.

They almost made it to the exit when Razor Swatan, a Skull who they knew and often exchanged information with, stepped in front of their path. His sudden appearance caught them all by surprise.

"Excuse me?" Lita did her best to come off as nonchalant.

"Sorry," Razor whispered. "I hope you don't hate me for this."

Razor Swatan disappeared as quickly as he had arrived. Watching him run off, the three shook their heads and started to walk again. Or, at least they would have, if The Bam Slicer wasn't blocking their way.

"Walleye Disdain, Lita, and Jinnion Crust," his low voice rumbled like a Harley. "So glad you could join our festivities."

Walleye and Jinnion began exploring escape points. Bam gave a brief shake of his head. "Don't worry, you are all safe. I just came to pass on a message to the three of you."

The three of them looked expectantly at The Bam Slicer.

"The message is from Flair."

All three gulped. That Flair had a message for the three of them frightened them. The message itself scared the living shit out of them. The Bam Slicer almost smiled as he watched all three hightail it out of the Stadium.

14

Enchanting. Magical. Spellbinding. If Jacy had to pick a word to describe what she was seeing, those and any other adjectives would never be enough.

"Where…what…where…?" she couldn't formulate a sentence. Jacy and Gravigo stood at the top of another glass stairway, though this one was different than the first one. Rather than run straight and long to the ground, this one spiralled downwards.

It wasn't the staircase that caused Jacy's awe, though. Jacy's gaze flowed over acres and acres of plush, avocado grass leading to a beautiful shiny, white edifice. The structure was the most colossal building Jacy had ever laid eyes upon. The setting sun gave the building a roseate halo.

The beauty and grandeur of the place took Jacy's breath away. This place *definitely* wasn't Hell. Jacy didn't try to speak. She merely glanced at Gravigo.

"This," Gravigo swept his arm across the miraculous view." "This is it. This is everything."

Jacy looked at the magnificent building again. It was almost futuristic looking, with an old southern charm tossed in. Huge pillars rose up in front, spilling down marble stairs to the most amazing fountain Jacy had ever seen. She had no words to describe the fountain, or anything else, for that matter.

"Is this Heaven?" she said, almost dreamily.

Gravigo grunted in exasperation. "Jesus," he grumbled. "Would you knock off this whole heaven and hell thing?"

Jacy looked at him with raised eyebrows. Gravigo's look softened.

"Look," he said, gently. "You are not in heaven or hell. Neither of those places even exist, and…." He sighed again.

"Can we go inside?" Gravigo offered his arm to Jacy. "All this will be much easier to explain if I can start at the beginning."

Jacy started to speak, but restrained herself. It finally occurred to her that her interruptions were not getting her anywhere. She nodded, slipping her arm into the crook of Gravigo's elbow. Gravigo led her down the see-through stairs. Stealing a glance behind her, Jacy noticed the stairs disappear behind them. Gravigo saw her look back and chuckled.

"Yes, these ones disappear, too. You know, you were one of 18,723 to look back at the first set of stairs you saw?"

"You watched that?"

"Yes, I did," he looked almost sheepish. "I wanted to see you, of course, but I also wanted to check if the ratio was right."

They made it to the bottom of the stairs. Jacy looked back at the now departed stairs.

"Ratio?"

Yeah," Gravigo nodded. "Fatter Verb tells us the average is 1 in 12,226 who look behind them as they descend the stairs. I always thought those numbers of Fatter's a little low. I look forward to dispelling them to him."

Jacy didn't respond, too enthralled with the dazzling pathway they were walking on. The glittering path led long, straight, and true to the resplendent fountain guarding the entrance of the building. Jacy took a deep breath, willing the thoughts in her head to slow to lightning speed, at least. While her head was a jungle of queries and thoughts, she did feel calmer now that she knew she wasn't going to burn in Hell for eternity.

Everything else, though, was too surreal for her to comprehend at the moment. Was she actually in some form of after-life? Or was she in a coma and all this was merely some fantastic scenario being played by actors and actresses her morbid imagination harvested? Or was she really just a lunatic who…

Jacy halted her runaway train of thought. All in good time, she reminded herself. Buy the ticket, take the ride seemed like a great motto to live by, even if she wasn't actually technically alive. As they neared the incredible fountain, Jacy noticed sporadic individuals on their hands and knees on the vibrant grass. It almost looked like they were....

"Those are the Grass Counters," Gravigo spoke their name with a mixture of disdain and regret.

"Grass Counters? They're counting the grass?" Jacy scanned the endless horizon of the emerald hued ground.

Gravigo sighed. "It's a type of punishment."

Jacy returned her eyes to Gravigo. "Punishment for what?"

"For breaking the rules of the Game," Gravigo looked at Jacy with a half formed smile upon his lips, daring Jacy to ask her next question. She couldn't resist.

"The Game? What's the Game?"

Gravigo's eyes sparkled brighter than the glimmering pathway they were on.

"The Game? The Game is *everything*." And with that pronouncement, Gravigo did the unusual hand movement again and they disappeared.

15

"I'm so sorry, Lita," Maise Elantina spoke in a reverential hush. "It's never easy losing any subject, much less your first one."

Lita sat across Maise's elegant desk. When The Bam Slicer had uttered his horrific message, Lita knew it was going to be her that message was really being delivered to. The missive being sent Walleye Disdain and Jinnion Crust from Flair was an understated one. Lita's message, on the other hand, wasn't very subtle, at all.

'Don't fuck with me or the Skulls. Maybe you should go to the Gaming area and see what happens when you do.'

The three of them raced back as quickly as they could. Walleye and Jinnion's area was fine.

When Lita neared hers and saw Rusty Sleeves rapidly departing the area, she knew her fears were realized.

"Rusty Sleeves," Maise spoke his name as if it were a sewer microbe. "He's a fucking monster. Jesus Christ."

Lita felt numb. She knew the odds of losing your first one were against her; most, if not all lost their first one relatively fast. That didn't make it any easier for her, though.

"How?" Maise looked at Lita with eyes full of empathy.

"Wrong place, wrong time," Lita sighed. "Bullet in the back of the head while working."

"While *working*? Motherfucker!"

Lita smiled in spite of her current state. Maise Elantina was the most incredible woman she had ever met. And here, in Maise's spare yet classy, candle-lit office, hearing her spout profanities like a roofer; well, it caused Lita to like Maise that much more.

"He was repairing a gas fireplace in a condo downtown. Bunch of trigger happy hop-heads barged in for a drug rip or something, and blasted the owner and…and…"

Lita didn't cry, but her voice trailed off to nothingness. Maise leaned over, took Lita's hand, and gave it a reassuring squeeze.

"William, his name was William."

Lita scowled. "I know his fucking name, Maise. I just don't…I just don't get it, I guess. What the fuck did he do to deserve that?"

"Absolutely nothing."

"Jesus." Lita exhaled loudly, remembering something else. "Those fuckers, the ones who did it? They also got some poor sap in the hallway. The guy was just heading to go play floor hockey with his buddies, for fuck's sake. Now he's gone, too."

Lita shook her head in dismay, looking away from Maise. Maise waited her out.

"All this because we crashed that stupid meeting?" Lita wanted to know.

Maise smiled, shaking her head. "No, the meeting had nothing to do with it. Flair knows we're always there, just as the Hats are, and just as his people infiltrate ours and the Hats. No, this is Flair being Flair. Have you had any recent run-ins with Flair since you turned down his offer to join the Skulls?"

Lita remembered how she hadn't had a chance to bring Maise up to speed on her earlier incident with Flair. She left out the Hammer Coolie almost-offer, though.

When Lita finished, Maise nodded. "Well, what they did was over-the-top for even Flair, but that's what this is probably about. I'll make some inquiries and get to the bottom of this."

"What about Rusty Sleeves?"

"You let me deal with Rusty Sleeves," Maise Elantina's cool, blue eyes blazed with intensity. "There will be payback, and there *will* be blood on the floor. Not ours, just his."

There were times when Maise Elantina scared Lita more than Flair and The Bam Slicer put together. This was one of those times. And then poof, like only Maise can do, she returned to the calm, cool, collected leader she is. Maise leaned across the desk, and Lita automatically took both her hands in hers.

"I shouldn't tell you this," her blue eyes now void of the earlier venom that briefly inhabited them, "but William was dying soon, anyways."

"What?"

"He had the cancer."

Lita looked at Maise Elantina as if she had spontaneously sprouted four heads. "No, he didn't. Minus the aches and pains of a 54-year-old, he was fine."

"No, he wasn't," Maise shook her head. "He didn't *know* he had the cancer yet, but believe me, he did. We try to do this with everyone's first. William only had a couple good years left, then the rest, depending on how the treatments took, weren't going to be much fun."

"Well, shit," Lita looked down at her lap. She took a deep breath. "Either way, this still blows chunks."

Maise chuckled. "Yes, this still 'blows chunks'. Want some good news?"

"Yeah," Lita smiled in spite of her mood. "Yeah, I would."

"Awesome," Maise withdrew her hands from Lita's and clapped her hands. "I've already got your new subject ready for you."

"Really?"

"She's been ready for you for a bit, now, but because of your inexperience, we decided to hold her back until you were ready."

Lita looked downcast. "After William, how can you be sure I'm ready?"

Maise waved her hand as if shooing away a pesky gnat. "Oh, you are ready for Serena, that I have no doubt. We just didn't know if you were ready for more than one subject in your pod. Now with William gone, you can focus all of your energies towards Serena."

"Serena?" Lita's eyebrows leaned inwards.

When Maise finished bringing Lita up to speed on Serena, Lita felt a heavy weight grow wings and flutter from her shoulders. While losing William hurt, Lita knew she was more than ready for someone like Serena. She would take all the mistakes she'd made with William, learn heartily from them, and pour everything she had into Serena.

She'd never forget what Flair had done to William, though. While Lita knew she was ready for Serena, meeting Flair head to head was something she wasn't quite ready for. Yet. One day she would be, though, and when that day came, Flair better have his head on a swivel.

Heads up, and eyes open, Lita muttered to herself as she departed Maise's office. *I'm coming after you, Flair.*

16

"I really wish you'd stop doing that," Jacy complained as she found herself in a spacious office, standing opposite a vast desk from a sitting Gravigo.

"You don't like it?" He seemed a bit surprised.

Jacy sighed. "No, it's not so much that. It's just…I just…."

Jacy could feel her tranquil feeling start to disintegrate. She felt like she had two feet on separating ice floes, stretching, stretching, stretching, until…

Snap! And she did.

"I mean, fuck, Gravigo," she saw Gravigo wince at her vulgar language, but she didn't care. "What the fuck do you want from me?! This isn't hell, this isn't heaven, I'm dead, I'm alive, I'm black, I'm white, I'm fuck, fuck, *fuck*!"

"Jacy, please sit and…" Gravigo motioned towards the chair beside her. Jacy stepped back from it like it was a naked Jabba the Hut.

"Fuck no, I am not fucking sitting down! I want some goddamned answers!"

Jacy mimicked Gravigo's voice. "Derian's alive, Beau's alive, your life as you know it is over. Nyah nyah nyah!"

"Jacy…"

"Disappearing stairways?" Jacy was now leaning over Gravigo's desk. "Those crazy lines of people? And then this?"

Jacy copied the curious hand movements Gravigo did just before they would reappear somewhere new. "Like what the fuck is that, Gravigo? Motherfucker…."

"Neva?" Gravigo nodded at something behind Jacy.

"What? What the hell is a Ne…" Jacy ended in mid-sentence as she felt an iron grip on her shoulder. Before she could turn around and see what it was, Jacy was lifted three feet from the ground and roughly slammed down onto the chair.

"Hey!" she yelped as she felt the mighty grip release. "Who the…"

Jacy finished in mid-sentence once again when she saw who her escort was. Standing before her was the tallest, most muscle bound woman she had ever seen. This behemoth looked to be at least ten feet tall, and was probably taller.

"Ummmm…I…."

"Jacy, this is Neva Tezremsy," Gravigo chuckled. "Neva, Jacy."

"Nice to finally meet you," Neva's voice was a wonderful feminine melody, totally incongruous with her appearance.

"I…nice to…I…." Jacy took a deep breath. "Likewise."

Jacy returned her attention to Gravigo who seemed to be enjoying this a little too much for Jacy's liking. Jacy threw him her most hostile glare, which only seemed to delight Gravigo more.

"Excellent," he clapped his hands together. "My turn?"

"Sure, now that your bodyguard is here," Jacy couldn't help herself. She knew Gravigo was losing his patience, and she didn't blame him. She couldn't blame herself, though, either.

"Look, Jacy…"

"No, you look, Gravigo, you rotten son of a…"Jacy felt Neva's elephantine hand cover her entire face. Neva let go before Jacy could even put up a fight. Jacy stood and turned to her. She knew she was no match for this mountainous female physically, but she figured she could get a few verbal jabs in.

"Mmmmphuuuuuuph!" was her brilliant attack.

Jacy looked incredulously at Neva, whose face abstained from any emotion. Jacy reached up to take off whatever was gluing her lips shut. Nothing was there.

"Grmmmmmmmmmphhhhguuurrrr," she attempted to speak a second time.

What the fuck? Jacy looked at the no longer smiling Gravigo. He nodded at the chair for her to sit. Fat fucking chance of that happening. Jacy did her best to laugh derisively, but sounded like she was severely constipated, instead.

"*Mmmmmmffffffppppprrrroooooogggggg!*" she wailed, just before she threw a looping roundhouse right at Neva's jaw, even though in reality she couldn't reach Neva's left tit. Neva smiled, catching Jacy's clumsy punch with her right hand. With barely a flick of the wrist, Neva twirled Jacy in an airborne cartwheel, spinning her a full 360 degrees before bringing Jacy crashing down into the seat. Neva leaned in, placing her hands on both of Jacy's forearms. Before Jacy could blink, her arms were fastened to the chair.

Gravigo offered a golfer's applause to Neva, who curtsied before resuming her post behind Jacy's chair. Gravigo turned his eyes to Jacy.

"Finished?"

Jacy's shoulders sagged as adrenaline and energy oozed out of her every pore. She nodded meekly. Gravigo smiled.

"Sorry about those," he gestured towards her invisible restraints, "but I just need you to listen for a bit, okay? You'll have ample opportunity for questions later."

Jacy had lost the gumption to even glare at Gravigo. She barely nodded.

"Okay, now that I have your undivided attention," he clapped his hands together, "let's start at the beginning. Let's commence with the creation of life on the planet you call Earth."

Gravigo stood, running his left hand over the top of his expansive desk, about six inches off the top of it, while he raised and lowered his left hand, which caused the lights in the office to dim. Jacy's eyes widened in surprise as a miniature model of her solar system suddenly appeared.

"This was your arm of the galaxy before my colleagues and I arrived," Gravigo stepped back to admire the sight hovering half a foot above his desk. "It took us a pretty long time to find the perfect place for our project."

Jacy became even more confused than she already was. Their project? Gravigo didn't notice her perplexity. He stared at his desk with unadorned fondness.

"I mean, of course, we found similar sites for what we wanted to do, but this place, *this* place was the best, and when I say the best, I mean absolutely perfect." Gravigo tore his eyes from his desk to look at the bewildered Jacy. "We had found forty-seven other uninhabited planets that met our specifications, but there was always something a little bit off. A couple degrees in temperature here, a longer revolution around the star there, whatever." He returned his gaze to the desk.

"But this place," he sighed, "was 100% magnificent."

Jacy tore her eyes from the miniature model of the solar system to look at Gravigo, who was wearing a proud yet almost sad smile on his face. She couldn't quite comprehend what he was saying to her.

"So, once we found the perfect nest, so to speak, the rest was pretty basic. We sent the basic building blocks of life to earth and waited to see what happened."

Jacy looked askance at Gravigo. What in the hell was he trying to say? Was he saying that he, this little chubby man was the reason for life on Earth? Jacy couldn't help the chuckle that tried to break through her glued lips. Gravigo didn't miss her disbelief.

"Oh, it's true, it's true," he said, returning his gaze to the miniscule solar system. He held his hand in a fist over the corner of his desk and slowly opened it. A small, bright blue light formed and began a slow trek towards earth.

He looked at Jacy. "You look a bit uncomfortable and overwhelmed. If I have Neva take your mouth guard off, will you promise to behave and let me explain everything?"

Jacy was still semi-pissed off, but also logical enough to know she was getting nowhere with her attitude so far. She gave one emphatic nod of her head.

Gravigo looked at Neva, who came over and brushed her fingertips along Jacy's lips. "Sorry 'bout that, honey," she soothed.

"You okay now?" Gravigo asked.

"I guess," Jacy answered.

Gravigo gave her a benevolent nod. "I know it's a lot of information to take in, but please hear me out, that's all I ask. Then you can ask any questions you may have."

Jacy nodded, looking down at her arms which were still attached to the chair. She glanced back at Neva.

"I'm going to leave those on for a bit," Neva smiled.

Jacy shrugged, returning her attention to Gravigo. She watched as he ran one hand over the model, erasing all the planets from his desk. He used his other hand in a swirly motion and up popped a laboratory setting, with six miniature figures working.

"This was my team and I, I guess around," Gravigo appeared to be calculating something in his brain, "four and a half billion years ago, give or take a few hundred thousand years. In your timeline, of course."

"What?!" Jacy couldn't contain herself. "Four and half billion years ago?! Jesus Christ, Gravigo, what in the…"

Jacy never did see Neva reach around and sew her lips tight again.

"Thanks," Gravigo smiled at Neva, before returning his eyes to Jacy. "You weren't anywhere *near* this annoying back on Earth, you know."

He returned his gaze to the miniature figures. "Anyways, yes, this is us, over four billion years ago. The timeline of my universe is infinitely different and far more exceptional than yours. The whole timeline thing was probably the largest flaw in our project, but in our defense, we had no idea our little experiment would grow to the size that it has."

Gravigo looked at Jacy and smiled. "This will be one of your greatest hurdles to face here. Time does not exist in your current definition of what time is. Time is quite fluid here. We can slow down a hummingbird's wings or have a decade of your time pass in an eye blink."

Gravigo stood and sauntered around the gigantic desk. He moved in front of Jacy, leaning on the edge of the desk. "I apologize; I really do, from the bottom of my heart and beyond.

This is only the third time we've ever had to explain this to one of you, and it doesn't seem like I'm very good at it."

Jacy looked away from Gravigo and watched the three little men and three little women work away. She was riveted to what Gravigo was trying to explain to her, she just had troubles soaking it all in. Diverse timelines, assorted life forms, these wacky little figures who were supposed to be models of Gravigo and his team more than four billion years ago?

Gravigo sighed, leaning in closer to Jacy. "I know, I know," he said in a voice so caring Jacy's heart nearly melted. "This is all so mind-boggling for you.

He reached out slowly, gently caressing her cheek. He then tousled her hair. "But you'll get it. I know you will." He stood and returned to his side of the desk, looking down at the little workers.

"This is not how we actually look, of course. I made us human-like in this model to make things easier to comprehend. This is the original team- Maise Elantina, Flair, Granny Mandible, who was known as Mother Atlas back then, Fatter Verb, Octavio Tosiri, and myself. Our project was to see if we could create a life form on a previously uninhabited planet. This was easy enough stuff, for a team of our intelligence."

Gravigo chuckled, looking at Jacy. "I know that probably sounds very egotistical to you, but I don't say that with any vanity. I only speak the truth." He returned his look to the mini-people, still toiling away on his desk.

"Creating life on a planet wasn't good enough for us, though. That's why we searched so hard and long for a planet like Earth. As I said earlier, we found many capable of hosting life, but we wanted more than that. Our project had to be perfect."

He smiled at the moving model on his desk.

"And we did it, we really did it. Not only did we create life on a planet, we created one that would evolve. Of course, we had no idea it would evolve to the extent it did when we first started this project. Flair, that egotistical bugger, likes to try and take credit for this, but if we're all completely honest about it, we know this was done by pure chance. Basically, it was a galactic fluke."

Gravigo looked at a wide-eyed Jacy.

"See, while we were waiting to see if life was going to take hold on Earth, we researched the other planets in your arm of the galaxy. We were studying the orbit path of the planet you call Uranus, when we discovered this."

The word Uranus made Neva giggle. Gravigo erased the model on his desk with his right hand and used his left hand to create another model. Jacy's eyes widened as she watched an eight-inch triceratops graze in a field of overgrown grass.

"These life forms were astounding. They were like nothing we had ever seen before. But there was one more part that was even more astonishing."

Gravigo raised his eyes to meet Jacy's, practically glowing as he warmed to this most obvious favourite topic of his. "We could control them."

Jacy's eyes registered a state of disbelief that delighted Gravigo to the point of giddy laughter. Did he just say they could control dinosaurs?

Gravigo clapped his hands, and heaved a nice, after-belly-laugh sigh. "We could control them, Jacy. Like puppets without strings. I could make this xjjytrrt...sorry, I'll use your terminology. I could make this triceratops attack a Tyrannosaurus Rex. I could control a whole damn herd of triceratops, if I wanted. We all could. We could make all and any dinosaurs do our bidding."

Jacy exhaled the best she could with sewn together lips. Creating life? Controlling dinosaurs? This damn invisible vise on her lips? She was at the stage of collapsing. She squirmed against her arm ties and muffled out whatever sound she could from her compacted lips. Gravigo held up a finger.

"Hold on," he said, slowly running his hand over the desk, creating a vast array of different species of miniature dinosaurs on his desk. "I'm just about finished my introduction."

Jacy watched all the different dinosaurs, recognizing some, ignorant of others. Her wide-eyed look fell upon an Allosaurus. She watched it with fascination. "You always liked Allosaurus'," Gravigo's words broke her interest. Jacy's eyes rose to him with raised eyebrows.

"I never really knew why," he smiled at her with that father/daughter look she caught him giving her earlier. "I remember you receiving an 'A' on that 5th grade report you did. I felt you deserved a higher mark, but apparently that's as high as those teachers of yours will give."

Jacy was almost as shocked at this last statement of Gravigo's as she was when he told her he and his buddies created life on Earth. Gravigo either didn't notice or care about her befuddlement as he had already returned his attention to the dinosaurs on his desk.

"Anyways, this was all so very remarkable, but it also became really, really boring," Gravigo continued. "We had to control everything they did. Eating, sleeping, procreating…"

Neva snickered again.

"It all became too much for us to take care of these guys properly," Gravigo gestured towards a huge dinosaur munching on the leaves of a tree. "Christ, do you know how many leaves it takes to fill an Edmontosaurus up?"

Gravigo looked at Jacy.

"So," he sighed, "we decided to bring in some help from home."

He shook his head, mournfully. "At the time it was the best decision we could make, it really was. Unfortunately, the people we went to for help screwed us royally."

17

Maise Elantina paused at the bottom of the cracked and faded concrete stairs, taking in her environment. She sighed, wishing she was meandering one of her favourite walking trails, instead.

Maise didn't like the area she was in. Glancing casually to her left and right, she wasn't surprised to see both directions of the dilapidated ghetto area devoid of any activity. This wasn't the kind of place one enjoyed hanging out in.

The eyes, she knew, though, were on her. Maise had made too many trips here to think otherwise. As she took the first step, she heard the massive front door of the decaying building creak open. Just like clockwork, she thought. She didn't bother looking up, focussing on the crumbling stairs, instead. She knew who would be waiting for her at the top when she reached the front door, anyways.

There'd be Dickie, Joey, and Lucy; each of them a shade under the age of five years old, and each of them looking cuter than buttons and sweeter than cotton candy. At least until they opened their mouths, that is.

"Jingle Bells," Dickie sang as Maise neared the top stoop the three children were now lounging on.

"Deck the halls," Joey sang next.

Maise made it to the stoop and looked down at the curly, raven-haired Lucy.

"Maise Elantina sucks donkey balls!" Lucy sang-shouted, her eyes blazing into Maise, causing Dickie and Joey to burst into gales of toddler laughter.

"She said 'donkey balls'!" Dickie hooted, causing Joey to cackle with glee.

Maise looked at the boys and smiled, their laughter too infectious to cause anything else. She had to fight to keep the grin on her face as she turned her gaze to Lucy, though.

"Fuck you, you dirty tampon," Maise's eyes twinkled. The retort caused the boys to snort and lose their breath.

"Lucy's a tampon, Lucy's a tampon," Dickie tried to chant in between hoots of snickering, but failed miserably. Lucy's eyes narrowed.

"Fuck you, Dickie, you motherfucking fuck...." Maise slipped through the door and closed it, muffling Lucy's profanity laced tirade against poor Dickie.

"Why must you bother to engage them?" a frail woman's voice came from a room off to Maise's right. Maise strode into the room, smiling at the toothless, grand lady she had come to see.

"Because they'd be disappointed if I didn't," Maise answered. "How are you doing, Granny Mandible?"

"I'm doing as good as an old woman can do, I reckon." Maise Elantina nodded, though not in agreement. Maise never let Granny Mandible's appearance fool her. Granny was one smart and tough lady. "You here for pleasure or business?"

Maise smile dazzled. "Granny Mandible, it's *always* a pleasure to come see you, you know that."

Granny Mandible waved away the compliment as she stood from her rocking chair, her knees quavering. Maise Elantina gave Granny a warm hug.

"Yeah, yeah, whatever," Granny muttered, fussing with the faded orange shawl that rested upon her bony shoulders as she extracted herself from Maise's embrace. "Save the bullshit for when you need it, pretty lady. Come, come, let's have us some tea."

Maise followed Granny Mandible into her cramped and dungy kitchen, sitting on one of the two mismatched chairs. Granny puttered around, finding a dented kettle to put water in. Maise smiled, marvelling at how long the two ladies had known each other. All the way back to the beginning. There were troubled times, and happy times. Peaceful times, and ferocious ones. Maise Elantina and Granny Mandible made it through all of them, though, which was astounding when Maise considered some of the nastier episodes.

This was one of the main reasons why Maise rarely dwelled upon times such as those. It was too arduous to proceed forward when one was towing a heaping load of troubled past along. She only wished Flair and Gravigo would share a similar philosophy.

"I expected you to come see me before now," Granny scolded her, bringing Maise from her reverie.

"My sincerest apologies, Granny Mandible. Things have been…well, they've been kind of hectic lately."

Granny snorted as she placed the kettle on one of the old stove's elements. "Hectic, schmectic. Things are always chaotic. Now I hear things have gone to fucking rot, too. "

Maise wasn't sure what to say. Granny Mandible knew all.

"I told Flair when he was by the other day that this whole thing is stupid. This has gone on *way* too fucking long. He and Gravigo need to just have this thing out and move the fuck on. Now we have this…this…" Granny waved her hand around, "what's her fucking name again?"

"Jacy. Jacy Morgan."

"Yes, yes, that's right. This bloody Jacy Morgan is going to cause more trouble and havoc here than ten Buzzed Rottids ever could, mark my goddamned words, Maise, mark my stupid, fucking, goddamned words."

Maise Elantina smiled, not willing to meet Granny Mandible in this argument. "You may be right, Granny…."

"Oh, no, no maybes about it. I can feel it in my rickety old bones," Granny Mandible stopped talking, eyeing Maise for a brief moment. Granny then began to cackle with laughter.

"That's right, I keep forgetting," Granny Mandible fetched a crumpled Kleenex from the counter and wiped at a drip of spittle that had escaped the corner of her mouth. "You have one of those human cretins in your group, don't you? That…that…oh, what's her name? That spicy, black bitch?"

"She's not a bitch, Granny Mandible, and besides, you love Lita," Maise grinned at Granny.

"Lita still a Bone?" Granny sat down in the other chair opposite the cracked Formica table that separated them. Maise hesitated before answering. Granny nodded.

"Not for long, eh?"

Maise chuckled. "Probably not. She'll end up with Hammer Coolie, eventually. Until then, though, she is still a Bone and she's one of the reasons I came to see you today."

Granny Mandible gestured with her right hand for Maise to go on. Maise told her what transpired.

"Rusty Sleeves," Granny Mandible sneered, as she rose on wobbly knees to get the now-whistling kettle. "Just the sound of his name makes me want to shit in my granny panties."

Granny Mandible took the kettle and slopped some hot water into two cups. She searched the grimy cupboards for some tea bags. "I'll have something in store for Rusty fucking Sleeves, and that's a freebie, too. That one I'll do just for fun. Now, why don't you tell me the real reason you've come here?"

Maise Elantina couldn't help smiling at Granny Mandible. The woman was incredibly perceptive.

Granny discovered the tea bags, dropped them into their cups, and handed one to Maise. "Knock that puzzled smile off of your face. Do you forget how long I've known you for? Shit, I knew you when you were just some perky priss who was so dumbstruck in love that you didn't know your tits from your ass hole."

Maise didn't say anything to this. Granny Mandible loved to throw around the age and wisdom card when in reality, there was little difference between the two of them, physical appearance notwithstanding. Maise tried everything to get Granny to pay more attention to her physical self, but to no avail. Granny Mandible was content with who she was.

Granny placed a wobbling cup on the table and sat down. "Now, we all know how much you love those wacky walking trails of yours, but I hear you've been overdoing it, even for you. Tell Granny what's going on in that lovely little head of yours."

Maise sighed, looking away to collect her thoughts. Dickie, Joey and Lucy had quietly re-entered the house and were passing by in the adjoining room. Lucy sneered at Maise and gave her the middle finger. Maise didn't bite this time. She returned her attention to Granny Mandible, looking her dead in the eyes.

Maise Elantina began talking. She talked and talked and talked. Granny Mandible listened. She listened and listened and listened. When Maise finally finished speaking, Granny Mandible sat silently for a few long moments. Finally, Granny slapped the table with an open palm and cackled with laughter.

"Child, you are chock full of a whole bunch of what the fucks, ain't you? God love you, Maise, you definitely keep things interesting around this place."

"But can you help me?" Maise Elantina leaned towards her, both elbows on the table. Granny stopped laughing, but her eyes twinkled with merriment.

"Of course I *can* help you. The million-dollar question is will I?" Maise Elantina and Granny Mandible sat stone quiet at the table, both refusing to blink. Granny broke the calm with a raspy chuckle.

"Looks like you and me have some business to discuss," she declared.

Maise nodded, smiling. She expected nothing less from Granny Mandible.

18

"See, when we sent the call home for assistance, that's all we were asking for. *Assistance*. Maybe some more bodies, which would help us get a handle on things," Gravigo waved his hand over his desk top, erasing his team of mini-people.

"Our minds were blown by who came to us."

Gravigo used his left hand to scan over the middle of his desk, producing three very imposing figures. It may sound weird to call three little six-inch people imposing, but even at this scale model, the three figures were pretty intimidating.

"The Three Generals arrived amid a cloak of deep secrecy," Gravigo too seemed awed by the miniature figures. "As I said, they were the last people we thought would show up. Sir Sullen Slow, Tzarina Rebel Hew, and Last Sentinel. Last Sentinel was promoted recently, and they took one of our original team, Tosiri Octavo, to replace him, but at the time, Tosiri was one of us."

Gravigo's paused for a moment at this statement; then shook his head. He looked up at Jacy.

"The Three Generals are the epitome of power," he nearly whispered. "For them to show an interest in our tiny project was almost implausible. Or devious. Take your pick."

Gravigo looked down at the Three Generals again. "The Three Generals were at the infant stages of harnessing an asteroid's power as a military weapon. Of course, they knew a huge asteroid would demolish a planet, but they were studying the effects of what smaller, more pin-pointed ones would do."

Gravigo sighed heavily. "And they were very curious as to the effects on living creatures who could somehow survive an episode like that."

Gravigo looked at Jacy with unadorned sadness. "They decided to blast Earth with an asteroid."

Gravigo sighed again and stood. He ran his right hand over the corner of his desk to produce a leaf munching brachiosaurus. He lumbered towards the mini dinosaur, watching it fondly. "These animals were so beautiful. They were living, breathing organisms. We created them."

He held his hand in a fist over the dinosaur; then unclasped his hand, causing the dinosaur to burst into ash and smoke. "And then we failed them."

Gravigo waved his hand over part of the desk to create Earth, as it would look from space. He used his other hand a short distance away to produce a streaking fireball. "We argued the best we could, but it was in vain, of course. You can't argue with The Three Generals, nor should you. We took a heavy personal risk by merely disagreeing with them."

Gravigo and Jacy watched the asteroid get closer and closer to Earth. "We managed to get some of the life forms away from the planned place of impact. At least we got that much. We didn't have the time, nor were we allowed to save many, but we did get some out of the way."

Gravigo and Jacy both silently watched the asteroid collide with Earth, a mini-explosion erupting on the desk. Jacy slumped back in her chair after watching a massive hole punched into her planet. She was unable to tear her eyes from her ruined home.

"And that was it," Gravigo waved a hand over the devastated planet, leaving an empty space on the desk that Jacy continued to stare at. "The Three Generals did their follow-up research in short order and returned home, giving us the highest praise and the best marks possible for our project. We were allowed to remain here for a while, and we did our best for the few surviving creatures. It wasn't long, though, before we were summoned home for an emergency and had to abandon our assignment."

Gravigo plopped into his chair and stared at Jacy for a moment or two. Jacy hoped he would remove her restraints, but Gravigo's story wasn't quite finished, yet.

"Little did we know, though," a sparkle returned to Gravigo's eyes, "that in our absence, all the fun began."

19

Flair watched Sultana Yelp attempt to take his massive cock into her mouth. Sultana could get most of the head of Flair's monster penis in before she began to gag, which was more than any other Lady Skull could accomplish. It was more than a few Bones and Hats ladies could do, as well. Of course, Sultana Yelp had more practice at fellating Flair than most, which partly explained her limited success.

Movement of white caught his eye. He glanced over at his assistants, all white frocked and taking notes. The four of them would have absolutely no participation this evening. They were to observe and take notes only.

Sultana languidly licked the entire length of Flair's engorged member, storing her energy before she attempted to stuff him into her mouth again. Flair returned his attention to her, mentally ranking where Sultana Yelp should be situated on his ladder of his favourite ladies.

She was a lock for top 10, with an outside shot of hitting his Top 5 was Flair's decision just as a gulping Sultana attempted to swallow him again. Since his split with Maise Elantina eons ago, Flair never found himself another permanent partner. There was maybe one female here he would deign to consider giving number one status to, but that was it. Since there was zero chance of that coupling occurring, Flair played the field.

Getting slightly bored with Sultana's latest unsuccessful excursion, Flair checked out the activity going on around them.

Not a bad orgy, he surmised after scanning the area. There was a little bit of everything happening tonight. Two sexy ladies rubbing their oiled bodies together, which he found pretty sexy. Two males locked in a sixty-nine, which he didn't. Gay men didn't bother Flair one way or the other, it just wasn't what he was interested in. Moving on, Flair watched triple, quadruple, and quintuple groups of naked bodies, all entangled in a jungle of moans and sweat so he couldn't tell exactly which body part was connected with which body.

His assistants paid special attention to each and every coupling. The whole sex thing confused the bejesus out of Flair. One way or the other, Flair was determined to unravel the mysteries of sex.

After glancing at a persistent Sultana Yelp, Flair scanned the crowd again. Of all the carnal fun taking place, the sight that caught his eye was The Bam Slicer, who was actually partaking in tonight's festivities. Flair watched him screw a purple haired beauty with ample breasts doggy style while a cute young blond thing stood over top of her, grinding her crotch into The Bam Slicer's face.

Flair nodded to himself in approval. It was nice to see Bam enjoying the fruits of his newfound success as #2 of the Skulls. Flair returned his attention to Sultana Yelp who had now straddled him, trying to guide his penis into her vagina without much success.

"Christ, Flair," Sultana Yelp panted, her dark hair cascading down and sweat running between her naked breasts. "This fucking thing will *never* fit in there."

"Keep trying," Flair murmured, trying to keep his mind in the moment, but failing miserably.

Gravigo. It was always that piece of shit-stained fuck Gravigo that interfered with all things Flair. He grunted in exasperation, which Sultana misunderstood as appreciation, so she bore down harder to take even more of Flair's hard on inside her.

Flair's mind was miles away, though. Fucking Gravigo, ruining a good goddamned orgy.

Gravigo was irking Flair because in the original deal, Gravigo only got to meet the new one and explain the situation in a ballpark way. Then the three groups, the Skulls, the Hats, and the Bones, all of them received a free and fair shot at recruiting her.

Gravigo was taking way too fucking long to explain things to Jacy, though. Was he already recruiting her? Flair wouldn't put it past him. On top of the Gravigo thing, he had the whole Hammer Coolie issue going on, weird whispers about Maise Elantina, all the leader activities that was expected from him, etc. etc. How much could a guy take?

Frustration and anger boiled over Flair so swiftly he didn't even notice it was there before it was too late. Growling, he grabbed Sultana's hips and flung her to the side, causing her to squeak in surprise. He quickly got on his knees, turned Sultana over so her ass was high in the air, and positioned the head of his dick against the opening of her vagina.

"Jesus, Flai...."

Without pause, Flair buried himself as far as he could into Sultana's hot pussy. Sultana screamed, causing some of the orgy participants to see what was going on. Flair grabbed both of her hips and began to pound into her with all he was worth. He wasn't even fucking Sultana Yelp anymore, he was fucking his anger, his frustration, his hurt.

Sultana whimpered out wordless grunts as he continued to pound into her mercilessly.

"Holy shit, she's taking the entire thing," Flair distantly heard a female to his right say. He was surprised to see he had a bit of an audience congregating. This aroused him even more. As he felt the pressure in his balls begin to build, he grabbed the neck of one of the female bystanders. She was a cute little pixie-haired thing with a mischievous glint in her eye.

"Down here," he commanded, pushing her head down so her cheek rested on Sultana's ass as he pulled out of Sultana. With his other hand he grasped his throbbing cock and started to stroke it, unable to fully wrap his hand around it. The girl watched in fascination as the head of Flair's dick seemed to grow even larger in the split second before he exploded what seemed like gallons of cum all over her face. She tried to take as much in her mouth as she could, but it was impossible to hold it all.

Spent, Flair leaned back on his haunches. He looked at Sultana, lying there like a rag doll, barely able to move. Take that, Gravigo, Flair thought. And you, too, Hammer Coolie. Take that *everyone* in this whole place. I am going to fuck each and every one of you worse, or better, than how I just fucked Sultana.

For the first time all evening, Flair allowed himself to grin.

20

Gravigo waved his hand over the Three Generals, erasing them. His desk was now completely empty.

"When we left, we expected all life forms who had somehow survived the asteroid blast to die off. After all, they needed us to eat and survive. Without us, we assumed they'd all die off naturally."

He smiled at Jacy, his eyes dancing. Gravigo waved a hand over the nearest corner of the desk from him, creating a miniature member of his team, working in a lab-like setting.

"This is Flair," Jacy couldn't tell if Gravigo said this with fondness or loathing, but she leaned towards the latter. "Flair was the youngest member of our team, a brilliant hot-headed little bugger."

Gravigo shook his head at the Mini-Flair before returning his eyes to Jacy. "When we were summoned home, Flair's duties became quite minimal and he wasn't very happy about that. He accused us, me in particular, that we had slighted him somehow. Nothing was further from the truth, but his resentment remained unabated."

Gravigo looked back at the miniature Flair. "Because his duties were so minimal, I asked him to check up on Earth from time to time. He wasn't to do anything special, just keep tabs on what was happening here, if anything. I felt it was the best thing to do, as his erring anger towards me was getting to us all."

Gravigo waved his hand over Flair, making him disappear. "Flair reported back from time to time, always quite vague with his reports. From those skimpy accountings, though, I detected something else going on. At my first opportunity, I did an unannounced drop-in here."

Gravigo waved his hand over the center of his desk and a group of mini-men appeared, maybe twenty or thirty of them. He then waved his hand over the corner of his desk and a tiny, Neanderthal-like man appeared.

"Flair stumbled onto something miraculous back here. Well, he'll tell you he created it, but whatever. That's not true. The bottom line here is that life not only continued on in our absence, but it evolved, as well."

Gravigo motioned towards the little caveman. "Along with the obvious physical evolution, another advancement had taken place, too. We could no longer control these new beings, as we once could with the dinosaurs. But, while we couldn't control them, we could give them an urge."

Jacy's eyebrows furrowed as she watched Gravigo study her. An urge? They could give man an urge?

"Somehow, these new life forms carried with them an echo of what we had with the earlier life forms. So while we couldn't control their every movement as we could with the dinosaurs, we could give these new life forms a nudge, an urge."

Gravigo leaned on his desk towards Jacy. "Or, to put it more accurately, we could give them a gut feeling. And thus, the Game was born." Gravigo leaned back and chuckled at Jacy's incredulous reaction.

"I apologize," he motioned at Jacy's muzzle. "I've been so immersed in my explanation of the origins of the Game that I forgot you still had that on." He nodded at Neva who promptly extracted Jacy's gag and arm restraints.

"You okay?" she asked Jacy in that melodic voice. Jacy nodded and looked at Gravigo as Neva Tezremsy returned to her post.

"Sorry for being such an ass," Jacy apologized.

Gravigo waved her apology away. "It's okay. This is a ton of stuff to take in all at once. You should've seen ole Baz, remember, Neva?"

Both of them shared a chuckle over whatever Baz's reaction was.

"Can I ask a couple questions?" Jacy asked.

Gravigo erased all the activity off of his desk. "Of course. Go ahead."

Jacy struggled to focus her ruminations. She probably had close to a billion questions to ask, and each one of those would lead to a billion more, but she had to start somewhere.

"The Game," she began. "The Game is your control of human beings? We are merely game pieces for you?"

"No," Gravigo shook his head emphatically. "Your people are not game pieces at all. The dinosaurs could've been considered game pieces, as we could fully control them. You humans, though, we can't control. We can only give humans gut feelings. Whether you choose to follow those gut feelings is entirely up to the individual."

Gravigo regarded Jacy seriously. "Make no mistake about this, Jacy. Humans are entirely sentient beings. Human beings are unique life forms, not puppets. This is integral for you to understand."

"Okay, I think I get that, sort of," Jacy nodded slowly. "You don't have the ability to control us, but through gut feelings, you have the ability to help us."

"And harm you, as well," Gravigo nodded gravely. Jacy's eyebrows arched in query. Gravigo let out a long, slow breath.

"We have three main groups here in the Game, Jacy. The White Hats, which is my group, The Skulls, who Flair is the leader of, and the Bones. Each group has very different views on how we help or harm humans."

"I'm guessing the White Hats are the good guys…"

"…and the Skulls are the bad guys."

"Where are the Bones?" Jacy asked.

"Somewhere in the middle," Gravigo answered after pondering the question for a moment or two.

"Okay," Jacy sighed, "so the White Hats are the good guys, the Skulls are the bad guys, and the Bones are somewhere in between good and evil?"

Gravigo hesitated before answering. "In theory, that's it in a nutshell."

"In theory?"

Gravigo sighed again. "The White Hats, or the Hats as we are better known as, will give gut feelings for what we think is good. The Skulls will give gut feelings for what they think will create havoc. But we are not infallible, not by a longshot."

"I don't think I understand," Jacy admitted.

Gravigo stood and slowly paced behind his desk. "Let me put it this way. The Hats have done more good than bad, and the Skulls have done more bad than good. But sometimes, we make mistakes. I may give someone in my pod what I think is a gut feeling for something good, but it could turn out I was wrong."

Jacy slowly nodded her head in understanding. "So in that case, you actually gave that person a gut feeling to do something bad."

Gravigo slapped the corner of his desk and cackled. "Exactly! Just another wonderful wrinkle in the Game."

Jacy pondered this for a moment before she eyed Gravigo evenly. "So where do I fit into all this, Gravigo?"

The light that was once there in Gravigo's jolly eyes extinguished with Jacy's question. He looked away for a long moment before returning his now sad eyes to Jacy. "You weren't supposed to die. A rule was broken here, and you died as a result of that broken rule. If a rule is broken, restitution must be paid."

Gravigo sat down, resting his forearms on his desk. "I couldn't bring you back to life, Jacy. We can do many things here, but restore life on Earth is not one of them. There are other things we can do, though, on top of the punishment that the rule breaker receives."

Jacy held Gravigo's eyes with hers. "Was I in your pod, Gravigo?"

Gravigo smiled such a gentle yet sad smile, Jacy almost burst into tears. "Yes, you were, and since I couldn't bring you back to life on Earth, I did the next best thing. I asked to bring you here, which is something that is rarely, rarely done."

"You mentioned I'm the third one."

"Yes you are. First Baz, then Lita, and now you. Bringing you here used up most of the restitution I was entitled to. I also requested and received 25 human years of safety for Beau and Derian."

It took a few seconds for that to register in Jacy's swirling brain. "Really? You did that?"

Gravigo leaned back in his chair and smiled. "That was the maximum I could get. Now, that safety doesn't cover natural causes, mind you, but for 25 years, neither Beau nor Derian can be harmed in any way by the actions of anybody here."

Jacy savoured this tidbit of awesome news. Derian was safe. Beau was safe. A tiny bit of the weight on her shoulders gently lilted away. And then just like that, she came crashing back to her new reality.

"But I'm still dead, right?"

Gravigo nodded. "Yes you are, but only on Earth. What you will find here is…"

"What I'll find here is not Derian and Beau," Jacy stood, noticing Neva step towards her. She looked at Neva. "Don't worry. I'm not going to go crazy again."

Neva looked at Gravigo, who nodded at her. She stepped back into place.

"Jacy, if you'd just let me…"

Jacy held her hand up to silence him. Gravigo acquiesced. Jacy walked to a corner of his office and studied an intricate and exquisite flower. At least, she assumed it was a flower, as she had never seen anything quite like it. She reached over and touched a petal of brilliant, purple hue. The petal was softer than silk, and the purple turned sunset red under her finger.

"It's from my homeland," Gravigo's soft voice told her from behind. "It's a favourite of my people."

Jacy turned and looked at Gravigo for another long moment. "This place isn't your home?"

"No, it's not."

"So where are we, Gravigo? We're not on Earth, heaven and hell don't exist, we aren't in your homeland. Where are we?"

"It's not easy to explain, I'm afraid. Are you familiar with the phrase 'seeing is believing'?"

"Of course."

"Well, where you are now it's the opposite. You need to *believe* to *see*. Do you follow?"

"Nope."

"Fair enough," Gravigo nodded. "Let's try it this way. What did you think heaven was? Did you really believe a place on the clouds, people with wings, large pearly gates, and all that?"

"No, of course not."

"So what did you think heaven actually was?"

"I'm not sure," Jacy admitted. "I guess heaven was always more like an idea than an actual place."

"Perfect," Gravigo smiled at her. "That's where we are right now. We are on a different plane of existence. We are here, and all of this is real. If you were on Earth, though, you wouldn't know we existed."

"If I was on Earth, I'd be with my daughter and husband, right now," Jacy frowned.

"Jacy," Gravigo stood and walked towards her. "I'm so sorry, if I could've saved your life back on Earth, I…" he looked down in disappointment. He was now within arm's reach of Jacy. She reached out and softly put her hand on his cheek.

"I know you would've done everything in your power to save me, Gravigo," she told him. He looked up at her with an alleviated look in his eyes. Jacy smiled and pulled Gravigo towards her. He seemed surprised by her gesture, but soon accepted and returned her warm embrace.

"I always wondered what a hug from you would feel like," he whispered in her ear.

Jacy pulled away from him and smiled. "Did it pass the test?"

Gravigo clasped her hands in his, his childish grin threatening to split his face in two.

"With flying colours," he laughed, tugging her hands. "Come here."

Gravigo led Jacy back to his desk. He then turned her so they both stood facing the long barren wall of his office.

"I know you have a million and one questions to ask me," he continued to hold Jacy's left hand.

"At least that many," she squeezed his hand, making Gravigo smile again.

"We have all the time in the world for that during your training."

Jacy's eyebrows turned inwards. "Training? Training for what?"

Gravigo's smile turned almost roguish. "Training for what, you ask?" Gravigo swept his arm theatrically in the air, causing his plain, bare wall to become floor to ceiling windows. Jacy's jaw dropped in awe.

"Training for this, Jacy," he led a speechless Jacy to the massive window. "Training for…"

Gravigo clasped her hand tightly.

"…the Game."

21

Maise Elantina watched Rainy Dissolve shuffle along the wooden walkway that led to Maise's hut. Maise's home was a bamboo hut that resided in the middle of a large, ripple-less lake. Maise rarely conducted business in her home, but for certain people at certain times, she did. Rainy Dissolve, the vice president of the Bones, was one of the few people Maise allowed in her personal place.

Rainy Dissolve had a good half mile walk to the middle of the lake, so Maise stood, and slowly wandered her deck. She drummed her fingers on the tall glass of iced water she held, recalling her meeting with Granny Mandible the night before.

Maise Elantina loved Granny, but that didn't mean Maise trusted the frail lady a full one hundred per cent. Maise believed Granny was on the same page as her regarding Maise's concerns, but Maise was a little wary as to whether they shared the methods on how to get what they needed.

"You okay, Ms. Maise?" The Fox intruded in her thoughts. Maise Elantina glanced towards the corner of the expansive deck, where her one of her few indulgences sat. Her home itself was a minimal bamboo hut, which was fine with her. Maise Elantina didn't need much in the way of material things.

She loved her music, though, so her one extravagance was a live cloned band called The Lion, The Bear, The Fox.

"I'm fine, Fox. Thanks for asking. Could you guys play something mellow?"

The Fox nodded as all three picked up their weathered acoustic guitars. The Lion counted them in to a quiet version of their song 'Shine.'

Maise smiled, letting the music awash her as she stared out at the serene lake. She wished her brain and heart were as calm as the water's surface and song. It was times like these she actually missed Flair. For all of his foibles, Flair always was a cool balm on Maise Elantina's psyche.

Of course, the beginning of Flair and Maise's relationship was anything but calm. After discovering how life evolved from dinosaurs to humans, all six of the original team returned, took the form of humans, and barrelled head first into creating the Game. It was such an incredible time. Maise took a sip of water, her eyes glinting at the memory of it.

At the time, Granny Mandible and Flair were fucking. Granny Mandible looked entirely different then, of course. She was known then as Mother Atlas and was so damned beautiful, she almost stung your eyes. Maise, going through a bit of a wild phase, accompanied them in more than a few threesomes.

Over time, though, Granny and Flair grew apart and Maise and Flair grew together. There were never any hard feelings on Granny's side. Granny took up with Fatter Verb, Gravigo and Tosiri Octavo had whatever it was they had going, and Maise and Flair fell in love. Business carried on without skipping a beat.

The last thought broke Maise Elantina's tranquil feeling. *Business.* They had to take care of business. What would become of their people if....

Rainy Dissolve's shuffling up the stairs caught Maise's ear. Shaking her head from earlier thoughts, Maise met Rainy at the top of the stairs. She gave Rainy a large hug, feeling the poor girl shrink from even that minor affection. Maise led Rainy to a table with two wicker chairs surrounding it.

Maise smiled at Rainy as they sat; Rainy looking at Maise with attentive, cloudless eyes. Maise Elantina knew others found Rainy Dissolve's appearance uncomfortable to look at, but as Maise told many and all who would listen, she thought Rainy Dissolve was the most beautiful person she ever laid eyes on.

Rainy Dissolve wore her greasy black hair over her face as best she could, as if she were trying to cover the scars that covered the entire right side of her face. Her nose was bent as if broken a half dozen times in the past, and three large warts resided on her lower left jawline. Rainy's lips were chapped, and the few times Maise saw her teeth, they were crooked and broken.

The reason Maise Elantina rarely saw Rainy's teeth was because she never spoke. Not once. Rainy had been number two in the Bones since their origin, and Maise never heard Rainy speak a single word. Whether that was by decision or design, no one knew. In fact, nobody could recall how Rainy Dissolve became number two of the Bones in the first place. Maise herself couldn't recall ever meeting Rainy, she was just there. Always. Forever.

Maise Elantina smiled at all of these thoughts as she looked at Rainy, clad in all brown. Brown shirt, brown pants, brown boots. The only colour visible were her frosty blue eyes, though one rarely saw those as she was always looking away and down.

As always, Maise Elantina shrugged away all of that as the only thing that mattered was that Rainy Dissolve was the best number two in the Game. Hell, she was probably the best in the Game, period. Flair often told Maise that if Rainy Dissolve would speak one word, just one tiny word, she could be leader of any of the three groups. She was just that damn good.

Nobody knew how or why, either. Rainy was this mysterious being, she would arrive with nobody knowing and exit without anyone really even aware that she had been there. Maise had been with Rainy long enough to not be surprised nor unsurprised if Rainy was or wasn't there. It's just the way things were.

At the end of the day, though, Rainy Dissolve succeeded in everything she did. She was so good that once Maise gave her a task, Maise never thought of it again. It was if merely asking Rainy Dissolve to do something meant it was done.

"We have a few things to deal with here," Maise told Rainy, and for the next hour Maise spoke on what needed to be done. Being the largest group, there was always a ton of housekeeping issues amongst the Bones. Maise and Rainy kept on top of it, though. Maise Elantina leaned back in her chair and sighed, looking at Rainy.

"If I tell you something, can I trust you'll keep it to yourself?" Rainy's expression didn't change, she merely regarded Maise with her head slightly tilted to the right. Maise winked at her and smiled. Rainy's expression didn't waver.

"I think," Maise leaned forward, resting her forearms on the table, "and I hope I'm wrong, but I think there's something heavy coming down the tracks at us. Not just us, the Bones, but us, as in everyone."

Maise sighed, looking towards the band as they moved into a quieter than normal version of their song, 'Freedom' for a moment before returning her regard to Rainy. "If I'm right, things could get a little crazy around here. I need to ask you to do a few things if this ever comes to pass, no matter what I say in the future. If this…this apocalypse or whatever you want to call it comes to fruition, I need you to do these things no matter what. Do you understand me?"

Rainy Dissolve's expression remained unchanged.

"Good, here's what you'll need to do," Maise Elantina spoke until the sun began to dip below the horizon and the band ceased to play. When Rainy Dissolve left the deck, Maise Elantina walked to the outdoor bar, and poured herself a glass of cabernet sauvignon. She took a long sip, hoping everything she just told Rainy would never happen, but something told her it would.

Despite the warmth of the early evening, Maise Elantina hugged herself. Suddenly she felt a little chilled.

22

"Oh….my…God…." Jacy spoke in a revered whisper after Gravigo's office wall became a floor to ceiling, wall to wall window. "This is…This …is…"

Gravigo clutched Jacy's hand and gripped it tight. "*This* is the Game, Jacy, right before your very eyes."

Jacy stepped closer to the window, extending her free hand until it came to a tentative rest against the glass pane. The scene took Jacy's breath away.

"They're playing the Game right now?" Jacy attempted to take it all in, but flunked. She could see enormous, crowded tables and lonely, near empty ones. Some tables were boisterous like a riotous drinking party, others as subdued and studied as a chess match.

Jacy was having a tough time wrapping her mind around everything that Gravigo told her and what she now saw with her own eyes. She didn't know if all this was some illusion or hallucination or if everything Gravigo told her was the gospel truth.

'Buy the ticket, take the ride,' Hunter's advice rang through her muddled brain with startling clarity. For now, that's all Jacy was able to grasp.

"Yes," Gravigo's eyes never left the scene that mesmerized Jacy.

"It's all so hard to fathom," she almost whispered, eyes trying to take in all the outside action. "People live and die by what goes on here. Wars are started, wars are stopped. Disasters evaded, disasters invited."

Gravigo looked over at Jacy with arched eyebrows. "I wouldn't give the Game quite that much credit, Jacy."

Jacy tore her eyes from the Game and looked at him. "But you said the Game gives us humans our gut instincts. Our gut instincts, well, mine anyways, were almost 100% correct."

"The Game does do that, but do you know how often people don't listen to their instincts? Do you know how prevalent it is for humans to ignore their gut instincts?" Gravigo waved his arm, making the window a wall again.

"Much stronger than the gut feelings we can give is human instinct itself. Believe it or not, there have been times where the Skulls and the Hats have worked together to avoid bloodshed and wars, only to have those efforts die in vain. Take your 2003 invasion of Iraq or the 1994 genocide in Rwanda as more recent examples of our failures."

Jacy returned to Gravigo's desk, nodding at the Amazonian Neva as she did. Jacy decided it never hurts to have a giant on your side. Neva nodded back, returning the smile to Jacy.

"So who controls human instinct?" Jacy asked.

"Humans do," Gravigo sat back down across from Jacy. "Do not over-estimate our power here, Jacy. I could give you feelings on how to get to a crossroads, for example, but I could never make you choose which path to follow."

Jacy nodded slowly. "But you could give me a gut feeling on what would be the best choice, right?"

"On what I believed to be the correct choice, yes. But you had to actually follow that nudge, that advice."

"I must've frustrated the shit out of you, didn't I?"

Gravigo chuckled. "More than you'll ever know."

Jacy laughed. Gravigo clapped, and stood up. "Look, as I said before, I know you have at least a million questions. I promise they'll all be answered in time, but for now, let's take a little walk."

"A walk?"

Gravigo merely smiled and did that increasingly annoying thing with his hands again. He and Jacy disappeared once more.

"Jesus, Gravigo, I wish you'd quit..." Jacy stopped in mid-complaint as Gravigo wouldn't have heard her anyhow.

"So, what do you think?" Gravigo leaned in so he was inches from Jacy's ear. He had to yell to be heard due to the all-out aural assault being waged on Jacy's ears. The outlandish din was a combination of a very large crowd coupled with music blaring at eleven. Maybe eleven and a half.

"Where are we?!" Jacy bellowed back into Gravigo's ear.

"We're on the Gaming Floor. This is where it's at, baby!"

Jacy couldn't help but smile at Gravigo's infectious enthusiasm. He was a man clearly in his element. "Why the loud music?!"

Gravigo ripped off an air guitar riff that would make any teenaged boy proud. "We can't get enough of your music!"

Jacy listened to see what the song was.

'Sunspot baby, you sure had me way outguessed...'

"You're all Bob Seger fans?!"

Gravigo laughed, swiping his hand across him. The music's volume receded to just-prior-to-bleeding-eardrums decibel. "Not just Bob Seger fans. We're dedicated fans of *all* your music. My people don't know how to create it!"

"What?! Really?!" Jacy looked at Gravigo to see if he was pulling her leg. Disappearing stairways, giving humans gut feelings, that weird thing he did with his hands. All of that and they couldn't make music?

"Scout's honour," Gravigo gestured towards the song being played. "We can *play* this song note for note. In fact, we can play every song you have verbatim, but for us to put three chords together in an original and ear-pleasing way, well...that's outside our area of expertise. Music is a trait that is singularly human. It's all yours."

"You don't have music in your homeland?" Jacy asked, as Gravigo led her through the jungle of tables.

"We have sounds," he answered over his shoulder, "lots and lots of sounds, but nothing anybody would ever classify as music. My people have very little time and patience for any kind of art."

Jacy sensed Gravigo's disappointment with his people as she followed Gravigo through a section of the Gaming Area. The mood in this room was almost celebratory, like a Vegas casino, or a hopping night club. There were hoots of pleasure, howls of derision, the clapping of hands, and the slapping of foreheads.

And the people! The people were every shape, size, and design one could imagine. Blacks, whites, Asian, Latino, you name it. Men in suits, casual attire, naked. Females in showy dresses, regular clothes, or nothing but a G-string. Midgets, tall people, fit people, fat ones. Jacy had a tough time keeping up with what her eyes were seeing. She tugged on Gravigo's hand, causing him to stop.

"Can we slow down for a bit, please?"

"Sorry, Jace," Gravigo nodded. "I just wanted you to get a taste of the Gaming Area before you started your training."

Jacy scanned the hodgepodge of humanity around them. "Gravigo, I'm only the third human here, right?"

Gravigo nodded.

"So, all these people are from your homeland?" she asked.

"The majority are. Some come from other places in the universe, but not many. The standards to get here are pretty high."

"Okay," Jacy had no idea what he was talking about, "but why is everyone here human? Is this what people look like throughout the universe?"

"No, no," Gravigo shook his head. "We don't look like this at all. It was decided that this is the form we'd take when we…"

"Jesus Buddha, Gravigo!" Jacy exclaimed. "I just saw Marilyn Monroe!"

Jacy scanned the crowd more closely now. She saw a muscle bound guy in a tight speedo. She saw a regular, Jane Doe female. She saw another guy in full military regalia. She then saw…

"Holy fuck, is that Sean Penn? What the…"

"That wasn't Sean or Marilyn," Gravigo patted her hand.

"Then what…how…who…"

"That's step one of your training," and with another ridiculous movement of his hands, they were gone again.

23

Johnny Bazinski, better known as Baz, tallied blade of grass number 351,647,222 and sighed. Pinching that blade of grass tight enough not to lose it but loose enough not to tear it out of the ground, Baz slowly rolled his neck around, stretching his tense shoulder muscles.

"Hey Baz," a voice called from his left. "You hear about the new human chick that showed up yesterday? Maybe she'll have a hankering' for some Polish sausage."

Baz looked over at the snickering Ugly Earful with a bemused expression. Ugly Earful had situated herself in Baz's counting vicinity when his grass count neared its first hundred million. Baz didn't mind her being around. He could do much worse for company.

"Ugly," Baz mused aloud, "please don't refer to my cock as a mere sausage. I'm wielding a knock of bratwurst down there. The thing is gargantuan."

Ugly Earful erupted into laughter, holding up one of her hands while the other clung to the last piece of grass she counted.

"Please," she wheezed in between giggle bursts. "No more, I'll lose my place."

"You started it," Baz teased, but he quit making her laugh, too. If one lost their place counting, they had to start at the beginning again. Baz had to do that twice so far, and he knew how bad that sucked.

Everything about being a Grass Counter was horrible. There were a million rules to break or not break in this crazy place, but there were basically only three that resulted in being sentenced to count grass forever. One, don't physically enter the Game; two, you can't change your appearance without letting everyone know; and three, no funny business during the Weaning Fest.

Pretty bloody simple. If one broke any of the other rules, the worst punishment they'd receive would be some time in a Re-Education camp. Not Baz, though, no way. He had to fuck up one of the major rules and end up here, counting blade after blade of grass forevermore.

Baz sighed and thought of the new human, Tracy, or Lacy or something like that. It would surprise people to know how fast gossip made it to the Grass Counters, given their low station here, but Grass Counters received fresh information all the time.

Baz shook his head. He felt for the human lady, whatever her name was. This place was beautiful and amazing, yes, but it was cruel and cold, too. He hoped she'd never have to discover that fact.

Sighing again, Baz resumed his count.

351,647,223. 351,647,224. 351, 64....

24

"Can anyone else do that?" Jacy asked, after finding herself in a large room alone with Gravigo.

"Do what?"

"That stupid herky jerky thing you do with your hands."

"Nope, just me and Maise and Flair," Gravigo's brow furrowed a bit as he said Flair's name.

"Maise?"

"Maise Elantina. Leader of the Bones, and former partner of Flair. We'll get to the both of them later."

"Okay," Jacy nodded and let it go. "So what's this?" Jacy gestured towards an enormous, complicated looking machine that stood in the middle of the cavernous room.

"This," Gravigo beamed as he led Jacy closer to the crazy looking contraption, "this is the Transmogrifier."

Jacy looked at Gravigo to see if he was joking or not. He was smiling, but he didn't seem to be pulling her leg. "The Transmogrifier?"

Gravigo chuckled. "That's our nickname for it," he ran his hand over the gleaming silver side of it. "Its actual name is Klhthdc, but we enjoy the term Transmogrifier much more."

"So what does it do?" Jacy admired the sleekness of the machine.

Gravigo raised his eyebrows at her. "You enjoyed the Calvin and Hobbes comics. I'm surprised you ask."

Jacy looked at Gravigo. Calvin and Hobbes? What would Calvin and Hobbes have to do with this? Then it hit her. Calvin 'invented' a transforming machine that could convert him into whatever he wanted to be. The machine was called the…

"…Transmogrifier," Jacy said aloud. "You named this high tech baby after something in a comic strip?"

Gravigo laughed. "Your comics were never quite the same after Bill Waterson and Gary Larsen retired. They were brilliant."

"I agree," Jacy sauntered alongside the machine, Gravigo following.

"I thought this would be the best place for you to start," Gravigo told her, motioning towards her attire. "I figured you may want to change into something, oh, I don't know. Something more you, perhaps."

Jacy looked down at her now-oversized Oakland Raiders sweatshirt she had borrowed from Beau. Jacy hadn't even thought of her clothing with everything else going on. Not that she had ever paid much attention to it back on Earth, either, but normally she was better clad.

"Thanks," Jacy nodded at Gravigo. "Now that you mention it, I'd like to change into something a little nicer."

"Okay," he clapped his hands together while leading her to the entrance of the machine. "The Transmogrifier is really quite remarkable. See, when we set up the rules for the Game, we decided we should all look human, as well. It kind of adds a bit more authenticity to the Game, if you ask me. Anyway, we brought out the Transmogrifier to allow this to happen."

"So…" Jacy wasn't fully grasping what Gravigo was talking about.

"You walk into here," Gravigo gestured towards the entrance, "and think of how you would like to look. Then bingo, you walk out the other side exactly how you imagined. That's how you saw Sean Penn and Marilyn Monroe back there."

"What? Are you kidding me?" Even with all Jacy had seen and been through so far, this seemed like a bit of a stretch.

Gravigo nodded enthusiastically. "Let me show you," he pointed towards the other end of the machine. "Go over to the exit and watch me come out."

"Okay," a skeptical Jacy complied, heading to the exit of the Transmogrifier. She turned around when she got there.

Gravigo gave a thumbs-up and entered the machine. The Transmogrifier immediately began to hum and lights on the outer shell flickered intermittently. Before Jacy realized it, Gravigo was emerging through the exit.

"Good evening, Jacy. What do you think?" Grav…No, it wasn't Gravigo who strolled out of the machine. This new figure had Gravigo's voice and exited the same machine that Gravigo recently entered, but this person *definitely* wasn't Gravigo.

Standing before Jacy now was a male of similar age to her who looked as if he just stepped from the pages of Esquire magazine. Jacy slowly circled this new being, checking out the form-fitting suit on this new, dashing figure.

"So what do you think?" he asked again, still in Gravigo's inimitable voice.

"I like, I like," Jacy studied the handsome face. "Is this really you, Gravigo?"

"You bet," he spun a little circle. "That's how simple it is to use the Transmogrifier."

Gravigo turned to a side wall that was a floor to ceiling mirror. He played with the collar of his stylish shirt. "When you get to the Gaming floor, you will see a vast array of human forms. Some people like to look like celebrities or other famous people, some like to be extremely attractive, others merely like to be comfortable."

Gravigo tore his eyes from his reflection to look at Jacy and smile. "That's why I chose the form I did. It just feels right to me. Even though I am far more eye-pleasing like this, it's just not me."

With that, Gravigo returned to the entrance of the Transmogrifier and stepped in. The machine hummed again and deposited the Gravigo Jacy knew out the exit.

"Better? Or worse?"

Jacy looked at him closely, understanding Gravigo's meaning. The looks Gravigo chose suited him much more than some male model.

"Better," she smiled. "*Much* better."

"Well, I'll trust you are being truthful and not merely trying to be polite," Gravigo glanced at himself in the mirror before smiling and gesturing towards the entrance of the machine. "Your turn."

Jacy let out a little sigh and headed towards the entrance of the Transmogrifier. What was she going to want to look like? She looked back at Gravigo. "Do I get more than one shot at this?"

"Of course," he nodded. "You can have as many turns as you like, but keep in mind. Once you choose a look, you can't change it without permission."

"Or you'll send me to my room?" Jacy teased.

"Or you could end up sentenced to be a Grass Counter," Gravigo raised his eyebrows.

"Oh," Jacy nodded, swearing to herself she wouldn't change her appearance without asking permission first. She peered inside the machine. More than a little apprehensive, she took a deep breath, and, with Hunter's advice of "buy the ticket, take the ride" ringing through her brain, she pictured an image in her mind and walked through the Transmogrifier.

"Ta-daaa!" Jacy posed for Gravigo as she stepped from the machine.

Gravigo did a double take. "Wow!"

Jacy spun in her Dolce and Gabbana designed dress that hugged her now 38-24-36 body like white hugs rice. As she pirouetted on her Christian Louboutin heels, a shimmering diamond necklace swung along with her.

"You approve, monsieur?" Jacy checked out her high class self in the mirror. She could feel Gravigo studying her, not saying a word. She turned to look at him.

"Well?"

Gravigo grinned, reddening slightly. "You look smashing, Jacy, you really do. I...I've just never seen you look like this."

Jacy admired herself in the mirror for a moment more, and then nodded. "You're right," she said, returning to the front of the machine. "Check this out."

She entered the Transmogrifier again, noticing how thoroughly boring it was on the inside. Gray, gray, gray.

"Well?" Jacy stepped out.

Gravigo clapped and whistled. "Bravo, braaaaaavooooooo!"

Jacy giggled as she twirled, checking out her seventeen-year-old self wearing her favourite blue dress in the mirror.

"Prom dress, right?" Gravigo asked.

Jacy looked at Gravigo in the mirror. "You saw my prom?"

Gravigo began to look a little uncomfortable. "Uh, just enough of it to make sure you were safe."

Jacy remembered what happened after her prom. She suddenly felt self-conscious. She continued to scrutinize Gravigo.

"What? I'm serious. Scout's honor." Gravigo held his right hand up as he put his left over his heart. Jacy wasn't sure if she entirely believed him or not, but decided to let it go.

"Check this one out, Grav," Jacy scooted back to the entrance and stepped in again.

"Jesus, you were cute as a button," Gravigo spoke to a six-year-old version of Jacy as she stepped out of the Transmogrifier. "I almost forgot how cute you were."

Jacy did a little girl spin in her bright green dress. Gravigo walked up behind her, locking eyes with her in the mirror.

"You know," he said, looking almost wistful," I remember back when you wore that dress to your grandparent's Easter party."

"I remember," Jacy nodded.

"Do you remember when your Grandpa was pushing you on the swing in the backyard?"

"When my Grandma gave him shit for letting me get this dress dirty?"

Gravigo laughed. "Yes, but do you remember the conversation you and your Grandpa had?"

Jacy looked at Gravigo's reflection in the mirror for a few moments. There was something there, nagging at the back of her brain.

"I...I kind of..." Jacy shook her head, the image fading.

"You asked him...." Gravigo coaxed her.

"What's on the other side of the clouds, Grandpa?" Jacy smiled at Gravigo in the mirror. Her grin was returned ten-fold.

"And he said...."

"Everything. Everything is on the other side of the clouds."

Gravigo was still smiling. He gave Jacy a solemn nod. "Seems like Grandpa knew what he was talking about."

Jacy thought about this, moving back towards the entrance to the Transmogrifier. Her brain bordered on overload, and memories of her grandparents and childhood seemed like a *way* too much to be on her mind at the moment.

"You okay, Jace?"

Jacy nodded as she neared the entrance to the machine, willing her mind to slow to an easy crawl. Buy the ticket, take the ride. All her unanswered questions would be answered in time.

"How about this one, Grav?" she said and an instant later she popped out the other end, all decked out Madonna-chic, circa 1986 or so.

Gravigo laughed and cheered as she preened in front of the mirror. "True blue, baby, I love you," Gravigo sang.

What followed was a goofy assortment of different forms Jacy experimented with. Jock, diva, hobo, policewoman, stripper, which made Gravigo look away and blush. Every style, occupation, and nationality Jacy could think of, she tried it.

"Is this the form you want?" Gravigo asked in an incredulous tone.

Jacy recently emerged from the Transmogrifier as a male body builder. She watched herself in the mirror as she ran her fingers over her naked pecs with an almost sensuous look in her eyes. "No," she sighed, "I probably wouldn't be able to keep my hands off myself."

Jacy entered the machine for the last time, and when she emerged, Gravigo let out a soft, wolf whistle. Jacy studied her pre-pregnant body in the mirror. Half shirt, faded blue jeans, sensible shoes.

"Just like back on earth," Gravigo commented, "but your boobs are a little bigger and your bum is a little smaller."

"Poetic licence," Jacy shot back as Gravigo pantomimed zipping his lips shut. She looked in the mirror, adjusting her breasts. "And besides, they're not *that* much bigger, they're just a teensy bit firmer."

Gravigo raised his eyebrows. Jacy playfully glared at him, daring him to say something. He shook his head and smiled. "You look fantastic, Jacy, you really do. I'm really happy you chose your normal looks. Now come on," he reached out and touched her arm, "there's someone I want to introduce you to."

"Wait."

Gravigo looked at her with raised eyebrows.

"You said you guys took the human form to make the Game more authentic, right?"

Gravigo nodded.

"So what do you guys really look like?"

Gravigo sighed. "Jacy, it'd be hard to…"

"Okay, okay," Jacy took Gravigo's hand. "Not quite yet, I get it. But at some point, I want to see what you guys really look like. Deal?"

"Deal," Gravigo nodded, after a brief hesitation. And with that plus a hand wiggle, they were gone.

25

Gravigo led Jacy, clothed in attire more to her liking, through the Gaming area to a quiet corner where four or five tables held only one or two players each. The thrashing sounds of Guns N Roses' 'Paradise City' faded a bit as her and Gravigo approached a table where a pretty, black woman sat. She was the lone occupant of the table.

"Lita?" Gravigo asked/called to her.

Lita didn't flinch. She was doing some kind of weird hand movements over the table, entirely engrossed in the centre of the table. She was in the middle of one movement that looked like she was pulling melted mozzarella cheese from the table when Gravigo called her name again, a little louder this time.

"Lita!"

Lita's hand movements didn't miss a beat, but her gaze flickered towards the two of them for a split second.

"Hey, Grav," her eyes settled on Jacy. "I was curious when you'd bring the rookie over." She finished her hand dance with a flourish.

"How's Serena?" Gravigo nodded towards the empty table.

"The girl will be the death of me yet," Lita sighed. "Well, that would be true if I wasn't already dead, eh, Gravigo? Maybe she'll be the 'life' of me, instead." Lita followed her statement with a wonderful laugh. She offered her hand to Jacy.

"My name is Lita, honey. You must be Jacy."

"Nice to meet you," Jacy shook Lita's firm yet inviting handshake.

"I thought it'd be a good idea if…" Gravigo began.

"…you introduced Jacy to one of the only two humans in this crazy place," Lita finished Gravigo's sentence. "And there was no way you were going to introduce her to Baz, eh, Grav?"

Gravigo did his best to ignore Lita's comments. "Why don't you sit with Lita for a few moments? I've got a couple things to check on. I'll be back in a bit," Gravigo left before Jacy could answer. She watched Gravigo's departing back with her response stuck in her throat.

"Sit, honey," Lita pulled out an empty chair directly to her right. "Grav'll be back. He's still a bit uncomfortable around me, that's all."

Jacy sat in the offered chair. "How come?"

Lita smirked and leaned towards Jacy. "He's still pissed I turned down his offer to join the Hats. He'll get over it, though. He'll come around."

Jacy studied Lita and guessed her to be pretty close to her own age of 33. Lita was definitely attractive enough, but that wasn't what was so eye-catching about her. Lita just looked like fun.

"He asked you to join the Hats?" Jacy asked.

"Sure, you'll be getting the same offer. You'll have to choose between one of the three groups when your training is done."

Lita started to mention the fourth unofficial group she was thinking more and more of becoming a part of, but decided against it. Though on the surface Jacy seemed to be taking all this pretty well, Lita knew from experience that inside she was an emotional tornado. Lita returned her look to the middle of the table.

"Goddamn that girl," she muttered before resuming her shamanistic hand movements once again.

Jacy looked where Lita's gaze was fixed She saw nothing but a dark section of the table. "Goddamn which girl?"

"Goddamn that Serena, that's who…." Lita stopped in mid-sentence, furrowing her brow at Jacy. "Is this the first time you've sat at a table, sugar?"

"Yes," Jacy nodded. "I just came from that Transmogrifier thingamajig to here."

"Well, scoot over here, Jacy," she motioned towards a chair beside her. "Let's bust your cherry."

"Pardon me?" Jacy slowly moved towards the offered seat.

"The Game, sugar. Want your first taste of it?"

Jacy's question meter had rung up well into the millions, but she tired quickly of getting answers that made no sense to her anyways. She looked over in the direction where Gravigo went, and was surprised he hadn't made it too far. He was now in a heated discussion with some biker looking dude. Shrugging, Jacy sat in the chair beside Lita.

"Get ready, Jacy-girl," Lita smiled brightly. "You are about to have your mind blown like it's never been blown before."

One thing Jacy learned about Lita was that Lita did not exaggerate things. Jacy's mind *was* blown.

26

When Gravigo left Lita and Jacy, he sighed. He knew he was spending too much time with Jacy, but he couldn't help himself. What happened to her back on Earth was wrong, but at the end of the day, Gravigo blamed himself. Jacy was one of his pod, and it was his job to get her home safe, every single day. He failed fantastically, and now almost hated himself because of it.

Someone else may have taken solace in the fact that the cheating Skulls had to break the rules to kill Jacy, but Gravigo wasn't the sort to do that. The good Gamers, the great ones, adjusted to wrinkles on the run all the time. That's what made them great.

The sad thing, in Gravigo's mind, was that *he* was considered one of the eminent ones. One didn't become the leader of one of the Big Three by being just a good player. No, to get to that spot one needed to be remarkable.

So even though cheating caused the death of Jacy, Gravigo had a hard time letting go of the feeling that he betrayed her. Both Neva and the logical side of him argued against this, but Gravigo wouldn't accept it.

Jacy was dead, plain and simple. Sure, she was here, which Gravigo loved, but Jacy was human and humans belonged on Earth. Earth was her home. She should be cuddled up with Beau or cooing over Derian right now, not trying to wrap her brain around concepts that even Stephen Hawking would struggle with.

Gravigo shook his head. He decided that leaving Flair and Maise waiting for the chance to meet Jacy was the least of his worries. Right now he needed to...

"Hey, Fat-ass!" an all too familiar voice called out. Gravigo sighed, watching the swarthy figure of Flair weave through the crowd towards him. Gravigo waited until Flair got closer before narrowing his eyes into a hostile glare.

"Moi? Fat-ass? The depth of your vocabulary truly astounds, you big dummy."

Flair halted about ten feet in front of Gravigo. Gamers around them eased away, creating an empty space consisting of only Gravigo and Flair.

"When do we meet the human bitch?"

Gravigo didn't bite. He stared at Flair until Flair looked away, rolling his eyes. "Fine, when do we meet Jacy?"

"I was just coming to look for you and Maise to see what would work best for you both. I know Maise's calendar is quite flexible, but yours must be chock full with all the problems you are having with your own people and…"

"Spare me the sermon, cheese hog. When?"

"Soon," Gravigo took a deep breath, trying to hold his anger in.

"Not good enough, Fatty. When?"

Once, just once Gravigo would love to *lose* it on Flair in public. He never does, of course, as being leader of the Hats carries a level of decorum that must be met and held. Once, though, just *once*….

"Hello, you fucking stupid…"

"Tomorrow. Will that suffice?"

Flair looked like he was about to say something, but didn't. Instead he only nodded, eyeing Gravigo as a semi-smile appeared. "Okay, tomorrow, first thing in the morning. Training room 3B. Got it?"

Gravigo let go of a deep breath. He understood. Jacy was to receive nothing extra than the other newcomers. Gravigo wasn't going to be able to shelter her forever, though if she joined the Hats after her training was done, that was exactly what Gravigo planned to do.

Gravigo seethed as he walked off. He didn't have much time left with Jacy before the others would latch themselves upon her, trying to get her to be a Bone or a Skull, or maybe even worse, a free agent. Flair tossed a closing insult at him that he didn't hear. Gravigo had too much on his mind to worry about the thoughts of a foolish dingbat.

27

Jacy looked down at the table as Lita continued her voodoo hand motions. Her breath ensnared in the back of her throat.

There, clear as a bell, stood Serena, fiddling with a locker in a high school hallway. She wasn't like those six inch figures Jacy watched on Gravigo's desk. Serena was a full size, actual human being. It was tough for Jacy to wrap her brain around exactly how she was seeing Serena merely by looking at the middle of an empty table. Nevertheless, she viewed her, sort of like a movie, but kind of not.

Jacy closed her eyes for a moment and inhaled a palliative breath. 'Buy the ticket, take the ride,' a recognizable voice spoke from within. Jacy respired the breath she held and opened her eyes again.

"Sorry, I know it's a little overwhelming at first," Lita smiled, never removing her eyes from Serena. Lita's hand movements became more fluid. "This is a high school in New Westminister, close to your home. You ever been to New West?"

"Many times," Jacy nodded.

"Beautiful place, your province," Lita paused as she stole a glance at Jacy. "Serena's a good girl, but well, she's a teenager, right?"

Jacy was mesmerized by what she observed. "She's a pretty little thing," was all she could offer for the moment.

"She sure is," Lita's smile brightened the room. "I just wish she could see what a freaking knockout she is. She thinks she's gawky with no boobs."

Jacy laughed, recalling a similar feeling at that age. Jacy leaned forward, studying Serena, trying to gauge her age. Watching Serena made Jacy feel old, which is a remarkable feat when one is already dead.

"She's 16," Lita spoke, reading Jacy's mind.

"Wow," Jacy chuckled. "Has it really been 17 years since I've been her age?"

"We got to live two of Serena's lifetimes," Lita was still smiling, though it lost its radiance a bit. "Ain't that a kicker?"

Jacy looked at Lita, feeling the best she had since she took her first step in this crazy place. Maybe it was finding someone like herself, maybe it was her personality. Jacy didn't know, and didn't care. All she knew was that she felt better being in Lita's presence.

"She's a good girl, though?" Jacy returned her gaze to the centre of the table.

"Yeah, she is," Lita never took her eyes from Serena. "She gets A's and B's, mostly B's, has a part time job at Petro-Can, and volunteers at the local hospital as a candy striper. On top of all that, she plays the saxophone and babysits her little brother a ton. He's a total pain in the ass."

"She sounds like an angel," Jacy compared herself to Serena when she was that age and felt somewhat intimidated. When Jacy was that age, her main three occupations were the phone, beer, and boys; not necessarily in that order, either.

"She is an angel," Lita nodded, "most of the time, anyways. Remember what I said. She *is* a teen-aged girl. She definitely has her moments."

Lita's voice held a touch of pride in it. Jacy smiled as they both watched Serena fish some textbooks from her locker.

"Is Serena your only one?" Jacy asked.

"Yeah, I did have…" Lita's face darkened for such a quick instant, Jacy thought she imagined it. Lita's face returned to its original glow. "Yes, Serena is my only one."

Jacy looked towards Gravigo and noticed he was still in a heated conversation with the biker dude. "You said you turned down Gravigo's request to join the Hats?"

"Yep," Lita nodded. "I turned him and Flair both down. I'm a Bone. I could never join the Skulls, they're just plain bad news. I like Gravigo and all, but the Hats are a little stuffy for me. I was totally drawn to Maise Elantina and the Bones, but now am unsure."

Lita sighed and looked at Jacy. "Keep that under your hat, though, okay? Who knows where I'll end up? Maybe I'll be the female version of Hammer Coolie."

"Who?"

"Hammer Coolie. He's the top free agent in this place, not to mention the finest piece of ass I've ever seen, alive or dead."

Jacy laughed at Lita's hungry smile. "What's a free agent?"

Lita tore her eyes from Serena, reached out, and patted Jacy's hand.

"Look, I know all of this is over the top, shit house rat crazy. I was in your shoes not that long ago. After you're finished your training, you'll understand all this stuff better, I promise."

Lita looked down at Serena again, still keeping her hand movements to a minimum. Serena held her books and was about to close her locker.

"A free agent doesn't belong to any of the three sides," Lita explained, monitoring Serena. "A free agent can cut deals and work with or against any of them. Of course, you don't have a safety net of a team behind you, either, but that's what makes the dreamy Hammer Coolie so good at what...oh shit."

"Oh shit, what?" Jacy noticed a scowl cross Lita's face as her hand movements became sharper.

"Meaning 'Oh shit, here comes Scott'," the way Lita said Scott's name made it apparent he wasn't welcome.

Jacy looked down and saw Scott, his stringy hair not covering the hoop earring in one ear, but reaching down onto the Bon Jovi patch on the back of his jean jacket.

"Are we back in the 80's?" Jacy giggled.

"Everything comes back in style, sooner or later," Lita chuckled, too. "Let's hope they leave the crimped hair back where it belongs."

"What's wrong with Scott?" Jacy asked as Scott sidled up to Serena's locker.

"Shhhh," Lita shushed Jacy, her hand movements picking up momentum. Jacy obeyed and watched the action below.

"Hey Serena, whazz up?" Scott leaned against the neighboring locker. Serena averted her eyes, blushed, and pretended to be busy with the books she just extracted. Oh Buddha, Jacy thought. Serena has a crush on this guy. Jacy looked at Lita who wore a look of total concentration.

"Hi Scott," Serena said, acting as nonchalant as a love struck, teenaged girl could.

"What's up tonight?" Scott asked.

"Nothing with you, you little perv," Lita mumbled as her hand motions sped faster.

Serena looked down at the hallway floor. "I have to babysit my brother tonight."

"Atta girl, that's my girl," Lita soothed, her hand dance becoming more rhythmic.

Scott looked away as if something more interesting caught his eye, before returning his youthful gaze to Serena. "Want me to pop over and help babysit?"

"*Oh no, she doesn't!*" Both of Lita's hands drooped down about an inch off the table, and then moved graciously upwards.

"I don't think tonight's a good idea," Serena told Scott. "I've got to take the little shit to baseball practice, and I've got a Biology test tomorrow as well…"

Scott held up his hands as if he were surrendering to an oncoming army.

"Hey, no prob. Maybe another night," Scott said as he walked away, leaving Serena to sigh when she thought he was out of earshot. She leaned her back against her locker.

"That's my girl," Lita wore a triumphant smile as her hands settled down.

Jacy did her best to absorb the happenings before she asked the obvious question. "What's so wrong with Scott?"

Lita looked at Jacy as if she'd just sprouted fifteen heads. "You *saw* him, didn't you?"

"I did," Jacy shrugged. "He wouldn't be my type, but Serena is crushing on him."

"Exactly," Lita frowned. "And before Serena, Betty Surowski liked him, too, until he fucked her in the bush and blabbed about it to the entire school. Poor Betty is now the school slut, even though Scott was her the only one."

"I see," Jacy looked down at Serena who still rested against her locker.

"And you want to know what else that little gigolo did? He...uh-oh...hold on..."

Serena straightened up. "Scott?"

"No, baby, no, hon, what are you..." Lita's hand did a graceless jive.

"Yeah?" Scott was part way down the hallway when he turned back towards Serena.

"No, Baby no, Baby no......" Lita pleaded.

"9:00 sound okay? My parents won't be home until at least 11:00."

Scott smiled the way Jacy imagined a wolf did when invited into a chicken coop.

"I'll see you then," he said, pointing both fingers at Serena in a 1950's sort of way, making his way down the hall. Serena, after a moment's hesitation, broke into a huge smile.

Lita, on the other hand, banged her forehead against the table. "Stupid, stupid, stupid..."

Jacy wasn't sure what to do. She wanted to console Lita, so she reached out and put her hand on her shoulder while looking for Gravigo. He would know what to do.

When she looked to the last place she saw him, though, she realized he was gone.

28

Neva Tezremsy wasn't surprised when Gravigo returned to the office nostril-flaring mad.

"*DO YOU KNOW WHAT THAT....*" Gravigo sputtered when he appeared out of thin air, halting in mid-rant when he saw Neva's hand raised. Gravigo looked confused until Neva tilted her head in the direction of the office corner. Gravigo followed her lead.

"Cruder Stiletto. And Unsay Moon. I'm deeply sorry for being late."

After nodding his thanks to Neva, Gravigo approached the two visitors. They both stood to shake hands.

"Is everything okay, Gravigo? You seemed a little flustered when you appeared," Cruder Stiletto asked, her shrewd eyes boring into his.

"I'm fine, everything's fine," Gravigo assured her.

"If everything is fine, why did you show up here so angry?" Unsay Moon asked.

Gravigo sighed. "It's nothing, really. Just a couple Skulls getting under my skin, that's all."

"If there's anything I can do for you, Gravigo, please just say the word. I am here for you," Unsay Moon declared solemnly.

"Ditto," Cruder Stiletto's mouth barely moved as she spoke.

"And I thank you both," Gravigo patted both of them on the shoulder. "The offers are very much appreciated. Now, how is the agenda looking?"

"We are working on the framework right now and..." Unsay Moon began.

"Gravigo, may I have a moment?" Neva's honeyed voice carried across the room. Gravigo walked over to Neva and held a swift, whispered conference. Gravigo nodded, and Neva exited the office.

"Cruder Stiletto and Unsay Moon," Gravigo called to them. "My sincerest apologies again, but there is something I need to tend to. Please continue to work on..."

"With all due respect, Gravigo, we need to get this agenda finished today and we need you to…" Cruder Stiletto's face was grim.

Gravigo held up a hand. "I leave the agenda's framework in both of your capable hands. I will not be long. We will iron out the details when I return."

"But…"

It was too late. After a quick hand movement, Gravigo was gone. He reappeared in another office where Neva awaited him.

"Thanks," he mumbled, making his way to the personal bar in the corner of this less spacious work space. "I need a drink. Care to join me?"

"No, thank you," Neva, in her full bodied, tight, leather bodice folded her muscular frame into a chair opposite Gravigo's personal desk. Gravigo returned with two three fingered glasses of 1924 Royal Brackla. Neva shook her head at the glass Gravigo placed in front of her.

"I said, no, thank you," she repeated.

"Suit yourself," Gravigo shrugged, placing both glasses in front of him as he took his seat across the desk from Neva. "Okay, what's up?"

Neva sat up straight and spoke in a professional manner. "Unsay Moon is plotting to overthrow you."

Gravigo sipped his scotch as he took this information in. Neva misunderstood Gravigo's pause as surprise.

"I know it's a bit of a shock. I thought if anyone it would be Cruder Sti…" she started.

"No, it's not that shocking. In fact, it's not a bad move. Unsay Moon has always been the shrewder one. How much support does he have?" Gravigo placed his glass down.

"Not enough, but he does have some. The other Hats feel you've spent far too much attention on your feud with Flair, and not enough on the big business at hand."

Gravigo nodded and shrugged simultaneously. "And they're probably right. Let's put out gentle reminders in the right ears and let's have a proper embarrassment for Unsay Moon at the convention to stop any momentum he may currently have. I will reign in my interest in Flair; publicly, at least."

"Yes," Neva nodded. "Any preferences as to what kind of embarrassment?"

"Surprise me," Gravigo clapped his hands, and shot the rest of his first scotch. "Is there anything else?"

Neva hesitated. "Two things. I know you only like facts, but I'm hearing some loud whispers about something potentially very big in the planning stages."

"Already?" Gravigo shook his head. "Jesus Christ, we're still dealing with the fallout of the whole Jacy thing. Are the Skulls really going to strike heavily again so soon?"

"From what I hear, it's not the Skulls who are in on this one. "

Gravigo frowned, reaching for the second glass. He sipped and mulled this latest revelation from Neva. He looked at her again. "I take it there is some pretty reliable whispering, as you wouldn't bring me rumours and innuendo."

Neva nodded. She didn't like doing this, as crazy rumours take away too much valuable time. Neva felt a heavy element of truth to this one, though. If it was as big a deal as she felt it was, they needed to be on top of it.

"Any suggestions?"

"A loose tail on Maise Elantina," Neva's voice went quiet.

Gravigo raised his eyebrows and took another drink. He wouldn't ask Neva who her sources were or why she suggested a loose tail on Maise. His trust in Neva was complete. Neva kept certain secrets from Gravigo, for sure, but she would never betray him or the Hats.

"Okay, keep it *very* loose, though. She's too good an ally to show her we may distrust her," Gravigo nodded, then shot the remains of his scotch. "Number two?"

"Pardon me?"

"You said you had two more things. What's the second?"

"I'm curious if you intend to tell Jacy the real reason for our mission here."

"Our mission is to help humans become the best species they can be."

Neva didn't blink. She never unlocked her eyes from Gravigo's. Gravigo continued the staring contest but his heart obviously wasn't in it.

"Look, Neva," Gravigo sighed. "No matter what other reasons we have for being here, you know we all want what's best for human beings. Even Flair wants what's best for humans."

"Your people, though...."

"Yes, yes, my people. You know my feelings on this. I believe we can get what we need without bringing harm to an innocent species."

"Innocent?" Neva smirked.

"Innocent to our mistakes, I mean," Gravigo slapped his desk. The two of them had this discussion many times before.

Gravigo glowered hard at Neva before asking, "Do you think we should tell her?"

"I'm not sure," Neva shrugged. "On one hand I feel she's bound to find out from someone, so why not us? It might give us the inside track on getting her to join the Hats."

Gravigo nodded. "And on the other hand?"

"On the other I feel she's not ready yet to hear the real reason we are here. It's a tough decision."

Gravigo remained silent for a moment before answering. "Let's both think on it for a bit, okay? The poor girl has been through so much. Let's let her get her feet under herself."

Neva nodded and stood. Gravigo did the same. "These rumblings you are hearing. Are you positive the Skulls don't have anything to do with this?"

Neva shook her head. "Of course I'm not positive. They're the fucking Skulls. Look, you just get Jacy started on her training and get back here to take care of our business. And stop worrying about the Skulls so much, okay? I keep a *very* close eye on Flair."

29

Jacy didn't have long to panic about Gravigo's absence, as before she knew it, he appeared out of thin air. He watched Lita continue to head-butt the table before turning his attention to Jacy.

"Scott?" he asked.

Jacy nodded. Gravigo reached across the table and rubbed Lita's shoulder. "Don't worry, Lita. She'll come to her senses."

Lita didn't respond, but she had at least ceased coco-bonking the table.

"Come on, Jacy," Gravigo said. "We need to move on."

Jacy didn't want to leave just yet, but she didn't know what else to do. Lita raised her head, smiling a tired smile at Jacy. "Go on, Sugar, come back when you get a chance."

"It was nice to meet you, and thank…" was all Jacy got out before Gravigo waved his hands and Jacy disappeared.

"That's *really* starting to get on my nerves, Gravigo," Jacy frowned, and then stopped. "Whoa!"

"You like? This is my personal residence."

Jacy and Gravigo were standing on a large deck attached to a colossal log home. Jacy stared out at the fir covered mountain.

"This is breathtaking," she half-whispered.

"Thank you," Gravigo stared at the mountain, too. "Sometimes I worry it's a little too much, you know? But then other times, I feel I deserve it."

"Does everyone get homes such as these?" Jacy asked, meandering across the capacious deck.

"No," Gravigo answered. "Just the other two leaders and myself. Granny Mandible and Fatter Verb qualify, but they choose to live where they live. Come on."

Gravigo led Jacy into the cabin. Jacy marvelled at the beauty of it; this definitely was not a cabin one's Grandpa built with his own two hands. The place was incredible, with its 17 rooms, sprawling wood burning fireplaces, outdoor waterfalls, and more. The tour took at least 45 minutes to complete.

"So, you like?" Gravigo asked once they sat down in his personal study.

"I love," Jacy said. "It's a little more than I expected from you, though."

"It's minor compared to Flair's monstrosity," Gravigo waved his hand through the air. "But you're right. Sometimes I feel the same way, too, but it's not much different than leaders of your countries. Have you seen that hideous thing the prime minister of Turkey built?"

Jacy admitted she hadn't. She was starting to realize how little she paid attention to things on Earth that were outside her immediate surroundings. "How are your group's leaders chosen? Do you guys have elections?"

"Yes, we do," Gravigo gestured to a comfy chair for Jacy to sit down in. Gravigo took a seat on the other side of a much smaller, much more elegant desk than the one back in his office. "Our democracy works wonderfully here, unlike on your planet."

"What's wrong with our democracy?"

"One of the troubles with yours is that you allow money to enter the mix," Gravigo began looking through the drawers of his desk for something. "Money distorts democracy. Money perverts everything, actually. The sooner your people realize what an unnecessary evil money is, the sooner you'll become a superior race. If you add proportional voting to the elimination of money in your elections, it will be infinitely more fair than your loopy system. Neva, where is my remote?"

It startled Jacy when Neva moved past her, handing a large object to Gravigo, who nodded his thanks.

"Hi, Jacy," Neva smiled as she left the room.

"Hi, Neva," Jacy still wasn't too sure about Neva.

"When we first got to the cabin, you seemed a little perturbed about my method of transportation. That surprises me, as I thought you'd be impressed by it."

"It's just a little disconcerting, that's all. Can't you just walk like everyone else does around this place?"

"Said the woman who would drive her car to get milk from a store situated six blocks away," Gravigo muttered, spinning his chair towards the blank wall on their left.

"Touché."

Gravigo held what looked like an over-sized, elaborate T.V. remote in his hand, pointing it at the wall he was now facing. Jacy spun her chair to do the same.

"What are we going to watch? A little porn, perhaps?"

"Very funny," Gravigo punched a button on the remote while waving his other arm to dim the lights.

"The Skulls, The Bones, The Hats," Jacy read the words now illuminating the wall. "I've been meaning to ask you, Grav. Why haven't you guys brought some marketing guru to this crazy place? I bet they'd come up with some much cooler names for your little gangs."

"And I'm sure Neva could come up with some more mouth glue," Gravigo searched and found another button that he pressed, causing his own image to be emblazoned upon the wall. Jacy bit back a sarcastic zinger, tossing a furtive glance over her left shoulder. She didn't know if Neva wasn't lurking around in the back of the study somewhere. For a Glamazon, Neva had an uncanny ability to blend in with the shadows.

"Before you begin your training," Gravigo stared at his image on the wall, "I thought we'd start at the end."

"That makes sense."

Gravigo looked at Jacy with raised eyebrows and exhaled loudly. Jacy pretended to zip her lips shut.

"Thank you," Gravigo nodded in the direction of his picture. "During your training period, you will meet, amongst a wide variety of trainers, with each of the three leaders. Myself, who you've already met…"

He pushed another button on the remote. "Flair…"

Jacy immediately recognized Flair as the guy she saw Gravigo arguing with on the gaming floor. She studied Flair's face, framed by his shaggy blond hair. She was surprised that the word 'interesting' popped to her mind. Hot on that word's tail were 'dangerous' and 'sinister', though.

"Maise Elantina…" Gravigo clicked the remote to reveal the pretty face of the leader of the Bones. Jacy furrowed her brow, as Maise Elantina looked exactly how she thought she'd look. This weirded her out, though, as Jacy didn't have a pre-conceived notion as to how Maise Elantina might look.

Gravigo clicked more buttons, causing a montage of faces to appear and disappear on the lit wall.

"All of those faces may be involved in your training. You will be given in-depth history lessons of the Game, its groups, its rules, everything. Most importantly, you will be taught the skills in how to play the Game."

Gravigo looked at Jacy with a gentle smile. "Try not to stress about this, okay? I know it's overwhelming, but you'll be well trained and an expert on all things here before you become a player."

Gravigo quit hitting the buttons, halting at a picture of a ridiculously long table with three comfortable looking chairs alongside it. "After you have completed your training and have met with all three of us individually, you will be summoned to meet all three of us together. This is where you will choose which one of the groups you'd like to join."

"Haven't I already met with you individually?"

"Not in the training phase, yet, you haven't. Others, specifically Flair, thinks I've had more than enough time to give you an overview. You and I will still meet privately before we get to the decision making time."

Gravigo's hardened features which sprang up on his peaceful face when he mentioned Flair's name didn't go unnoticed by Jacy. She returned her gaze to the wall, and decided a change of topic was in order.

"You mentioned that I get to make my own decision to join one of the three groups."

Gravigo nodded in affirmation.

"What if my choice is to not join a group?" she asked.

Gravigo waved an arm, the study brightening immediately. Apparently Jacy's choice of subject wasn't the correct one. "Has Lita already been babbling like a love-sick teenager about her ridiculous infatuation with Hammer Coolie?!"

"Hammer Coolie?" Jacy attempted to look thoughtful. "You know, now that you mention the name, I seem to recall her using it in passing."

Gravigo harrumphed. "Lita has *never* spoke of Hammer Coolie 'in passing'. The woman is incorrigibly enamoured with that man, much to her future detriment, I might add."

"Why?" Jacy asked. "What's wrong with him? Why is it so bad to be a free agent?"

"Free agent, my bum hole," Gravigo waved his arm to re-dim the lights as he clicked another button on his remote. The picture of a rugged looking male in his late thirties or early forties appeared on the wall. Too rough looking to be called attractive but with enough character to be considered handsome, Hammer Coolie, with his five o'clock stubble stared back at them.

"Lita and all others of Mr. Coolie's ilk, like to describe themselves as free agents, not the fence jumpers they truly are." Jacy could tell Gravigo wasn't particularly fond of Hammer Coolie, but his disdain was muted compared to his hatred of Flair.

"Fence jumpers?"

Gravigo stared at Hammer Coolie for a long moment before answering. He then extinguished the portrait on the wall and made the lights regain their full strength before answering.

"That's, in a nutshell, what they do. One day they work with the Hats, the next day they assist the Bones, the day after that with The Skulls. And they have no qualms that on each of those days, they'll be working against someone they had worked alongside with the day before. They're basically mercenaries, answerable to nobody but themselves."

"And their pod, I would assume."

"Yes, and their pod," Gravigo exhaled. "But are they really doing what's best for their pod? Going out alone on a limb may be required from time to time, I grant you that, but always, all of the time? I don't understand how that's best for them or their pods."

"How come?" Jacy asked. "Isn't everyone here only doing what's best for the people in their pods?"

"Look," Gravigo said, leaning his forearms on the desk, facing Jacy. "I've worked with Hammer Coolie before. He's a nice enough guy, and I'm sure he has the false belief he is doing what's right. It's just that players like Hammer Coolie don't get quite the same cooperation they would if they belonged to one of the three groups."

Jacy looked puzzled. Gravigo sighed again.

"Okay, I'll admit it, when I've been forced to work with a free agent, I rarely give 100% and when I work against one, I probably go at it a little harder than I need to. And don't go thinking I'm some whiner who does this because he doesn't get his way. All the Hats, and most of the Bones and Skulls feel the same way I do."

"But why?"

"Because nobody fully trusts free agents. It's like an Independent who runs for political office. That person may seem appealing and a bit of a maverick, but in the grand scheme of things and without the power and numbers behind him or her, what do they really accomplish? 99% of the time, not a whole lot."

Jacy nodded, more because she was getting confused than her agreeing with what Gravigo espoused. Gravigo stood, rounded his desk, reached out and tousled her hair.

"It's a lot to take in Jace, I know. When we first started this whole thing, we didn't have a clue what we were doing. We learned, though, through trial and error, to get where we are today. Think of it, this way. When we first began, all of this was like a sandlot baseball game. Vague rules, no umpires, crappy equipment. Today, though, we are like Game 7 of the World Series. That's how far we've come, and I think it shows down on Earth, too. The changes are reflective of the other."

Jacy stared blankly at Gravigo. He smiled.

"All of this will become crystal clear when you have completed your training. Believe me, your training consists of a ton more than merely learning how to give your people gut feelings. You will be taught the ins and outs of the entire machinery here." Gravigo smiled that gentle smile of his that Jacy was becoming increasingly fond of. "After your training and studies are over, you will be confident and will be able to make the important decisions you will find yourself facing."

Jacy reached over and took Gravigo's hand. She looked up at him and smiled. "Thanks for your faith, Grav. I hope I won't let you down."

Gravigo squeezed her hand tightly. "You'll never let me down, Jacy. I'm positive of that."

"So when and where do I start my training?"

"Well," Gravigo's features darkened a bit, "apparently I've ruffled a few feathers in spending so much time with you giving you the overview. Your first trainer isn't someone I would've chosen to be your first hands-on trainer...oh, whatever. While I may not personally like the person you are to meet with, I do have trust in his abilities. You'll learn a lot from him."

"Who is it?" Jacy asked, suddenly feeling a little bit alarmed.

"I'll take you to him and..." Gravigo was about to do that goofy movement with his hands when Jacy stopped him.

"Can we walk there? Maybe you can fill me in a bit on what to expect."

"Walk there?" Gravigo appeared to toss this idea around before he dismissed it as out of hand. He did his weird hand movement and they disappeared again.

PART II

TRAINING DAYS

"If you do not change direction, you may end up where you are heading."
—Lao Tzu

1

Hammer Coolie tossed a piece of driftwood on to the crackling, early evening campfire. As the wood snapped and popped in protest, he did a slow observation of their newest, temporary rebel camp and nodded in satisfaction. Set-up was becoming more and more efficient.

Hammer sighed as his gaze returned to the campfire. Every once in a while a melancholy feeling threatened to envelop him about not having a more permanent home base. The feeling never lasted, though, as their constant mobilization was part of who they were as a group. He also secretly enjoyed the consternation their constant movement caused Agent Ninny Mop and the rest of his security goons, too.

Hammer did have a permanent base of sorts, of course, though no one outside of his inner group knew about it. Well, at the moment he believed that no one outside of that was aware of its location, but the way things were leaking like a runny nose in this place, Hammer wouldn't be shocked if his belief was a false one.

"Hey," a mug of steaming tea held by a female's hand suddenly blocked his view of the flames. "A toonie for your thoughts?"

"Thanks," Hammer took the offered beverage from one of his inner group, Karma Twin. "Except my train of thought is a bunch of empty box cars at the moment, so save your money for something more valuable."

Karma Twin took a place on the log beside him, blowing softly on her cup of hot coffee. "I don't believe you, but if you don't want to share, I'll do my best not to weep." She took a sip of her coffee.

Hammer chuckled as he wrapped both hands around the warm mug. Karma Twin was probably the strongest person he knew, even tougher than him. She didn't look it physically, at 5'2", sinewy arms and legs, small but perky breasts, and permanently dishevelled sandy blond hair. In this place, though, looks were deceiving. More than once Hammer witnessed her cause much larger men and women shrivel into a pool of tears. If the day came that Hammer Coolie decided to take this entire place on alone, Karma Twin would be one of the two or three people he'd choose to have his back.

"While you're holding in those tears of yours, I'll tell you that I've taken your advice and have been keeping a water-tight watch on my pod. I haven't been able to detect where the threat will come from, though."

"Keep watching. It's coming."

Hammer nodded as he sipped his tea. Karma Twin was always right. *Always*. There was no point in discussing it any further.

"Oh," Karma Twin nodded across the fire. "Look who's coming for a social call. And darn it, we're wearing the same outfit once again."

Hammer looked up and noticed another member of his inner group approaching, Trichina Flame. He smirked at Karma Twin. "Play nice, please."

"Fuck her," Karma rolled her eyes, making to stand. Hammer put a hand on her knee.

"Please. Stay?" It was a request, not an order. There were never any commands given with the rebels, or The Free Ones as Hammer and his cohorts liked to refer to themselves as. Karma Twin grumbled, but didn't leave. Hammer gave her knee an affectionate squeeze and looked up to greet their guest.

Hammer felt like laughing aloud, but he didn't. If there were two more opposite looking people, he had yet to see them. Trichina Flame was a six-foot-tall, smoldering beauty. With her flowing auburn locks that tickled the middle of her back, her 42 DD breasts, and hourglass figure, Trichina Flame caused both men and women to stop dead in their tracks.

This evening was no different as camp dwellers' eyes followed Trichina, all decked out in a body hugging scarlet dress, black stockings, and flaming red high heels. With anybody else, this ensemble might seem incongruous in a camp, but not with Trichina Flame. She could carry all and any looks in all and any places.

There were two curve balls to Trichina Flame, though. One, Trichina Flame was a transsexual; and two, she was Karma Twin's lover.

Hammer asked Karma Twin about the odd coupling once.

"I know it's a little different for those who don't get it," she admitted, "but Jesus, Hammer, look at her. She's fucking fabulous. I can't get enough of those big tits and her cock is incredible. What else can I say?"

The only thing Hammer Coolie could say about it was that he wished their apparently flawless intimate life extended outside of the bed they shared. Work-wise, their competitive nature seemed one boil away from erupting into violence. If one didn't know the two were fucking, they'd think they were mortal enemies.

Bickering and sex notwithstanding, Trichina Flame and Karma Twin were integral parts of Hammer's inner group. Hammer was lucky he had Tagger Merrino in the group with him, or he'd get steamrolled by Trichina and Karma on a regular basis.

"Good evening, Hammer," Trichina's smoky voice carried a hint of summertime in it. "And good evening to you, too, Karma."

Karma Twin grunted, but her eyes lingered on the distinct bulge under Trichina's tight dress. Hammer, on the other hand, was drawn into Trichina's mulberry eyes.

"Hello, Trichina," Hammer greeted her. "Care to join us?"

"I'd love to, but I was hoping to drag Karma away once I pass on some news to you," Trichina's eyes wandered from Hammer to Karma. "I've had a long, long day. I'd really love to lick your pussy right now."

"Okay," Karma perked up, her professional grievances forgotten.

Trichina's look fell back Hammer. "One of your pod is in imminent danger."

"We already know that," Karma rolled her eyes. "Amateur."

Trichina Flame chuckled, her eyes glowing with a hint of mischief as they sought out Karma. "Yes, but does he know when? Because I do."

"What?!" Hammer and Karma Twin blurted out together. "When?!"

"Three days from now," Trichina chuckled at their surprise. "I haven't been able to discover which one they'll target, but the time is set in stone. You really pissed them off with that gig in Wisconsin, Hammer."

Hammer nodded, remembering what one of his pod did. Hammer knew when it happened there would be unintended consequences, but he was proud of it all the same.

"Nothing the Skulls didn't deserve," Karma Twin remarked.

"I agree," Trichina nodded. "I'm hearing that it wasn't the act itself that pissed them off so much, it was the fact that what you did threw off all the dominoes that were supposed to fall because of it. Apparently those dominoes led all the way up to Flair's pod."

Hammer nodded, more to himself than to Trichina's words. He suspected as much, as he had been caught a little off-guard by the Skulls reaction to what transpired. Sure, Hammer Coolie knew the Skulls would be irked by what he did, but the rage expressed wasn't expected if you took the one act and kept it solitary. Once you added the other plans that may have relied upon this one, though, well, wasn't this part of what made the Game so addictive?

"You okay?" Karma and Trichina were both watching him.

"Yeah, yeah," he looked up at Trichina. "Thank you. Thank you both for everything you do."

Trichina was aware her grandstanding on this work issue may have annoyed Karma Twin. "Are we okay, Hon? Because it feels like forever since I've tasted you. Can we go back to our tent?"

Karma's loins overpowered any displeasure she felt about Trichina discovering the 'when' before she did. She reached up, took Trichina's outstretched hand, and stood.

"Thanks, Trichina, I owe you one," Hammer said.

"No, you don't, but you're welcome," Trichina Flame tossed a hungry smile at Karma Twin. "Good night, Hammer."

"G'night," he replied, watching them walk off. Trichina's hand slipped down and caressed Karma's cute ass as they leaned their heads together, whispering and giggling. Hammer shook his head. He had some work to do to be ready for whatever was coming from the Skulls three days hence.

He'd be ready, though. Hammer Coolie was *always* ready.

2

The Bam Slicer wasn't in a happy mood at the moment. Actually, The Bam Slicer usually wasn't very cheery at *any* moment, but today was worse than usual.

That morning's meeting went well. Flair, he, and the five lower table officers of the Skulls got a satisfactory amount of business accomplished. Both he and Flair were satisfied with the clean-up of all the shit that accumulated since the Buzzed Rottid incident, which was why The Bam Slicer was taken aback at the order Flair had given him once the table officers had left the meeting.

"Really?" The Bam Slicer said after hearing Flair's wishes. Truth be known, it felt kind of good for The Bam Slicer to now be able to question Flair's orders. He wouldn't have dared done that before he reached the position he now held.

Flair explained his rationale, and The Bam Slicer concurred. He knew from the start he would follow the orders. Questioning them was just his way of letting Flair know he wasn't happy about it. This errand Flair sent him on could've and should've been given to someone of much lower ranking than The Bam Slicer. Hell, a common Skull foot soldier could handle this crappy task.

Nevertheless, there was an enormous difference between questioning the boss and disobeying him, so The Bam Slicer did as he was told. That still didn't make him any happier, though, and now that the person he was to meet was late, he became even angrier.

As if on cue, the door opened in time with this thought. When The Bam Slicer saw who was standing there, he rolled his eyes.

"Get out," he commanded.

"I just want to…"

"Out," he pointed towards the door the figure just walked through. "This is not what Flair agreed to. Go."

The intruder started to speak up, but then conferred with the person standing behind him. The Bam Slicer tolerated the muffled whispers for ten seconds longer than he wanted to.

"Out, or I'm leaving."

The figure harrumphed loudly, whispering to his companion before storming away, leaving Jacy in his wake. She frowned at The Bam Slicer.

"Nice manners, big fella."

The Bam Slicer would've grinned at this if he were the type to smile.

"Sit down, female," he gestured towards the chair across the wooden table from him.

"No." Jacy didn't budge.

The Bam Slicer felt his blood begin to heat, but then remembered his own studies when he was a hopeful soldier trying to claw up the ranks. 'Save your anger for those who really deserve it.' The Bam Slicer continued to stare at the feeble human standing in front of him, realizing she didn't deserve anything at all from him; least of all his anger which he long ago had turned into one of the most useful tools in his arsenal. He attempted a more welcoming approach.

"Would it help if I said 'pretty please'?"

"Maybe," Jacy shrugged, checking out the bare room they were in. "That, and you can address me by my name."

The Bam Slicer held strong to his patience, trying to recall any tidbits of information from his studies that may help him here.

Nope, not one. He was about to try a new tact, but Jacy surprised him by speaking first.

"Why are you named The Bam Slicer? Do you 'bam', or do you 'slice'?"

The Bam Slicer looked at Jacy as if she spontaneously combusted.

"Or do you do both and are just indecisive?" Jacy carried on. "It'd be tough, I guess, because there is so much value in both bamming and slicing, to decide which name to go with. I think if it were me, I'd…"

"Whoa, whoa, whoa," The Bam Slicer held up a hand to halt Jacy's dissertation. Her voice already gave him a headache. Jacy stared at him with raised eyebrows and a bemused expression on her face. The Bam Slicer locked his steely eyes with hers with a venomous gaze that normally brought much stronger ones than her to their knees.

Not this time, though.

"Oh, please," Jacy rolled her eyes. "Save your oh-look-how-fearsome-I-am face for someone else. I'm here for part of my training, and for some goofy reason, I'm here with you. Can we get started?"

The Bam Slicer remained mute, but not for his customary reasons. He was having a devil of a time getting a read on this one. Is this why Flair sent him to do this? Did he know what a royal pain in the ass this human female was?

Just then, a voice from his past echoed through the fog of his brain. Ironically enough, the voice belonged to Buzzed Rottid.

"Never believe the surface answer," Buzzed told him when The Bam Slicer was young and green. "Constantly question things, and don't stop until you are at the root of what you're seeking."

The memory of Buzzed Rottid carried no nostalgia to it. It was the lesson Buzzed taught him that mattered.

The Bam Slicer looked away from the weakling female as his contemplations burrowed deeper. Flair wouldn't have sent him just because this human was an annoying twerp. If anything, this kind of scenario would fit perfectly in Flair's wheelhouse. He'd be slapping this wimpy woman in the forehead with his meaty dick and howling like a wolf.

So why, then? Why didn't Flair, who'd been all consumed by this human since she died, want to meet her at the first available opportunity? Was The Bam Slicer supposed to soften her up?

The Bam Slicer shook his head. No, that wasn't it, as Flair would've given him stricter orders on how he was supposed to behave.

"Just give her the first stage of training like you would any other rookie," Flair told him.

The Bam Slicer was on the right pathway of thought, though. Flair deliberately didn't ask him to soften her up because he assumed The Bam Slicer would just do it naturally. Flair was right, too, but now that The Bam Slicer had met this woman, this Jacy Morgan, he realized his normal way of doing things wouldn't suffice.

"Hello?" Jacy waved her hand before his eyes. "Is anyone home?"

The Bam Slicer nodded slowly, and attempted to smile, but knew he failed miserably when he saw a flash of fear pass over the human's face. This raised The Bam Slicer's spirits. He spoke to her in an ugly, gentle voice. "It looks like we got off on the wrong foot, Jacy. Maybe we can try this again."

The Bam Slicer stood and gestured towards the empty chair across the table from him. "Please have a seat, Jacy, and we can begin your training."

3

Still too astonished for words, Jacy slowly raised her right hand. The bunny (*her* bunny!) lifted his head and looked over to the right. After a moment of surveying its surroundings, the bunny reverted his attention to his meal.

"Good, very good," The Bam Slicer's rumbling voice intoned. Jacy stole a fast glance at him, before returning her look to her bunny. After a bit of a rough start, she and The Bam Slicer slid into the role of trainer/trainee quite smoothly, minus the fact that this mountain of a man scared the bejesus out of her. She did her best to not show her fear, though, and The Bam Slicer had been a pleasant surprise as a teacher. He was far more patient than she originally gave him credit for.

"Okay, let's see if we can get him to do something," The Bam Slicer instructed.

Jacy looked up at him, keeping her hands very still, about a foot off the table that separated the two of them. "But Cletus isn't finished his lunch yet."

"Cletus?" The Bam Slicer regarded her as if it were her, not him, who was a complete and utter lunatic. Jacy shrugged, somewhat embarrassed.

"He looks like a Cletus, doesn't he?"

"God of Fuck," The Bam Slicer muttered. "Don't name the goddamn things. Do you know why hog farmers don't name their pigs?"

"They don't? I would."

The Bam Slicer shook his head, trying to retain his patience. "Look, Jacy, it's best for you if you don't name your bunnies, okay? Just trust me on this one. If you name them, it'll be that much harder when they die a violent death."

Jacy stared at The Bam Slicer in horror. "Why would Cletus die a violent death?"

The Bam Slicer sighed, as they both looked down at the feasting Cletus.

"This is a training session, Jacy," The Bam Slicer tried to speak in a gentle tone, but as with most things The Bam Slicer aimed to be soothing at, he sucked. "It's your first, for that matter. It's not uncommon for accidents to occur to our training subjects."

Jacy watched her cute little bunny. "Are you saying I might kill Cletus?"

"No, I'm saying you might kill the rabbit. Cletus doesn't exist."

"But Cletus does exist. He's right there eating lunch."

The Bam Slicer wore an exasperated look. Jacy's feeling of satisfaction for causing that exasperation was short lived, though, when The Bam Slicer spoke next.

"Well, it looks like now may be a good time to get him away from there, because if you don't, 'Cletus' may turn out to be someone else's lunch."

"What?!" Jacy screeched. "What do you mean?!"

"Look," The Bam Slicer pointed towards a circling bald eagle, causing Jacy's eyes to widen in terror.

"Holy fucking shit," Jacy's hands fumbled, causing Cletus to involuntarily lurch ten yards or so to his left.

"Careful," The Bam Slicer rested his hands on top of Jacy's. "You could give the poor guy a heart attack. Remember the movements I taught you."

The Bam Slicer gently helped Jacy's hand movements begin before removing his hands. "You don't want to overcome him with so much fear he'll go off all helter skelter. You just want him to be aware of his safety spots."

"Don't I want him to know that he may be murdered by a marauding eagle?" Jacy eyed the flying monster.

"No, the rabbit…."

"Cletus."

The Bam Slicer sighed. "No, *Cletus* is already aware of the danger. Remember, we aren't puppet masters. Every living being has its own way of doing things, and creatures like Cletus here, for example, don't need our assistance in finding things to eat or to be aware of predators. They can do that all on their own."

"So what *are* we doing?"

"We're trying to find out what Cletus' options are if that eagle decides to swoop."

Jacy scoped out the barren lot that only a minute or so ago felt like a safe haven for Cletus. The lot was bare, though, minus a few tufts of grass decorating the gravel space.

"What do you think?" The Bam Slicer asked.

"I don't see anyth…. wait," something caught Jacy's attention.

"What is it?"

"A road, about 100 yards away. I can see some cars travelling on it," Jacy's eyes burned as she studied the surroundings. Cletus, for his part, sat there and pooped.

"What about the road?"

Jacy looked up at The Bam Slicer, leaning back in his chair.

"Well, wouldn't an eagle be less tempted to swoop down and snatch poor Cletus if there were cars speeding by?"

"Good, very good," The Bam Slicer looked impressed. Jacy was worried he would attempt another smile, and she really wished he wouldn't. He tried one earlier and it wasn't very pretty.

Jacy returned her attention to her and Cletus' enemy. She couldn't be sure if it was her imagination or not, but it looked to Jacy as if the eagle's circles were growing tighter and lower to the ground. She looked at Cletus who was now finished his business.

"Okay, Cletus, here we go," Jacy spoke quietly as she moved her left hand over top of her right. Apparently she gave Cletus a little too much juice, though; Cletus took off like he was shot from a gun.

"Not too much," The Bam Slicer spoke but kept his hands off of Jacy's. "You don't want to…uh-oh."

"What the fuck, uh-oh?" Jacy asked but didn't need to look. If the eagle hadn't noticed little Cletus before, the high-tailing bunny was definitely on the predator's radar now. The bully eagle dropped even further, slowly breaking its circle pattern. It now followed Cletus in a straight line.

"Oh, no," Jacy moaned, urging Cletus to move faster. "Bam…."

"Just keep him going towards the road. That's all you can do."

Jacy stole a quick glance at The Bam Slicer, expecting him to be to be looking smug about what was happening. He looked concerned, though, making Jacy like him a tiny bit.

"Fuck me!" Jacy watched the steadily descending eagle get too close to Cletus for her comfort. Jacy was never a great judge of distances, but she guessed this feathered beast was twenty or thirty feet above poor Cletus and moving closer by the second.

"Come on, Cletus, come on," Jacy forgot her lesson about hand movements and worked on total instinct and adrenaline now. Her hands were getting tied up in complicated knots, they were here, there, everywhere, like there was super glue taffy on the table and she was trying to escape it. Up, down, right….

"LEFT!" Both Jacy and The Bam Slicer yelled in unison. Thankfully Cletus obliged, the eagle's talons missing him by mere inches.

"Breathe; gentle hands…" The Bam Slicer coached Jacy from across the table.

Jacy slowed her hands to a more fluid motion as the eagle rose up and began pursuing Cletus once again. Jacy slowed her rapid breaths, starting to feel a little more comfortable. She was starting to feel…

"RIGHT!!" Both she and The Bam Slicer cried out together, and once again Cletus listened, cutting a precise 90-degree angle that left an eagle talon clutching air.

Jacy gently steered Cletus towards the road as the eagle rose again, following Cletus' charted path. Jacy narrowed her eyes at the eagle, trying to guess if he had enough room to make another strike. She guessed Cletus was about thirty yards from the road. She watched his little legs pump like pistons and felt an immense rush of relief when the eagle, with an angry squawk, peeled off and flew away. Jacy slumped back in her chair, exhausted.

"Jesus, Bam, that was fucking close."

"Jacy…"

"I mean, I would've felt the complete shits if Cletus died here."

"Jac…."

The adrenaline and euphoria Jacy felt raced through her veins at lightning speed. It was a feeling that she could not put into words. It almost…

"LEFT!!" The Bam Slicer bellowed, and Jacy did instinctually attempt to move Cletus to his left. The problem was, though, she was a split second too late.

Cletus ran directly onto the road. Jacy heard the sick bump and saw the squeamish face of the driver whose tires squashed poor Cletus into the asphalt.

4

When Hammer Coolie sat at his regular playing table, his anxiety level rose exponentially. This was it. Today was the day of the return attack. Doing his utmost to radiate his usual self-confidence and coolness, Hammer joked and greeted most of the fellow players at his table.

"I hear Agent Ninny Mop caught wind of your camp," Wondered Dawns, a Bone whom Hammer knew and liked, leaned in to whisper as Hammer sat. "Word is they're planning a surprise visit this evening."

"Thanks for the tip," Hammer nodded, unconcerned as the camp was being folded up and transported. Karma Twin told him about the surprise visit yesterday morning, causing no small amount of distress to Trichina Flame who was usually the one to discover when the raids were coming. Judging by the passionate moans emanating from Karma and Trichina's tent this morning, though, they obviously made up.

Hammer tried a breathing technique Neva Tezremsy taught him eons ago in hopes of slowing the rapid flutters inside him, but he must have forgot how to do it properly because nothing quelled his apprehension. To make matters worse, Hammer needed to not show he suspected anything out of the ordinary was happening today. Trichina Flame was very clear with her instructions.

"The counter attack *will* happen," she spoke to him over a steaming cup of coffee last night, "but if you show any signs of knowing, they'll back off."

"They'll back off if we show up en masse to protect Hammer," Tagger Merrino argued.

"Yes, but then what?" Karma Twin interjected. "Then we're back at square one, hatching a million plans for what may or may not happen. This is our best chance."

Hammer agreed with Karma and Trichina and despite Tagger's disagreeing words, Hammer showed up at the table alone. He did his best to make himself appear composed and that today was no different than any other day at the office. He made small talk with his fellow gamers, taking note he knew most everyone there. He would pay closer attention to the three newcomers in recent days; two Hats and a Skull.

Hammer glanced over in their direction, noticing the two Hats ignoring the Skull, who was doing his best to show that he could give a rat's ass about *any* fucking Hat, let alone these two peons.

A less experienced Gamer than Hammer would focus more energy and time than what was needed on the new Skull. Hammer's knowledge, most of it learned by the bumps and bruises of experience, made him suspect everybody. Hammer trusted Trichina's information that the Wisconsin business pissed off the Skulls, so that made it most likely that's where the attack would come from. But in reality, the attack could come from anywhere, a Bone wanting to move into the Skulls, or a Hat needing to repay a favour to a Skull, perhaps. The counter attack could come from all and any angles.

Hammer took a large swig of water from the bottle he brought to the table with him and tried to slow his brain which was beginning to catch up with the flurries within.

You are Hammer Fucking Coolie.

Fuck them.

Hammer's silent prayer grounded him a little, as it always did. He'd been through battles and hardships far worse than what he'd face today.

So why the heightened anxiousness now? Hammer couldn't put a finger on that one, which caused his foreboding feeling to enhance. Hammer could only grit his teeth in frustration.

"Hey, Hammer, come on," Nine Franc Jeweler, a Hat who was a regular at the table called out. "Put a tether on your little Don Juan here, would you?"

"What's going on?" Hammer pulled himself from his reverie to focus on the Game.

"I've been working hard with Wondered Dawns to set up a relationship and hopefully even a marriage with a couple of our subjects here. Your boy down there isn't helping things," Nine Franc Jeweler complained.

"A marriage to a Hat? You that desperate?" Hammer spoke softly to Wondered Dawns.

"Orders from above," Wondered rolled his eyes. "Could be worse, like a Skull or a rebel."

"Fuck you," Hammer retorted good-naturedly. He and Wondered Dawns enjoyed a good, professional relationship; not exactly friends, but both held a healthy respect towards the other. Nine Franc Jeweler, on the other hand, was a simpering idiot in Hammer Coolie's opinion.

"You want out of this?" he spoke out of the side of his mouth to Wondered while smiling across the table at Nine Franc Jeweler.

"I'm not asking you for a favour," Wondered Dawns sighed, "but no, I don't want out of it. Maise Elantina will be happy if I'm successful with this."

Hammer nodded, understanding the request from Wondered. It was proper etiquette to state clearly if one was asking for a favour or not. A favour would be expected to be repaid somewhere down the line; a nice gesture set the table for a mutually respectful relationship.

Hammer looked down at what was going on, and smirked at the situation.

Nine Franc Jeweler's subject was a cute, little coffee shop waitress and Frankie, one of Hammer's pod, had his charm and wit cranked up to eleven. Hammer chuckled aloud at Nine Franc's subject. She looked as if she were about to pull her skirt up and let Frankie fuck her right there on the table.

Hammer raised both his hands slowly, then dropped and raised his right hand three times fluidly. Hammer felt that recognizable surge of pride as he watched Frankie immediately obey his gut feeling, pulling back his flirtatiousness a little at a time so by the time the conversation was done, Nine Franc Jeweler's subject returned to work thinking what a nice guy Frankie was, silently chided herself for thinking Frankie had been putting the moves on her.

Frankie admired her shapely ass as she departed, and then opened his tattered notebook he carried everywhere. Frankie was the singer of an indie punk-country-folk-rock outfit, called the Sulk Loungers. The band had been harping on him to come up with some lyrics to put to some cool riffs they came up with at a recent rehearsal. Maybe he'd write a song about an appealing, coffee shop waitress with a sexy ass.

Hammer lowered his hands and smiled, nodding to accept Nine Franc Jeweler's gratitude. Frankie was one of Hammer's favourites. Of course, he loved and treated his entire pod equal and fair, but Frankie, Kate, Josh, and Marley were the favoured ones of his pod of 3,762 subjects.

Doing his best to remain normal and nonchalant, Hammer did a brief check on each of his subjects. Each and every one of them was fine.

Hammer couldn't ask for more from his current pod. Every one of them were good, hard-working, peaceful folk, who always seemed to do what was right in Hammer's eyes. Be nice. Don't hurt. Be happy. Of course, some in his pod needed more attention and time than others, but that was to be expected for a pod of his size. All in all, he was proud of every last one and would defend them to the end.

The question of the moment was, though, who was going to do the attacking, and who would be the one attacked? Feeling an unspoken presence cast a shade over the table, Hammer raised his eyes from the table to the newcomers who just arrived.

"Hey, Flair," Hammer nodded, ignoring Flair's two sidekicks. "Is this a social call, or are you *finally* ready to go mano y mano with me?"

5

"Don't feel so bad, Sugar," Lita spoke over her shoulder at the following Jacy. "You should've seen my first training session."

"What happened?" Jacy asked, as they rounded a hallway corner of a bizarre looking apartment complex.

"I had the cutest, little baby mouse," Lita's voice had a reflective note to it. She halted in front of a door. "I had him for less than a minute before I ran him straight into the paws of a one-eared alley cat who chomped his cute head off."

Jacy laughed in spite of herself. "Cletus was awfully cute, too."

"I'm sure he was, Sugar, but do you know how many bunny rabbits there are down there? They multiply like, well, like bunny rabbits." Lita held up her hand to a blue-lit hand imprint on the wall and the door clicked open. She smiled at Jacy. "Ta-daaaa! Here we are."

Jacy stepped into the room and realized that using the term 'room' was generous. She looked around, taking inventory. Two single beds, two wooden chairs, a side table, and a window.

"It's very, um, sparse," she wasn't sure what to say.

"It's a fucking cubby hole," Lita snorted. She lay down on the bed nearest the door. "It's fine for what it is, though."

Jacy strode the three or four steps it took to traverse the room and looked out the window. She was glad it afforded a view of the magnificent fountain. Besides its beauty and grandeur, Jacy couldn't put into words why she was so enchanted with it; she just knew it grabbed her. She walked back from the window and sat down on what she presumed would be her bed. Lita rolled onto her side to face her.

"See, we don't need to eat, drink, or sleep in this place, so we don't have to have a home, per se. We get these cubby holes to add to the authenticity of the Game, and besides, it's nice to have a place to decompress once in a while. Once you're done your training, you'll be given the choice of your own room if you want one."

"I wouldn't call Gravigo's home a cubby hole."

"Ooooh, already been to his house, have you? Clicking heels with the big shots," Lita teased her. "But yeah, the higher ups get the fancier places. Wait 'til you see Flair's."

"You mentioned we don't need to eat or drink, but I saw people eating and drinking on the Gaming floor," Jacy pointed out.

"Yeah," Lita paused, wondering how deep she wanted to get into the Game with Jacy at this early juncture. She knew Jacy would discover everything in time, but Lita wasn't positive telling Jacy now was the right thing to do. "We all eat and drink, but it's strictly for pleasure as we don't require nourishment."

Jacy looked puzzled.

"It's a foreign concept, I know," Lita smiled. "It took me awhile to grasp it, too. Think of it this way, though. You can forget about all those yucky healthy things we needed back on Earth and you can eat all the hot buttered popcorn you want without gaining an ounce. Pretty cool, huh?"

Jacy nodded in an absent way. "Pretty cool."

Lita frowned, pulling herself into a sitting position so she faced Jacy. "You okay, Sugar?"

"Yeah," Jacy shook her head, "I am *so* not okay.

Lita scooted over to Jacy's bed. She reached out and put a hand on Jacy's shoulder. "It's been a bit of a whirlwind, hasn't it?"

"More like a fucking cyclone."

"It does get better, Sugar, I promise you," Lita chuckled.

Jacy fought some tears that threatened to escape. "My baby, though, Lita, my baby daughter Derian, and Beau, and…." Her struggle with her tears became a dismal failure as they now tumbled and jumbled down her cheeks. Lita pulled her close, hugging her tight.

"Your daughter is safe, Jacy," Lita whispered as she stroked Jacy's hair.

Jacy pulled away and stood, attempting to re-assemble herself. She wiped at her cheeks as if she were afraid her tear stains would entrench her face. She walked towards the window and gazed out.

"But I'm not *with* her," she whispered.

Lita pulled her knees up, hugging them. "No, you're not. She's there, and you're here, but…"

"Where is 'here', though?" Jacy interrupted her. "Where is here? I know all that bullshit Gravigo spewed about controlling dinosaurs and giving people gut feelings and the Skulls, the Hats, the Bones, but…"

Jacy trailed off into silence. She looked at Lita. "What the fuck is going on here, Lita?"

Lita smiled a sad, sad smile. "This is all déjà vu for me, Sugar. It doesn't seem that long ago that I was standing in that same exact spot saying those exact same words to Johnny Bazinski."

"The third human?"

"Actually," Lita shook her head, "Baz was the first. I was the second, and you are the third."

Lita walked over to where Jacy stood and peered out the window as if she were searching for something. She then pointed to a Grass Counter, way off in the distance.

Jacy squinted, barely able to discern what the smudge in the distance even was. "How can you tell from here?"

"I just know," Lita stared at the figure for a long moment. "I'd know Baz anywhere."

Lita shook her head and stepped away from the window. She took Jacy's hand and led her to one of the two wooden chairs that were separated by a small table. A newspaper sat upon it. Jacy glanced at it.

"The Daily Sneer?"

"It's a rag that a couple Skulls started to keep tabs on possible trades, pick-ups, local gossip, what have you."

"That makes sense," Jacy deadpanned.

"I'll explain the Daily Sneer to you later," Lita laughed. "It won't come in handy until after your training, anyways."

"After my little episode with Cletus today, I doubt my training will be completed anytime soon."

"Bah," Lita swatted Jacy's comment from the air. "Cletus was merely a test from the bigwigs to get a handle on where to start your training. Don't you think it was a little early for them to throw you into the frying pan like that?"

Jacy rolled her eyes. "I have no fucking idea what is up or down in this place, Lita. I don't know if it was early or late."

"Well, you listen to me, Sugar," Lita reached out and patted Jacy's hand. "Not many are tested that early around here. Baz and I weren't, that's for sure. And on top of all that you actually did pretty good."

"Pretty good?" Jacy chortled. "Cletus is flatter than a crepe right now."

"True," Lita conceded, "but you did save Cletus from that eagle. With no prior experience or knowledge, you saved him from the primary threat of danger. Granted, Cletus didn't fare very well with the secondary source of danger, but hell, there's experienced Gamers who don't handle secondary sources very good, either."

Jacy put her hands up. "Whoa, Lita, you're talking over my head here."

"Sorry," Lita smiled. "I got carried away. I'm just trying to boost you up a bit, to show you did pretty damn good regardless of the outcome for poor Cletus. And to tell you the truth, I wouldn't have put it past The Bam Slicer to have snookered you into pushing Cletus under that car."

"Really?" Jacy frowned. Even though The Bam Slicer frightened her, Jacy thought him to be a fair and able teacher.

"You never know with the Skulls, sweetie," Lita shrugged. "Either way, word out there is that all three groups have some high hopes for you."

"Thanks for the boost of confidence," Jacy sighed, "but what I really need is just a better understanding of where the fuck I am."

"I know how you feel, Sugar," Lita nodded and smiled. "I really do."

"I guess you do, don't you?" Jacy studied the pretty Lita. "How did you get here, Lita?"

"Same way as you. A rule was broken…."

"….and restitution was paid," Jacy finished for her.

"I take it Gravigo explained that part to you," Lita chuckled.

"Were you part of Gravigo's pod, too?"

Lita laughed loud and long. "Oh, Sugar, if you knew me back on Earth, you'd know there wasn't a dilly bar's chance in hell that I was being watched over by a Hat."

"Really?"

"Hon, you wouldn't believe half of it. But no, I definitely wasn't in Gravigo's or any other Hat's pod. Not a Bone's, either."

"Then…." Jacy looked confused. Lita locked her brown eyes on Jacy. She now wore an embarrassed smile.

"Believe it or not, Sugar, but I was one of Flair's girls."

6

"Hammer," Flair pretended to be offended, "why the disrespect? You're not worried about anything are you?"

Hammer cursed himself. The entire table turned silent and watched the two leaders square off.

"Worried isn't the correct word," Hammer replied casually. "Vomitus is more apt to how I'm feeling right now, though I'm sure it'll go away when you slither off and hide up at the Big Tables."

Hammer Coolie nodded towards the section where all the big gamers played, a section raised ten feet taller than the rest of the Gaming Area. Hammer's table was as close as one could get before being in the high roller's area, but as of yet, only Hats, Skulls, and Bones made it to that lofty height. Hammer was determined to change that one day, though. Being the highest ranking rebel, he stood the best chance, too.

"Ahhh, yes, the old 'I'm in the trenches while you sip expensive champagne' angle," Flair's eyes danced with devilry. "You and your shtick are getting tired and old, Putty Knife."

Flair's oft-used derogatory nickname drew a few laughs from the table, mostly from the Skulls. Hammer shrugged it off, peering over at The Bam Slicer.

"How about you, Number 2?" Hammer almost sang the request. "Care to dance?"

Unlike Flair and Hammer's talents of keeping a cool and calm disposition, The Bam Slicer radiated rage and violence. "I'll fucking tango all over your fucking…"

Flair raised an arm and squeezed Bam's left shoulder, never taking his icy blue gaze from Hammer Coolie.

"Nice try, Putty Knife," Flair snarled, "but we've got *way* bigger game to bag than the likes of you. No slumming for us, today, I'm afraid."

Hammer shrugged, upset with himself for giving away his tactical position. It looked like they knew he was ready for them, and they were now going to pull back and strike another day. He returned his attention to his pod.

"On the other hand," Flair's voice raised a notch in volume, "maybe my other friend here is in the mood to play."

Hammer looked up at the third Skull. Hammer needed no introduction, and he wasn't fooled by his slender, meek appearance.

"For those who don't know him, his name is Ridded Snot, and he's in the mood for a game," Flair spoke to the entire table before narrowing his eyes at Hammer. "And once he makes quick work of one of you, he may find one when he returns to his regular table."

Flair left with a flourish, The Bam Slicer scowling at Hammer Coolie before falling into Flair's wake. Ridded Snot looked at Hammer while the other Skulls at the table laughed and whooped and whinnied. Hammer eyed Ridded Snot, nodding towards an empty chair across the table from him, two seats to his left.

Ridded Snot was no Flair or Bam, but he was considered an excellent Gamer. He would also be Hammer Coolie's toughest opponent to date.

Ridded shook hands and greeted those around him at the table with grace and courtesy. Unlike most of his brethren, Ridded Snot was lean, fair, and well-dressed. He carried an almost effeminate quality to him, but somehow exuded a masculinity impossible to ignore. On Earth during 1960's England, Ridded Snot would be classified as a 'mod'.

Once Ridded had finished with the pleasantries, he took his seat and nodded at Hammer.

"Mr. Coolie, it's a pleasure to meet you, finally. I've heard much about you," he intoned in a surprisingly soft voice.

"The pleasure is mine, my good sir," Hammer hammed it up, causing a few muffled chuckles. Ridded appeared to not notice or care. He stared at Hammer Coolie, 30 seconds, a minute, a minute and a half. There was nothing hostile in Ridded's studied gaze, but his black irises crowned with flecks of gold could easily unnerve someone with less vinegar than Hammer.

Hammer would hold Ridded Snot's gaze for as long as Ridded chose, and it took two minutes and thirty-eight seconds for Ridded to understand that. Breaking eye contact first, Ridded Snot clapped his hands together and giggled.

"Splendid," he exclaimed. "This is going to be fun."

Ridded Snot returned his now smiling face to Hammer Coolie. "Are you ready?"

Hammer nodded.

Game on.

7

"Ha-ha, I wish I had a camera to take a picture of you, Sugar," Lita guffawed. "You look absolutely shocked."

"Well…I…because…" Jacy sighed. "I guess I am."

"Not half as shocked as I was, believe me," Lita reached across the table and patted Jacy's hand. "Look, you've had a ton to digest in a short period of time, so I'll do my best not to pile on too much more. Gravigo explained the whole Hats, Skulls, and Bones thing to you, right?"

Jacy nodded.

"And since you're so green here, it seems to you that the Hats are good, the Skulls are evil, and the Bones fall somewhere in the middle, correct?"

"In the proverbial nutshell…"

"Clamshell."

"Huh?"

"I hate clichés," Lita chuckled. "I like the term clamshell."

"Okay," Jacy smiled, "in the proverbial 'clamshell', that's exactly how it looks to me."

Lita leaned forward, her sturdy breasts resting on the table top.

"And in that clamshell, you'd be right. Skulls bad, Hats good, Bones in the middle. But," Lita held a finger in the air, "that's only *inside* the clamshell. Believe me, Sugar, once you get outside that clamshell, all the fun begins."

Jacy looked at Lita with raised eyebrows.

"Fair enough," Lita chuckled, "I'll stop there. I'll just ask you to always keep reminding yourself of one thing in this place."

Jacy nodded.

"Things are not nearly as black and white as our minds were programmed back on Earth to think like. There is an incredibly large grey area here where everything gets tossed upside down, and pulled inside out."

"Deal," Jacy sighed. "I'll do my best to remember that, even though I haven't a clue on what you're saying to me."

Lita giggled. "You'll get it, Sugar, you'll get it."

Jacy laughed, too. She looked at Lita. "So were you really a member in Flair's pod?"

"What a size twelve to the ass *that* was to find out," Lita slapped the table with an open hand. "I mean, I was no angel back on Earth, far from it, but son of a bitch. A member of *Flair's* fucking pod?! Get outta here!"

"What were you like on Earth?"

Lita paused for so long Jacy thought she wasn't going to answer.

"Sorry, I didn't mean to…"

"No, it's okay, Sugar," Lita attempted to smile at her. "It's still a tough thing for me to talk about, you know?"

"You don't have…"

"I was in Medford, Oregon. It's really close to the California border. It's a mostly white, retirement kind of town. I was an LPN at Providence Medford Medical Center."

Lita looked down at her lap as she spoke in a low voice. "It was a boring town for me. I was brought up in Portland, which was really cool. Medford was alright, but it wasn't Portland. I was kind of wild, Jacy, and I'm not proud of it."

Lita looked at her with moist eyes. "But I didn't deserve what I got, no fucking way."

Jacy didn't speak. She reached out and held one of Lita's hands. Lita looked down at their clasped hands.

"I was seeing this guy from Grants Pass, a town not far away. Nothing too serious, just horsing around, mostly. Anyways, one Friday night he comes to my place after work with a friend of his.

They've got a bunch of cocaine and I've got a cupboard full of whisky and rum, so we proceed to have a little party."

Lita sighed. "Some time after midnight, a porn movie ends up on in the background as we're snorting and drinking and talking. At some point my guy suggests we have a threesome."

Lita shakes her head. "As I said, I was no angel back on Earth, and there's some decisions I made that were so fucking stupid I cringe. This was one of those times."

Lita's eyes found Jacy's and held them for a long moment before looking away.

"We get into it and we're all naked and laughing on the living room floor. At one point I'm going down on my guy as his friend eats me out. At some point his buddy comes up and helps me give my guy a blowjob."

Jacy's eyes widened. Lita chuckled.

"I'm sure that was the look on my face, too, but I'm all coked up and drunk and it seemed pretty hot at the time. My guy totally digs it, and he starts getting super-hot. So hot, he blows his load really quick. He's a little embarrassed, but we make him feel better and soon we're all laughing about it. We take a break, snort some more, drink some more. At some point, my guy starts licking me and he reaches out and touches his buddy. His buddy scoots over so we're laying side by side. My guy takes turns servicing both of us."

A single tear runs down Lita's right cheek but she doesn't wipe it away. "Things get a little hazy for the next little bit, but I remember at one point his friend started fucking me. My guy loved it at first, but at some point he went to the bathroom. 'Don't stop,' he told us, 'this is really hot.' As I said, I can't remember all the details because we were all so fucking wasted. At one point I think we noticed that my guy hadn't returned yet, but we kept fucking, anyways. At some point, my guy comes back, and he's really pissed off."

Lita shook her head. "He lost it on his friend. They fought, nothing major. A few drunken punches, mostly wrestling around. I managed to break it up, and told the friend he better leave. I tried to calm my guy down, but he kept calling me a slut and a whore."

Lita took a deep breath, and continued on. "I finally managed to calm him down enough, and get him to bed. I was so fucking wired still, I couldn't sleep, so I began to tidy up and have another drink so maybe I could sleep. Again, things go away here for me. The next thing I recall is my guy back in the kitchen, accusing me of thinking he was a fag. He kept screaming it over and over."

More tears fell from Lita's eyes. "I rented a place that sat on 5 acres, so I had no neighbours. I finally got scared enough to call 911, but by then it was too late. He grabbed a large kitchen knife and he began to stab me. Over and over and over and over again."

Lita looked at Jacy with such vulnerability in her eyes, Jacy began to cry, too. "He was so *angry*, Jacy. He just kept stabbing me. Flair told me later I had been stabbed 27 times. Why? Why did I deserve that? Just because I was acting like a slut?"

"I don't know why he did that," Jacy answered.

"Neither do I," Lita's voice was nearly a whisper. "Next thing I know, I'm at the bottom of some cliff and Flair's trying to explain everything to me."

Jacy watched her new friend pull herself together. "What was your murderer's name?" Jacy finally asked.

"Hmmm?"

"The guy who killed you. You never said what his name was."

Lita's face hardened. "He doesn't get a name, Jacy. He doesn't deserve it. One thing Flair helped me with during my training was scouring his name from my memory bank."

Jacy didn't know what to say about this. She said nothing.

"And I don't know who's pod my murderer was a member of, either," Lita went on. "My death wasn't mean-spirited up here. The official word was some lazy asshole who got tired of trying to keep one of his members between the ditches. Apparently he gave up on my killer; it was as simple as that."

Lita stood, rapping the table twice with her knuckles as if to signal a change in topic. "Anyways, enough of the depressing shit. Who are you off to see next?"

"Some guy named Agent Ninny Mop. What's up with all these goofy names, anyways?"

Lita laughed. "You'll get all that with time, Sugar. Enjoy your time with Agent Ninny Mop. He's a good guy to have on your side."

"Buy the ticket, take the ride," Jacy murmured.

"Oh, you've already bought the ticket, but don't just take the ride, Sugar. Embrace it. Enjoy it. Go soak up everything you can from Agent Ninny Mop to Flair to Maise Elantina to Gravigo. I will always be here to help fill in the blanks."

Jacy stood, taking both of Lita's hands in hers.

"Thank you, Lita, I mean that. Thank you so much."

"You're welcome, hon, but don't bother thanking me again. We're roommates, and I bet we'll be even better friends. I think we're going to be helping each other out a whole bunch in the future."

8

The patient Agent Ninny Mop waited for his next task. Standing close to the heart of the Grand Fountain, the sound of falling water failed to register with the Security Director. Lots of other things were picked up by his highly trained ears and eyes, though.

"…. last night at the clearing…." A couple of Skulls passed by.

"…a new rebel camp sprouting…." A Bone and a Hat.

"…that fucking Gravigo and his…." A Skull and two Bones.

Agent Ninny Mop took all this in while standing as tall as a skyscraper and straighter than a preacher. His gangly seven foot eight-inch frame, made even taller when one took his bright red, curly mop of hair into the equation, was both relaxed yet alert. His mind automatically discarded the two snippets of gossip he'd heard while filing the piece about the rebel camp. Ninny and his crew had yet to catch a rebel camp, but it wasn't from lack of trying.

Agent Ninny Mop's next task caught his eye, pushing all thoughts away. He sighed. Ninny hadn't come to terms with how he felt about the human female, yet. The task itself was simple enough. Show one of the new rookies the lay of the land. Ninny had completed this easy duty thousands of times. Usually he'd hand it off to one of his underlings. The word came from way up high that in this case, though. Agent Ninny Mop was to take care of this one personally, which helped cause the tension he felt.

Human beings were alien to him. Jacy would only be the third one he ever came into contact with. To be efficient and correct at his job, Agent Ninny Mop had zero affiliation with any of the groups or players. A Hat was a Skull and a Bone was a free agent as far as Ninny was concerned. Everybody was equal.

And while Agent Ninny Mop did his best to conceal it, humans intrigued him, no matter how many times he scolded himself for it. He was too new to the job when Johnny Bazinski was still a player and Lita was too recent for him to get a fair read on. Now, this third human was here and....

Ninny sighed again as he pushed all and any thoughts from his mind. "Good morning, Mrs. Morgan. How are you?"

Jacy paused at the title "Mrs. Morgan" before replying, "I'm fine Mr. Mop. How are you?" Before Ninny could answer, Jacy crinkled her forehead and added, "And please. Call me Jacy."

Agent Ninny Mop handed her a tablet and an ultra-thin belt. "Thank you, Jacy. And please refer to me as Ninny. This way?"

Jacy took the offered tablet and moved in the direction of Ninny's outstretched arm. "What are these for?"

"The belt is a communication device," Agent Ninny Mop pulled up his shirt and revealed his. The belt was so thin you could barely see it, except for a blue button. Ninny pushed the button and said the name 'Cereal Jenny'. Seconds later a voice came through the belt, clear as air.

"Yeah, boss?"

"Nothing, Cereal Jenny, just testing my communication belt. I'm out." Agent Ninny Mop returned his attention to Jacy. "It's that easy."

He motioned towards the tablet in Jacy's hand. "That has a wealth of information in it, but today we'll only use it as a map to help you until you get to know the lay of the land here." Ninny led Jacy away from the fountain area and onto one of the numerous sparkling paths that led through the vast expanse of evergreen grass. "I'll show you how to use it once we get to the intersection."

"The intersection?" Jacy tried her best to pay attention to what Agent Ninny Mop told her, but she was having a tough time. Right now she noticed one of the Grass Counters staring at her. Jacy knew enough by now that this particular Grass Counter was a Skull, decorated with his arm sleeve tattoos, scarred face, and full on biker regalia. He and Jacy continued to hold eye contact as her and Agent Ninny Mop passed him by.

"All of these trails lead to…." Ninny immediately picked up on the eye contact. He stopped talking and walking, and stared hard at the Grass Counting Skull.

"Can I help you?" Agent Ninny Mop spoke in a steely tone that conveyed that was the last thing in the world he wanted to do.

The Skull held Jacy's gaze for a moment or two longer before giving her a subtle nod. Ninny's eyes narrowed as the Skull returned his attention to the grass. He touched Jacy's arm and they started moving again.

"As I was saying before that scumbag interrupted us," Ninny tried to make his voice sound jovial but came up short. "All of these trails meet at the intersection. It's the best spot to centre yourself."

"Centre myself?"

"This is a really big place," Agent Ninny Mop answered. "It's easy enough to get discombobulated and lose your way around here.

Of course, you can always centre yourself from the Gaming Area, too, but when you're outside it's easier to…. what are you doing?"

Agent Ninny Mop's voice raised in concern as Jacy bent down, about to feel the grass.

"Fuck you, Sister!" a kneeling Grass Counter snarled at her.

"Enough from you, Kernel Bats," Ninny snapped at the woman. He grabbed Jacy by the elbow and helped her to her feet. "Let's go."

They marched in silence for a bit before Jacy spoke. "I'm sorry, I just wanted to feel the grass."

"I know; *everyone* just wants to feel the grass. Well, except for Grass Counters. They hate it." Agent Ninny Mop stopped walking. He looked at Jacy.

"It's rude to touch the grass unless you're invited onto it by one of the Grass Counters. Each one of them," Ninny waved an arm, "have a different counting strategy. Some do it in blocks, some in lines, there's hundreds of different tactics. If you trample a part down they haven't tallied yet, then you make an impossible job even harder."

Jacy stared out across the fields. She could see hundreds of Grass Counters. "I can't even begin to imagine doing that," she said.

"Good," Agent Ninny Mop liked hearing that. "Don't break the rules and you'll never have to."

Jacy didn't bother asking what the rules were. They'd been drilled into her head already.

"Doesn't counting grass strike you as a harsh penalty?" Jacy asked, instead.

"No," Ninny shook his head. "Grass Counting is reserved only for the most egregious rule breakers. If it's a more minor infraction, one ends up in a Re-Education Camp," Agent Ninny Mop looked sharply at Jacy. "Still, just don't break the rules. That way you'll be fine."

"What happens when someone finishes counting?" Jacy asked as they started to move again.

"They start at the beginning again. Now…"

"What?!" Jacy interrupted. "Why do they have to start over?"

"A Grass Counter has to be within one hundred blades of grass of the actual number to be allowed back in the Game again. If they're wrong, they have to go back to the beginning."

"Has anyone ever got it right, or at least within a hundred?"

Agent Ninny Mop shook his head. "No, Nibbled Saltwater would've been the closest, but she was 2,725 off. It's a tough job…"

"It's an impossible one," Jacy cut in.

"Well," Agent Ninny Mop shrugged his shoulders, "I don't think that *anything* is impossible, but yes, Grass Counting is a difficult task, I'll give you that. Ahhh, here we are."

Ninny pointed to an area they were approaching. They walked to it in silence.

"So, this is the Intersection?" They stood in the middle of a large circle. Dozens of glittering pathways shot off in all directions.

"Some call it the child's sun," Agent Ninny Mop looked down at the ground.

"Huh?"

"To some it looks like the sun an infant would draw." Agent Ninny Mop moved over so he stood directly beside Jacy. "Okay, right now we're facing the Gaming Building, correct?"

Jacy nodded.

"So press this button here," Ninny pointed to the edge of the tablet she was holding. She did as she was told and the tablet came to life.

"Cool," she said.

"I know," Ninny gestured towards the screen. "As you can see, this place is set up much like Earth."

He pointed at the trail leading directly behind them. "Follow that one and you'll find the South American Gaming Building."

"There's another gaming building?" For some reason this surprised Jacy.

"There's another five gaming buildings."

"One for each of the continents," Jacy nodded as she looked at her tablet. "How many people are there in this crazy place?"

"At last count we had 6,549,672."

Jacy let out a low whistle. "Wow, that's a lot."

"Depends on your perspective, I guess," Agent Ninny Mop shrugged. "See, the average Gamer has 1,064 humans in their pod…"

"What?!" Jacy looked incredulous. "How can someone look after that many?"

"The good ones have much more than that. 1,064 is the average. You start with one human, and as your talent grows, so does the population of your pod."

"I get that," Jacy nodded, "but how can someone look after that many?"

"It's easier than it sounds, to be honest. Since time is a fluid concept here, it's quite easy to manage that number of humans, especially since they don't need us for the essentials, such as eating, drinking, and sleeping. Great gamers, such as the Flairs and Gravigos of this place have over 5,000 in their pods."

Jacy shook her head in dismay.

"So when you do the math," Agent Ninny Mop went on, "six and a half million people here isn't all that great a number. Take our building, the North American building. At last count there were 497,180 gamers. That's roughly the size of Atlanta, Georgia."

Ninny gestured in the direction of the South American building.

"That building holds 362,782 gamers, approximately the size of Pittsburgh." He pointed to a path that led away from their right.

"That one will take you to the European Gaming Building, which is slightly larger at 694,549, or near the size of Dandong, China. The Asian building is the largest as it has to hold close to four million gamers. The African building is near a million, while the

Australian one is quite small in numbers. It doesn't take long to reach six and a half million."

"It's hard to fathom," Jacy slowly shook her head.

"Only if you look at the actual numbers, but six and a half million is akin to the size of, ohhh," Agent Ninny Mop furrowed his brow in concentration, "let's say a little more than half the size of Sao Paulo, Brazil."

"I've never been to Sao Paulo," Jacy said.

"Okay, then take the cities of Vancouver, Dallas, and Chicago. That is basically our entire population."

Agent Ninny Mop smiled at Jacy and spoke in a gentle voice. "I know this is a lot for you to take in, Jacy, but you will get it all, I know you will. For now, though, use this tablet. It contains almost everything you need to know."

"Do I get to keep this?"

"Why would you want to carry that cumbersome thing around all the time? Just grab one from the main foyer when you plan to go out exploring."

"Fair enough," Jacy nodded. "I won't have much time for stuff like that due to my training, anyways."

"Training will keep you very busy," Agent Ninny Mop agreed, "but you will have some downtime. Come on, I want to show you something."

"Where are we going?" Jacy asked as the shiny path they were on gave way to a dirt path.

"There are numerous walking paths here. 286,412, to be exact. You will find these paths helpful to unwind a little during your training and when you're playing the Game. The Game is so all-consuming, it's a necessity to have some place or thing to ground yourself from time to time."

Jacy nodded, marvelling at the size and grandeur of the trees now enveloping them.

"I thought I'd show you my favourite shorter route. I have a favourite longer one, but you and I still have some formalities to cover back at the Gaming Building."

Jacy noticed what wouldn't exactly be a trail, but a definite tamping down of the foliage. "Where does that go?"

Agent Ninny Mop grunted. "That leads to the Clearing. Believe me, Jacy, you *don't* want to know what goes on there."

"Well," Jacy teased Ninny, "*that* statement definitely piqued my curiosity."

Agent Ninny Mop looked uncomfortable. "The Skulls use it for…. for…."

Jacy dipped her head and raised her eyebrows. "For…"

"For fornication parties, and I hope you'll never attend one. It's disgusting what they do to each other there." Agent Ninny Mop frowned in displeasure towards the direction of the clearing.

"Okay," Jacy sensed this wasn't a favourite topic for Agent Ninny Mop to discuss. "I won't go. Ever."

Ninny couldn't help but look relieved. He chuckled in embarrassment. "Look, Jacy, I'm not some humdrum prude," they began to stroll again. "I just don't like what happens there."

"Fair enough," Jacy said. If she wanted to know more about these 'fornication parties', she would ask Lita. "So where to, now?"

"A couple minor things, then off to your next training session. Who do you see next?"

"I'm meeting someone named Flair."

"Well, you'll have to meet him sometime. If you can get past his boorishness, huge ego, and his over extravagant tastes, he's one of the best Gamers there is." Agent Ninny Mop led Jacy to the edge of the trail to an exquisite looking flower.

"Now, this is something worth discussing. Flowers and plants are my hobby. This is called The Ghost orchid. It's a rare plant that was thought to be extinct on your planet for almost 20 years. The plant is so rare because it is basically impossible to propagate. It needs a specific fungus in close contact with its root system to feed it. The Ghost orchid can live underground for years, and will only bloom when…"

Jacy admired the pretty flower, but bored quickly of Ninny's talk. She wondered what her meeting with Flair would be like. She didn't have very high hopes about it.

9

Jacy exited the Hennessey Venom GT in front of the most opulent, incredible mansion she had ever seen.

Flair's driver gave her the rundown on the place during the twenty-minute drive to his private abode. 250,000 acres of property, almost 100,000 square feet in building space, including the 63,000 square foot main castle. 123 bedrooms, 61 bathrooms, tennis courts, a movie theatre, indoor and outdoor swimming pools; the list of extravagance bored Jacy to tears.

While the driver's tour guide spiel didn't impress her, seeing Flair's home in all its lavish glory was another matter.

"Wow," Jacy muttered to herself as the driver pulled away, leaving her in front of this grand palace, feeling both tiny and alone. Her ears were soon tickled by the faint guitar chords of a Steve Earle song. The song was one of her favourites. Jacy followed the music to the left of the castle.

"Oh!" Jacy and another female startled each other at the side of the house. The girl hopped back, her naked breasts bouncing along with her movements.

"Sorry," the girl giggled. "You spooked me, that's all."

"Please, no need to apologize," Jacy smiled. "I'm looking for Flair."

"Isn't everyone?" the girl smiled. "Come on, I'll show you where he is."

The girl led Jacy across the sprawling lawn. Jacy noticed that the girl was naked from the waist down, too. She struggled to act nonchalant around this naked woman, but it wasn't easy. The girl nodded at a gorgeous, tattooed woman behind a bar situated on the side of the grass.

"Care for a drink, Jacy?" the girl asked, looking over her shoulder.

"Ummm, no, thanks," Jacy wasn't sure how the naked girl knew her name. "Thanks anyways, though."

The music grew louder.

"Holy shit!" Jacy exclaimed as a concert stage came into view. Far from being canned music, a perfect rendition of Steve Earle was up on the stage, with dry ice, flashing lights, the works.

"Well, I was born by the railway tracks

The train whistle wailed and I wailed right back…."

The girl pointed out Flair, gave Jacy a lingering kiss, and departed with a wicked grin. Jacy blushed, unsure how to respond. Chuckling to herself, she turned her attention to Flair. He had an undeniable coolness as he kept time with the drum beat on the table while two rowdy looking animals were blabbering about him. She walked towards the table.

"But Flair…." One of the ugly goons pleaded as she approached. Flair noticed Jacy and smiled, finally addressing his two companions.

"Gentlemen. Big boobs. Go discuss."

The two behemoths got up and left, animatedly discussing the most preferential size and shape of a female's breast.

"Jacy," Flair stood, pulling out the chair next to his for her to sit. "I've been looking forward to meet you."

"Pretty classy company you keep," Jacy smirked as she took the offered seat.

Flair ignored the barb and resumed watching Steve Earle. Being a huge Steve Earle fan herself, Jacy wondered if this was all a ruse to butter her up. She watched a seemingly captivated Flair view the show. With the final notes of 'I Ain't Ever Satisfied' echoing in the smoky air, Flair turned his attention to Jacy.

"Goddamn it, that man can write the tunes, can't he?" Flair appeared authentic in his love of Steve Earle. "Tell me one thing. How is Mr. Earle not recognized as *the* best songwriter of your generation?"

"To some of us he is."

Flair grunted. The holographic Steve Earle launched into 'Devil's Right Hand,' Jacy's personal favourite.

"Take this song," Flair observed the stage. "This one should be a classic, a standard, yet more of your people can recognize some computer generated crap than a piece of art such as this…"

Flair halted his speech with a loud exhale.

"I'll get down off of my soap box," he said with a winning grin. "Thank you for coming to meet with me. It's a pleasure to finally meet you."

Jacy nodded approvingly towards the stage. "I love your taste in music."

"Just in music?" Flair smirked. "What do you think of my place?"

"Well," Jacy didn't want to offend him. "It's a little over the top, isn't it? I mean, even for this crazy place, it's pretty extravagant."

"Maybe," Flair shrugged, "but it's based on a similar home on your planet."

Jacy chuckled. "Point taken. It's wonderful. It's just not my kind of thing, that's all."

"We can move to some place to your liking," Flair offered.

Jacy returned her attention to the flawless Steve Earle imitator.

'Then I went and bought myself a Colt 45

Called a Peacemaker but I never knew why…'

"Sounds good," Jacy replied, "but after this song, okay?"

"Deal," Flair sat back in his chair and the two of them watched the rest of the song in silence. Once the tune came to a raucous end,

Flair made a distinct hand motion to someone up near the rafters. The stage lights went black, and when they came back on seconds later, the singer-songwriter was gone. Only dissipating dry ice remained.

"Ready?" Flair asked.

Jacy barely nodded in agreement before Flair did a similar to Gravigo's hand shimmy.

"Wow!" Jacy exclaimed, seated at a cliff top table seated for two, overlooking the entire gaming complex, grass-counters and all.

"This is my favourite place to come unwind," Flair gazed out at the vista before returning his look to Jacy. "Especially when I'm in the company of a woman as pretty as you."

Before Jacy could reply, a waiter appeared, dressed in a tux with the arms cut off.

"Ahhh, Johnny Kneed," Flair greeted him. "How are you this fine evening?"

"I'm excellent, Mr. Flair. Would you like your usual?"

"Please."

"And for the lovely lady?"

Jacy had been studying the muscles of Johnny Kneed's impressive arms. She looked at Flair with a dumbfounded look on her face. "Ummmmm......"

"Your favourite?" an amused Flair asked her.

"Sure," an embarrassed Jacy looked away.

"One *very* strawberry margarita," Flair told Johnny Kneed who slipped away as quickly as he had come. Jacy had seen enough of this place to know better than to ask how Flair knew what her favourite drink was. She started to have creepy feelings, though, about what these people knew of the intimate details of her life. She shuddered at the thought.

"Are you cold?" Flair inquired.

"No," Jacy realized she didn't want to broach this subject at this point in time. She looked out at the magnificent view. "This view is amazing."

"Yes, it is," Flair didn't take his eyes off of her. Jacy couldn't contain her laughter.

"Oh please, come on, Flair," she said once she stopped giggling. "Knock off all the sweet talk bullshit. Let's hear why I should become a Skull."

Flair started to speak, but stopped when Johnny Kneed appeared with their drinks. Flair thanked him and their waiter departed.

"Cheers," Flair held up his scotch glass towards Jacy. Jacy returned the gesture and took a sip of her drink.

"Wow," she gazed at her drink in disbelief.

"Not bad?"

Jacy took a bigger swallow, marvelling at the perfect combination of strawberries and tequila exploding all over her taste buds.

"Not bad," she tried her best to remain nonchalant, "not bad at all."

"Johnny is a whiz at mixology," Flair rested his scotch upon the table and removed a cigar package from his pocket. He popped one into his mouth, lit it, and then offered the pack to Jacy.

"Want one?" he exhaled four perfect smoke rings.

"I don't smoke," Jacy took another sip of her marvelous margarita.

"You smoked cigarettes when you were a teenager."

"And I quit when I turned twenty," Jacy shot back, before adding, "Smoking will kill you."

Flair raised his eyebrows at her last comment. He took a long, slow drag and exhaled as Jacy burst into laughter at the absurdity of her statement.

"Jesus Christ," she leaned across the table and grabbed the pack. "Give me one of those fucking things."

Flair leaned forward and lit the cigar dangling from Jacy's lips. Jacy took her time drawing in the smoke, before leaning back and exhaling a cloud of blue smoke. She nodded at Flair, who was taking a slow pull from his scotch.

"Okay," Jacy smiled. "I'm ready for the Skull spiel."

Flair shook his head, his blond locks fumbling along his forehead. "No spiel, Jacy."

"Oh, come on," Jacy laughed. "The Steve Earle concert, the best margarita I've ever tasted, the sweet talk? Please don't."

Flair chuckled as he took a drag from his cigar.

"First of all," Flair's blue eyes burned into Jacy's, but in a non-threatening way, "Steve Earle is my favourite songwriter. Second of all, I didn't concoct that delicious margarita, Johnny Kneed did. And third of all…."

He took another sip of his scotch.

"….ahhhhh," he sighed. "And third of all, I meant what I said. No spiel."

"Really? No sell job?"

"Nope."

Jacy pondered his answer for a moment. She gazed out at the grandiose view, sneaking a puff from her cigar in between sips of her drink. She looked at Flair.

"Why not?"

Flair stubbed his cigar out on the table. He picked up his drink, leaned back in his chair, and smiled.

"Honestly, Jacy?" Flair's magnetic gaze held Jacy hostage. "Unlike Gravigo, I know the two of us have an ice cube's chance in Maui of getting you to join either of our teams. Even better, I'm pretty sure I understand why."

Jacy butted some ash on the ground and leaned closer to Flair. "Care to enlighten me?"

Flair took another pull from his scotch. "I understand, because I'd probably feel the same way you do if I were in your situation."

"And how is it that I feel?"

Flair studied her for a few moments before responding. "You blame each of us for you being here and not with your daughter and husband right now."

Jacy's eyes hardened like stone at the mention of Beau and Derian. She looked away to contain her rising anger, snubbing out her half smoked cigar and pushing her drink to the side. Neither of them tasted very good at the moment.

"See?" Flair nodded. "There is *so* much shit going on here right now that you don't know what is up, down, or sideways. Everything is racing at you a million miles an hour, and you're being spun around blindfolded even faster than that. It's overwhelming for you."

Flair leaned forward, leaning his elbows on the table. "But believe me, Jacy, you will get it, you will understand all of this," Flair swept his arm out at the view beyond the cliff, never taking his eyes from Jacy. "And when you do, you will blame us. Probably Maise, too. No matter whom it was or which group your killer belonged to, you will blame everybody here. Well, everybody not named Baz or Lita, anyways."

Jacy looked off again, trying to ease her galloping mind to a trot. She had no idea if Flair was right or wrong in his assumptions, except for the one about her being more than confused. She gazed out at the cobalt sky, but didn't really see it. Finally, she sighed and returned her eyes to Flair.

"Will you tell me who killed me?"

"No," Flair sighed, "apparently that's not for me to tell you. I can tell you it wasn't me, though."

Jacy nodded, regaining control of her mind. Deliberate and steady remained the key for her; too much too quick left her feeling helpless and in a rage.

"The Skulls are the type to do that kind of thing, though, right?" she asked.

"What kind of thing?"

"You know," Jacy shrugged, eyeing her neglected margarita. "You guys do all the evil stuff."

Flair laughed long and loud at her words. Jacy, realizing no good was going to come from abandoning her tasty drink, reached over and reclaimed it.

"Is that what that fat lout has been filling your head with since you got here?"

"What fat lout?"

"Oh, please," Flair swiped his hand through the air. "Gravigo, that's who. What a fucking meathead."

Flair leaned close to Jacy. "For your information, Gravigo and the Hats kill people, too, you know."

This took Jacy back a little. "Pardon me?"

"Oh, yes," Flair chuckled. "I know Gravigo has probably given you the perception that the Hats are good, the Bones are in the middle, and the Skulls are the evil incarnate ones. Am I right?"

"Well…." Jacy tried to look away from Flair, but couldn't.

"Don't stick up for the fat fuck, okay? He's far from perfect, as are his Hats. See, Gravigo and his group kill people, too, you'll discover this. Gravigo will attempt to justify it, though."

"Justify killing someone?" Jacy's eyebrows furrowed.

"Yep," Flair took another cigar out of the pack and lit one. "See, he'll give some long winded answer that his group only kills as a last resort and only if it's for the greater good."

"The greater good?"

"Yeah, you know," Flair did a fair imitation of Gravigo's voice. "You see, everyone, we could only save those five hundred people by sacrificing those two lives, so we did what had to be done for the greater good."

Jacy smiled at Flair's Gravigo imitation as she pondered what he said. "Is he wrong in that way of thinking, though?" she finally asked.

"I'm not saying he's wrong or right," Flair shrugged. "I'm just saying that Gravigo and his ilk kill people, too."

"For the right reasons, though."

"For what they *perceive* to be the right reasons. Killing two people to save five hundred makes a ton of logical sense. Except…"

Flair paused, exhaling a stream of smoke in perfect heart rings.

"Except?" Jacy prodded.

Flair's eyes flashed brilliantly at her. "Except for the two people who had to die. It makes absolutely no logical sense for them at all."

10

Hammer Coolie surveyed his charges as he simultaneously tried to figure out who was Ridded Snot's target.

The most obvious target would be Josh. Not only was he one of Hammer's favourites, but Josh was also involved in the whole Wisconsin incident. Involved, hell, he *was* the Wisconsin incident. Hammer sighed, wishing his foe was someone like The Bam Slicer. The Bam Slicer's way of playing was simple; straight ahead, pulverizing power and violence.

Ridded Snot, on the other hand, played the Game much like Hammer himself played it. Balance and gamesmanship. Players such as Ridded Snot and Hammer Coolie viewed the game as chess-like with strategies, counter-strategies, plans, and broken plans. Other players like The Bam Slicer viewed the Game like a parking lot brawl with chains, bats, and switchblades.

Neither way was right or wrong, they were merely different.

Hammer did a second quick check on his favoured four:

Josh – In Uptown Library, Kenosha. Josh was doing some research on the dangers of privatizing public water. He had been there for the past hour or so and deep into his reading. Hammer knew he'd be good there for a while more.

Kate- The 42-year-old mother of three had just picked up her youngest child from a gruelling day of Grade 7 at Sacajawea Middle School in Bozeman, Montana. She now headed to pick up her eldest two from Bozeman High School. Hammer nodded in satisfaction; she'd be fine for the time being.

Marley – The seventeen-year-old ball of adorable fire from Campbell River, B.C. exited Carihi Secondary School with her two BFF's chatting excitedly about their Friday evening. Hammer would be keeping a close eye on her.

Frankie – Still at the coffee shop in Toronto with a half page of lyrics but now playing googly eyes with Nine Franc Jeweler's waitress again. Hammer stole a swift glance at Nine Franc who wore raised eyebrows and a pleading look. Hammer sighed, giving Frankie an urge that it was time to leave. Frankie dutifully followed the message by picking up his notebook and pen, and after sneaking one last peek at the waitress' ass, departed the shop. Hammer would keep a close eye on him, too, as he and his band had an important gig that night at the venerable Horseshoe Tavern; home to a stage that once held The Rolling Stones and The Ramones at varying points in their careers.

Hammer completed the same loyal check on each of his pod, noting which charges were in what stages of danger. This was the tough part of matching wits with someone like Ridded Snot. Hammer had helped his charges evade dangers such as falling cranes and homicidal maniacs, only to lose other subjects when they were sitting on their couches in the safety of their homes only to be killed by a runaway vehicle or exploding plane debris raining down from the sky.

Hammer chanced a sly glance at Ridded Snot who was a balanced mix of studying the playing field while chatting amiably with his table mates.

"Any idea where he's going to hit?" Wondered Dawns murmured, staring at Ridded Snot with undisguised loathing.

"Narrowing it down," Hammer responded. Ridded glanced at Wondered Dawns, then Hammer, then back to Wondered who still stared at Ridded Snot. Hammer caught the slight downturn of Ridded's right eyebrow. Hammer gave Wondered a sharp nudge with his knee under the table.

"Knock it off," Hammer smiled to disguise his words.

"I'm not scared of him," Wondered Dawns listened to Hammer's advice, though, and looked down to his own charges.

"You should be," Hammer sighed. "I am."

Wondered looked over at Hammer Coolie with slight surprise.

"Fuck him, Hammer," he whispered, keeping his face as neutral as possible. "I've been having some troubles with him, lately, but have been holding my own. You can take that asshole."

"What kinds of troubles?"

"Nothing I haven't been able to handle so far," Wondered Dawns smiled. "I may make the big tables, yet, huh?"

Hammer nodded in agreement, and he was being truthful. Wondered Dawns was an able competitor, and with a notch or two more in his belt, he may very well make the big leagues.

"Just don't underestimate that little fucker," Hammer tossed another look over at Ridded who was no longer addressing his fellow gamers. Ridded Snot was now full focus. Hammer did another speedy check of his charges and his blood ran cold.

The clock on the wall of the Uptown Library read 8:55 PM, almost closing time. Josh was saying his 'see ya laters' to the helpful library staff and about to exit the building. Hammer squinted at Ridded who nodded.

"Shit," Hammer muttered to himself. Time for the real work to begin.

Hammer's mind raced. Safest route home, Hammer pondered as Josh opened the front doors and stepped into the evening's dying light. Which way to take home? The bus would be quickest and have more people for the safety in numbers angle, but walking the twenty minutes home would have more escape routes if Josh needed them.

Hammer scanned the sidewalks in search of any danger spots. He noticed a lady pushing a stroller on the other side of 63rd Street and two guys headed towards Soul Harbour PCG church on the corner. So far, so good. Hammer let out a long breath, his mind still racing a million miles per second, but slowing slightly. Hell, was Josh even the target? Ridded Snot was sly enough to use this as a ruse….

Wondered Dawns broke Hammer's train of thought by staggering to his feet and knocking his chair over backwards.

"You've got to be kidding me!!!" Wondered Dawns half-stood, his raging eyes glaring at Ridded Snot. "You fucking fucker!!!!"

11

Jacy knocked on the silver and black doors that led to Fatter Verb's office.

"It's open!!" a voice called out, beckoning Jacy to enter the office, though the term 'office' was a generous term here. The entire room was about the size of Gravigo's desk. Jacy spied Fatter Verb sitting in a simple, green wing chair, staring out a floor to ceiling window.

"Mr. Verb?" Jacy raised her voice to be heard over the radio talk show that blared from unseen speakers. "I was told to come here for…"

"Just a second, please," Fatter Verb lifted a hand for silence.

Jacy used the moment to check out Fatter Verb. He looked to be in his mid-fifties, and had a bit of a mad scientist look to him, minus the white coat. He looked what Jacy guessed Denis Leary would look like if he got into a tussle with Gary Busey's hair, and lost.

Jacy looked out the window to see what was enthralling Fatter Verb. She could see the splendid fountain with members of all three groups meandering about. She could see the Grass Counters. Jacy tried to spy out Baz but couldn't from this distance. Jacy shrugged, unsure was so enrapturing. She turned her attention to the talk show.

"…and all of you stinking Chargers fans and your wives who are actually your sisters and…." Some caller rattled on.

"RRRRRRRRHHHHHHHH!!" the radio host screamed.

Fatter Verb slapped his knee and burst into a giggling fit.

"How many times have I told you clones that…" the radio host's voice faded to mute as Fatter Verb waved his hand, chopping the volume down to an almost discernible murmur.

"I wish we had that invention here," Fatter swivelled his chair to face Jacy.

"What invention?" Jacy looked puzzled. "The radio?"

"The manual buzzer. You use it when someone says something stupid," Fatter rolled his eyes. "Lord knows we'd use it a lot around this place. Didn't you ever listen to Jim Rome during your time on Earth?"

"Jim Rome?"

"The Pimp in the Box?"

"Huh?"

"Mr. Man Candy?"

"What?"

Fatter Verb made no attempt to conceal his disappointment in Jacy.

"Doesn't even know who Jim fucking Rome is," he muttered to himself, dimming the lights with one of his hands while raising his other to point at a bare wall. "What the hell are they sending me here?"

Fatter Verb made a circular motion with the index finger of his raised hand.

"Alright, let's start your lesson. Who is this?" he asked when the image appeared on the wall.

"Justin Bieber."

"And this?"

"Maggie Gyllenhaal. She's awesome."

"And this?"

Jacy stared at the stocky, pregnant, early human female making her way across muddy terrain. Jacy looked at Fatter Verb and shrugged her shoulders. Fatter Verb nodded as if this was nothing more than he expected.

"It's unsurprising you don't know who she is," he stared at the image on the wall. "She's only the mother of all humans."

"What?" Jacy found a chair and sat, staring at the woman on the wall.

"Well, there's the grand mother of all humans who would go back 200,000 years, but this fearless lady here, yes, she's all of your peoples' mother," Fatter took a sip from a drink sitting on a side table. "Approximately 70,000 years ago, her tribe began having difficulties finding food, so they crossed a drying up Mediterranean Sea and unknowingly changed the fate of the world. You are watching the first humans leave Africa."

"Holy shit," Jacy muttered to herself.

Fatter Verb nodded as he shut off the flickering image on the wall and returned the lights to their original glow.

"At least you have the good sense to be awed by what you just saw," Fatter Verb smiled. "It's nice to meet you, Jacy Morgan. I am Fatter Verb. How are you adjusting to your new surroundings?"

"New surroundings," Jacy chuckled. "That's a nice way of saying I'm dead."

Fatter Verb reached over and patted Jacy's leg. "What you call dying, I call rebirthing."

"You say ma-tour, I say ma-chure?"

Fatter Verb guffawed. "You dig, Jacy, you dig well."

"Did you make those projections happen with your finger?" Jacy asked.

"Mmmhmm," Fatter nodded. "It burns Gravigo that he has to use that cumbersome remote of his, but he can do that squiggly wiggly thing with his hands…"

"…that's annoying as hell," Jacy cut in.

"You find that annoying?" Fatter Verb looked surprised.

"Kind of," Jacy shrugged. "Where I come from, a lot can be learned from the journey, not the destination."

"Said the insipid inspirational poster," Fatter Verb muttered.

"Yeah," Jacy shrugged again, "but there's a certain truth to it."

Fatter shot Jacy a disbelieving look before going on. "You just came from seeing Agent Ninny Mop?"

"Yes."

"Okay, so he would've shown you how we separate buildings here by continent, not by the archaic tribal lines your people conjured out of thin air."

"Archaic tribal lines?"

"Yes," Fatter Verb dimmed the lights and illuminated a map of North America on the wall. "Take your home continent, for example. Here she is, in all her unadorned beauty."

Fatter Verb moved his ring finger in a circular motion. Bold lines showed the separation between Mexico, The United States, and Canada. He then moved his thumb and dotted lines appeared, showing the different provinces and territories of Canada, and the distinct states of the U.S.A. and Mexico.

"Not only did your fore-people carve up the continent with phony lines on a map and call them countries, they then carved up the countries into provinces, territories, and states. Archaic tribal lines separating the cavemen tribes; that's all your imaginary borders are."

"I like to think we've come a long way since we were cavemen," Jacy frowned.

Fatter Verb pondered this for a moment. "In some ways, I guess, but basically, nope. You're still cavemen. You are more comfortable cavemen, but you're still cavemen."

"That's a little insulting, Mr. Verb," Jacy's hackles began to rise.

"My apologies, I'm truly sorry," Fatter Verb put his hands up and leaned back in his chair. "My manners have eluded me."

Jacy simmered down. A little.

"What I was trying to show you," Fatter Verb tried a different tack, "were those imaginary lines you call borders are pure bullshit. The only people who are expected to follow them are your average human beings. Those other fictional objects, corporations and such, don't pay any attention to them in their pursuit of that man-made evil you call money. So why are your people expected to honour them?"

"I'm not sure," Jacy admitted, raising her eyebrows. "Are you saying we shouldn't have countries?"

"That's *exactly* what I'm saying. Look at your wars. Your young people go fight these senseless, idiotic fights while your companies rack up tremendous profits. Those conglomerates don't care which side they deal with, either."

Fatter Verb took another drink before continuing.

"During World War II, did you know that Coca Cola was told they couldn't sell their product in Germany? No worries, though. Coca Cola created a subsidiary named Fanta that sold its product to the same country that was killing so many of your men. Ford? They sold their products to Germany, too."

Jacy didn't know any of this, but didn't feel like admitting to it, either. Fatter Verb noticed her forlorn look and smiled.

"I'm sorry, Jacy, look at me ramble and spout. I love your people. You humans are beautiful, unique, and you hold a very special place in this universe. You're also dumber than a sack of mallets. Until your people learn they are *not* a herd of sheep, though, they will never take the next step."

"What's the next step?" Jacy asked.

"Well, the one that will save the planet they are fucking up, for starters. That will be one rung up from being comfortable cavemen," Fatter Verb grinned at her, making Jacy laugh. Fatter stood and moved to a messy shelf. He rummaged around on it, found what he was looking for, and returned to Jacy.

"Here," he handed her a flat, silver object. "Insert this into one of those machines Agent Ninny Mop taught you about, study, then come back and see me. I'm sure we'll have lots to talk about."

"Okay," Jacy stood, slipping the object into her pocket.

"Who are you off to see now?" Fatter asked.

"Maise Elantina."

"Ahhhh, I love Maise," Fatter smiled. "Go learn from her what you can, Jacy, she has a lot to teach you. And please don't forget to study. I look forward to our next discussion."

"Thanks…"

"RRRRRRHHHHHHH!" Fatter Verb manual buzzed her. "I never want to hear the words 'thank you' from you again, Jacy. I mean that. Just go and be the best Gamer you can be. That's all the thanks I need."

Jacy didn't know why, but she leaned in and kissed Fatter Verb on the cheek. This flustered Fatter, causing him befuddlement and clumsiness until she closed the door.

Buy the ticket, take the ride, right?

She left to go see Maise Elantina.

12

Ridded Snot tossed a bored glance at the hyper-ventilating Wondered Dawns and shrugged. Wondered Dawns grunted and pushed himself back from the table, stumbling on his overturned chair. Hammer stood, too, putting a hand on Wondered Dawn's shoulder. Wondered shook it off, never taking his eyes from Ridded Snot.

"You're…. you're…you're nothing but a homicidal fucking maniac…." Wondered Dawns sputtered as he rounded the table.

"Wondered…" Hammer called out, eyeing Agent Ninny Mop's security goons who had now taken an interest in their table.

"No, Hammer, you stay out of this! This has nothing to do with you!"

Hammer Coolie hoped that was true. Wondered Dawns stopped and looked at Hammer.

"Oh, it's true, Hammer. This…this…this fucking dirt bag," Wondered jabbed his finger at Ridded Snot, "has been pushing and sneaking and thieving his way to get to Alecia, and well…."

Wondered Dawns glanced back at his playing spot with a mournful look. Hammer recalled many a story Wondered Dawns told him about Alecia. She was obviously one of his favourites. Wondered Dawns looked as if he was about to burst into tears.

"Wondered…." Hammer grabbed the fallen chair and set it upright. Hammer gestured towards it, hoping Wondered would return.

"Now, what?!" Wondered Dawns ignored Hammer and refocused his fury towards Ridded Snot. "Now, what, Ridded? You've got her. Your douchebag subject beat her soul down so fucking much, you've finally got her!"

The tears that were threatening to fall were now in free-fall. Security redeployed to advantageous points around the hushed and beguiled table. Wondered Dawns had no attention for anything else other than Ridded Snot, who for his part, looked both bored and amused the same.

"Answer me, you fucking scumbag," Wondered Dawns voice was pure raggedness. "You've stolen her self-esteem, her support systems, her dreams. And now you've made her a fucking junkie whore! Jesus Christ, she's only 17 years fucking old!"

Wondered Dawns moved so swiftly, Hammer lost sight of him for a moment. Apparently security didn't, though, as by the time Hammer got a clearer view, two of them had Wondered Dawns in a double hammer lock.

"What now?! What now?! What now?!" a blubbering and babbling Wondered Dawns repeated over and over.

"What now?" Ridded Snot finally deigned to stand, facing an debilitated Wondered. "Why, I guess she'll spread her legs like a gutter whore and take a few thousand strangers' cocks up her ass before she ends up in jail or a grave by the time she's twenty-one."

Wondered Dawns let out an anguished bellow before being dragged away. Ridded Snot watched him leave before returning his attention to the table. He seemed surprised to find the whole table watching him.

"What?" Ridded Snot looked genuinely puzzled. "That was merely a guess. Shit, like I know how to read the future."

Hammer leaned over to his left and sought out Rotten Jaws, another Bone. "Better get someone to watch Wondered's pod."

Rotten Jaws nodded and departed the table in a hurry. Hammer Coolie returned his attention to Ridded Snot who revisited his seat. He eyed Hammer with an alarming intensity.

"Touching, wasn't it?" Ridded sneered and shook his head. "Some people take this shit so seriously; I just don't get it."

Ridded Snot leaned forward, resting his elbows on the table. "But now that that's out of the way, Mr. Coolie, why don't you and I have some fun?"

Hammer sighed, centring his brain on his charges. He couldn't read the future, either, but he was pretty sure that whatever Ridded Snot had in mind wouldn't be what Hammer Coolie considered as being 'fun.'

13

The lone picture Jacy saw of Maise Elantina when she first arrived here did not do Maise justice, in Jacy's eyes, at least. Maise wore her blond hair shoulder length, not too long, nor too short. She wasn't slim, but neither was she plump. She wasn't drop dead gorgeous, yet she definitely wasn't unattractive. She bore a regal, yet common air. Maise Elantina was like no other woman Jacy had laid eyes upon before. She could be a first grade teacher or a leather clad dominatrix. Maise Elantina would suit either role perfectly.

They met at the magnificent fountain, where Maise found Jacy watching the Grass Counters.

"Did Agent Ninny Mop or one of the others explain the Grass Counters to you?" Maise Elantina's voice could melt the largest iceberg on Earth. Maise slipped her arm through Jacy's and they began to walk.

"Yes," Jacy answered, getting the sense someone was watching her. Bingo. The same Skull she noticed the last couple of times watched her again. He busied himself with a blade of grass once Jacy spotted him.

"Does that particular Grass Counter interest you?" Maise's gaze followed Jacy's own.

"Kind of, I guess," Jacy said. "I've noticed him staring at me a few times."

"Do you know who that is?"

"Nope."

"That's Buzzed Rottid. He used to be Flair's right hand man."

Jacy whistled softly. "Pretty high up dude to get stuck as a Grass Counter."

"He was," Maise nodded.

"I'm surprised someone that important up ended up here," Jacy commented as they started to stroll.

"You shouldn't be surprised. We can't buy justice like you can on your planet. Here, you either fuck up or you don't."

Jacy smiled, liking Maise Elantina more and more with each word that escaped her lips. Maise was assured, but not cocky. Swift, but not rushed. And Jacy was no lesbian, but she couldn't stop thinking about groping the perfect ass of Maise Elantina.

"Well, he must've royally fucked up, as you so eloquently put it, to be a Grass Counter," Jacy said. "What did he do to become one?"

Maise Elantina's eyes found Jacy's and held them like a steel vice. As matter-of-factly as one would tell another they had a flat tire, Maise spoke.

"Why, he's the one who killed you, hon."

14

While Hammer Coolie had always liked Wondered Dawns, he didn't have a moment to waste thinking about him. Apparently the whole business between Wondered Dawns and Ridded Snot was a mere housekeeping item for Ridded. Now that he had dealt with that issue, he could focus all his attention on Hammer.

Hammer did a quick re-check of his entire pod, again focussing on his favoured four. Hammer sighed.

All four were doing things which could, depending on how things unfolded, be fraught with danger. Frankie was stopping by his pot dealer's apartment on the way to their gig; Kate was dressing for a long overdue night out with her husband; Marley was at a party with her two buddies; and Josh stood outside the library in the darkening, cool air.

Hammer sighed. He almost nudged Josh home a few hours earlier, but didn't. Hammer cursed himself. He was falling into the same trap he worked so hard to avoid. Trichina Flame would be disappointed, as she coached him many times about this exact thing.

"Stop falling into 'safety first' mode," she warned him. "Accidents happen. Shit happens. Your concerns of potential danger can never outweigh your subjects' need to experience life."

"I don't want them to die, though," Hammer argued.

"Of course, you don't, no more than they themselves want to die," Trichina snorted. "Their desire to live, though, far outweighs their fears of dying. Otherwise, nobody would ever leave their homes."

The debate went back and forth, though Hammer knew Trichina Flame was right. He struggled with the whole grey area of it all, but he understood. Just then he recalled something Karma Twin spoke about that same night.

"When the time is right, a good offense is truly the best defense."

Hammer glanced over at Ridded Snot. He seemed to be taking stock of his own charges, too.

What if I attack him first? Hammer speculated. He took a longer look at Ridded Snot's part of the table and felt a small surge of hope. Hammer Coolie knew exactly where to hit him.

15

Jacy felt as if a bullet train drove through her. Maise Elantina wore a puzzled look before her eyes softened to a billowy blue. She took Jacy's hand and squeezed.

"Oh, fuck, Jacy," Maise grabbed Jacy's other hand and squeezed that one, too. "I'm such an asshole. None of us have much experience in dealing with humans."

Jacy continued to hold Maise's hands as she stared back at her murderer. Her murderer, for Buddha's sake. How fucked up was she becoming? One moment she's admiring another woman's ass, the next she's watching her murderer count blades of grass.

"Here, come sit," Maise Elantina led her to an intricately carved bench made from marble. Jacy didn't notice the bench's beauty. She could've been sitting on a carving of an elephant's phallus, for all she knew. She couldn't tear her eyes from Buzzed Rottid.

Maise continued to hold one of Jacy's hands as she used her other hand to guide Jacy's cheek towards her. "I'm truly sorry, Jacy. Will you forgive me for being such a heartless jerk?"

"Of course," Jacy tossed a hasty glance at her slayer. "Why would he kill me?"

"It is all so convoluted and webbed with deceit and mystery," Maise sighed. "I'm not sure the true answer will ever be known."

Jacy returned her look to Maise. "Well, thanks for clearing that one up for me."

Maise Elantina let out a melodic laugh, which didn't surprise Jacy in the least. Was there *anything* about this woman that wasn't likeable?

"I apologize, again, Jacy, but there are so many half-baked theories and conspiracies floating around this place. Don't clog your head with all of it, which will be 99% bullshit and innuendo."

"Fair enough," Jacy nodded. "What do *you* think the reason he killed me was?"

Maise looked out at the Grass Counters before responding.

"I believe there was a royal fuck-up somewhere," she declared.

"You're telling me," Jacy deadpanned.

"Oh, Jacy, this must all seem so cold-blooded to you," Maise took hold of her hands again. "I assure you, though, that we are not. Your death caused an uproar here we hadn't experienced in eons. Finger pointing, scandals, eternal bonds shattered like fine China meeting the horns of a bull. In the end, we have the highest ranked member of any group sentenced to Grass Counting, only the third human admitted to the Game, and every single person looking over their shoulder. Your death caused chaos, here, believe me."

Maise Elantina sighed. "Your death on Earth was given the highest regard and attention here. Unfortunately, we still don't have the answers, but it hasn't been from lack of trying."

Jacy did her best to absorb all of what Maise said. "Okay, but you still didn't tell me what *you* think."

Maise shook her head. "I can't tell you what I don't know, Jacy, but I will tell you this. I know Buzzed Rottid and Flair very well. In fact, I saw Flair the night you died. He was shocked at what happened to you."

"Really?" Jacy asked.

"Really. Flair can't bullshit me that good. He honestly didn't know you were going to die. And Buzzed, well, I can say with absolute certainty that Buzzed Rottid would not have traded a minor victory over Gravigo for a lifetime of being a Grass Counter. Something happened, but whether it was a simple miscommunication or some grand double cross, we just don't know."

Maise Elantina stood. "I have some feelers out there, as I don't believe in coincidences here. It's not lost on me that both the leader of the Skulls and the leader of the Hats lost one of their favourite members in such a small time frame. I promise you I will let you know when I find out something more concrete."

Jacy thought for a moment, looking one last time at Buzzed Rottid before returning her attention to Maise.

"Okay," Jacy nodded, "one last thing, though. Why was I *so* important to Gravigo? Being one of the head cheeses like he is, wouldn't the people in his pod be bigwigs, too? You know, like presidents, CEOs, rich muckity mucks?"

"Oh, Jacy," Maise laughed. "Because we see all here, most of your 'muckity mucks' don't mean squat shit on the true canvass of life. Everything in the universe, though, is connected in a very intricate snowflake. A rich asshole may be nothing; a street sweeper or pregnant Canadian housewife may be everything."

Jacy snorted. Maise turned serious. "Remember the snowflake I spoke of, Jacy. Maybe it wasn't even you who was so important. Maybe you were a strand *leading* to something important."

"So maybe it wasn't me, per se," Jacy nodded her head in understanding, "but maybe it could be…"

"…. your daughter," Maise wore a grave look before adding, "or grandson. Or great-great-great-great-granddaughter."

Jacy exhaled in frustration. Her head felt like it was about to explode.

"Come on," Maise Elantina led her towards the entrance doors. "Let's get to work. I've got this amazing charapa turtle in Peru's Pacaya-Samiria National Reserve that we're going to train you on today."

Jacy followed Maise into the building, struggling to understand it all.

16

Hammer Coolie made up his mind what to do when he noticed Josh stop in front of the library and chat with a group of guys he knew from school. He'd be safe for a while there.

Instead he focussed on Terry, a twenty-year-old male in his pod who just left the Elite Ju-Jitsu Academy in Pocatello, Idaho. This was in an area very close to where Hammer noticed one of Ridded Snot's characters lurking about.

"Want to take the bus?" Terry's buddy asked him, gesturing in the direction of the bus stop. Terry nodded and started to follow when he stopped.

"You know what?" Terry asked. "It's a nice night. Why don't we head down 7th and grab a half sack of beers?"

Hammer smiled at how quick Terry responded to his gut feelings. The young tended to heed them much more than the older humans, and for that, Hammer was grateful.

Terry's friend was pretty easy going and agreed to the idea. As they turned to head in the direction of the liquor store, Hammer checked his others out. Josh was still chatting with his friends, Kate and her husband were on their way to a movie, and Marley looked to be behaving herself, as far as drinking teenaged girls conduct themselves.

Hammer glanced at Ridded Snot who didn't seem to notice what Hammer was doing. Ridded no longer chatted with others, though. He was in full on Game mode.

The timing couldn't have been better. Terry and his buddy, chatting about girls, rounded the corner when they saw Ridded Snot's guy dart out and knock a woman to the ground. He grabbed the woman's purse and fled. Terry and his buddy didn't even think. They raced after him.

Hammer Coolie noticed Ridded look over at him, but Hammer didn't take his eyes from the scene below. Terry and his friend caught the guy within the block, subduing the skinny drug addict with ease. The guy squirmed on the ground, pleading to them.

"Come on, guys, I'm on probation," he bargained. "Let me go, and I won't do this again, okay?"

Terry and his friend pretended to ponder this before laughing.

"Go fuck yourself, dude," Terry's friend said. "That could've been one of our mothers that you just did that to."

Terry's friend called 911 as Terry held the thief down. The lady who had her purse stolen caught up to them, thanking them profusely. It was only then that Hammer Coolie allowed himself to look up at Ridded Snot.

A smiling Ridded nodded at Hammer and gave him a little golf clap.

"Well played, Mr. Coolie. I rather liked little Jason down there, despite his appetite for drugs and thievery and such, but you played that well. I didn't see that one coming. I wonder, though…"

Ridded Snot's smile vanished.

"Did you see *this* coming, Mr. Coolie?"

17

"Where in the hell are we?" Jacy murmured to Lita.

"Why are you whispering?" Lita's eyes glinted with amusement as they passed under a dull street light.

"I…." Jacy began to answer but reconsidered while as she checked out their less than savory surroundings. She shrugged.

"I don't know why I'm whispering," she continued to whisper. "Probably so I won't draw attention to us from the murdering gangs of thugs that are lurking around here. Jesus Christ, Lita, look at this fucking place."

Lita giggled as Jacy swept her arm around the desolate, darkened neighborhood they were in. Jacy frowned at Lita. "And you laugh? Seriously, Lita, this place gives me the jeebies."

"It's okay, Sugar," Lita put her arm around the small of Jacy's back. "We are 100% safe here, I promise you."

Jacy raised her eyebrows, not sold on Lita's reassurance. Jacy had never seen as rough a neighborhood as this one.

"Where are we going?" she moved closer into Lita after hearing something scurry in the darkness, rattling a garbage can lid. Lita led her across the deserted, litter-strewn street.

"There's someone you need to meet," Lita replied as they set upon the opposing sidewalk. "This person will not be on your official training schedule, but believe me on this. She is just as important if not more so than all of the trainers you will see."

"Really?" Jacy's spirits sagged alongside her shoulders. "*More* training? This is my first night off since I got to this bizarre place, and you take me for more fucking training? Goddamn it, Lita, I…"

"Shhh, hon," Lita removed her arm from Jacy and grabbed her hand, instead. "This isn't official training; this is just going for a cup of tea with a sweet, little old lady, that's all. Just pay attention, okay?"

Lita cocked her head, tossing a smirk at Jacy. "I promise, I'll take you to the strippers after this, okay?"

Jacy pretended to perk up. "Strippers? Male or female?"

"Your choice."

Jacy furrowed her brow in pretend thought. Lita laughed as they came to a halt before a set of crumbling, concrete stairs leading up to an imposing building.

"Okay, you ponder that for a bit," Lita gently elbowed Jacy. "But take this visit seriously, alright, Sug? Granny Mandible will be very important to you here."

The front door creaked open and the very cute Dickie, Joey, and Lucy stepped out, taking their positions on the top stoop.

"Oh, look how cute…." Jacy stopped talking when Dickie produced a cigarette and lit it. Jacy's eyes widened. She looked at Lita. "What the fuck?"

"Just ignore them, hon," Lita took Jacy's arm and led her up the stairs. They made it within ten steps of the seated Dickie when Joey's voice rang out in the quiet night.

"Deck the halls!"

"Jingle Bells!" Dickie responded, exhaling a lungful of cigarette smoke.

Lucy's eyes locked on Jacy. "Jacy Morgan's vagina smells!" she spat the words with venom. Jacy's eyes widened, her mouth hanging open as the boys' belly laughed.

"Fuck you, you little whore-bag," Lita's voice was cut and mean. "Her vagina smells better than your breath."

Both boys howled uncontrollably, now.

"Lucy has pussy breath! Lucy has pussy breath!" Joey did a funny dance as he sang his words. Lucy glared at him.

"Fuck you, Joey Small Dink," Lucy snarled. "I'm going to kick you right in the…"

Lita slipped herself and Jacy in between the squabbling kids and through the door. She closed it, causing the voices to muffle.

"What the fuck was that?" Jacy whispered.

"Oh, don't pay any attention to…"

"Jesus fucking Christ, Lita, why do you and Maise always have to engage the children? It's not their fault they are the way they are." Jacy turned in the direction of the disembodied voice. Lita led Jacy into a gloomy living room.

"Oh, come on, Granny," Lita left Jacy by the entrance. She approached the seated Granny Mandible. "You know how cranky they get if I don't join in with them. How are you doing?"

Lita leaned in to give Granny Mandible a kiss on the cheek. Granny took Lita's hand and held it.

"I'm doing fine, but have been wondering what it is I've done to offend you."

"Offend me?"

"Yes, I must've really pissed you off to make you come around as rarely as you do. Is your life too hectic to come visit a lonely old lady like me?"

"I'm never too busy to come see you, Granny, you know that," Lita offered the old lady a gentle smile.

"Maise Elantina comes to see me three times as much as you do," Granny Mandible pushed herself out of the rocking chair. "Shit, even fucking Flair comes around more often than you. And *he* doesn't rile up the kids the way you do."

Lita shrugged, defeated.

"I'm sorry, Granny Mandible," she spoke in a soft voice Jacy hadn't heard from her before. "I should definitely come by more."

"Yes, you should, child," Granny moved closer to Lita and gave her a frail hug. "More importantly, though, you will, right?"

Lita nodded as Granny Mandible's gaze fell upon Jacy, still standing by the living room's entrance.

"Well, come on, don't be a fraidy cat," Granny waved Jacy into the room. "Let me get a closer look at the one who's caused all the shit balls to start flying around here."

Lita met Jacy halfway into the living room. She took Jacy's hand and led her to Granny. "Granny Mandible, this is Jacy Morgan. Jacy, Granny Mandible."

"It's nice to meet you," Jacy spoke as Granny Mandible studied her face. Lita continued to hold Jacy's hand as Granny did a more thorough inspection. Granny circled the back of Jacy, making the odd grunt here and there. Jacy was curious whether the noises were made in admiration or derision, but she held her tongue. She attempted to speak, though, when Granny returned to her front, reached out with both hands, and jiggled her breasts.

"Uhmmm…" Lita crushed Jacy's hand like a vise. Jacy tossed an annoyed look at Lita.

"Sorry, sweetie," Granny said. "Your tits remind me of mine back in the day. Mine were bigger and firmer, though."

Jacy wasn't sure what she was supposed to say to that, so she kept silent. Granny peered into Jacy's face again, and smiled.

"I can see why Gravigo loves you so much, though. Come here," Granny Mandible drew Jacy into a warm embrace, positioning her mouth close to Jacy's right ear, the one opposite Lita.

"Trust no one," Granny whispered fiercely before breaking off the hug and stepping back from a quizzical Jacy. "Now, I look forward to hear how you are getting along here, Jacy. But first, I was wondering if I could discuss some quick business with Lita here. Would you mind making us some tea?"

"Uhhh, sure, okay, I guess…"

"Thanks, sweetie," Granny Mandible gestured towards the hallway outside the living room. "The kitchen is that way. Take a right down the hallway."

Jacy followed Granny's directions and found the dingy kitchen without trouble. Grabbing the dented tea kettle from the counter, Jacy puzzled over Granny Mandible's message to her as she filled the kettle with water. Lucy walked into the kitchen.

"Fuck you, you fucking slut," Lucy snarled, opening the fridge door.

"Why are you so mean?" Jacy asked, turning off the water and putting the kettle on the stove.

"Who's being mean, twat lips?"

"You are," Jacy turned the element on, put her hands on her hips, and stared at Lucy. "Where I come from, kids don't act like you do. They are kind and gentle. They don't know how to be assholes until they are older."

Lucy gaped at Jacy for a moment before responding.

"Fuck off," she said, leaving the kitchen. She halted before she exited and looked back at Jacy for thirty seconds or so. "Just fuck off."

Jacy shrugged when Lucy left. She had enough on her mind to be worrying about some foul mouthed brat. She finished making the tea and went to the living room to see Lita and Granny Mandible.

18

Hammer Coolie looked down at the table and immediately saw what Ridded referred to. Josh left his friends and was just rounding the corner onto 24th Avenue.

It seemed both Hammer and Josh heard the revving of the engine and the screeching of the tires at the same time. Josh glanced back and saw a truck he knew all too well. Hammer didn't need to give any urges whatsoever. Human instinct took over. Josh dashed down 24th.

Hammer saw the four guys in Levi Johnson's '89 Dodge. They spotted Josh and headed after him. Hammer glanced over at Ridded, who rewarded Hammer with a wink.

Hammer couldn't do much as Josh now worked on adrenaline and fear. Hammer urged Josh to turn right and scoot down 61st in hopes Levi and his thugs wouldn't notice and would drive right past it. Josh made the turn just past the burgundy bungalow on the corner as Levi and his friends rounded onto 24th. With any luck, they didn't notice where Josh went.

Hammer would've made different choices here had Josh been accepting of gut feelings, but Josh was far past that, now. Josh dashed down 61st and turned left where Daisy's Vanity Shoppe stood. Hammer breathed a sigh of relief as he watched Levi skip past 61st street and stay on 24th while Josh sped down 23rd.

It was time to check on the rest of his pod, as Hammer Coolie didn't come this far by merely being pretty good. He was an excellent Gamer, and the best Gamers knew that things weren't always the way they looked. This whole play for Josh could be a decoy.

The only one who stood out for him was Marley. Her friends were really drunk. Marley was buzzed, but still in good shape. Marley's friends wanted to go for a ride with three boys to another party, but Hammer didn't like the looks of them. Marley appeared to be thinking about it, so Hammer hit her with a pretty hard gut feeling. Soon enough, Marley shook her head and wandered back inside towards the party.

Atta girl, Hammer thought, returning his attention back to Josh, after double checking Frankie, Kate, and doing a rapid sweep of most of his pod. Hammer gritted his teeth. Poor fucking Josh. He didn't deserve this. Josh was a good kid.

Josh originally attracted the ire of his pursuers with only minimal urges from Hammer. Josh knew a wrong had been done and he did his best to correct it. He noticed some postings and pictures on Facebook about a school friend of his being really drunk and having sex with four or five different guys at a party. For some reason he printed the postings, as at the time he had no idea what really transpired.

A few days later, it was revealed the girl wasn't merely drunk, she was passed out. All the sex happened when she was unconscious.

By the time this came out, though, the Facebook postings and pictures were down. The whole sordid episode turned into a he said/she said until Josh turned in the pictures he printed off to the police. One of the postings, 'stupid bitch didn't even know we was fucking her,' was especially damaging. All of it was pretty incriminating evidence.

Unfortunately, the town was split on the whole thing. Some blamed the girl for being drunk, others blamed the boys. It was still a red hot issue, and it didn't stay secret long as to who showed the Facebook postings to the authorities.

Screeching tires brought Hammer back to full focus. Josh rounded the corner by Bombay Louie's and flew down 60th street. Levi and the other bullies were deciding which way to go on 60th when one of them noticed Josh. They turned right and started down it, engine roaring.

This turned out to be good for Josh, though, as he decided to cross the street then while he had enough space. If he didn't do that, he may have been stuck with the option of racing inside the Citgo gas station for help. Instead he was on the left side of the street and managed to burst through Finney's Pub's doors. His waitress Mom saw him huffing and puffing at the entrance. She sighed.

"Anybody want to please help get whoever is chasing my son off of his back?"

Five or six of the regulars all stood, patting Josh on the back as they exited the bar to face Levi and his friends. Josh's mom went to him and hugged him.

"Let's get you some water," she murmured into his ear and led him towards the bar.

Hammer let out a long breath, not realizing he was holding it in. He looked up at Ridded Snot, who nodded at him.

"Well played, again, Mr. Coolie. You are really quite good."

Hammer didn't say anything.

"Unfortunately," Ridded nodded at one of the Skulls at the table. "I'm quite good, too. I win, Hammer Coolie. You lose."

Hammer didn't even get the chance to give Marley a gut reaction. He watched helplessly as the car creamed into her from behind. Hammer watched her fly forwards, skidding along the pavement and gravel. Her ravaged body rolled down the embankment leading away from the road. She came to a stop against an overgrown brush in the marsh.

The car sped away as Hammer looked on in horror.

19

Jacy originally intended to go explore some of the walking trails, but instead found herself lost in her thoughts, wandering one of the sparkling paths amongst the Grass Counters. Jacy relived an exciting morning of training that led to a very successful episode with a giant pangolin in Burkina Faso, Africa. It was only when she sensed someone watching her that she pulled herself from her reverie.

Jacy was surprised to find herself 50 feet or so away from Johnny Bazinski. Jacy stopped walking and stared back at him. She was unsure how long they remained like that, but a female grass counter's chuckle broke her trance.

"Hi, I'm Jacy," Jacy said.

"And I'm Baz," he smiled at her. "Care to sit for a spell?"

Jacy almost stepped onto the grass before catching herself.

"It's okay," Baz said, "thanks for thinking of us. Just come to me in a straight line and it'll be fine."

Jacy followed his direction and sat where Baz indicated.

"Well, it's nice to finally meet you, Jacy. How are you doing in this demented place?"

"Okay, I guess."

"That's not what I'm hearing," Baz chuckled. "I hear you're getting close to graduating from your training and will be in the Game before long."

"Really? Who did you…how did you…" Jacy looked perplexed. Baz laughed.

"You'd be surprised what we hear out here, Jacy. Most of it is good information, too," Baz motioned towards a female grass counter not far from him. "That's Ugly Earful. She's a beacon of information, that one."

Jacy looked at Baz, unsure on what to say. She felt a kinship with him, being one of the only humans in this place and all, but she found it difficult to start a conversation with him.

"How are you holding up?" she finally asked.

Baz looked down at the limp piece of grass he was retaining between his thumb and forefinger of his right hand.

"I'm holding up as well as this cursed piece of grass is, I suppose."

Baz laughed a joyless chuckle that broke Jacy's heart. She looked across the acres and acres of plush grassland and couldn't begin to fathom what Baz was going through. She surveyed the area that Baz already counted.

"Well," Jacy tried to sound hopeful. "You're more than half way there."

Baz nodded slowly, gesturing to someone way back near the beginning of the counting field.

"See that guy over there?"

Jacy nodded, squinting to see who he was referring to.

"That's Weapon Lush, one of Flair's old comrades," Baz said. "He finished, ohhhh, about two months ago or so."

Even from this distance, Jacy could see the saggy shoulders and defeated spirit of Weapon Lush.

"He was 12,658 blades of grass off," Baz shook his head. "And that's not a horrible number to be wrong by, either."

Jacy didn't know what to say to that.

"You need to be within 100. It takes roughly 80 Earth years to count this field. That was Weapon Lush's third attempt."

Jacy's mind could barely fathom it. She reached out, placing a hand on Baz's shoulder. "Oh, Baz," was all she could say.

"Bah," Baz patted her knee with his free hand. "Listen to me becoming some bitter old fart. I made my bed and deserve to lie in it."

Jacy was about to ask what he did to become a Grass Counter when her communication belt went off.

"Jacy?"

"Yes, Maise?"

"Can you please meet us in Conference Room 74 B?"

"Okay," Jacy answered. "See you soon."

"Looks like you're closer to graduating than we heard. Congratulations."

Jacy stood, careful to stay in the line she walked in on. "Think that's what this is?"

"Yes, I do," Baz nodded. "You'll be expected to choose one of the three groups when you get there."

Baz chuckled at Jacy's facial reaction. "You don't know which group you want to join yet, do you?"

Jacy shook her head. Baz sighed.

"Well, you have two choices. Make your mind up before you get there, or…" he went on to explain the only other option Jacy had.

Jacy listened, and thanked Baz. She promised to return soon, before heading for her big meeting.

20

"Come on, Hammer, you're better than this," Tagger Merrino looked at his friend through the smoke of the campfire. Hammer Coolie had been in such a daze after what happened to Marley that he forgot the new camp had been moved. Karma Twin and Trichina Flame found him wandering near the previous one. Trichina returned to the tables and stepped in for his pod, while Karma led Hammer to the new one.

Karma went back to fetch Trichina Flame. Hammer sat slumped against a log. Tagger shook his head at him.

Tagger paced. "Look, I know she was one of your favourites, but come on, man...."

"She would be dead, if not for Rainy Dissolve," Hammer didn't look up as he spoke.

"Oh, wow, really? Do you hear yourself, Hammer? Fuck, who the hell cares how she survived, alright? She's alive, that's all that matters."

Trichina Flame and Karma Twin appeared at the fire, holding hands. Trichina looked at Tagger.

"How is he?" Trichina asked.

"Fuck, ask him yourself," Tagger muttered. He looked at Hammer. "Look, amigo, I'm not being heartless, I'm just making sense, okay? Get your head out of your ass, quit crying, and carry on. That's what the Hammer Coolie who I know would do."

"Tagger...." Karma started.

"Bah," Tagger waved his hand at them and stalked off. Trichina Flame ignored him. She knelt down beside Hammer.

"She's going to live, Hammer. That guy of Rainy's spent three hours looking for her. He could hear her; he just couldn't see her. The guy saved her life."

"The guy looked for her for three hours?" Karma asked.

"Yeah," Trichina nodded. "Pretty wild, eh? He lived close by. He stepped outside for a smoke just before bed, though, and he heard a female's voice. He started to search for her right then."

"Why didn't he call it in?" Karma asked, watching Hammer.

"He didn't put two and two together at first. He didn't realize Marley had been hit by a car. He thought it just might be someone sleeping off a drunk or something."

"What are the other injuries?" Hammer finally looked up.

Trichina Flame looked at Karma Twin. Karma shrugged.

"Too soon to tell, Hammer, I...."

"I'm guessing she'll be lucky if she walks again," Hammer stood. "That car hit her awfully hard. Thank you both."

Hammer started to walk away.

"Wait. Are you alright?" Karma asked.

Hammer stopped and turned, nodding.

"I'm okay," he waved a hand in the direction that Tagger left in. "Tagger had it wrong. I wasn't sulking. I was stopping myself from doing something stupid and crazy. Marley is going to need me more than ever, now. I plan to be there for her."

Hammer started to leave, then turned. His eyes blazed.

"Of course, I won't rest until I hunt down that fucking Ridded Snot, either. Put a watch out for him and let me know when you hear something."

Hammer walked off to help Marley.

21

"Okay," Gravigo rapped a gavel on the oak table he, Maise Elantina, and Flair sat. "Now that the pleasantries are over with, let's get this meeting under way."

Jacy wasn't too sure which pleasantries Gravigo referred to. In the last three minutes, Gravigo and Flair bickered like a couple of whiny school kids, and Flair called Maise an 'amateur bitch', which caused Gravigo and Flair to natter at each other again. It all came to a crescendo when Flair cut a roaring fart which elicited an 'amateur flatulator' comment from Maise.

With that eloquent beginning, they were ready to begin. Jacy waited to see why she'd been summoned. She wasn't sure Baz was correct in his assumption as to what this meeting would entail.

"Jacy," Gravigo spoke in a warm tone. "Speaking on behalf of all of us, I want…"

"Who gave you the right to speak for me?" Flair interrupted.

Maise Elantina rolled her eyes and Gravigo harrumphed. Jacy decided that no one harrumphed better than Gravigo. She should know. She caused those harrumphs many times since she'd been there.

"Flair," an exasperated Gravigo whined. "We agreed it was my turn to chair the meeting because you were the chair last time."

Gravigo softly elbowed Maise. "Remember how well *that* meeting went?" he chortled.

"You have the right to chair the meeting," Flair barked, "but you don't have the right to speak for me."

Jacy looked at Maise Elantina who tossed her a wink. Gravigo stared at Flair for a long moment before speaking. "May we proceed?"

Flair waved his assent. Gravigo restarted the meeting.

"Jacy," Gravigo's warm tone returned, "all three of us have watched you with immeasurable pride. You've passed your training with near perfect marks…"

"Except for that poor Chihuahua in White Rock," Flair snickered.

Gravigo continued without pausing.

"...so we are proud to say that you have graduated and are now ready to be a participant in the Game. Congratulations."

All three clapped. Jacy acknowledged their well wishes with a smile and a nod.

"You've fit in wonderfully here, Jacy," Gravigo carried on. "Considering the difficult circumstances that brought you here, I can do nothing but shake my head in admiration."

Jacy thought of Derian and Beau, feeling a stab of guilt. The thought of her family returned rational thought.

"Now, since you have officially graduated, this is the time for you to choose between being a member of the Skulls, the Bones, or the…"

Flair ripped another loud fart.

"Sorry," Flair looked at Jacy. "I should have added an 's' to that."

Jacy couldn't help but giggle. Neither could Maise.

"You're such a pig, Flair," Gravigo wasn't laughing.

"Me? A pig? You know, Gravigo, you are the last person who should…"

Jacy watched another insult-fest. Maise looked at Jacy, mouthing the word 'boys' before rolling her eyes.

This little outbreak gave Jacy a chance to reflect on what she was going to do. She still wasn't 100% sure, yet. She had a tough choice ahead of her. Gravigo had become a bit of a father figure to her, and Maise was almost her mentor. Even Flair and the Skulls trainers she had were great to her. Of course, being a Skull was out of the question. That left either the Bones or the Hats.

"Oh yeah? What about Mahatma Ghandi, huh? You guys…." Gravigo was worked up now.

"Fuck that, Gravigo, you can't…" Flair bellowed back.

Jacy put her hands up, asking for quiet. It took a moment or two, but Flair and Gravigo finally shut up. They looked at her with raised eyebrows.

"I've made my decision," Jacy said. She told them her choice.

PART III

THE EUGENE CHAPTERS

"It's fine to celebrate success, but it is important to heed the lessons of failure."

—Bill Gates

1

This was it. No more bunnies, dogs, or kitty cats. No more ferocious lions on the plains of Namibia, and no more wolves on Mount Lucania. Jacy's newest subject was an actual *human being*. She slow walked to the table and sat down, rubbing her hands on her thighs in an attempt to settle her hopping nerves.

Eugene. Eugene Thompson. Eugene Earl Thompson, born in Sausalito, CA in 1965. Today, Eugene was a 49-year-old widower deli manager at Haggen's Market in Ferndale, Washington.

"He hasn't sunk into a bottom-less pit of depression," Maise Elantina explained to Jacy during her debriefing of Eugene, "but he is a little fragile."

Fragile was a good word to describe Eugene, and Jacy kept that tenuous image in mind. The other word best used to describe Eugene was normal. He was normal weight, normal height, and normal looking. He wore normal clothes, drove a normal car, and had the normal interests of any middle-aged, American male.

Eugene, Eugene, Eugene. Fragile and normal, normal and fragile. Jacy felt the name Eugene was one of the most beautiful names she ever heard.

During her resolute studying of Eugene's background, Jacy ended with the conclusion that Eugene was spinning his tires. He was neither rich nor poor. Neither happy nor sad. He wasn't too sure where he was going, and a little wary of where he had been.

Eugene was pretty close to his brother Earl. All Thompson males had the first or middle name of Earl, after a semi-wealthy great-great grandfather. Earl did his best to pull his older brother from the funk Eugene found himself in since his wife of 17 years perished from a heart attack two and a half years before.

Jacy took a deep breath and looked down at the table, stretching her arms and fingers. She felt an unwelcome guest join the nervousness and excitement that resided in her belly.

The intruder was doubt. Jesus Buddha Christ, was she really going to be able to pull this off? Eugene was an actual living, breathing human being, not some barn cat in Nebraska. Jacy was about to have a very large say in this man's life. Whether Eugene listened to her or not was entirely up to him, but still, what if she was wrong?

Jacy looked down on Eugene, watching him slice some Black Forest ham for a customer he idly chatted with.

"Sure glad the 'Hawks locked Sherman down," Eugene said. Jacy's football knowledge wasn't the best, but she knew Eugene was a huge Seattle Seahawks fan.

"Still too tough to repeat, though," the customer teased Eugene who took the jibe good naturedly.

Jacy watched and smiled, appreciating the beauty of human beings from a vantage point she never looked from before. From cells to fish to dinosaurs to apes to voila. Your average, every day human being. Humans went from cold caves to mud huts to a deli counter in Washington. Humans lived and loved and learned and adapted; always stumbling, but usually moving forward.

Eugene represented a microcosm of all of that. The uncertainty in Jacy's stomach expanded. What if she wasn't good enough? What if she messed up and Eugene missed his life's calling because of her? What if she directed him into the path of a runaway bus? What if….

"You're going to do fine, Jacy," a voice startled her. "Just relax and be yourself."

Jacy looked up, surprised to see Flair standing at her table. "A little overwhelming at first, isn't it?" Flair nodded towards the centre of the table.

"No, no, I, uhhhh…I…." Jacy rolled her eyes in exasperation, shaking her head. "No, not a little. A lot."

Flair smiled, spun a chair around, and sat so he was straddling the back of the chair. "Good. People who aren't overwhelmed by this scare the piss out of me."

"Why?"

"If you're not nervous, then you don't care. And if you don't care, then you'd be reckless, letting your subject do everything and anything regardless of the consequences to your subject and others."

Flair's cool blue eyes bore directly into Jacy's. "So you being nervous shows me you care. And caring about your subject is *the* most critical piece of the game."

"Do you really feel that?" Jacy looked unsure.

"Absolutely," Flair chuckled. "Don't believe all the rumours and innuendo you hear about me."

Flair leaned closer to Jacy, his twinkling eyes growing serious. "No matter what you hear about me, Jacy, please believe this. I love my subjects, every last one of them. I care about all humans, not just the ones in my pod. People can say and think what they want, but if they're being truthful, they can't take that away from me."

He leaned back and gestured towards the table. "It warms me to know you feel the same about Eugene. We may be more kindred spirits than you think we are."

Jacy laughed. "How can we be kindred spirits, Flair. You're a Skull."

Flair cocked a half grin. "And you are…."

"…not a Skull."

Flair waved his hand. "A difference in politics, that's all. You don't have to buy the black and white bullshit that flies around here, Jacy. All of us, Skulls, Hats, Bones, free agents, we're all far more alike than we are comfortable in admitting."

Jacy chewed on that statement for a few moments, unsure if she was buying into Flair's 'thug with a heart of gold' speech.

"Anyways," Flair stood, rearranging his chair to its original place. "You'll do great, Jacy. I know you will."

"I wish I had as much faith in me as you do," Jacy didn't return his smile.

"My faith is well placed," Flair departed. Jacy watched him walk a few steps before calling out to him.

"Flair?"

He turned and raised his eyebrows. This time Jacy smiled at him. "Thanks. I appreciate the pep talk."

"The pleasure was all mine," Flair gave an exaggerated bow, then spun so quickly he bumped into an oncoming Gravigo.

"Whoa, sorry 'bout that, big fella," Flair did a drum solo on Gravigo's stomach, before turning back to Jacy. "Remember what I said. And don't worry, you'll be fine."

With that, Flair was gone. Jacy looked at a grumpy Gravigo.

"Soooo," Gravigo wasn't very talented when trying to mask his annoyance. "I didn't realize you and Flair were so close."

"Give it a rest, Grav," Jacy rolled her eyes and looked down upon Eugene who was making small talk with one of the cashiers who came by the deli section for her lunch. By the way she looked at Eugene, Jacy decided she had more on her mind than just the sandwich of the day. Jacy disliked her on the spot.

"Was Flair trying to recruit you?"

"Yep," Jacy lied. "He offered me the #2 spot with the Skulls. Can you top that?"

Gravigo refused to take the bait. "Why do you toy with this heart of mine?" he half whined.

Jacy laughed. "Okay, straight goods. He merely came by to wish me luck. He knew I'd be apprehensive and nervous as shit, so he stopped by and gave me a little pep talk. Nothing more, nothing less."

Gravigo eyed her for a moment or two before responding. "I was coming to do the very same thing, and I would've beat him to it, too. Unfortunately, I was waylaid by a rookie Hat who was having an issue with one of his subjects."

Jacy gave Gravigo a genuine smile. "Waylaid or not, thanks for coming by. I mean that."

"I could be of the same aid to you, but oh, that's right, you're not a Hat," it wasn't hard to tell that Gravigo was still hurt by her decision.

"I'm not a Skull or a Bone, either. I've merely delayed giving my answer by provisions provided me in your own bylaws," Jacy told him for probably the twentieth time since she had made her choice to not belong to any of the groups for the time being. Jacy knew Gravigo was pained by her decision not to become a Hat, but she didn't appreciate his attempts to make her feel bad about what she felt was the best path for her to take.

"I never should have introduced you to Lita," Gravigo muttered.

"It wasn't Lita who told me about the bylaw." Jacy wasn't going to tell him it was Baz who informed her about it.

"Either way, I still feel...."

Jacy listened to him with half an ear as she watched the cashier, whose name was Terri. Terri with an 'I', of course. How else would you spell Terri when you're a woman in her late forties, peroxide blond hair, gallons of cheap make-up, and a too tight blouse that showed off her no longer perky assets?

"Buzz off, Terri," Jacy muttered, moving her hand as Eugene looked over at the clock.

"Terri? Who is Terri?" Gravigo interrupted his grievance long enough to check out what was going on.

"Someone who's trying to sink her panther claws into Eugene," Jacy made another hand movement and smiled when Eugene moved away from the counter. He grabbed a fat turkey breast and moved towards the meat slicer. Terri, with a pathetic, flirty smile, took her chicken salad sandwich and ambulated on.

"Good boy, Eugene, good boy," Jacy whispered.

"We don't like Terri?" Gravigo asked.

"No, we don't."

Gravigo watched Jacy for a long moment and then smiled. "You're going to be an awesome player, Jacy, I really believe that. I would offer you my wishes of good luck, but I get the feeling you're not going to need any luck. Your skills will be sufficient enough."

Jacy sighed, smiling back at Gravigo. "I wish I had as much confidence as you and Flair seem to have in me."

Gravigo's eyes darkened. "I've got much more faith in you than that oily rat Flair...." Jacy tuned out this new batch of squawking and focussed on the only thing that mattered to her at the moment.

Eugene, Eugene, Eugene; her wonderful and beautiful Eugene.

2

Lita felt the pressure constrict against her throat just as she felt a hand move dangerously close to her exposed vagina. Far from panicking, though, Lita feigned a movement of defense she knew her assailant would be expecting. Just as she anticipated, Lita felt the grip around her throat tighten.

"Come on, Lita, you're better than..."

Lita countered so swift it caught her opponent off guard. With a quick twist of her neck and rattlesnake spin move, Lita avoided the choke hold and pussy seeking hand. She was now on her foe's back, administering a perfect half nelson.

For further immobilization, Lita wrapped her legs around her challenger's legs, using her feet to spread the calves apart. Lita briefly smiled at her opponent's muffled grunts and attempts of escape. As the body beneath her jerked and flopped, Lita seized the opportunity and slid her right hand underneath. She pushed her hand hard against her challenger's genital region and began to massage roughly. Her foe's cry of mixed anger and pleasure delighted Lita.

"Don't fight it, Sugar, just say the words," Lita purred into the left ear of the struggling body.

"Fuck you," came the hoarse reply.

"Well," Lita chuckled, "it looks like you may be doing that very thing."

Lita felt her opponent relax slightly and a moan escape as Lita's hand worked its magic. She wasn't fooled, though. Lita's rival was deceptively strong and clever. She couldn't allow her guard to droop for a second.

"Just say the words, Sugar," sweat dripped from Lita's chin onto the neck of her opponent as she spoke. For emphasis, Lita forced the legs apart and thrust against her opponent's.

Her opponent gasped in joy and exasperation but wouldn't concede defeat. This came as no surprise to Lita. She had never defeated her opponent before. This was the farthest any of their bouts had gone, though.

"Come on, baby, you know you want…" Lita's words were cut off by a flurry of spastic movements. Lita found herself bucked in the air, and before Lita could blink, she was on her back. Her assailant's naked body pinning her to the ground, their faces inches apart.

"Really, Lita?" Karma Twin panted, sweat oozing from every part of her taut body. "You may be improving, but you're not better than me, yet."

Karma Twin then began grinding her groin against Lita's, causing a tidal wave of glee to course through Lita's fatiguing body. Against her better instincts, Lita matched Karma's gyrations.

"That's my girl," Karma groaned. "Say the words, sweetheart."

Despite the decadent pleasure she felt, Lita cursed herself for getting cocky earlier with Karma Twin. There was a reason neither Lita nor anyone else had ever beaten Karma Twin in this kind of fight.

Karma was just that damn good.

Lita marvelled at how these types of bouts came into being for her. Lita first visited this place in a hunt for exercise and physical activity. This gym was known as a place where you could find all different sorts of pugilistic activities. Boxing, wrestling, mixed martial arts; you name it, it was here.

While some people enjoyed walking or running as a healthy pastime, others liked to pound each other in the face. Lita fell into the latter group. There were a couple significant difference between Lita and her group and the others who trained at the gym, though.

One, Lita's training group was the best of the best. And two, no one in Lita's group turned their pain receptors off. This was a quirky choice, as most others shut them down so they wouldn't feel the pain of having their nose broken or their eye gouged or their front teeth knocked out. They'd just head to the Transmogrifier pain free and heal themselves up.

Lita and her group used the Transmogrifier to mend, too, but they went there feeling all their bumps, bruises, and contusions. Feeling the pain of her wounds made Lita feel as close to human as she could in this crazy place.

Because everything is balanced, if one's pain receptors were turned off, then their pleasure receptors were off, too. Hence, if the pain receptors were left on, then ditto for the pleasure receptors.

From the onset, Lita received no sexual pleasure from her training so she had no idea her pleasure receptors were on. It only came evident to her when she was in an MMA fight with a tough, muscled up dude named Longer Tonsil. Lita had just converted a clean take down and held him to the mat with her own body. She lay there for a moment or two, plotting her next move when she felt something growing between them. She looked at Longer Tonsil, dumbfounded.

"Jesus, Longer, do you have a boner?"

Longer Tonsil showed no embarrassment. "Give me a break, Lita. You're pretty hot, you know."

Lita shook her head in dismay, but found herself caught up in the absurd fun of it during the match. Longer Tonsil, despite his impressive physique, was no match for Lita. She could have put him away in the first round, easily.

She was enjoying herself, though, so she let the match go on longer than it should. Sometimes she worked on some of her techniques she felt were rusty, and other times she played around with Longer. She'd get him in a compromising position and tickle his balls or rub his ass. One time she got him in a leg lock and gnashed her groin into his face.

Lita got so caught up in it that after she finally made him submit, she yanked down his shorts, pushed hers to the side, and slid his cock deep into her. She rode him for less than a minute before they both exploded in orgasm.

Lita rolled off of Longer Tonsil panting when she was shocked back to reality by a round of applause. Horrified, she sat up and saw Karma Twin with 2 females and three males.

"Well, done, Lita, but come on. You could've wrapped that thing up two rounds earlier," Karma walked over.

"What…"

"Longer Tonsil gets *really* turned on when he wrestles females. Actually, he gets turned on when wrestling males, too, but that's beside the point. We wanted to see how you would react, as we need one more female for our special training group. Care to join us?"

Lita only knew Karma Twin by her reputation around the gym and by her closeness to Hammer Coolie. When she eyed the others in the group and noticed they were all top fighters in the gym, she accepted Karma's invitation.

Thus started a brutal training regimen for Lita. She became expert at Bokator, an ancient form of Cambodian martial arts. She studied Combato, an extremely lethal form of fighting used in WW II by Canadian Armed Forces. Kajukenbo, Sambo, and Kalarippayattu were all added to her arsenal.

As a break from the harsh training, they'd challenge each other to sex wrestling. The object of the fight was to get the other to surrender, and the winner would get to have their way with the loser. Lita had beaten and lost to everyone in her group, except for Karma Twin.

So that was the trail that had led Lita to being underneath Karma Twin who was still rubbing her naked pussy against hers. Back on Earth, Lita considered herself 100% hetero sexual. She still considered herself that here, but somehow Karma Twin sauced Lita's apples.

Lita reached around and cupped Karma's ass cheeks, pulling her tighter to her. Karma stayed close, but stopped her gyrations.

"Say the words, baby," she said in a husky voice.

"I surrender to you," Lita whispered.

Karma groaned and restarted her pelvic thrusts. Their sweaty bodies slid against each other in a sensuous dance as their moans of pleasure rose and mixed together above them. It wasn't long before they both shuddered in orgasm.

Not quite satiated, though, Karma spun around and planted her pussy on Lita's face. Lita licked her clit softly as she felt her own clitoris being sucked into Karma's hot mouth. Minutes later, they both came again. Karma collapsed beside Lita, nuzzling her nose into the crook of Lita's neck. They lay in each other's arms until they regained their composure.

"I don't know why lesbians say tribbing is not a thing," Karma said.

"It works for me," Lita smiled, "but it's definitely a work out."

They stood and began to dress.

"How's Hammer doing?" Lita asked as she pulled her bra and panties on.

"Still wants Ridded Snot's balls on a pole, but he's coming around," Karma was well aware of Lita's feelings for Hammer Coolie. "Have you decided when you're going to present your idea to him, yet?"

"No," Lita exhaled, wiggling her tight jeans on.

"Well," Karma shrugged," I don't know if Hammer would be receptive to it or not, but it's not the worst idea in the world."

"Thanks for the vote of confidence," Lita winked at her. "Ready to join with me and present it together?"

Karma laughed. Their training group made a pact to keep things clandestine. It wasn't as if they were ashamed or embarrassed; they just preferred to keep things to themselves.

"How's the human girl doing?" Karma asked.

"She's doing good, better than I was at the end of my training."

"Really? You were pretty decent."

"I was better than that, Rusty fucking Sleeves or not," Lita's voice hardened. "But yeah, Jacy's a good one. I like her."

Karma cocked an eyebrow. Lita laughed.

"Not in that way, oh sexy one," Lita grabbed Karma's ass cheek and squeezed while planting a kiss onto receptive lips. "She's become a good friend, though. I will have her back."

"Good," Karma nodded. "From what I hear, she's going to need someone like you watching out for her."

LIta eyed Karma. "Do you have anything concrete?"

Karma Twin shook her head. "Just mutterings, but they're coming from all sides. I'll tell you when I hear something."

Lita stepped in and gave Karma a long hug. "Thanks, Sugar. See you next week?"

"Same time, same place, sweets," Karma blew a kiss and walked out into the night.

Lita watched her leave, thinking how lucky Karma Twin and Trichina Flame were. Each knew the other played around on the outside from time to time, but they were still a couple in love. Lita would never be comfortable in that type of relationship, but hey. Each person mashes their own potato.

Lita wasn't ready for a relationship in this crazy place, but she realized more and more that she liked having someone to go home to each night. Even if it was just a friend, it felt nice. Smiling, Lita headed out the door and went home.

3

Much like back on Earth, Jacy realized things could change in an eye blink here.

Things started well for Eugene and Jacy. Well, Jacy would say it started good. Lita called it 'boring as fuck'. While she adored Lita, Jacy didn't give a shit about what Lita thought in this case. Three months of time on Earth passed, and Eugene was still alive and healthy. Humdrum to some, absolutely exhilarating to Jacy. Some say Bon Eye-ver, others say Bon Eeee-Vair.

So there they were, after another day of work where Eugene didn't slice a finger off in that horrible meat slicer and a lunch break's worth of fending off Terri's sexual attacks, and Jacy was hovering over Eugene as he made his short walk home.

When he stepped into the fading daylight, though, a voice called out to him. "Well, well, well, you are still alive."

Both Eugene and Jacy looked to the source of the voice and were both surprised to see Earl, Eugene's younger brother standing outside Hagen's doors. Well, Jacy was startled. Eugene, on the other hand, felt guilty about not returning the three or four phone messages Earl left for him in the past two weeks.

"Earl," Eugene grinned. "I was going to call you tonight."

They shook hands in that special way brothers shake hands. "Looks like I saved you a phone call then. Wanna go grab a beer?"

Earl's invitation threw Jacy for a moment. She and Eugene had fallen into a set routine for his life, and that custom didn't allow for out of thin air invites to Buddha knows what dive bar Earl wanted to visit.

"Ummmm," Eugene hesitated before answering.

Jacy furrowed her brow. She knew what others felt about the way she protected Eugene, but what was wrong with being predictable? The chances of getting knifed in a bar fight or dying of a parachute malfunction or falling prey to a desperate panther like Terri were the kind of things predictability fended off.

Besides, it wasn't as if Eugene was wasting away. He worked full time at a job he liked, he bathed every night, he read the newspaper or a book after that, and then finished off the night with a sitcom rerun or the local news. On his days off he'd toss in a walk, a visit to the local library, or a lunch out somewhere.

Jacy failed to see what was improper with that. Did everyone have to participate in some extreme activity to be considered as living a full life?

Apparently the surprise invite didn't faze Eugene, though, as he accepted Earl's offer before Jacy could react. With a growing sense of trepidation, Jacy watched the two walk towards a local watering hole.

"Come on, Jacy, snap out of it," she admonished herself, feeling a bit of a killjoy. It was only two brothers going to get caught up over a few cold ones. It wasn't like they were going cliff diving or anything. She watched them cross the bridge over Nooksack River, smiling as Eugene listened to Earl's tales.

Jacy felt even better when she saw the little establishment they were going to. It was called Babe's Place. Apparently Earl was steering clear of the waitress at the Martini Bar and for some reason Outlaw Saloon was closed that day. Babe's was a small, quiet place with nice customers. It was perfect.

Eugene and Earl evaded the front diner and another waitress Earl was attempting to dodge by entering through the side door to the bar. They ordered a couple of Budweisers and picked a table which afforded them a good view of the ball game on the television above the bar.

"Mariners are on a nice little run," Eugene remarked.

"I hope they keep it up," Earl answered. "They could do some damage in the playoffs with that pitching rotation."

"All hail King Felix."

"Hear, hear," Earl clinked his bottle against Eugene's. This was good. This was fine for Jacy. She quit reprimanding herself for being such a worry wart. To see Eugene's obvious happiness over this brothers-bonding-over-beers experience made her feel warm inside.

Jacy guessed her feelings were probably similar to a mom whose child plays football or hockey. The mother's main concern, of course, is the child's safety, but when they see the joy that those activities bring, they are forced to put those concerns in their back pocket and let their children live the lives they have.

Within reason, of course, Jacy thought, as she did her best not to intrude too much on their conversation. She did listen with half an ear, but she didn't eavesdrop. On top of keeping Eugene safe and alive, she also adopted a policy of not stepping over the line when it came to certain private areas of Eugene's life.

For example, if Eugene were to find a woman good enough for him, she wouldn't play the voyeur and watch their intimate moments. She was still unsure how much Gravigo saw of her private life and felt disconcerted by it.

As it was, though, Eugene didn't have a woman in his life. The only intimate moments he had in that area were with his hand and internet porn. Besides the one time to see what his porn likes were and what size his penis was, Jacy respected his confidentiality in those instances.

This brotherly get-together held a similar intimate feeling for her. Eugene and Earl drank beer, watched the ball game, laughed, and chatted. Earl flirted with the waitress a little. All was harmless fun. Jacy let her mind wander.

As usual, her brain went to Derian and Beau. She missed the two of them so much her stomach ached. She laid in bed at night scheming on how she could get them into her pod, but she didn't know so much as where to even start. She soon surmised that any hopes of that happening depended on her success or failure with Eugene. She knew the first person in her pod was a probation period of sorts to see how Jacy held up. Only after a series of successes would she be able to expand her pod and then maybe explore how she could get Derian and Beau in there.

By the date on Eugene's calendar, she deduced that almost two years had passed on Earth since her death. She missed so much of Derian's life already. This thought depressed her, so she refocused on Eugene and Earl. It was a good thing she did, too, as she realized that three hours of Earth time had passed and Eugene and Earl were on their eighth beer. Just then a very unwelcome guest plopped down on the chair across from her.

"Well, hello there, Jacy," The Bam Slicer's left side of his upper lip curled into a half sneer. "Mind if my guys join Eugene's party?"

4

With the echo of Eugene's laughter over a lewd joke Earl just told as a backing track, the bottom of Jacy's stomach crashed into a dizzying freefall. Jacy stared at The Bam Slicer. What the fuck would a Skull want to do with somebody like Eugene? Jesus Buddha, Eugene's idea of a crazy time was to forego decaffeinated coffee once in a while.

And not just any Skull was here now, threatening her Eugene, but The Bam Slicer. The #2 guy in their organization. Gilligan to the Skipper. Richie Cunningham to the Fonz. Well, The Bam Slicer didn't seem so bad once compared to Richie Cunningham. Maybe she could try playing nice and use her charms to sway him from harming poor Eugene.

"What the fuck are you fucking doing fucking here?!" Jacy half screamed at him, tossing her wooing strategy straight into the crapper.

The Bam Slicer let out a grunt that constituted a belly laugh for him.

"Things looked boring over here, so I thought I'd liven up the joint a bit," he growled, then looked down at the table. Jacy's eyes followed his and she gasped as four hard core looking dudes rolled into Babe's Place amid laughter and bravado.

Jacy snuck a quick glance at Eugene who noticed the guys come in but didn't pay them much attention. Earl glanced at them, too, but the two of them were pretty engrossed in their conversation and the ball game to care much about the newcomers. Jacy looked at The Bam Slicer.

"Come on, Bam," Jacy hated the pleading note in her voice. "Eugene and his brother aren't causing any shit, they're just minding…"

The Bam Slicer's hand movement cut her words short, and Jacy saw one of the newcomer's hands grab the ass of the waitress who Earl flirted with earlier. The waitress spun around and backed away, not making much of a scene.

It had been a big enough of a commotion to catch Earl's eye, though. He looked questioningly at the waitress who gave him a quick shake of her head. Earl nodded, taking a long sip of his beer as he evaluated the new arrivals. None of them discerned Earl or Eugene. Jacy took another stab at Bam.

"Why are you doing this, Bam? You and I get along fine, don't we?" Jacy looked down again. She noticed the waitress talking to her manager, who was shaking his head and gesturing towards the table of Bam's guys. Visibly upset, the waitress grabbed some beers from the cooler and carried them over to the new arrivals. Earl tried his best to watch everything nonchalantly. Eugene remained unaware, caught up in a bases loaded, one out situation of the ball game.

"Heard you weren't letting this fucking asshole live, that you were smothering him. I trained you better than that, Jacy," The Bam Slicer punctuated the end of his speech with a sharp hand movement downwards. Jacy's sight caught one of the rough guy's hands come up and grab the wary waitress by the crotch. Earl wasn't sitting still for that.

"What the fuck?!" He yelled and stood. "Leave the lady alone!"

Eugene looked up at his now standing brother in alarm. "Earl, what…"

"Mind your own business, fuck wad," one of the guys at the table sneered. Jacy looked around the bar and besides an old drunk at the bar and the chicken shit manager, Earl and Eugene were on their own.

"Keep your hands to yourself, and I will," Earl looked at the waitress. "You okay, Lola?"

The Bam Slicer looked at Jacy with what might be called a half grin.

"Here we go, Jace. Game on," he said, his hand carving down at a right angle. Jacy watched one of Bam's guys rise from the table and approach Earl.

"Oh shit," she muttered, her shaky hands rising above the table.

"Who the fuck do you think you are, shit face?!" This one was definitely the meanest looking of the bunch, with his full beard and angry scar running from his left eye down underneath it. Jacy moved her hands. It was time to get Eugene out of this place.

Eugene stood, saying, "Hey, what's going on...." Poor Eugene didn't stand a chance. Bam's guy swung a meaty fist and caught Eugene square in the jaw. Eugene dropped like a sack of bricks. Earl went after the guy at exactly the same time Jacy began to leap over the table at The Bam Slicer.

"Hold on there, mon cheri," a sexy voice accompanied a hand on her shoulder, restraining her from attacking Bam.

"Really?" The Bam Slicer looked annoyed at their new visitor. "What kind of skin does Trichina Flame have in a game such as this?"

"About as much as you do," Trichina purred, sitting in a chair to the right of Jacy.

"And her?" Bam now looked uncertain. He cocked his head towards the person now sitting at Jacy's left. She hadn't even noticed someone sit down.

"Rainy has some football playing friends of Lola's down there. In fact, they are just about to enter the bar," Trichina smirked, and then looked at Jacy. "Hi, hon. I've been meaning to introduce myself, but haven't had the opportunity. My name is Trichina Flame and this other pretty lady is Rainy Dissolve."

Jacy glanced over at Rainy Dissolve and didn't think she would use the 'pretty' adjective when describing her. She definitely didn't think of her as ugly as others described her, but Rainy Dissolve was a hefty throw from attractive.

Jacy could give two shits about that right now, though. Her Eugene was unconscious on the floor of some bar right now.

"It's nice to meet you both," Jacy managed as she watched Earl swing at Bam's goon. He connected a few times, too, but Bam's guy was just plain tougher. He was about to throw a heavy left hook when the bar's door pushed open.

"These assholes grabbed my vagina!" Lola yelled at the door. "The two nice guys were sticking up for me!"

Three burly defensive tackles stood in the door. Actually, they had to stand single file as the three of them couldn't fit in the doorway. Jacy loved them at first sight.

"You okay?" one of them asked Lola. She nodded and the three bull rushed The Bam Slicer's henchmen. Bam frantically moved his hands to get his guys out of there but didn't have much luck. Rainy Dissolve's football players made short work of his guys.

"Okay, okay. Uncle," Bam muttered. Rainy Dissolve's eyes narrowed as she looked at Bam, but lightened up on her movements all the same. By the time they tossed the last of Bam's guys through the doors onto the street, Lola was on her knees with a towel full of ice helping an awakening Eugene.

"You okay?" Earl looked concerned.

"I'm fine," Eugene took the ice and held it to his bruised cheek and stood with Earl's assistance.

"Thanks, you two. Thanks, everyone," Lola said meaningfully, glaring at the manager who still stood behind the bar. "Next round is on the house."

Jacy wasn't so sure she wanted Eugene remaining at the bar, but by now the football players were clapping Eugene and Earl on the back thanking them. Jacy had some thanks to give as well.

The Bam Slicer stood. He glared at the three women across from him.

"I wasn't going to hurt him," he glowered as he spoke, focussing his attention on Jacy. "Let the asshole live. Quit smothering him."

"Go play with people your own size," Trichina retorted.

Rainy Dissolve stared at The Bam Slicer with her vacant eyes. Bam looked uncertainly at Rainy for a moment or two before grunting and walking away. Jacy sighed and sunk back into her chair.

"Wow," she gushed. "I can't thank either of you enough for what you just did."

"Bahhhh," Trichina Flame smiled a glorious smile. "Us girls need to stick together, don't we, Rainy?"

Rainy nodded, but wouldn't look at Jacy. Jacy studied her closer, and began to see glimpses of what Maise Elantina told her during her training.

"Sometimes I think Rainy Dissolve is the most beautiful being I've ever laid eyes upon," Maise remarked to her during one of their walks. Jacy could see how under the warts, the scar tissue, and the crooked teeth Maise just might be right.

"Well, thank you all the same." She looked down at Eugene, who was now doing Jager Bombs with his new friends. "I think I should probably get Eugene home. He's had a pretty exciting day."

Rainy Dissolve stood and departed. Trichina watched her scuttle away, smiling wistfully.

"She's a good girl, she's just a little shy," Trichina Flame stood and Jacy couldn't help but marvel at her statuesque nature. Jacy wasn't sexually turned on by her, but she could appreciate goddess like beauty as much as any red blooded male. Trichina nodded towards the table.

"The Bam Slicer wasn't 100% wrong, though, hon," Trichina hoped Jacy could take gentle criticism. "Our subjects do need to live to have fulfilling lives. Over protecting them can be just as harmful as not protecting them."

Jacy started to say something, but stopped. "Thanks, I'll chew on that. Maybe I'll let Eugene stay and enjoy this night."

"They definitely look like they're enjoying themselves," Trichina Flame smiled again before leaving. "Let's meet up for a drink in the next couple days. You up for that?"

Jacy thought for a moment. "Yes. Yes, I am."

"Perfect. I'll be in touch, hon." And with that, Trichina Flame swayed from the table, leaving Jacy to end the day just as she started it.

Eugene and her. At this point, that's all she fucking cared about.

5

Rainy Dissolve ignored the evening dampness and made her way through the place most referred to as 'The Bowels.' Rainy may not talk much, but she wasn't stupid. She knew it was a derogatory nickname, but she didn't care. Let others call it 'The Bowels.' She just called it home.

"Beeyoolip, beeyoolip, beeyoolip," Mewing Gnawn, a toothless gnome of a man sat on a cracked cobblestone planter talking to himself as she passed by. Rainy Dissolve smiled, pulling from her thoughts from the human woman. She didn't know why she was thinking of Jacy. She and Trichina Flame had helped her out of a jam over a month ago, but had no contact with her since then.

Rainy bent over and placed a gentle kiss on the kips of the stunted man. Mewing Gnawn's face broke into a humongous grin that ate up half his face and he repeated the word 'beeyoolip' faster and faster. He fell in behind Rainy and followed.

Rainy Dissolve continued on into the dreary, dizzying maze of alleyways full of stink, despair, and darkness. That's how all others saw it, anyways. Rainy and her community felt the truth, light, and hope that these passageways truly offered.

"Rainy Dissolve," a voice called from one of the countless balconies above. She and Mewing Gnawn both halted, pretending to squint up to see who the voice belonged to. In reality, both knew full well who called out before the croaking laugh rained down upon them.

"I love you, Rainy Dissolve. You are more beautiful than a dying swan's song," Granddad Roadaxle called out. Granddad Roadaxle was the unofficial gate keeper of The Bowels, a perpetual watcher so their communal secrets and home would remain safe.

Rainy Dissolve gave a harmonious smile, holding her hands over her heart before spreading her arms as if she were releasing her heart to fly into Granddad's waiting arms. Out of nowhere, a dule of doves flew at the sky, mere feet from Granddad's face. Granddad Roadaxle broke into giddy laughter, as Rainy and a waving Mewing Gnawn moved on.

Rainy and Mewing Gnawn took a left turn followed by two hasty rights. She smiled as her shuffling step took on a peppier one as she neared the place she loved the most.

She knew what was happening. A facsimile of the band Ages and Ages played a song called 'Divisionary (Do the Right Thing)'. Her sisters would be at their tables with beer tankards in hand or perching in the upper balcony, feet dangling, looking down upon the dance floor as they drained their highballs. They would be singing the unofficial anthem of The Bowels, though outsiders would be dumbfounded to know this. The lyrics are opposite of what they believe inhabitants of The Bowels to be.

Rainy Dissolve's smile grew an inch as she could almost hear the faded music. She could see all her sisters singing along with the band, the males, too, but not quite as boisterously. They'd be hovering on the outer circle, a shade apprehensive as to whether they would be picked to warm a bed this evening, or left to another night alone in the commons area.

Rainy Dissolve began humming the song as she halted, tilting her head. Changing direction, she and Mewing Gnawn rounded a false bend in the alley. Sure enough, a group of roughneck males were surrounding two rolling, biting, punching counterparts. The whooping circle dropped silent as she approached. The two fighters sensing the alteration in tone and stopped bashing at each other. The only sound heard was Rainy Dissolve's faint humming of The Song, as people of The Bowels referred to it. She put her hands gently on both of their shoulders and delivered an almost imperceptible shake of her head.

The males bowed their heads, nodded, and shook hands. The whole lot of them, dusty and sweaty in their white tank tops and ripped jeans followed the departing Rainy Dissolve and Mewing Gnawn. They became a jubilant group, but not noisy. They didn't have to be. If one looked, all one would see was joy.

Rainy Dissolve reached the stairs first, of course, and began shedding her black jacket, her black gloves, and her black headband as she ascended the stairs. She heard the muffled music and singing. She hummed along with the band and her vocal people as she stopped and pulled off her black motorcycle boots with the silver buckles drooping down the sides. She left her garments behind as she climbed the stairs. Mewing Gnawn retrieved what his little arms would hold as the gang of menfolk picked up the rest.

Two more flights of wooden stairs to go. Rainy Dissolve shed her black tank top, revealing, surprise, surprise, a black bra. She undid her only non-black accessory, a jangly silver belt, and paused to pull off her ripped, black jeans. She climbs the final set of stairs in her black cotton panties and bra.

Rainy and her followers heard the loud and clear voices from behind the old, mahogoney doors.

'So what you're up against all the disingenuous

They wave you along and say there's always room for us

But we know better than to take them serious

Still don't let 'em make you bitter in the process'

A faded and cracked mirror hung on the outside door. Rainy stood on the top stoop, staring at her distorted reflection as the next verse washed over her. She whispered along with it.

'And when the light is up, this is how it oughta be

We'll make it alright, they'll come around eventually

They say it's nothing but that ain't the reality

They may take us on but they can never take us easy'

No sounds beyond Rainy Dissolve's soft singing voice and the muted voices beyond the doors are heard. Mewing Gnawn and the roughneck boys held their breath as Rainy studied the scar tissue covering her forehead and crawling down the side of her face. She scrutinized the warts on her jawline. She saw parts of her crooked and broken teeth behind her gentle, singing lips.

'Cuz they ain't moving, they're just moving around

So if you love yourself, you better get out, get out, get out…'

Rainy Dissolve nodded at her reflection and two burly stepped up to the doors. Just as the last 'get out' was sung, they kicked the doors open. Mewing Gnawn scattered in, as a spinning Rainy Dissolve, clad in only bra and panties, entered the room.

The entire room erupted in cheers and louder singing voices as Rainy Dissolve continued to spin. It was impossible to see, but if this was done in slow motion, one would see her ugly teeth straighten with every turn. They'd see the mean warts break off, and the scar tissue melt away. They'd witness her greasy, black hair give way to lustrous blonde locks.

When Rainy Dissolve ceased her swirling, she was clothed in a beautiful gold gown. Rainy's lengthy hair was accessorized by a purple gerbera; her eyes blue as ice.

Only ice in appearance, though. The openness, love, and joy dancing in them was irrefutable. The band repeated the chorus over and over again, and singing sisters came to greet the queen of 'The Bowels.'

'Do the right thing, do the right thing

Do it all the time, do it all the time

Make yourself right, never mind them

Don't you know you're not the only one suffering'

Rainy Dissolve greeted her well-wishers, kissing and hugging each of her sisters as they welcomed her. No males dared approach yet, as they waited their due turn. Ages and Ages sang louder and with more passion, acknowledging Rainy Dissolve's grand entrance. The ladies above sang, called out, and raised their glasses towards her.

Rainy Dissolve smiled at them all, lighting up the cavernous room. She loved everybody here, and they all loved her back. She would always 'do the right thing' by them. That would never be questioned.

The song ended and the place became quieter than a mole. Rainy Dissolve did one more final, looping spin before proclaiming aloud, "I love you all."

The place blew up into a hail of boot stomps and hearty cheers. Jinnion Crust approached her with a generous smile.

"My Lady, the council awaits you. Will you allow me to accompany you?"

"Yes, Jinnion Crust, I would like that," Rainy answered, doing her best to conceal her disappointment. She hoped to spend more time with her people, but took Jinnion's arm all the same. Her people and the music would be here when she returned from her meeting of the council.

6

Jacy sat down at her table. Alone again, as the song is sung. Jacy preferred it this solitary way, though. Despite what a growing chorus of voices attempted to tell her, Jacy no longer gave a shit. Her first and only job was to protect Eugene.

She smiled as Eugene glanced through the morning paper and ate his normal breakfast whole wheat toast with raspberry jam. He rinsed his plate when he finished, then went to brush his teeth.

"Just like clockwork, honey," Jacy whispered. "Keep it up, no surprises."

Jacy felt he was safe enough to leave alone for the moment. She recently began easing back into her privacy policy, which lapsed since the bar fight two months ago. She wouldn't let him take a dump in the first week without hovering over him like a momma bear.

Jacy watched Eugene re-enter the kitchen and retrieve the lunch he packed the previous night after watching an old Mork and Mindy rerun. Jacy nodded her approval as he exited his apartment and double checked his lock to make sure it was secure. Sighing, Eugene trundled along towards the elevator.

"Maybe not today, Eugie," Jacy spoke, raising her right hand in a slow arc, giving him a gentle nudge towards the stairwell. Eugene hesitated at the stairway door before looking up the hall towards the elevator.

"Uh-uh, baby, Mama knows best," Jacy gave him a more forceful nudge this time.

Eugene took two steps towards the elevator before stopping with a shrug and another sigh. He retraced his last two steps and took the stairs instead. One day, future Jacy would look back and cringe at the present Jacy for bullshit such as this. Afraid of a freaking elevator? What the fuck?

Present Jacy knew all the dangers associated with elevators, though. Cables could snap, causing the car to plummet to the ground floor where Eugene would be smashed to smithereens. Power outages where Eugene would be locked for hours before rescue crews could get to him, setting him up for a lifetime of claustrophobia issues.

None of that was going to happen to Jacy's Eugene. Besides, the four floor jaunt was better for Eugene's cardiovascular system than some stupid metal box and its faulty pulley system. Eugene stepped from the stairwell into the lobby, mumbling 'good morning' to a tenant whose name Jacy forgot. This tenant lived on the floor above Eugene's and had invited him to a poker game the previous week. Jacy had nudged Eugene into begging off of it.

"Hey, Eugene," the guy said. "You missed a great game the other night. We set up another round for next week. You want in?"

Jacy rolled her eyes. Goddamned sharks, just lingering around trying to bamboozle poor Eugene out of his hard earned dollars. Fuck them. Jacy moved her left hand in a slow, diagonal direction.

"Oh, Gosh," Eugene said. "When...when is it?"

"Next Friday. Five other guys, a few beers, ball game on mute. What do you say, amigo?"

"He says to go find some other sheep to fleece, *compadre*," Jacy did a quick stop and go motion with her left hand.

"Ummmm," Eugene did a slow walk towards the front door. "Can I get back to you on that? Something tells me I might have something going on that night, but I'll check and get back to you."

Jacy knew Eugene's co-tenant would be disappointed to lose what he no doubt thought of as a Golden Goose, but to Jacy's surprise, he did a fantastic job of hiding that sorrow.

"Sure, sounds good, Eugene. Give me a call by next Wednesday. How does that sound?"

"Of course, yeah, awesome," Eugene said, already at the door. "I'll do that. I'll call you." The glass door shut by the time Eugene said 'I'll call you.' Eugene looked sad as he stared at the closed door.

Fucking Christ, Jacy thought. How difficult did things have to get for poor Eugene? Death trap elevators, financial sharks in the lobby, and now he was on his way to the bus stop where Buddha knew what other dangers and vermin awaited him.

"Slow and easy, hon, easy and slow," Jacy murmured as Eugene, shoulders slouched, made his way to the bus stop. It was only two blocks away, but Jacy watched for any potential pitfalls that might engulf poor Eugene. Eugene made his way down the not-too-crowded sidewalk, avoiding eye contact and clutching his lunch to his chest. Jacy frowned as a homeless guy made his way towards Eugene.

"Hey, buddy. Can you spare a buck for a cup of hot coffee?" He held his hand out towards Eugene.

Jacy's frown grew deeper as she tried to figure out what degree of danger he was to Eugene. She picked up her hand movements to try and steer Eugene clear of the dirty man.

"Hi there, cutie," a voice snapped Jacy's head up so fast she almost threw her neck out. "Mind if I join in?"

It had been so long since someone sat at Jacy's table that it took a moment for it to register that she wasn't alone.

"What the fuck do you want?!" she half-shouted.

"Ummm," the newcomer looked uncertain all of a sudden. "I was hoping to meet your acquaintance. My name is Befriending Track."

Jacy gave him a shooing motion with her hand. "Well, move along, Mr. Befriending. I don't need any more acquaintances."

"What…."

"Buzz the fuck off!" Jacy snarled. "I mean it!"

"Wow," Befriending Track rolled his eyes as he stood. "Maise Elantina told me you were quite approachable and…"

Jacy tuned him out as she refocused on Eugene. Apparently he was a little out of sorts and was lurching down the sidewalk. He took another glance over his shoulder at the grungy guy he left in the dust when he felt a strong hand on his shoulder.

"Whoa, dude, slow down!"

Jacy was as out of sorts as Eugene was. Now who the fuck is this guy?

"What…who…what…" Eugene stammered.

"You almost walked out into the intersection, bro," the guy let go of his shoulder. "You okay?"

"Yeah, yeah…I…uhhh…" Eugene looked at the intersection that was busy with Ferndale's morning rush.

Jacy glared at Befriending Track. "Do you see what you almost fucking did?"

"What I did?" Befriending looked at Jacy as if she were an axe wielding lunatic.

"Yes, what you did!" Jacy's eyes were wide as she nodded. "You and your loser fucking subject almost ran Eugene into a busy intersection!"

"That's crazy," Befriending Track answered. "All he did was ask for a fucking dollar. He's a little down on his luck right now, that's all."

Jacy noticed gamers at nearby tables trying not to stare at the scene this bozo caused. She looked down at a troubled Eugene.

"Sorry, man, and thanks," he mumbled to the guy.

"No worries. You sure you're alright?"

Eugene nodded. Jacy looked at her table to see who sat down without her noticing and saved Eugene. The table was empty. Befriending Track shook his head.

"Nobody is here," he said. "Most humans do the right thing without needing to be prompted. Didn't you learn that in your training?"

"Yeah, yeah…I….it…I….it just slipped my mind, that's all." Jacy plopped down into her seat with a sigh.

"Maybe you need to go back and brush up on your training a bit," Befriending said. "Looks like you've forgotten a bunch of things."

"Please just go away," Jacy whispered. Befriending Track left without another word.

7

"So," Jinnion Crust patted Rainy Dissolve's arm that rested in his crooked elbow. "Any chance you'd like to see me later?"

They walked down the cob webbed hallway towards the Council Chambers. Rainy Dissolve returned the pat. "I picked you the last time," she teased. "People are going to start thinking you are my favourite."

"Aren't I?"

Rainy Dissolve tilted her half grinning, half serious face. "I have no favourites, Jinnion. You know that."

Jinnion Crust was not surprised, just a little disappointed. He loved Rainy Dissolve from the first day they met. He wasn't on the council as no males were allowed, but he was a trusted and cherished ally of Rainy's.

"Of course, my lady. My apologies."

Rainy Dissolve rolled her eyes and smiled. "No apologies needed, my wonderful friend. How are things going with you, by the way? We seem to have so little time to talk nowadays."

"Things are fine," Jinnion sighed. "I'm not getting much traction in discovering what's going on, though. If it's this secretive, it must be something big."

For the first time since she returned to the Bowels today, the smile slipped from Rainy's face. She and everyone else were feeling the same frustration as Jinnion. Of course, it didn't help that they all had to use the ultimate in discretion in their searches to evade raising the wrong eyebrows, but that didn't lessen the uneasiness they felt. Rainy patted Jinnion's hand as they neared the Chamber door.

"Don't fret, Jinnion. We're all feeling the same. We just have to keep at it. Maybe some from the council have discovered something useful."

"I hope so," Jinnion put a brave smile upon his face. "I fear time is growing short."

Rainy Dissolve felt the same, but she didn't vocalize that. They came to a halt before the circular Chamber entrance.

"My lady," Jinnion nodded and headed off.

"Thanks for the walk, Jinnion," she called after him. She watched him depart until he turned a corner and was gone. Rainy sighed as she turned the handle set in the middle of the intricately carved door. She pushed it open, and entered the room.

"Rainy," a familiar voice greeted her as she closed the door.

"Cruder Stiletto," Rainy Dissolve approached her, hugging her tight. "How are things going on your end of things?"

Cruder made a dismissing sound through her pursed lips. "I've discovered nothing. Nada. Zilch. I'm afraid I'm losing my patience with this one."

"Please don't be so hard on yourself," Rainy ran a gentle hand along the woman's cheek.

"But I've had the perfect opportunity handed to me. Unsay Moon was trying some kind of silent siege on Gravigo and got his ass handed to him at our convention last week. Gravigo is so caught up in that stupid human girl...."

"Jacy." Rainy spoke her name firmly, causing Cruder to stop talking and look Rainy Dissolve directly in the eye.

"Yes, of course. My apologies, Rainy. Gravigo has been so caught up in Jacy and the Skulls that this has been a perfect time to be a little bolder in my hunting. But still, nothing." The distaste on Cruder Stiletto's face spoke volumes. Rainy's voice softened.

"It's okay, my friend. It is not our fault that whoever is planning this is incredibly crafty."

"We just have to be craftier," a voice spoke from behind. Rainy Dissolve turned and smiled again.

"Trichina Flame and Karma Twin. How are you both?"

Rainy approached them. Karma was perched on Trichina's lap, licking Trichina's neck, but turned as Rainy came over.

"Hey, sexy Rainy, care to join us this evening?" she asked.

Rainy Dissolve hesitated. It had been awhile since she joined the two of them, and the last time had definitely been fun. "We'll see," she winked at them.

Trichina pretended to pout. "Don't tell us Mr. Jinnion Crust is hogging you all to himself. That's not fair."

All three ladies broke into giggles. Rainy looked to the door as it swung open to reveal the final member of the Council.

"See you soon, Galore," the lovely figure said, looking down the hall at the unseen Galore. Rainy Dissolve shook her head. Of all the strong men or seductive women the last member of the council could fall in love with, she lost her heart to a non-descript, bespectacled, five foot nothing wisp of a man named Galore. Of course, there was much more to Galore that meets the eye, but still, the unyielding love for Galore was a great mystery to those on the Council.

"Sultana," Rainy greeted her. "How are things with you?"

"Ugh," Sultana Yelp rolled her eyes as she entered the room. "Our assignment notwithstanding, sometimes I wonder if it's worth it spending time with all those fucking creeps."

Rainy Dissolve opened her arms and the two women came together in a warm embrace. Of all the members of her council, Sultana Yelp concerned Rainy the most. She loved them all equally, but Sultana had to cavort with the worst of the worst.

"Oh, it's not that bad," Sultana reassured them at one of their previous meetings. "I turn off my pain receptors, let Flair stick his 'legendary phallus' into me and pretend that he's fucked me half to death. I also lick all sorts of pussies, cocks, assholes, and titties, and listen. It's amazing what people talk about when they think you're a garden variety whore. Except for the ache I get in being apart from Galore, I could have worse jobs."

Despite those reassurances, though, Sultana Yelp was a concern for the other ladies on the Council. Sultana drew the worst assignment, and they all felt protective of her.

Rainy Dissolve pulled back from their hug, but continued to hold her by the hips. "Is there anything we can do?"

"Give me more time with Galore?"

"We can do that," Karma Twin hopped off Trichina Flame's lap and came to hug Sultana. "Let's get this meeting over with so you can go have some quality time with him."

The ladies all took their respective seats around the circular room. Their meetings were never of the formal Roberts' Rules type of meeting. It was more of a discussion type atmosphere, but one with order and meaning. No gossiping, no talking over another person. Say what had to be said, and then move on. Rumours and innuendo were reserved for the beer tables or pillow talk.

The only other rule, and probably the most important one, was that none of them, save Sultana Yelp, would ever deceive the leaders of their respective groups. Rainy Dissolve served Maise Elantina proudly, and would continue to do so. Cruder Stiletto may not be as fond of Gravigo as Rainy was of Maise, but she held honour, truth, and character in such high regard she would not double cross him. And Trichina Flame and Karma Twin? Except for the minor deception they planted about being professional rivals, they would protect Hammer Coolie with their final breaths, if need be.

The original reason the Council formed was the concern of the Earth's future. They loved and cherished the humans who inhabited Earth with all the love they could muster, but if it came down to the lives of humans and the life of Earth, well….

"I think there's something to the walks Maise Elantina has been on," Trichina Flame looked at Rainy Dissolve as she spoke. "Can you get any closer to her when she goes on one?"

"I will not spy on Maise during those times, you know that," Rainy said. Remembering something, she looked over at Cruder Stiletto. "And really, Hairyoak Animal as a loose tail on Maise? He's more noticeable than Neva Tezremsy."

"Gravigo's choice, not mine," Cruder chuckled.

"Back to Maise's walks…"

"Enough of that," Rainy's voice rose. "You know where I stand on this. I will tell the Council when I discover something relevant, but I will *not* forsake my vow to Maise Elantina. She is not part of whatever plot is being hatched, I swear to all of you. "

"She may know something valuable without realizing how precious it is, though," Trichina said.

"Yes," Rainy nodded, voice returning to normal volume. "I understand that, which is why I am all eyes and ears when performing my Bones duties."

"I may have something small," Sultana offered.

"We'll take anything at this point, hon," Karma Twin said.

"Flair and The Bam Slicer have been discussing Granny Mandible a lot lately."

"So what? All the leaders go to her for advice," Cruder said.

"I know, but she's being talked about a lot. I think Flair is going to visit her more often." When nobody spoke, she added, "It may be nothing, I know. I just thought I'd mention it."

Karma Twin looked at Cruder Stiletto. "How about Gravigo?"

She shook her head. "No more or less than usual."

"Hammer's frequency of visits hasn't changed, either" Trichina Flame said, and Karma nodded in agreement.

"Maise has been to see her a bit more than normal, too. Not copious amounts, but the appointments have increased," Rainy Dissolve looked thoughtful. "Thanks for bringing that up, Sultana. Maybe that's something we can all keep an eye out for."

"It may not hurt to keep a loose eye on Granny Mandible's place," Trichina Flame offered. "Very loose, though. You know how Granny can get when she's mad."

"I'll take care of it," Sultana Yelp said. "It'll cost me a couple of blow jobs a week, but I know someone in the area."

"Make it so," Rainy said, nodding at Sultana. "And thank you, Sultana. Last thing, what about Jacy? I'm positive that somehow she is connected to all this."

"How?" Cruder snorted. "She's a bumbling rookie who's about to lose her first, from what I hear."

"Really?" Rainy hadn't heard that, and felt for Jacy. Every single one of them had lost their first. Nobody ever really forgets it. She looked at the others and surmised they were all thinking the same thing.

"Well, I think we all agree that sucks, but it will make her a better Gamer," Sultana Yelp looked over at Rainy. "Why do you feel she's connected?"

"Not in the way Cruder assumes," she smiled at Cruder. "Jacy just seems to take up a lot of Gravigo's and Flair's time. If we were to attempt pulling something big off..."

"...we'd use a diversion," Trichina nodded.

"Exactly," Rainy answered, and then looked at Karma Twin. "Karma, how is your relationship going with Lita?"

"Judging from her coochie tales, I'd say the relationship is going great," Trichina Flame chided. All the other Council members laughed.

"It's going well," Karma spoke after the laughter subsided.

"Maybe that's an angle to use?" Cruder Stilleto asked.

"Maybe," Karma spoke after a moment's thought. "Lita is pretty protective of her, so I don't know how close I can get. I'll try, of course."

"I think we all need to," Trichina Flame spoke. "Rainy is on to something here. If we all increase our efforts, maybe we can piece it all together."

"Fair enough, I think that's as far as we get today, ladies. Who would like to go for a beer and dance?" Three ladies cheered Rainy Dissolve's announcement, one wore a sheepish smile.

"Yes, after your Galore time," Cruder teased Sultana. Sultana cheered and raced out of the Chambers.

"Come on, ladies, we have some drinking to do," Trichina Flame announced, and the four ladies did just that.

8

With Eugene safely tucked in bed for the night, Jacy thought it was a good time for her to take a break and stretch her legs. Since the close call with The Bam Slicer and her gong show meeting with Befriending Track, she strayed from her table for nothing more than short bursts of time.

As she made her way to the entrance of the lobby she recalled Flair's visit to her table a few days' back.

"You've put Eugene in a cage, you know," he said to her, his arm muscles tightening as he leaned on her table. "Remember when you were back on Earth and how much you hated zoos?"

Jacy did her best to hide her surprise from him. The unfairness of keeping animals in the zoo was a pretty intimate belief she kept mostly to herself. She didn't care much for the fact Flair knew this about her.

"What you have now," Flair gestured towards the centre of the table with his chin, "is a chimpanzee in a zoo cage. Sure you can feed him and let him live to an old age, but is that a fair trade with the fact that he'll never swing from the vines of a real jungle?"

Jacy pushed through the door and thrust Flair's argument from her mind. She needed to clear her head from him, Gravigo, everyone.

Jacy paused to take a deep breath of the warm, sweetened air. The temperature was perfect, the weather was flawless, and once again, the fountain was as resplendent as the first time she laid eyes upon it. Without any clear destination in mind, Jacy began to ramble around the fountain and onto one of the glittering paths.

Gosh, how long ago it seemed to Jacy that Gravigo first led her down one of these paths. Was it yesterday? Three decades ago? Did it even matter?

Jacy sighed, her eye catching a Grass Counter staring at her. She gently shook her head. Nobody except her friendly neighborhood murderer. For the first time, Jacy didn't divert her gaze from Buzzed Rottid, all clad in his Motley Crue 'Girls, Girls, Girls' regalia. The strange realization that she didn't out and out hate Buzed Rottid anymore crept through her belly. She couldn't see herself going on a summertime stroll with him anytime soon, but to be truthful, she no longer loathed him.

Jacy's emotions were a constant juggling act for her in this place. At the table she would feel all and any emotions. Hope, joy, despair, fear, anger, satisfaction, everything.

Away from the table, though, all her negative emotions were strangely muted, so cloudy that any hatred she may have felt for someone like Buzzed Rottid became nothing more than a faint echo. He had become a song that she struggled to recall.

Her negative feelings became elusive. She knew she should despise Buzzed Rottid, but try as she might, she couldn't summon the dark feelings of hatred. Strangely, she almost sensed something similar in him right now. Now that they locked eyes, he didn't smile some victor's smile, nor did he bow his head in shame. She couldn't be sure, but she thought he gave her an almost imperceptible nod of the head.

Wow, nothing like clearing the old head with an avalanche of new issues. Jacy broke eye contact and moved on. Now that she had Grass Counters on her mind, though, she felt she may as well go visit Baz. It had been too long, and she felt slightly guilty about it. She'd been to see him five or six times since she first met him, and really took a liking to him.

It didn't take too long to wind her way back to Bas's area. When she got there, she was impressed by how far Baz was with his counting since her last visit. She walked until she was parallel with him.

"Have you counted this section yet?" She recalled how Grass Counters absolutely hated it when someone trampled down a section the Grass Counter hadn't tallied.

"Yep," Baz counted for a minute or two longer to get to an easier number to recall. He held the last blade that he counted between his forefinger and thumb of his right hand and looked over at her.

"Thanks for asking," he smiled. "Come. Sit."

Jacy couldn't contain her giggle. Baz furrowed his brow, not understanding.

"Sorry," she apologized making her way across the lush grass to him. "It's just that you remind me so much of Jean-Luc Picard when you say things like that."

"Like what?"

"When you said, 'Come'. It's exactly the way Jean-Luc Picard would say it."

"Jean-Luc who?"

"Picard," Jacy smiled. "He was the main character in one of my favourite T.V. shows back on Earth. It was called Star Trek -The Next Generation. You remind me so much of him."

Baz pondered this for a moment. "Was he a good guy or a bad guy?"

"Good, very good. The ultimate good guy."

"Well," Baz shrugged, "I guess there are worse characters I could resemble."

"Could you do me a favour?" Jacy said.

"What kind of favour?"

"Could you say," Jacy lowered her voice to her lowest possible octave. "Tea. Earl Grey. Hot."

"Why the bloody hell would you want me to say something like that?"

Jacy shrugged. "Nostalgia, I guess. It was one of the things the Captain would say on the show."

"The Captain?"

"Captain Jean-Luc Picard."

"Ahhh," Baz shrugged. "Tea. Earl Grey. Hot."

Jacy clapped her hands and chuckled. "That was perfect. Just perfect."

"Well, if it was me, I would've said beer. Ice cold. Now."

"The Captain wasn't much for beer, I'm afraid."

"Then he wasn't much of a Captain, in my books," Baz looked up at her and smiled. "Anyways, what brings such a lovely lass out to a God forsaken place like this? I trust it wasn't merely to hear me imitate your favourite captain."

"I had a little time on my hands," Jacy said, sitting down a few feet from Baz. "I thought it'd be a good time to drop in and see how a friend of mine was doing."

Baz let out a prolonged sigh, looking out into the never ending field of grass.

"I wish I had only a 'little' time on my hands," he said, shrugging. "How's Eugene doing?"

"He's doing great. I didn't come to talk about…"

"Is he?" Baz held Jacy's gaze in that particular way that only Baz could. Jacy's shoulders slumped a little.

"Why? What have you heard?"

"It's not what I hear that's important, it's what you say that is significant," Baz smiled.

Jacy returned the smile. Baz had a way of slicing through bullshit better than anyone she had ever known. It was one of the qualities that so endeared her to him.

"Well, *I* think he's doing just fine. Everyone else thinks I'm smothering the poor guy to death by over protecting him."

"And are you?"

Jacy hesitated before answering, feeling her defenses dissolve quickly under Baz's watchful eye. She chuckled to herself. Baz was fucking awesome. "Maybe a little bit," she admitted.

"Just a little?"

"Probably a lot, okay? It was that stupid run in with that fucking Bam Slicer. It scared the shit out of me." Jacy took a deep breath. "Look, Eugene is a good guy. He doesn't deserve to be rubbed out for that asshole's entertainment, or any other asshole's entertainment, either. I'm scared for Eugene, and am doing my best to protect him."

Baz nodded, shifting his position while never losing contact of the single blade of grass he was holding. "Are you afraid for Eugene's safety, or are you scared you can't match wits with a member of the Skulls?"

Jacy calmed the indignant feeling she felt rising in her belly. She knew Baz wasn't trying to be mean or hurtful, but he was beginning to piss her off.

"I can outwit any of those scumbags," she snapped. "From a strictly gaming point of view, though, I'm not so sure I'm good enough to beat anyone quite yet."

Baz smiled. "But you are, Jacy, you are."

Jacy caught herself beaming, which made her feel embarrassed. All she heard lately was how bad she was messing things up. Baz's compliment felt like a cozy, warm blanket over her, evaporating any earlier bitchiness.

"Thanks, Baz."

"I should be the one thanking you," Baz nodded at a fellow Grass Counter about thirty yards to the right of them. "Whenever you come by to see me, Ugly Earful there gets so jealous she won't speak to me for at least a week. The silence is delightful."

Jacy chuckled again, and gave Baz a playful slap on the leg. "You be nice."

Baz shrugged, and the two of them fell into a comfortable silence. Baz appreciated the break in counting, while Jacy was deep in thought. There wasn't much competition about who was going to break the quiet first.

"Baz," Jacy looked at him. "How does one enter the Game?"

"Fuck," Baz muttered, looking away for a while before refocusing on Jacy. His look was loving, yet blazing the same. "You don't need to know that, Jacy."

Jacy nodded and sighed. "I'm not going to do anything stupid, Baz. I just thought I should know, you know, I should know how to just in case."

"Just in case you wanted to count blades of grass for eternity?" Baz barked out a laugh. "If you want to do it that bad, Jacy, come and take a load off of me. I'd love to sit back and sunbathe while you counted for me. You'd go nucking futs before you reached your first million."

Baz gave a long, slow shake of his head. "Nothing or nobody, and I mean *nobody* is worth this punishment, Jacy. Nobody. Take it from someone who's been there."

Jacy looked away for a moment before asking her question. "What about your great-great-great-great-great-grandson? Wasn't he worth it?"

Baz studied the horizon for a long while before responding. "Was my five times great grandson's life on Earth worthy of me counting blades of grass for all of eternity, is that what you're asking me?"

"Yes," Jacy nodded. "That's exactly what I'm asking you."

Baz blew out a strenuous breath before looking at Jacy again. "Forever is a very long time, Jacy. That's the most truthful answer I can give you."

While Jacy pondered Baz's reply, he carried on.

"And nobody can teach you how to get in the Game anyways. You just do it by instinct. When the time came, I just went. To tell the truth, I don't even recall how I even did it."

Baz's eyes burned with the intensity of a fevered man. "But you goddamned well listen to me, Jacy, the time is *never* right to enter the Game. Get that through your pretty head of yours, okay? It's never, never, never...."

Baz sighed, long and hard. "Forever is such a long time, that's all, hon." Baz's term of endearment took some of the sting out of his anger. Jacy had never upset Baz before, and she felt horrible for doing it. The poor man had enough on his plate, he didn't need her coming around, stirring shit up for him.

"Baz, I...."

"I probably shouldn't tell you this, Jacy, but what the fuck? It's not like they can punish me any more than they already have."

Jacy raised her eyebrows at him.

Baz nodded. "Good point, but fuck it. I figured Lita would've told you by now, but apparently she hasn't."

"Well, I haven't exactly been in the listening mood lately, anyways."

"Fair enough. Please listen to this, though, and don't tell anyone I told you this, okay?"

"Of course," Jacy said. "I swear."

Baz sighed again, looking around to see if anybody was within hearing distance. The closest person was Maraca Kabob, a Grass

Counting Bone who was too far to hear any talk, and Ugly Earful who was doing her best to ignore them. Baz leaned closer to Jacy.

"Forgive me for telling you this, Jacy, but Eugene has a life ending illness."

The words blasted Jacy like a Mack truck.

"What…"

"All first ones do. It's a bit of a safety net to assuage people's guilt when they do die. They don't tell you beforehand, because they don't want you to be reckless, but they realize rookies are rookies. Why give a bright and healthy newborn to someone who has only mastered bunnies and other animals? The next logical step is to give someone who is going to die."

"But…what…how…."

"They can't give you a person dying of old age, as you can't enhance your talents with them. It's the middle aged ones who don't know they're dying yet. Those are the ones that work best. They approach a Gamer who has someone in their pod that fits these criteria and the Gamer donates to the Rookie Pool. It's a bit of an honour, actually, and there's usually a benefit given to someone who contributes."

Baz took a deep breath, and let it out slowly.

"The average time a rookie's first member has is three to five years of Earth life left. When you lose him, you will be devastated, no matter if it's from the disease or because you made a rookie mistake. They tell you then to help ease the pain a bit."

Jacy looked at Baz as if he'd just sprung a second nose on his face. What the fuck was he talking about? Eugene dying? What the…

Something caught Baz's attention off in the distance towards the entrance's fountain. He squinted his eyes to get a better look.

"What's that idiot doing now?" he asked, more to himself than to Jacy. Jacy turned to see what Baz was looking at. She saw someone, he appeared to be a Skull, standing on the Fountain's edge with his arms raised. It looked like he was shouting.

"Who is it?" Jacy asked.

"It's Onerous Dray," Baz frowned.

Jacy watched Onerous Dray. The water of the fountain sprayed up behind him like a peacock's plume, and he pumped his arms up and down to go along with whatever he was chanting. Jacy couldn't quite make out what the words were.

"Oh, shit," Baz said, looking over at Jacy.

"What…" she was about to ask before the breeze carried Onerous Dray's words to her ears.

"…ne…gene…ugene…Eugene…EUGENE!!!"

Jacy's eyes widened and her throat constricted. "Eugene?"

Jacy scrambled to her feet and bolted in the direction of her table as fast as her feet would carry her. Onerous Dray's ugly chant sliced through her aching stomach.

"Eugene! Eugene! Eugene!"

9

Sultana Yelp pulled the cock out of her mouth just before it exploded its salty semen into her mouth. She stroked it vigorously and pointed it up at Laddie Nines belly. Arching his back, and letting out a loud moan, Laddie launched an impressive amount of cum all over himself.

He began to curse instantly. "Jesus fucking Christ! It got me in my eye!" he blurted out. "Quick, hand me a fucking towel!"

Sultana couldn't contain in her giggles as she searched the messy room for a towel. Not finding one, she found the next best thing and tossed it to him.

"Thanks…ahhh, fuck! A dirty sock? Really? Jesus, Sultana," but he used it anyway, getting most of the mess around his eye. He rolled onto his stomach and let tears and gravity take care of the rest of it. Sultana admired his taut, naked ass. Not as sexy as Galore's, to be sure, but not bad at all.

"It was a crusty one you handed me, you know," he tossed the dirty sock into the corner.

Sultana laughed harder. Laddie Nines looked at her sharply before chuckling, too.

"Okay, okay," he rolled over onto his back. "It was kind of funny. Let's keep this to ourselves, though, all right?"

Sultana pretended to zip her lips shut. She moved up on the bed, putting her head on Laddie's shoulder, gently stroking his muscular chest. For a Skull, Laddie Nines was one of the good ones. He wasn't a sick pervert who got off on demeaning or hurting women. In fact, he probably was a good lover. He tried his best to sway Sultana into letting him make love to her, but she held strong. She had to play this right, one step at a time.

"Anything interesting going on at Granny Mandible's house?" she asked.

"Oh yeah, I was going to tell you," he leaned over to grab a cigarette from the cluttered nightstand but only found an empty package. "Shit. You got a cigarette?"

Sultana shook her head. "I don't smoke."

"Oh yeah, that's right," he settled back down and she resumed gently running her fingers over his nipples and chest. "Anyways, those three little bastard kids are missing."

This wasn't the type of information Sultana was looking for, but it surprised her all the same. She and pretty well everyone else in this whole place had a run-in with Lucy, Dickie, and Joey at one point or another.

"Really? Any idea what happened?"

"No, and I think even Granny Mandible doesn't know. Agent Ninny Mop showed up there yesterday, and he's one dude who you never see go there."

This was interesting information, and she'd definitely pass it on to Council. "Anybody else of note visit her lately?"

"A lot of them. Flair, Maise Elantina, Gravigo. Hammer Coolie, too, but not as often as the other three."

"Anyone else? Come on, Laddie, this is important to me. I think that mind blowing blow job I just gave you is worth more than three missing, foul mouthed kids, and the leaders of all the groups, don't you?"

Laddie Nines kissed her on the forehead. "Baby, I've never had anybody slurp my gherkin like you. You should give a class on that or something. You'd make a lot of dudes happy if you could pass that skill on to their ladies."

"I've got some other skills you could experience firsthand if you continue to provide me with good information about the comings and goings across the street."

"Mmmm," Laddie Nines ran his hand through her tousled hair. "That's a deal."

Sultana Yelp leaned down, gave his right nipple a gentle nibble and kiss, then stood up and straightened her clothes. Laddie Nines leaned over to the other side of the bed where a mini fridge acted as the other nightstand. He extracted himself a cold beer and popped it open.

"Your earlier question, though," he said after taking a large gulp of the cold ale, "about anyone else of note? Usually Granny gets the higher up muckity mucks, but in the last week or so I've noticed Neva Tezremsy, The Bam Slicer, and even Hammer Coolie's buddy, what's his name?"

"His name? Not Trichina Flame or Karma Twin?"

"No, the guy, you know...."

"Tagger Merrino?"

"Yeah," Laddie took another swig of his beer. "Him, too. I mean, that place always gets a fucking ton of visitors, but it caught my eye seeing a bunch of number twos and such show up."

Sultana raised her eyebrows and nodded. This wasn't juicy enough to allow Laddie Nines to stick his tongue in her vagina, but it definitely warranted a return performance from her.

"I'll pop by next week some time," she said, putting her hand on the doorknob. "Keep your eyes open, okay?"

"And Rainy Dissolve," Laddie Nines said.

"Pardon me?" she took her hand off the doorknob and turned to him.

"You know her? The ugly thing with the scars and warts and all...."

"Yes, I know who she is. Go on."

"She visited Granny Mandible just the other day."

"Which day?"

Laddie Nines looked to the ceiling and took another gulp of beer. "Wasn't yesterday. Must've been the day…yeah, it was the day before."

Sultana was surprised at this. Rainy visited Granny Mandible after the Council meeting. Very interesting. It might not mean anything, but it definitely pricked her radar. Sultana Yelp walked across the room, bent down and laid a long, slow kiss on Laddie Nines' lips, slipping her hand under the covers, and gave his cock a nice squeeze.

"You promise to keep our thing a secret, right?"

Laddie Nines nodded. Sultana could feel his penis growing in her hand. "Good. Keep it that way, and keep giving me information like that? Well, you will be one *very* happy boy."

Sultana gave him another wet kiss and tug before standing. "In fact, if you keep it up, you may earn yourself a rusty trombone."

"What's a rusty trombone?"

Sultana Yelp smiled wickedly over her shoulder as she opened the door. "I will show you next week. Don't worry, if you thought tonight was good, next week will blow your freaking mind. Ciao."

The last thing she saw before she closed the door was Laddie Nines' hand move under the sheet and start stroking himself before she closed the door. She laughed as she walked down the dingy hallway. Men were so fucking *easy*.

10

Jacy came to an abrupt halt about twenty feet from her table. Ever since she re-entered the Gaming Area, the quiet crowd parted to let her walk a straight line to her area. The closest tables to her were silent. Jacy shuffled the remaining distance to the table, semi-noticing the two normally undisturbed chairs being askew. The sight registered in her brain, but did it really matter?

She crept to her chair, both sure and unsure of what she would find back on Earth. Her brain ebbed to numb as she put her hand on the smooth oak table and made her way to her seat, her fingers dragging along the table behind her. Pulling her chair out from where she'd left it before, Jacy sat down. She took one last long breath and looked down.

By the time the whole chaotic scene unfolded beneath her, the rest of her body joined her brain in Numbville. She stared at the lifeless body underneath the police blanket. Screams erupted from somewhere deep inside of her, but not a sound escaped her quivering lips.

Eugene, Eugene, Eugene...

Little bits and snippets registered in whatever part of the brain still functions in times such as these.

The Chrysler Intrepid: smashed through the front doors of the convenience store.

The shaken cashier: "He just bought a bag of Cheet-os, complaining he couldn't sleep and got bored..."

The elderly driver: "I just came to grab some Tums for the wife. Her stomach was acting up. I thought the car was in reverse, I really did. Oh dear, that poor man...."

The ambulance and police lights, flashing through the night sky...

Jacy shook her head as if to wake up from this nightmare. What the fuck just happened? Eugene turned off the bedside lamp after watching an old Married With Children episode, Jacy went to visit Baz, and Eugene was now squashed flesh.

Jacy noticed a small crowd of looky loos who amassed beyond the yellow police tape. She guessed things like this didn't happen much in sleepy Ferndale.

"You're too late, folks," she whispered. "I was too late. We're all too late."

Jacy looked up from her table and stared out into the Gaming Area, not seeing anything until she noticed both Flair and Gravigo watching her. Were they concerned? Did they care? Did they want to yell, "I told you so!?"

Jacy realized she didn't give a fuck. She slowly raised both of her arms in their direction, and she extended her middle finger of both her hands.

Fuck you both. *Fuck everyone.*

11

Hammer Coolie took a long hike with Tagger Merrino, a favourite ritual of theirs. They hadn't been able to spend much time with one another lately. They talked business all the time, of course, but it had been awhile since they got to just hang out.

"Come on, Tagger, or should that be Lagger?" Hammer called back over his shoulder when he noticed Tagger had dropped back twenty yards or so.

"Only if you want to be addressed as Putty Knife for the rest of the hike," Tagger replied.

Hammer grinned as he dug his hiking boots in. He knew Tagger Merino would keep up, and besides, he really needed this break from the Game. Ridded Snot had disappeared. Hammer and his crew couldn't recall anybody disappearing so thoroughly before.

Hammer enjoyed the burn in his quads as he pushed up the last 500 yards or so of trail to the lookout he and Tagger sought. He could hear Tagger's heavy breathing and the scuttling of pebbles from behind.

"Come on, Tagger Tiger," Hammer hadn't used his nickname of Tagger for so long, both men laughed when he said it.

"On your fucking heels, Hammer Head."

Both men pumped their sweaty, muscular legs for all they were worth. They were almost sprinting, when at the last second, Tagger threw his body in a perfect jackknife dive through the air. His hands broke through the fern fronds a half second before a surprised Hammer burst through.

"Oof," Tagger hit the ground with a thud and a gushing breath. Hammer found his usual stump and slumped down onto it, laughing.

"You're a crazy fucking bugger," he wheezed, wiping sweat from his face.

"A crazy fucking bugger who just beat your ass, though," Tagger rolled onto his back, revealing thin droplets of blood running in tiny rivulets down his ebony chest.

"You're bleeding," Hammer took a swig of water from the wineskin hanging from his neck.

"Nope, I'm basking in my win." All the same, Tagger winced as he sat up. Hammer handed him his wineskin and Tagger splashed some water on his chest. "It's all good."

Hammer nodded, taking the wineskin back. No true free one turned off his pleasure and pain receptors. That was for all the pussy Skulls, Hats, and Bones who didn't know how to live. Hammer's crew figured it out one time, coming to the conclusion that 100% of the free ones kept them on, and about 40% of the Bones did the same. The Hats and the Skulls were down around 10%.

"The pussiest of pussies," was how Karma Twin described that statistic.

Hammer looked out at the magnificent view the rocky lookout afforded them. They were high above the greenest of valleys. Hammer checked out one of the numerous waterfalls that fed into the winding, unseen river below.

Tagger Merrino enjoyed the view, too, before he asked his question. "How's Marley doing?"

"She's okay," Hammer answered after a moment's hesitation. "She's getting a handle on the wheelchair."

Tagger nodded, pausing a bit before his next query. "I went to Granny Mandible like you asked."

"And?"

"I think she knows," Tagger shook his head, "but she's not saying anything."

"Fuck," Hammer walked closer to the edge of the bluff.

Tagger Merino watched him, finished with the two topics he knew were tough for Hammer Coolie to discuss. He decided he'd gone far enough on their recreation day; he'd probe more when they were back to work. He changed the subject.

"That human chick, Jacy? They killed her first yesterday."

Hammer Coolie raised his eyebrows at that. Not about the actual news, he heard about it soon after it occurred. It was something else Tagger said that caught his curiosity.

"They? I heard it was Onerous Dray."

"It was," Tagger stood, stretching. "Onerous Dray is too low on the chain to take this on himself."

"So he had some help from an upper Skull," Hammer shrugged. He felt bad for Jacy as he liked her, but the first was the first. And *everybody*, him included, had a first who died.

"Of course, he did," Tagger shook his head as if Hammer Coolie was a blathering idiot. "Word is, though, is that the Skulls didn't want to take this one on alone."

Now Hammer looked at Tagger as if he was the loony one. "Are you crazy? The Skulls worried about hitting some rookie's first?"

"I know, I know," Tagger held his hands up, "but you know how Flair is about Jacy. He's still trying to win her over, so this makes a kind of weird sense, if it's true."

Hammer returned his gaze to the emerald valley as he pondered what Tagger said. He supposed it did carry a certain type of twisted logic, but whatever. There was nothing either of them could do about it now.

"Well," Hammer said, sighing, "she'll get a hearing out of it as she wasn't at the table when it happened. I'm still surprised Flair would've allowed the old 'elderly person drives through storefront' card on a rookie's first. They usually reserve those for someone more important."

"Yeah, that stumps me, too."

"Anyways, Maise Elantina is on the judiciary panel on this one, so Jacy will get a fair hearing. She'll probably get the minimum in retribution, at the least."

"Do you remember your first?"

"Of course I do. Don't we all?"

"I mean your first hearing, meathead," Tagger Merrino smirked.

Hammer did indeed recall his first hearing. "It was a little intimidating," he admitted.

"Fuck that, Hulk. It was *a lot* intimidating."

Hammer stood, not able to debate Tagger on the subject. Tagger was right, plain and simple. "Well, Jacy has Lita at her side. That means a ton."

"Are you ever going to finally fuck that poor girl? She pretty near orgasms any time you're within ten feet of her. Put her out of her misery."

"And ruin my legendary status in her eyes?" Hammer cocked an eyebrow and grin. "Why ruin what she thinks I could be? I would only disappoint someone that infatuated."

"I wouldn't be so sure. You could probably fart near her and she'd bottle it so she could smell it whenever she wanted. Eau de Hammer, cologne of the sex God."

Hammer didn't have a retort to that false claim. While far from celibate, Hammer Coolie kept his sexual liaisons low-key. Tagger

Merrino, on the other hand, was almost mythological with the number of ladies he bedded.

Hammer laughed instead, looping the wineskin's handle around his neck. He would have to deal with Lita's infatuation at some point in time, he knew, but today was not that day.

"Last one down sucks Skulls boners," he said as he dashed off of the bluff. A cursing Tagger Merrino was hot on his heels.

12

Jacy sat outside the hearing room, Lita by her side. Everything seemed blurry to Jacy. Somewhere deep down where any emotions were still alive, she felt enormous gratitude for Lita's friendship and guidance. Jacy was fine on auto-pilot, but that's all she was good for at this point.

When they were called in, Lita led Jacy to their seats. "Sit here, Sugar. I'm going to talk to Maise Elantina for a moment."

Jacy watched Lita walk up to the head table where the three adjudicators sat. She recognized Maise, but wasn't totally sure who the one seated to the left of Maise was. There was no mistaking the person on her right, though. Jacy would recognize The Bam Slicer anywhere.

It registered somewhere in Jacy that having The Bam Slicer on the adjudication panel didn't seem fair, but she had neither the energy nor the knowledge on how to deal with something like that. Jacy was sure that Lita was looking out for her best interests. And if she wasn't? Oh well, too. Jacy dimly saw Lita in a hushed but heated discussion. Lita appeared to be exasperated, and Maise Elantina looked troubled, but she continued shaking her head and shrugging her shoulders until Lita gave up and stalked back to Jacy.

"Is everything okay?" Jacy whispered.

Lita put her hand on Jacy's left knee and squeezed it. "Everything is going to be okay, Sugar. We'll get through anything as long as we stick together."

Jacy nodded as she absent mindedly scanned the rest of the room. Lita and Jacy were the only ones on their side of the room facing the judicial table. Onerous Dray sat on the other side of the room facing the same way. There were two empty seats beside him.

Somewhere deep down, Jacy supposed she should ask why there were two open seats beside Onerous Dray, but her query lay low in the muddied waters her insides had become. Jacy's gaze moved back to the head table, where Maise Elantina watched her with a look of concern on her face. Maise offered a sad smile to Jacy. Jacy attempted to return the smile, but she wasn't sure if she did or not.

Jacy heard the doors open behind them and felt Lita's hand on her knee tighten. Jacy looked back at the doors but the two figures had already moved through her line of sight in a blur. She heard the two figures take the remaining seats left in the room.

"It's going to be okay, Sugar," Lita leaned in to her left ear and whispered. "I promise you, we will get through this." Jacy heard this, but was too puzzled for the words to register. In her brain, she only had one, clear thought.

What were Flair and Gravigo doing sitting with Onerous Dray?

13

Maise Elantina rapped the elevated bench with her gavel. "I call Jacy Morgan's hearing to order."

Maise arranged the legal pad of paper in front of her, though she knew she wasn't going to take any notes. She, The Bam Slicer, and Rosy Situp, the third judge, already discussed the merits of the case. The sentencing guidelines were pretty clear. Precedence had already been set in this case.

This burned Maise Elantina a bit; there was nothing punitive they could do to Onerous Dray. He had the ironclad excuse for a death when the Gamer wasn't present at the table – Accidents happen. Further strengthening his case was the elderly driver at the wheel. Of course, Maise knew there was more to it than that, but this panel didn't allow for that kind of conjecture.

Maise sighed. She knew why this was one of those rare occasions where Flair and Gravigo worked together. And to tell the truth, she understood their positions. It was true that Jacy needed a wake-up call. Besides the countless offerings of advice, The Bam Slicer was sent to rectify the issue, and Maise herself sent Befriending Track when Bam failed. Nothing worked. While Maise Elantina had her own perspective on the methods used by Flair and Gravigo, she understood their reasoning.

She also knew why Gravigo and Flair were here together. Neither of them was willing to take the fall for this. Jacy was too important to them both. So the answer was either doing nothing, or take the fall together.

Tough love. It was ten pounds of shit in a five-pound bag, as one of Maise's own pod was fond of saying.

The only thing to be decided by the panel was what restitution Jacy would be afforded. Ironclad excuse or not, a gamer always received something in compensation for a subject dying when they weren't at the table.

Maise Elantina looked at Jacy, and her heart broke. Poor thing, she didn't have a clue what was going on. Add the baffled look on Jacy's face when she noticed Flair and Gravigo sitting together…. Maise brushed the corner of her right eye with the back of her left hand as nonchalant as she could. This is what caused Maise's and Lita's argument earlier.

"Look," Lita defended, "everyone in this room knows that fuck all is going to happen to Onerous Dray. Let's just skip to the restitution part and be done with it."

"I can't do that, Lita."

"Seeing Flair and Gravigo together might be enough to break Jacy's back. Can you do *that*, Judge Elantina?"

"Fuck you, Lita," Maise hissed. "You know how much I care for Jacy. I can't change protocol here; you know that."

Lita stormed off, then. The one saving grace Maise Elantina had in this was knowing someone like Lita had Jacy's back. The formal part of this almost farcical hearing was over in 45 minutes. Maise, The Bam Slicer, and Rosy Situp adjourned to a connected meeting room.

"Jesus," Rosy declared as The Bam Slicer closed the door. "I could barely look at Jacy, as I feared I would burst into tears."

"She'll get over it," The Bam Slicer took a seat. "And speaking of that, let's get this over with. We all know she's eligible to pick the next person of her pod, so let's give it to her."

"I wish we could give her more," Rosy stated.

The Bam Slicer rolled his eyes. "Look, you two are acting like this is the end of the fucking world for her. Well, let me remind you that it's not, okay? Every single one of us has lost our first, only the lucky ones manage to get them to die naturally. This isn't something horrible that has happened to her, it's a rite of fucking passage."

"You Skulls are always so heartless," Rosy Situp declared, before looking away from Bam and finding a perfectly good space of the wall to study.

"Jesus fucking Christ, Maise, would you…"

"Regardless of whether he's being heartless or not, Rosy, he's right," Maise Elantina closed her eyes. "There isn't anything more we can give Jacy in form of restitution…"

"Bloody right," The Bam Slicer stood up. "Let's go tell her and…"

"…hold on," Maise looked directly at Bam. "I'm not finished yet."

The Bam Slicer sat down, staring at Maise.

"Thank you. I would like to add the stipulation that Jacy does *not* have to make her choice right now."

"When, then? By tomorrow?"

"No," Maise shook her head. "I'm stipulating she gets to make her choice whenever Lita deems Jacy fit enough to make her decision."

"What?! No fucking way," The Bam Slicer shook his head. "Why would we give her that? Nobody else gets that. We can't play favourites here. We don't have the authority."

"We don't have the authority to go outside of precedence, but we can add stipulations if other related issues warrant it."

"What are the other related issues, Maise?" Rosy Situp asked.

"This is the first time we've had a human in a hearing for their first. I'm sure that will be enough to appease The Three Generals when they do their periodic review."

The Bam Slicer made as if to argue, but changed his mind. He cursed under his breath. Rosy Situp watched Bam with interest.

Maise knew Rosy Situp quite well, but they rarely worked with one another. Rosy wasn't anybody high up in the Hats officially, but if one wanted to get something done the unofficial route, it had to go through Rosy to get to Gravigo. That Gravigo allowed Rosy Situp to take the prestigious role of adjudicator in this hearing spoke volumes about how valued the sharp, spinsterish woman was to him.

"Okay, fair enough," The Bam Slicer conceded. "Let's say we can pass this through officially. Tell me *why* I would want to vote for this stipulation to be attached."

Maise Elantina was waiting for this one. "Well, we all had a hand in training Jacy, Bam. If we failed to properly prepare her for the Game, she shouldn't be punished for our failings."

Rosy Situp said nothing. She just watched The Bam Slicer with a bemused expression. Maise held her own smile at bay.

"Fuck you both," Bam snarled, storming out of the room.

Rosy Situp and Maise Elantina smiled at each other and nodded. Rosy stood.

"Rosy," Maise said, "could I have a few moments of your time after we give our ruling? There is something I would like to discuss with you. Confidentially, of course."

"Okay," Rosy seemed curious. Maise hoped what she was going to ask from Rosy Situp would never be needed, but Maise never left anything to chance.

14

Jacy wandered around the magnificent fountain. Her hearing concluded a few hours earlier, Lita had some important business to take care of with Serena and Jacy? Well, Jacy wasn't quite sure what she was supposed to do with herself now that poor Eugene was dead.

Parts of the hearing registered in her brain. Lita seemed a little surprised and quite happy with the retribution Jacy received. Jacy supposed that should make herself happy, too, yet she couldn't quite summon that emotion to the surface. Jacy wasn't surprised Onerous Dray received no punishment at all; Lita had prepared her for that eventuality.

Gravigo and Flair sitting there together, though? Even though the memory was clear, the meaning of it evaded her. Jacy ceased her rootless ambling. She stared at the kaleidoscopes of water shoot into the air.

It wasn't just Eugene dying that hurt her heart, though that reality alone was more than enough to crush her. Somewhere, way deep down inside of her, she realized her heart wasn't anywhere near this place at all.

Her heart was back on Earth with Derian. With Beau. Hell, with Eugene, too, though she hadn't known him back on Earth. Jacy's heart was with them and all of the people back on Earth. And not just people. *Her* people. Jacy had never thought of all human beings in that term before, and it hit her with all the subtlety of a steel toed boot to the crotch.

They were all 'her people,' weren't they? English, Russian, Chinese, Spanish, Brazilian, Scandinavians, Arabs, every single label put upon them. All the different nationalities, all the regions within those nationalities, all the communities within the regions that are within those….

"Are you okay, Jacy?" a voice barged into Jacy's newfound realization. She was surprised to see Maise Elantina sitting on the edge of the fountain.

"I…uh…I…" Jacy looked back at the shooting water and drew in a deep lungful of warm air. She looked at Maise again. "Did you know Gravigo was in on Eugene's death?"

Maise's lips became firm as if she were about to smile, but the edges didn't upturn to complete the process. "No, I had my suspicions, but the truthful answer is no."

Jacy approached her. "Why?"

"Why was he involved? I don't know that…"

"No," Jacy interrupted her. "Why were you suspicious?"

Jacy sat down beside her, and Maise took Jacy's hands in her own. Jacy didn't pull them away; she merely cocked her head a little to the left. Maise Elantina gave Jacy's hands a gentle squeeze.

"Do you recall hearing the story back on Earth about the angel who saved the devil?"

Jacy attempted to sort through her jumbled brain but conceded defeat in swift fashion.

"Well," Maise began the story. "One day the people of a small town realized they had captured the devil. Not just any devil, mind you. *The* devil. The very same devil that's hated and loathed from every corner of the globe. And the people of this small town caught her, right on the main street of their town."

Jacy listened.

"All the townspeople knew they had to kill their captive. She was the devil, after all. One of the guys punched the devil, knocking her to the ground. Another one kicked her. Another one smashed a metal bar across her back. Soon all the townsfolk were beating her to death with fists, bricks, and knives. At some point, the devil rolled over into the gutter, and the people gathered around to watch her die a painful death. Just as the devil's final breaths grew shallower and shallower, though, the clouds opened and an angel descended to the ground."

Jacy's eyebrows furrowed.

"The townspeople stepped back, dumbfounded. The angel knelt beside the dying devil and healed her. The townsfolk were too dismayed to do much when the devil rose, sauntered away, and flipped them the bird. Finally, a boy, a little, nine-year-old boy asked the angel, 'Why? He was the devil and we killed her. Why did you save her?' Others in the crowd nodded in agreement, and started questioning 'why', as well."

"Why?" Jacy squeezed Maise's hand. "What was the angel's answer?"

Maise Elantina smiled. "As the angel slowly ascended back towards the heavens, she looked down upon that small town and said, 'Don't you understand? If the devil doesn't exist, then neither do I.' "

The words did their best to sink in and mean something to Jacy. "So you're saying if the Skulls don't exist, then neither do the Hats," she whispered.

Maise Elantina nodded, raising her eyebrows for Jacy to finish.

"And if the Hats don't exist, then neither do the Skulls."

Maise squeezed Jacy's hands. "Exactly, Jacy. Flair and Gravigo don't really want to destroy each other. Yes, they can't stand each other and yes, they *definitely* want to claim victory over the other. But destroy one another? They can't, and won't do that. Ever."

Jacy looked at the sky, exhaling. "It must suck to need your mortal enemy," Jacy joked, yet there was no humour in her voice.

Maise chuckled. Jacy shook her head.

"What does Eugene have to do with it, though? I don't get that. Even if Eugene was going to die from some disease, why not let the poor guy enjoy the last little bit of time he had left on Earth?"

Now it was Maise's turn to shake her head. "That I don't know. What I do know is, though, is that Gravigo loves you like a daughter, Jacy. Yes, he's devastated you didn't become a member of the Hats, but I believe part of him is proud that you went your own way, too. Gravigo wouldn't agree to Eugene dying just because you didn't join the Hats. He would've only agreed if he felt it would be for the betterment of you."

Jacy extracted her hands from Maise's to massage her temples. It was almost easier for Jacy if some type of treachery was the death of poor Eugene, but in reality, his death laid upon her doorstep. If Jacy was honest with herself, that's exactly where Eugene Thompson's corpse belonged.

"Thanks, Maise," Jacy stood.

"Where are you going now?" Maise asked.

"It's been a tough few days," Jacy sighed, "I think I'll go lie down for a bit."

Maise Elantina nodded, and watched Jacy walk away. She wanted to help Jacy, but knew sometimes you needed to let people go through things their own way.

15

Flair's face was inches from Jacy's, spittle dribbling from his lips onto her.

"Get up, you lazy fucking twat!!! What?! Are you going to just lay here and bathe in your woman tears and be a pathetic lump of useless shit?!!! It's been six fucking days since you've been up!! Motherfucker, fatherfucker…"

Jacy's neutral expression never wavered. She heard this rant yesterday, too. She also heard the following words from the same, potty-mouthed Flair.

"...come on, Jacy, baby, you can come back from this..."

"...well, then, fuck you, you sack of...."

"...please come back to us, hon......"

Whether it was pornographic or cajoling words, nothing got Jacy to rise from her bed. Gravigo sat stone faced in the corner of the room.

"This is absolutely killing me to see her like this," he stated before leaving the room. Flair shook his head as he watched Gravigo leave before returning his face so close to Jacy's, their noses brushed one another. Flair launched into another tirade.

"I *know* you can hear and understand me, you fucking weakling!!!! Enough is enough of this stupid-ass charade...."

Flair was right about that, at least. Jacy heard and understood what was going on around her; she just didn't give a shit at the moment. Regardless of his tactics, it was oddly touching Flair cared so much, no matter how deep she hated the son of a bitch.

"Okay," Flair's voice returned to normal. He wiped the spit off of her face with the back of his hand. "I'm sorry, I just...I just... I just want you back here with us, okay? Things are better when you're around."

Damn, Flair was quirky. One moment he played the mean thug; the next he was the cool guy with a heart of gold. Sometimes Flair could be so very close to the truth or galaxies away from it, and yet he never seemed to know one way or the other. Jacy realized then how exhausting it must be to be Flair.

"But then again, I think, fuck you, you fucking cockroach!" Flair's voice rose in volume again. "You're wasting everyone's time with this little pity show of yours and..."

"What do you think you're doing?!" a new voice entered the room. Ahhh, Lita, almost on cue. Flair moved his raging glare from Jacy to Lita.

"Mind your own business, douchebag," he snarled. "I'm trying to help your worthless…"

"Get out!" Lita pointed towards the open door.

Flair's look softened as he stood to his full height. He bobbled his head back and forth in some kind of weird nodding fashion, before moving towards Lita and the door.

"Alright, okay, alright," he held his hands up in defeat. "I was only trying to help your friend. Sorry if you don't like my methods, but I truly am trying to help her."

"Get….out," Lita's voice dropped in volume, but not in disdain. She had her hands on her hips, looking half at Jacy, half at him. Flair scratched his ear as he stopped in front of Lita, gaping at Lita's tits.

"Jesus Christ," he shook his head. "Did you enhance your splazoingas or…." Flair reached to cop a quick feel but Lita responded with lightening quick reflexes. Flair's face was now mushed into the carpet, his right arm wrenched behind his back. Lita lay on top of his back, her lips touching his ear.

"If you *ever* try something like that again, you piece of…"

"Alright, okay, alright!" Flair shouted. "Get off of me, for fuck's sake!"

Lita sprang to her feet, just out of reach of Flair who pulled himself to his feet and turned to face her. He looked down at his waist.

"Jesus," he stared at the pup tent that was his pants, "would you look at that? You gave me a hard on."

Lita glanced down at his crotch and chuckled.

"Looks like your training with Karma Twin is paying off," he grinned.

Lita smirked, too, nodding her head towards the door. Flair bowed, and exited. Lita sighed, closing the door after him. She returned and sat on the bed beside Jacy. Lita put her hand on Jacy's cheek, gently rubbing it.

"Sorry, Sugar," Lita spoke in gentle tones. "I wanted to return sooner, but Serena is giving me a hell of a time, right now. How are you doing today?"

As was becoming custom, Jacy didn't respond. Lita stood, stretched, and flopped down on the adjacent bed.

"I freaking *love* Serena to death, but wow!" Lita stared at the ceiling. "I don't have any words for the crazy stunt she pulled today."

Lita rolled onto her side, looking deep into Jacy's sad eyes. Lita gave her a half smile.

"I know you're in there, Sugar. You'll come back to us when you're ready. Just remember you have lots of people who care about you besides me. Even Hammer Coolie asked me about you today, and me oh me oh me oh my, you should've seen how yummy that man looked today. Whooo-eeee, he was…."

Lita went into another one of her perpetual listings as to why Hammer Coolie was the sexiest man in the universe before launching into all the things she'd do to him if ever given a chance. Jacy lay there, tuning out Lita's current words, but reflecting on ones she said earlier. Lita was right. Jacy was here and she'd be fine. Lita, unlike all of the others, understood. While the rest of them chalked her state up to Eugene's untimely death, Lita knew it was much more than that. After all, Lita had gone through it, too. They just dealt with it in different ways.

It had nothing to do with losing their first, either.

"You're more contemplative than me," Lita remarked on the second day Jacy took to bed. "Me, I went out and learned to fight. I punched and kicked all the anger out of my system. You, you just need to sort all this shit out in your head and you'll be fine. I'm here for you when you're ready, Sugar."

The anger Lita spoke of wasn't about Eugene's death. Sure, Jacy was upset by that, but it wasn't the end of her world. It was just that everything caught up to Jacy at the same time as Eugene's passing. Jacy had been so tough mentally and kept buying the ticket and taking the ride, that when Eugene's death caused her to pause momentarily, everything else creamed into her like a blitzing linebacker from the blind side.

At first Jacy was pissed at everything and everyone. She was angry about her own death, about Derian having to grow up without a mom, about Beau's inevitable struggles as a single parent. Jacy was also livid she and everyone else of her people had been lied to back on Earth. There were no harps and fluffy clouds of heaven, nor were there heat and flames of hell, either. For a day or two, Jacy felt incredible ire at this.

Slowly, though, that resentment simmered down a bit, as Jacy realized she was as much at fault as all those who lied. Her wrath turned on herself as she realized how gullible and naïve she'd been to believe their words in the first place. Like, honestly, who the fuck really knew what the afterlife consisted of? Not anybody alive, that's for sure. Shit, Jacy *was* dead and she still didn't understand it.

This self-rage became a turning point for Jacy. The irritation she felt towards the loud-mouthed know-it-alls who pretended to know all turned into fury at herself for buying what they were selling. She literally vibrated when she recalled how casually she adopted the fact that those people knew more than her.

Now, she understood this better than ever. Sure, a mechanic could speak with authority on a vehicle's engine, but others waxing eloquently how others should live their lives? Fuck them.

"....and then I'd take that throbbing, 100% all beef thermometer and let him take my temperature the old fashioned way…" Lita's musings broke into Jacy's thoughts. Jacy tried to smile at her best friend, but her cheek muscles weren't quite ready for that, yet. Jacy closed her eyes and drifted off to sleep.

16

Fatter Verb sat in the same chair Gravigo perched in two weeks ago. When Fatter stopped by to check on Jacy, Lita told him she was sleeping. Lita wanted to check on Serena, so Fatter offered to sit with Jacy until Lita returned.

Fatter sighed as he watched Jacy doze. He heard the rumours about how broken Jacy was, but this was the first time he saw it with his own eyes. Jacy stirred, her eyelids fluttering open.

"How you doing, kiddo?" he asked. Jacy looked at Fatter Verb but said nothing.

"Fair enough," Fatter sighed again. "You don't want to talk, and I get that. I actually came to show you something, so you don't need to talk, anyways."

Fatter Verb used his right hand to dim the lights while pointing his left index finger at the bare wall closest to the foot of Jacy's bed.

"You see, my love," Fatter looked at Jacy again. "I know how much you loved and cared for Eugene. Everybody knows how much he meant to you. I'm willing to wager, though, that his death isn't the sole reason for you being where you find yourself at the moment."

Jacy remained mute, watching Fatter Verb with empty eyes.

"I believe," Fatter continued, "that Eugene's death was the final extra weight your already over-burdened shoulders couldn't carry. If I'm right, I believe what I have to show you may help you."

Fatter hesitated before flicking his left middle finger to begin his show. He had mulled this action over for the past week or so; he even spoke with Granny Mandible about it. Both of them admitted this may be risky, but decided that the positives outweighed the potential negatives.

Fatter dearly hoped they were right, and moved his middle finger in a circle. "Here is your beautiful daughter, Derian, at 10 years old."

Jacy's eyes darted to the wall. Fatter Verb smiled. She was more aware than most others believed. "Go on, take a look at her. She's angelic."

Jacy stared at her daughter, slow tears trickling down her temples.

"I wanted you to see this, Jacy," Fatter Verb spoke in a revered tone. "Derian and Beau have had many, many, many discussions about you. They continue to do so, of course. This one, though, is one I really thought you should see."

Fatter moved his left ring finger in a diagonal motion, and the still picture of Derian became a movie.

Derian sat at a wooden dining room table, drawing a picture. Beau entered the frame, stooping to kiss the top of Derian's head. He then stepped out of the frame.

"What are you drawing, honey?"

"Just doodling," Derian said, her voice sad. After a pause, Beau's voice spoke again.

"You okay, sweetie?"

"Yeah," Derian continued to sketch, never looking up from her picture. "I've been thinking about Mom a lot."

Fatter Verb stole a glance at Jacy. The tears ran heavier now, but Fatter deduced the last thing Jacy wanted was for him to stop the show. There was no going back, now.

"Yeah?" Beau returned to the frame and sat down beside her. "What kinds of things about Mom are you thinking about?"

Derian ceased her scribbling, but she didn't look up from her picture. "I don't know, Daddy. Lots of things. I think about her every day and still don't know why she had to go heaven."

Beau tried to smile at his daughter. "I don't know, either, baby. Heaven needed another angel, I guess."

Fatter contained his snort of derision. Jacy's tears flowed more.

"I don't want her to be an angel, though. I want her to be my mommy," Derian looked at her daddy with tear filled eyes. Beau's eyes filled with tears, but he did his best to shield Derian from seeing them. He hugged Derian close.

"She is your mommy, Derian," he whispered. "She's watching you and she's being your mommy every day."

Beau gave up trying to restrain his tears and now cried freely. The movie faded out, with Derian and Beau sobbing in each other's arms.

Fatter Verb brought the lights up to their proper level and was surprised to see Lita wiping tears off her own cheeks. She looked at Fatter, nodding slightly to him. Fatter nodded back and returned his attention to a wheezing, tearful Jacy. He stood and knelt beside the bed, laying his hand upon her cheek.

"I don't say this to be critical of Beau, but he said two bullshit things there. The first was when he told Derian heaven just needed another angel."

Jacy cried harder, gulping for air. Fatter looked to Lita, but she bobbed her head for him to continue.

"I don't blame him for using that familiar coping mechanism you humans lean on during times such as these," Fatter went on, "but that statement is pure crap. Destinies are only destinies until they become destined for something else. Does that make sense?"

Jacy was crying and wheezing so hard Fatter Verb was uncertain whether she understood or not.

"People die who aren't supposed to all the time, just as people who don't deserve to live get to keep living. It's the karmic universe at work, and like everything else, sometimes it works brilliantly, and other times it doesn't. Contrary to popular belief, there are such things as karmic accidents."

Jacy's tearful convulsions seemed to be waning.

"That's what your death was, Jacy. It was a worthless accident. Oh, sure it may have been carried out by Buzzed Rottid and it definitely shook things up here, but in the bigger picture, your death should have never happened. Never forget this, Jacy, but there is a bigger picture to this place, too."

Fatter was certain Jacy's tears were slowing. Now was the time to hit her with the big gun.

"Now, the other part that Beau wasn't speaking the truth about was when he told Derian that you were watching her every day.

Again, another human coping mechanism, not harmful but it's full of empty rhetoric."

Fatter Verb leaned even closer to Jacy. "But what if I told you I could help you make the last statement Beau told Derian become true?"

Fatter didn't have to surmise the waterworks were slowing, now. They came to a complete stop. "You need to get up and get out of this room. You need to make your death not worthless. I can help you, Jacy, but you need to snap out of this, first. If you do that, I will assist you in being able to see Derian every single day."

Jacy's eyes widened. Fatter Verb looked up at Lita who mouthed the words 'thank you.'

17

Jacy watched Fatter Verb stand after pecking her on the cheek. He walked over to Lita, and both of them stepped outside into the hall.

When she heard the door click, Jacy pulled herself up into a sitting position. How long had it been since she first lay down, she wondered? It had to be a couple of weeks, at least. Resting her back against the headboard and her knees bent, she grabbed one of her pillows and hugged it, burying her face in the soft fabric of the pillow case.

Her chest was sore, her head burned, and it felt like her eyes were hit by a drought. Yet, strangely enough, she felt the glimmerings of warmth in her stomach. She'd felt empty for so long, the feeling caused her to smile, a real smile. The first authentic one, actually, since she was last on Earth.

I will assist you in being able to see Derian every single day.

Those words of Fatter Verb's etched themselves in Jacy's psyche. She daydreamed about having Derian in her pod every day since she'd begun to understand this place, but never truly believed it to be true. And now here was Fatter Verb, telling her it could happen.

It never once occurred to her that Fatter may have just been trying to boost her spirits and give her the swift kick in the ass she needed. She trusted Fatter Verb. What he did was gut wrenching, and the cajones he must have to go through with it....Well, Jacy always believed anybody can tell you that you look good, but it takes a true friend to tell you to clip your nose hairs.

Jacy pulled her face away from the pillow and swivelled her ass so her feet were now on the floor.

This was it. No fucking around this time.

I'm coming, baby girl, and nothing is going to stop me now.

18

Lita shook her head as Coney Slut, one of Flair's numerous 'personal assistants' led her into a dimly lit room with soft spa music playing in the background. Coney didn't miss the look Lita gave her.

"Look, you said it was urgent to see him. It's no skin off my ass if you see him or not. This is the last possible time before Weaning Fest to see him."

Lita nodded. "My apologies, Coney. Thanks for doing this for me. I owe you one."

Coney Slut eyed her for a moment. "Will you give me a fight lesson? I've been studying kajukenbo. I hear you are one of the best at it."

Lita eyed Coney Slut in a new light. Coney didn't strike Lita as the person who would be interested in a fighting form that originated in the streets of a crime ridden area in Hawaii.

"I've never seen you train where I train," Lita said.

"I know," Coney Slut shook her head. "I'm too intimidated to go to the gym you go to. I practice here at our own gym. The Bam Slicer says I'm getting pretty good."

Lita smiled at the way Coney's chest puffed with pride when she said that.

"Well, okay, then," Lita agreed. "How about the afternoon before Weaning Fest? We'll have plenty of time to clean up before the big shindig."

Coney Slut swallowed her glee and tried to maintain her cool.

"Thanks, Lita," she motioned with her head into the room. "Go see him, now. This spa appointment usually takes an hour, but he hates being disturbed for the last half of it."

With that, Coney Slut walked off. Lita took a deep breath and entered the room. Lita had never seen a room quite like this. The room was unique enough. One of the longer walls was a water wall, with soft blue and red lights gently pulsing through the streams of falling water. Candles circled the upper perimeter of the other walls, casting their soft glow throughout the room. The soft music in the background was the perfect backdrop to it all. Lita wasn't positive, but she was pretty sure it was Breudi Siebert's 'An Adventure in the East.' Lita loved and knew her spa treatments, too.

The only thing marring the scene was a naked Flair lying on a massage table in the middle of the room.

Taking a deep breath in through her mouth and exhaling out through her nose, Lita approached Flair. As she got within ten feet or so, a discreet door opened, causing Lita to stop in her tracks. Through the door came a tall, handsome, muscular male. The man nodded hello to Lita and went to the table. Flair noticed he was no longer alone.

"Hello Lita. Hello Abs." Flair turned his head towards Lita. "Have you two ever met?"

Lita shook her head.

"Lita, this is Abs Tortonis. Abs, this is Lita."

"Nice to meet you, ma'am," Abs nodded to her.

"If you'd come over to the Skulls side," Flair winked at her, "you could be the recipient of Abs' world class massages, too."

Lita withheld comment. Abs Tortonis stepped over to a narrow side table full of different oils.

"What will it be today, Mr. Flair?"

"I think I need a number 4, Abs. I fear I may have tweaked my bulbospongius muscle in an entertaining five-some I had last night."

Lita rolled her eyes. Abs picked out an oil and returned to the table. "Ouch. I hope that's not the case, Mr. Flair, but let's check it out. Can you please get up on your hands and knees?"

Flair did as he was asked. Lita made a noise; half laugh, and half squeak of surprise. Both Flair and Abs looked over at her.

"Sorry," Lita tried not to look at Flair's oversized cock swinging between his legs like a pendulum but she found it hard not to. She wasn't going to give Flair the satisfaction in knowing that, though. She looked at him with raised eyebrows. "I didn't know you swung both ways, Flair."

Abs and Flair both laughed. "Get your mind out of the gutter, Lita," Flair got more comfortable, resting his chest on the table with his ass still high in the air. "This is strictly a much needed massage. There is nothing sexual about this, at all."

Abs oiled up his hands and reached between Flair's legs, using both hands to grasp Flair's manhood. Flair tensed, Abs studied the cock, and Lita tried her best to look away but likened it to watching a car accident. One didn't want to check it out, yet most did.

"For fuck's sake, Lita, move up here by my head. It's hard for me to relax when you're staring at my penis."

Lita nodded in agreement, but continued to watch Abs Tortonis' maneuverings as she made her way to the head of the table. Abs stroked Flair's penis with long, slow strokes with his right hand while his left hand pressed gently along other areas of the shaft. Flair winced a couple times, and Abs halted his prodding.

"Wow, Mr. Flair, you were right, but that's not the end of it. You've also twisted the ischiocavenous muscle, the deep fascia may be strained, and your frenulum is a little worse for wear. What were you *doing* last night?"

"Two acrobats, a gymnast, and a hypermobile hermaphrodite," Flair's face broke into a proud smile. "You may want to check my superficial transverse perineal muscle, too. The two acrobats were extremely pliable."

"Let's deal with one thing at a time, Mr. Flair." Abs Tortonis' head disappeared behind Flair's raised ass and Lita could no longer see him.

Flair spoke. "What's up, Lita? Why the rush to see me?"

Lita sighed and looked away. Coming to see Flair for a favour wasn't easy, but she sucked it up and made the last minute appointment. She found herself questioning that choice.

"You can stand there silent all you like," Flair moaned a little. "Or you can go give Abs a hand. He may need it when he starts working on my external sphincter muscle."

LIta chuckled, returning her look to Flair who was slowly swinging his upturned hips from side to side.

"Right there, Abs," Flair whispered. "A little more pressure."

"I want you to leave Jacy alone." Lita's voice was firm.

Flair looked up at Lita, astonishment on his face. "Nice fucking try."

"I'm not saying for good, Flair," Lita argued. "Just until she gets back on her feet, okay?"

Flair shook his head. "What's the fucking worry? Her daughter has 25 years of safety. We can't touch her. Ohhhhh, that's it," Flair closed his eyes and rested his head on the massage table again.

"Her daughter has nothing to do with this."

"Of course she does," Flair snorted. "Everyone knows she's going to ask for her daughter to be in her pod now that she's out of her pity party."

"She's not going to choose her daughter."

"What?" Flair raised his head, causing his ass to push backwards. "Ow! Jesus fucking Christ, Abs. Give me some warning when you do that. And remember the rules, no more than two knuckles."

Abs Tortonis' head popped up from behind Flair's recently invaded ass. "Sorry, Mr. Flair. I wasn't going there, yet. When you flinched, you backed into my oil bottle. My apologies."

"Yes, yes, just be more careful next time. Continue, please." Abs went back to work. Flair closed his eyes in appreciation. "Why isn't she taking her daughter?"

"I don't know," Lita lied.

"Don't bullshit me, Lita."

Lita sighed, looked away to gather her thoughts, then returned her attention to Flair. "Look, she probably doesn't feel ready, yet, okay? She got pretty shaken up with the whole Eugene thing. She just doesn't feel worthy. All's I'm asking is for you to give her a break and let her get her shit together."

Flair said nothing.

"Come on, Flair," Lita urged. "You just said there's nothing you can do to her daughter until she's 25 anyways."

"What's in it for me?"

"How about just doing it because you're such an upstanding guy?"

There was a moment's silence before all three of them shared a chuckle. Flair tossed a glance backwards at Abs.

"Sorry," Abs muttered, returning his full attention to his duties.

"Look, I'm giving Coney Slut a fighting lesson for getting me this appointment. I can give her more and you can tell her you got it for her. Kind of an employee bonus."

"Really? What kind of fighting?"

"Kajukenbo."

"Hmmm," Flair looked thoughtful. "I didn't realize she was getting good enough in her to turn to you."

"I don't know how good she is. I've never seen her fight."

"If she asked you, though, she must be pretty good. She looks up to you, for some stupid fucking reason. Ahh," Flair's body shuddered. He arched his back, closing his eyes. "Wow, that's the spot, Abs. Good work."

"Okay, Mr. Flair, that was a tough one. I'm moving on to the deep fascia massage now."

Flair looked at Lita. "Okay, tell you what. We back off until she gets back on her feet. Then all bets are off."

"Fair enough," Lita nodded.

"And keep me updated on Coney's progress, okay? She's my favourite personal assistant."

"Don't you mean your favourite vagina?" Lita snickered, but Flair didn't.

"No, actually, I didn't mean that at all. I know you think I'm the scuzziest of the scuzz, Lita, but I take care of my people. *Especially* people that are part of my inner circle. There is no crazy sex going on with them. Only idiots bring sex into the work place."

"I'm not here to judge you, Flair. Thanks for agreeing to lay off Jacy, though."

"Yeah, yeah, get out of here before I change my mind. Unless you want to stay and watch the fun part of the massage."

"Maybe I'll take a rain check on that, but thanks," Lita headed towards the door with both Flair and Abs' chortles bouncing around behind her.

19

Jacy let Lita talk her into going to Weaning Fest.

Actually, in all truth, Lita didn't put too much effort into it. Jacy had been knocked down, but she got back up, brushed the dust from her clothes, and moved on. Weaning Fest was the perfect place for her to be on this warm and early evening.

For the last month, Jacy threw herself body first into the Game. Not anything like she had done with Eugene, though. This time, Jacy was going to do it right.

For the retribution owed to her, she chose her cousin's son, Cade, to be in her pod. Cade was a good kid who fell in with some so-called friends who were lousy influences on him. He was 16, and the timing seemed perfect for Jacy to help him re-find his path.

Jacy's choice for her pod stunned almost all. Lita knew her plan, and so did Fatter Verb, but there weren't many others. Lita told Flair a small portion, but that was okay. Nobody needed to know her full plot until she implemented it.

Right now, the ideal and only way to employ that strategy was to become the consummate player she could. No more solitary nights at the table for her and her pod. Jacy talked to and picked the brains of every Hat, Bone, Skull, and free agent she could. She studied and learned and learned and studied.

It didn't take long for everything to come back. She was a good student during her training, and though she may have forgotten some important lessons during her time with Eugene, she was an astute re-learner.

Jacy knew she was on the right track when earlier that day, a lovely Hat named Yenken Inane, approached her.

"I just wanted to thank you, love," she said, kissing Jacy on the cheek.

"What for?" Jacy asked.

"I have Cade's mom in my pod. She'd been pretty worried about Cade, but today she had tea with her friend and remarked how she was sleeping better because she feels Cade has turned a corner. I know you've worked wonders with him. He was always a good boy, but he became sidetracked. You've helped him back. Thank you."

Jacy smiled as she recalled the conversation when she entered her first Weaning Fest. Weaning Fest was a let-your-hair-down type of dance/social occasion.

Weaning Fest had some important rules and traditions. There was to be no talk of the Game. None. No one was allowed to sneak off and sabotage someone else's subject, either. All humans were safe, separate from natural occurrences, during the evening of Weaning Fest.

There was also a tradition at the Weaning Fest called the Forgiveness Dance. Enemies who agreed to partake in the Forgiveness Dance erased all grudges and acts of revenge. Once the Forgiveness Dance was expended, the slate was wiped clean.

"Just giving you the heads up on that, Sugar," Lita told Jacy as they readied themselves for the festivities. "Whether you choose to partake in the Forgiveness Dance is your choice, and I will support you whatever you decide to do. I just want you to think on it before you're all caught up in the moment and do something you regret."

Jacy smiled as she recalled that conversation, too. Lita had been a rock for her, from day one, for sure, but she really rose to the occasion since Eugene died. Jacy looked over at Lita as they walked through the main lobby towards the huge ballroom where Weaning Fest was held. Eyes followed them as they strutted through, and Jacy didn't blame them.

"We look pretty hot tonight, if I do say so myself," Jacy winked.

"Damn straight, Sugar," Lita answered as they approached the front doors, music booming from within.

"It's the Wicked Drools!" Lita whooped as they entered. "They're fucking amazing. And they're doing my favourite Frank Turner song."

Jacy listened to the catchy song, but couldn't place it.

'The bands I like, they don't sell too many records

And the girls I like, they don't kiss too many boys

The books I read will never be bestsellers,

But come on, fellas, at least we made our choice.'

"I don't think I've heard of Frank Turner," Jacy spoke louder so she could be heard.

"I'm not surprised," Lita nodded. "We humans can be freaking dumb when it comes to good music. We eat the force fed pablum from soulless corporations when there is all this fantastic shit being put out."

Lita pointed out a long haired, dread locked guy standing at the sounding board. He was dancing and banging his head to the music.

"That's Piggy Nunook. He turned me onto Frank Turner, and many others, as well. I'll introduce you to him later."

"Sounds good!" Jacy swayed her shoulders with the music as Lita led her to the nearest bar.

"Two margaritas, I presume?" Jacy heard a voice to her right as they bellied up to the bar.

Jacy looked over and felt warm all over. Fatter Verb. She had only spoken to him once since his intervention on her, and that visit was too short for Jacy's liking.

"You are correct, my good man," Jacy laughed.

"Strawberry ones, to be more precise?"

"That is two for two, Mr. Verb," Lita leaned past Jacy and gave him a kiss on the cheek.

"You heard them, Lady Barkeep," Fatter Verb snapped his fingers towards the nearest, hovering bartender. "Two of your finest strawberry margaritas for these two equally, fine ladies."

Fatter Verb took a long sip of whatever it was he was drinking.

"Ahh," he sighed, turning his eyes towards Jacy. "It's nice to see you out and about. I hear good things about you, lately."

"Thanks in large part to you."

Fatter Verb waved her comment away as the bartender placed two margaritas on the bar. Jacy reached for the one nearest her, but Fatter reached out and blocked her hand.

"Not that one," he pushed the one Jacy was reaching for towards Lita. He gripped the other one, and stared into it intently for a moment before passing it to Jacy.

"This one is yours," Fatter Verb's eyes held Jacy's as he picked up his glass. "Cheers to you both."

"Cheers!" Lita and Jacy sang before taking a drink. Jacy stopped when the straw touched her bottom lip. Right there, in beautiful, dazzling blue script, the name 'John Peedpant' was written on the top of her drink.

Jacy stared at the elegant lines and repeated the name 'John Peedpant' silently to herself a few times to see if it rang a bell. It didn't. "What...."

"No shop talk, I'm afraid," Fatter Verb intoned, standing with his drink in hand. "Even with a woman as lovely as you. I see someone who appears to be checking me out. I'm going to go make her acquaintance. Enjoy your evening, ladies."

With that, he was gone.

20

Jacy watched Fatter Verb walk away as Lita stared into Jacy's margarita glass.

"Is everything okay, Jace?"

Jacy watched Fatter approach an older lady who looked delighted to see him. Jacy smiled and shrugged her shoulders. Fatter Verb was right. Weaning Fest was shop talk free. She would figure out who this John Peedpant was later.

"Everything is great," she clinked her glass against Lita's. "Cheers to you, my good friend."

Just then the Wicked Drools blasted into Hank Williams III's 'Crazed Country Rebel.' Jacy grabbed Lita's arm. "Oh my Buddah, this is one of my..."

"...favourite songs," somebody else finished her sentence.

Jacy turned her head to look at Flair. She hadn't spoken with him since the whole thing went down with Eugene, nor was she sure she wanted to. This being the Weaning Fest, though, she would adhere to its traditions.

Lita, on the other hand, didn't exactly share Jacy's charitable outlook.

"Why don't you make like a leaf, and fuck off, Flair."

Flair smirked. "I'm glad to see you are being as charming as ever tonight, Lita," Flair nodded at the bartender who handed him a scotch on the rocks promptly.

"I requested the song as soon as you walked in the door," Flair looked at Jacy. "I hoped it would make you smile. You look very pretty tonight, Jacy."

He glanced over at Lita. "You, not so much."

Lita chuckled.

"Were you hoping I'd dance a Forgiveness Dance with you, Flair?" Jacy asked.

Flair took a slow pull of his scotch and watched the band for a moment. He then swivelled his head in her direction, looking over his left shoulder at her.

"I don't know, actually. Maybe, but maybe not," he smiled. "I would like to have some fun with you, though."

"Keep it in your pants, Flair, you…." Lita blurted.

Flair didn't take his eyes from Jacy. "Not sex, Jacy. A duet."

Lita snorted. Jacy looked confused. "A duet?" Both Lita and Jacy spoke at the same time, causing them to laugh.

"Yes, a duet," Flair drained the last of his scotch. "I will leave it up to you to define what this duet is, whether it's in the spirit of forgiveness or not. I'd just like to sing with you."

Jacy and Lita stared at one another. Lita gave an almost imperceptible shrug of her right shoulder as if to say, 'This is your call.' Jacy cracked a half smile at Flair.

"Alright. What's the song?"

"It's a surprise," Flair did that same weird hand movement he'd used before with her and they disappeared. Now they were on the right side of the stage, just behind the curtain as Wicked Drools sang the last chorus of their song.

"Shit," Flair slapped his forehead. "We need some stage clothes."

Flair did another weird hand movement and he was instantly clad in new stage clothes; a silver blazer over a tight black t-shirt. A nice, gold chain hung from his neck.

"Wow, not bad, actually," Jacy nodded.

"And now you." Flair did another hand movement and Jacy was now clad in a black corset, black fishnet, ass-less stockings, and stiletto heels. Jacy looked down at herself with wide eyes.

"Are you crazy, Fl...."

"Okay, okay, keep your dick in your panties," Flair studied her for a moment, as Jacy attempted to cover herself up.

"Flair, I will…"

Flair waved her off. "Did you like Joan Jett?"

"Everybody liked Joan Jett, Flair. If you don't change me…"

Flair did another hand movement. Jacy now wore red leather pants and jacket, black tank top, and black studded belt. Jacy took a survey of herself, then looked for a mirror.

"There," Flair pointed to one against the wall. Jacy headed over to it to check out her new duds. Standing in front of the mirror, she admitted she liked what she saw.

"You look hot," Flair said as the song wound down. "Come on."

Jacy scooted over to Flair and he took her hand, leading her out on stage. The crowd cheered when they saw Flair and Jacy appear. Flair stopped to talk to the singer/guitarist of Wicked Drools. He nodded and signalled something to the band.

Flair returned to Jacy's side with two microphones. He handed her one. "You ready?"

"I don't even know what song we're doing," she hissed.

"Don't worry," he laughed. "You'll love it."

Just then a screeching guitar note was struck and hung there. Jacy recognized it immediately, as another of what she called her

Deserted Island songs back on Earth. Jacy always had a playlist of songs that she would need to have if she were ever to be stranded on a deserted island. 'Girly' by Roger Clyne and the Peacemakers was one of them.

The crowd roared its approval as Flair stalked the front of the stage, pumping his fist in the air. Not to be outdone, Jacy went to the left side of the stage and did the same, causing a louder roar. Flair laughed as he strutted towards her, putting the microphone to his lips.

'I'm going to the hardware store,

Going to buy you a really big hammer

Girly won't you pull these nails from my heart.'

The men in the crowd whooped wildly. Jacy spun on her heel and prowled towards him, singing the next line of the song.

'Well, I'm going to the sporting goods store

Going to buy you a really heavy baseball bat

Boy, won't you knock these thoughts out of my head'

The females in the crowd cheered louder when Jacy sang her lines. By now she and Flair were practically nose to nose at the center of the front of the stage. They started to sing together.

'Beat me 'til I'm black and blue and I'm

Hangin' by a thread

Then I can get back up and we can

Do it all over again.'

The crowd gave its frenzied approval as the guitarist stepped between them to do his descending guitar riff.

Flair moved towards the left side of the stage and Jacy to the right. She spied Lita in the crowd who raised her arm and whooped. Jacy laughed, and began to high five people congregated near the stage.

Jacy let the music and lyrics guide her feet and actions. While earlier she may have struggled looking Flair in the eye, she now stared him down, belting out her lines. The buzz in the crowd intensified until it could almost be declared as a roar.

As for Jacy, she felt the anger and hostility she had for Flair drip off her like melting ice. Jacy sang, danced, and smiled. Oh, how she smiled. For the first time since coming to this place, she felt good.

21

"Remember when we were full of piss and vinegar like that, Fatter?" Duna Lunar, a sprite of a woman laughed in his ear, watching Flair and Jacy's performance.

"Oh, Duna, you can't fool me. I *know* you're still full of that p and v."

"And don't you forget it," she playfully swatted Fatter's shoulder. "I may be older, but I've still got the goods."

Fatter Verb chuckled as the song came to an end. He clapped long and loud.

"Bravo," he said. "I had no idea Jacy could sing like that. She's pretty good, isn't she?"

Duna Lunar applauded, too. "As a singer, yes. What are your thoughts of her as a player, though?"

Fatter stopped clapping and looked at Duna. "Jacy is going to be just fine. Nobody needs to worry about her."

Duna Lunar eyed Fatter for a moment before nodding and changing the subject. "Where's Granny Mandible? I was told she was attending this evening's festivities."

Fatter Verb filled Duna's wine glass from a half filled carafe. "Granny's feeling under the weather. She said if she were feeling better later, then she would come."

If Duna didn't believe Fatter, she gave no sign of it. She nodded her thanks for the refill and took a small swallow before smiling. "We sure had fun together when we were young, didn't we, Fatter?"

Fatter nodded in agreement, though he wasn't entirely positive what times Duna was referring to. There were entertaining times during the Game, to be sure, but there were also some pretty fun times outside of the Game, as well.

"Do you recall the time when one of Granny's favourite subjects got into that melee in Mexico?"

"In Irapuato, of all places. Of course, I remember."

Both shared a laugh and momentary silence, as both recalled the scene where Fatter had to call in many favours to assist Granny Mandible. Duna Lunar did her part, too, but Fatter paid the biggest price, having to agree to marry one of his subjects to a Skulls'. He got over that, but it still carried a pang of regret for him.

"Let's you and I go have our own fun tonight," Duna put her hand on Fatter's knee, slowly moving it up towards his groin.

"What about your escort?" Fatter nodded towards Unitary Sam, the young, muscular, good looking guy to her left.

"Do you want him to come watch?" Luna's eyes sparkled.

"Uhhhh, no, no I don't."

"Okay, fine," after a brief look of disappointment Duna looked at Unitary Sam. "Sam, off you go. I will see you tomorrow."

If Unitary Sam was happy or sad about being dismissed, he showed neither. He bid his tablemates a good evening and disappeared into the crowd, leaving a leering Luna and a smiling Fatter to themselves. Duna's hand found Fatter's crotch and squeezed.

"Oh my, some things never change," Duna took another drink of wine, before looking deep into Fatter's eyes. "Is my vagina crying, or are you just incredibly sexy?"

Fatter Verb laughed.

"Before we get to that, though" Duna smiled, taking a sip of her wine, "I'd like to have a talk with you."

"About?"

"About whatever it is that Granny Mandible is conspiring to do."

"Umm, it's the...."

"...Weaning Fest, I know," Duna looked into Fatter's eyes. "I just need you to pass on a message to Granny Mandible for me, that's all."

Fatter Verb made a non-committal sound which Duna Lunar took as a yes. She leaned across the table and whispered in his ear for at least a minute. Fatter sipped his drink, listened to Duna, and nodded to her at the end.

"I will pass that on," he set his empty glass down on the table.

"Promise?"

"Scout's honour," he held one hand up.

"Then let me thank you for that," Duna smirked before sliding under the table. Fatter Verb smiled as he felt Duna unbutton his pants and take him into her warm mouth. All of a sudden he was *very* glad he came to the Weaning Fest tonight.

22

Lita and Jacy piled out onto the outdoor patio, closing the French doors to the loud strains of Jeremy Loops' 'I Wrote This Song For You.'

"Whoooo!" Lita whooped, leading Jacy towards the outdoor bar.

"Let's check out the fountain from here," Jacy led Lita to the deck's outer railing. Sure enough, the glowing fountain was visible from here. They both admired it before Lita threw and arm around Jacy's shoulder and gave her a kiss on the cheek.

"I love you, Jacy."

Jacy looked at Lita and smiled. "I love you, too, hon. I really need to thank you, too."

"Bah," Lita swiped her hand through the air. "I didn't do much. You would've come out of your stupor sooner or later."

"I'm not just thanking you for that," Jacy said. "I'm thanking you for everything."

Lita's smile dazzled in the moonlight. "And thank you for everything you do for me."

Jacy leaned out over the railing, breathing in the warm evening air. "I miss Beau and Derian," she whispered into the darkness.

Lita put her arms around Jacy from behind and hugged her tight. "I know you do, Sugar."

They stood like that for a while. Lita broke the silence. "Can I ask you a really personal question?"

Jacy disengaged herself from Lita's arms and turned to look at her. "Of course, you can."

Lita looked momentarily uneasy, before breaking out into a huge grin. "Want another margarita?"

Jacy burst out laughing. "Another margarita," she agreed.

Lita slapped Jacy on the ass, and they headed off towards one of the two outdoor bars. They made it halfway before a voice from behind stopped them.

"Jacy?"

Jacy turned around and almost didn't recognize him at first. With his slicked back hair, clean shaven face, and dashing suit, it took her a moment to recognize the person standing before her.

"Bam?"

The Bam Slicer looked uncomfortable, though whether that was from being dressed up or from being in Jacy's presence, she didn't know.

"You...you look...you look very nice tonight," he said with all the confidence of a thirteen-year-old boy on his first date.

"Jesus fucking Christ, you guys just keep crawling out from the woodwork," Lita complained, before looking at Jacy. "I'll go grab our drinks. You okay with Mr. GQ here?"

Jacy nodded, turning back to The Bam Slicer.

"Thank you for your kind words, Bam. You look nice, too," Jacy answered, her emotions bouncing clumsily. On one hand, she really didn't like The Bam Slicer. He was scary, mean, rude…She could go on and on. On the other hand, he was a tough yet fair trainer. While Jacy doubted she'd ever be bosom buddies with the guy, she had no reason to hate him, either.

"Nice night, huh?" he nodded towards the darkness.

Jacy couldn't contain herself anymore so she did what she normally did when in uncomfortable situations. She giggled.

"It's nice to hear you laugh," he spoke softly, his eyes devoid of the usual rage and violence that normally resided in them.

"For real?" Jacy raised her eyebrows. Bam let out a rare chuckle.

"For real."

Someone propped open the doors, and the opening strains of U2's 'Sometimes You Can't Make it On Your Own' filtered onto the deck. Both Jacy and The Bam Slicer looked towards the band. Bam looked back at Jacy.

"Would you dance with me, Jacy?" he almost whispered his invitation.

Jacy raised her eyebrows at him. "Are you asking me for a Forgiveness Dance, Bam?"

"I'm asking for any kind of dance you'll give me."

"Oh, Bam, you are so sweet and tender it's bringing tears to my eyes. Why are you being such a fucking wuss?" Jacy hadn't noticed Lita return with their drinks.

"Lita," Jacy whispered, grabbing her drink from her.

The Bam Slicer's eyes returned to their hardened state at the sight of Lita. Lita didn't look away, though, meeting his eyes with a stony glare of her own.

"It's okay," Jacy whispered to Lita, handing her drink back to her. "I'll be back in a minute."

Jacy held her arm out to The Bam Slicer and he took it. He didn't lead her to the dance floor, though. He stopped in the middle of the deck and turned to her.

"Would it be alright if we danced under the stars?"

Jacy nodded, and they began to waltz to the words of Bono's love for his father. The Bam Slicer's dancing astonished Jacy. She considered herself a pretty good dancer, but Bam was graceful and smooth, much more adept than Jacy would've given him credit for.

After a dance that Jacy enjoyed more than she would ever admit, The Bam Slicer led her back to a waiting Lita. As they walked, Jacy leaned in closer to Bam's ear.

"As far as I'm concerned, that was a Forgiveness Dance, Bam," she whispered.

He stopped, relief flooding his features. He squeezed her hand. "Thanks, Jacy. I mean that."

They returned to Lita who looked as if she were attempting to extract something from her front pocket. "Oh Bam, I almost forgot. I've got something for you."

The Bam Slicer watched as she pulled her hand from her imaginary front pocket and held her hand up, the middle finger raised. "Oh, here it is."

Bam's eyes hardened, but he held his tongue.

"Always the lady, aren't you, Lita?" was all he said before returning his attention to Jacy. He took both her hands into his. "Thanks for the dance, Jacy. I enjoyed it more than you'll ever know." Before Jacy could say anything in return, he walked away.

"I'm sure you did, you pervert," Lita shot at his departing back, but The Bam Slicer paid her no heed.

Lita handed Jacy's margarita back to her. "Are you finished with all this business? I could just set up a Skulls bukkake if that's what you're into."

Jacy swatted Lita's shoulder. It was time to carry on, to move to the next chapter of wherever this adventure was taking her. Lita and Jacy clanked their glasses together and danced long into the night.

PART IV

RETRIBUTION

Forget the past—the future will give you plenty to worry about.
—George Allen Sr.

1

It didn't take much sleuthing to discover where John Peedpant was. Jacy investigated the day after Weaning Fest, and once she found some spare time, she sought him out.

Still unsure why Fatter Verb wrote his name in her drink last week, Jacy watched the non-descript John Peedpant enjoy a mellow round of his game. There were five others at the table with him. Just by watching for a few minutes, Jacy knew that John Peedpant was a Bone, through and through. He never seemed to get too excited or too down. He played the Game at a nice, even pace.

John Peedpant seemed to be quite the solid player. Two Skulls, after a couple attempts to cause some shit, quickly moved on. The other two at the table were obviously Bones, as all shared an amiable chuckle and chat once the Skulls departed. Jacy took a deep breath and approached the table.

"Mr. Peedpant?" Jacy asked, as John looked up to the newcomer.

"Sorry, no Mr. Peedpant here," it was tough to decipher his thick Scottish accent.

"Oh, I'm sorry," Jacy pondered her mistake. "I was told John Peedpant played here. My apologies for disturbing you."

Jacy started to leave the table, confused with her erroneous information.

"Well, why didn't ye say so," the Scottish brogue cut into her thoughts. "There is a John Peedpant here, just not a *Mister* Peedpant, that's all."

The others at the table laughed. Jacy stopped and smiled. John Peedpant stood and offered his hand to her. "And he'd be proud to meet the lovely Jacy."

Jacy frowned. "Did Fatter Verb tell you I was coming?"

"Fatter Verb? Hell, no. I haven't talked to that bastard in years," he offered Jacy a seat next to his.

"How do you know who I am, then?" Jacy sat.

"Do ye hear the lass?" John Peedpant chortled with his fellow Gamers before returning his attention to Jacy. "You're pretty famous, my dear."

It was Jacy's turn to chuckle. "Yeah, a famous failure."

"Ahhhh," John Peedpant patted her hand. "Don't be dwelling on Eugene, my love. Shit, you shoulda seen what I did with me first. Poor bugger didn't make it to his 22nd birthday."

"What was his name?" Jacy asked. The question replaced John's look of joviality with one of sadness and regret.

"Eino Sinisalo," he sighed. "He was a good Finnish boy who I couldn't save from a couple of bastard Soviet soldiers."

John Peedpant looked at Jacy. "So you see, my lovely Jacy. You are not the only one nursing a broken heart over their first. Christ, I moved to a different country and still couldn't outrun my guilt."

"Where did you go?"

"Brazil. Can't ye tell by my accent?" John Peedpant laughed at his own joke. "Naw, I went to Austria, where I had me a pretty good run. Even had a doctor in me pod at one point."

Jacy warmed to John Peedpant. She was still unaware why Fatter Verb pointed her in his direction, but she liked him all the same. "You and your pod are in North America, though."

John looked down at the table. "Aye, I've got the restless blood, I suspect. I get the itch every once in a while, and am beginning to feel the starting of another one. Which is why, I expect, Fatter Verb sent you to me."

Jacy furrowed her eyebrows. "I'm not sure I follow you."

John Peedpant smiled a wonderful smile. "Ye really don't know, do ye, Lassy?"

Jacy shook her head. John looked at her for a long moment before beckoning her closer with a cock of his head. "Come here, my lovely Jacy. I expect Mr. Verb wanted you to meet a couple of people in my pod."

Jacy's pulse scrambled.

"Would ye like to be meeting a certain Beau and Derian Morgan, my love?"

2

Jacy felt all the air suck from her lungs. Then it felt like she was smacked on the side of the head by a 2X4. Following that was a feeling reminiscent of being struck by a runaway bus.

"Oh my," John Peedpant clutched Jacy's arm. "I threw ye for a bit of a loop. Are ye okay?"

Jacy shook her head, not in reply to his question, but more to try and get her brain working. Or maybe she needed it to slow down. Hell, maybe…

"I'm sorry for spooking you so, Jacy," John's words cut through her addled brain. "I expect I could've done this with a bit more diplomacy."

"No, no," Jacy leaned back in her chair and sighed. "You've done nothing wrong. Like you said, it just threw me for a loop, that's all."

John Peedpant noticed his fellow Gamers staring at Jacy. "Ye mind? Christ Almighty."

The two Gamers stood, giving Jacy a profuse apology before leaving the table.

"I'll meet ye for an ale afterwards," he called to their retreating backs before restoring his concentration on Jacy. He studied her for a moment.

"So, Lassy," he patted her hand. "Where would ye like to go from here?"

Jacy studied John, afraid to speak as the hundreds, thousands, millions of questions that may escape would drown the poor man. Where was she to go from here? Was knowing Derian and Beau were safe and alive enough for her? Would her brain and heart be able to handle anything more than that? What about…

John Peedpant patted her hand again. "Would ye like to hear a little about them? They're very good people."

"Are they?!" Jacy's eyes squirted out tears as she blurted out her query. "Are they good people?"

"*Very* good people," John nodded. "Want me to bring ye up to speed on what transpired since ye traded that crazy place down there for this daft place?"

Jacy took a deep breath and wiped her sweaty palms on her jeans. She flattened her feet to the floor, and pressed her hands hard to her knees. She exhaled, long, slow, and easy.

"That's probably a great place to start," she whispered.

"Okay," John Peedpant sat back in his chair, draping his left leg over his right one. "I take it you know that you three were in Gravigo's pod."

Jacy nodded.

"Well, about that same time that you came to join us, I was in the process of moving from Austria to Canada. I told ye about my restless blood, right?"

Jacy nodded again.

"Good. See, Gravigo needed extra time to spend with you, and he wanted to know Derian and Beau would be well taken care of. He needed someone he truly trusted."

"And he picked you," Jacy broke in, causing John Peedpant to guffaw and roll his eyes.

"Lassy, Gravigo hardly knows who I am," he slapped the table with an open hand. "He gave them to Maise Elantina."

"Maise Elantina had Derian and Beau in her pod? She never…."

John Peedpant held his hands up. "No, no, she never had them in her pod. Gravigo gave them to her and she gave them to me."

"Why you?" Jacy frowned.

"Well," John leaned back and brushed his chest with an exaggerated air. "You might not think it to look at me, but I'm pretty highly regarded by most of the Bones' higher ups. Maise Elantina in particular likes me, so she figured me perfect with my upcoming move to the Great White North. Then voila, ye and I are sitting here having this conversation."

"Okay," Jacy's brain decelerated from its frenzy.

"Not to brag too much, but I've done a fairly good job here. Of course, the 25-year safety net I had made me job a mite simpler, as I didn't have to deal much with Flair and his ilk. Beau and Derian, though, minus a couple bumps and bruises along the way, have done very well."

Jacy attempted an easy breathing pattern to calm herself. "How old are they right now?" Jacy closed her eyes.

"Derian graduated this week from high school, which makes her 18. That'd make Beau…"

"51," Jacy did the math for him.

"Aye, that'd be about right. Derian gave a beautiful speech for him at his 50th birthday party last year."

Jacy leaned forward, her breasts against the table, her face a few inches from the surface. She wondered if her lap would catch her galloping heart if it somehow managed to beat its way out of her chest. Graduated from high school? Her baby had lived 18 years and Jacy had missed every single one of them?

John Peedpant reached out and rubbed the back of Jacy's neck. "It's okay, Jacy. They've both done very well, considering how much your death hurt them. Beau's been a hell of a dad, and Derian, well, she's bloody amazing. She's enrolled in university for the upcoming semester and…"

Jacy's head snapped up. "Derian's going to university?"

"Aye, she is."

Jacy sighed in relief. Unknown to her conscious thought, she'd been concerned Derian may have gone off the rails a bit not having a mom in her life. She had faith in Beau that he'd be an incredible parent, but two parents were optimum. Jacy looked at John Peedpant and smiled. "John, please, if it wouldn't be too much for you, I would like to know everything I can about them."

John Peedpant smiled at her, taking both her hands into his. "It's almost breakfast time. How'd ye like to meet them?"

3

"I'm proud of you, Derrry. You did the right thing last night," Beau said to his daughter as she pushed a fork full of French toast into her mouth.

Jacy sat in stunned silence as she watched her husband and daughter talk over breakfast. John Peedpant reached over and gave Jacy's knee a squeeze. "Ye okay, Jacy?"

Jacy nodded or gulped or breathed or farted. She didn't have a clue what she did at that exact moment. She could tell you, though, every single thing about her baby girl. How when Derian smiled she looked like Jacy. How when she spoke she looked like Beau. The barely visible cleft in her chin came from a grandfather on Beau's side. Jacy tried to hold back her tears, but the attempt was futile.

"She's great, isn't she?" John Peedpant remarked.

"She's spectacular," Jacy sniffled.

Jacy looked at her husband. He aged, of course, but looked more handsome than ever. He had salt and pepper hair, with more pepper than salt. A few extra lines on his face, and Jacy was pretty sure his 6 pack abs were a thing of the past. She didn't care, though. Both her husband and daughter were here in living colour, right before her eyes. Jacy marveled, and continued to cry.

"What's Beau proud of?" Jacy wiped at the tears on her cheeks as she recalled his earlier statement.

"Yer daughter used that pretty little head of hers last night. She was at a party with some of her friends. There was a wee bit of drinking involved…"

"Drinking? My baby was drinking?!" Jacy looked at John, aghast.

"Actually, Lassy, she's not much of a baby anymore. She's 18 years old."

Jacy rubbed her eyes and temples with her fingers, nodding. John Peedpant had a point. The legal drinking age in Canada is 19, and well, if Jacy were to recall the number of drinks she had in her teenage years…

"Okay, sorry. Point taken."

"Nothing to be sorry for, Jacy. I imagine this is a lot to take in," John patted her knee. "Anyways, some of her friends hopped into a car with a boy who was drunk. Derian here didn't. She called her papa for a ride, just like he taught her to do."

John Peedpant looked down upon them with genuine fondness. "They're really good people, Jacy. I'm extremely proud of them."

Jacy nodded, her admiration for her family doubling with every second she watched them and each anecdote she heard. Her daughter Derian. Her husband Beau. They were both so….

Jacy's concentration wavered when a good looking seven or eight-year-old boy entered the kitchen. He teased Derian about something. Derian laughed.

"Who's that?" Jacy asked.

John Peedpant looked like a deer caught in the headlights. "Aye, I probably shoulda said something about him."

Just then a pretty red headed lady waltzed in. Jacy looked at John again. "And I probably shoulda said something about her, as well."

Jacy didn't comprehend what was going on here. She felt like she should be grasping it, but it wasn't registering. John Peedpant let out a heavy sigh.

"Jacy, that's your husband's wife and son."

4

"Beers in the afternoon?" Lita asked as she approached the bar table in a quaint, rustic pub. "I'm not complaining, but this is not normally your scene, Jacy. What's up?"

"Thanks for coming, Lita," John Peedpant said, signalling beer for Lita.

"No worries, John, thanks for calling."

Jacy looked at them both. "You two know each other?"

"Of course," Lita nodded. "I had no idea he had Beau and Derian in his pod, though."

John Peedpant shrugged at Lita's withering glare. "Maise Elantina swore me to secrecy until the time was right. When Jacy showed up at my table looking for me, I figured that was a pretty good sign that the timing was now."

Lita nodded, though it was clear she wasn't happy. Her look softened when she looked at Jacy. "How did it go, Sugar? How are they?"

Jacy sighed, waiting as the waitress deposited a mug of beer on the table and left. Only leaving out Fatter Verb's part in it, Jacy told Lita everything, right up to the breakfast she witnessed this morning.

"His wife and son?" Lita raised her eyebrows.

Jacy shot her a sharp look. "Don't laugh, Lita, don't you dare…."

Jacy's warning came too late, though, as Lita fell into a snicker fit. Jacy sat there watching her for a moment before breaking into giggles, too. John Peedpant, figuring it was safe, began to laugh, as well. Once the laughter subsided, John Peedpant filled them in on how it happened.

"Beau went eight years without even looking at another woman. He was that focussed on Derian. One day, though, out of the blue, he realized he enjoyed talking to Derian's softball coach. She asked him out for coffee one day, six months later they were an item, and two years after that Derian had a half-brother."

"Eight years?" A surprised Lita looked at Jacy. "He sure must've loved you. Most guys I knew back on Earth would've been trying to bang my pall bearers."

"Beau did love Jacy," John agreed, "and he still does. His new wife knows it, but since Jacy isn't returning to Earth any time soon, she's okay with it."

"How's Derian?" Lita asked.

Jacy took a long swig of her beer and started talking. She didn't stop until three hours later.

5

Jacy walked the paths that she and Lita traversed on a weekly basis. Today, though, Jacy walked solo as Lita wasn't comfortable in leaving Serena too long from her sight. Jacy didn't pry too much, but she sensed Serena was having some issues again.

"She's such a good person, Jacy," Lita told her the previous night. "Those stupid drugs fuck her brain up so much, though."

Jacy felt bad for her friend. Lita's pod had grown to fourteen, and her other thirteen were doing awesome. Serena, though, held a special place in Lita's heart, and Jacy knew it killed Lita when Serena went off the rails. Jacy sighed, pushing them from her mind. She would be there whenever Lita needed her. Right now Jacy had enough on her mind.

Number one on her mind was Derian. John Peedpant would be ready to move by the time her daughter turned 19. Jacy had a lot to do before then.

Ambling down the familiar dirt path, Jacy came to a fork in the trail. Normally her and Lita took the left path as they preferred the fauna on display on that path. Today, though, Jacy took the other path for a change in scenery.

There was no doubt Jacy would take Derian into her pod. John Peedpant offered Beau, his wife, and son to her, too, but Jacy passed. She loved Beau, but it was time to let that part go. It wouldn't be fair to Beau and his new family.

Jacy needed to set some things in motion before Derian could be in her pod, though. Number one, Jacy needed to choose a group. She evaded the decision long enough, and it was now time to make that choice. Jacy knew Derian would still have another six years of safety left to her, but Jacy wanted the security of being in a group.

Second, Jacy needed to hone her skills even more. She was doing awesome with Cade, so well that she recently was given Maggie, a housewife in Langford, B.C. Both were doing great, but Jacy wanted more than that for Derian. Jacy wanted to be at the top of her game, or even better than that.

Just as Jacy rounded a bend in the path, movement caught her eye. Something large was stirring the brush. Jacy furrowed her eyebrows. Why was Neva Tezremsy skulking through the thicket?

Shaking her head, Jacy carried on down the path for a half minute or so before she halted. Curiosity got the best of her. After a furtive scan to see if anyone was around, Jacy waded into the undergrowth, moving in a diagonal line back towards the direction she saw Neva heading in. Jacy moved through the scrub, thankful it was soft underfoot. There was no rustling of leaves or breaking of twigs to worry about.

Jacy stifled a chuckle, looking forward to telling Lita about her stealth-like tracking of the Glamazon. She eased herself between two drooping cedar branches before coming to a standstill when she noticed Neva standing tall in a clearing.

"Well, hello there," that incredibly feminine voice of hers reached Jacy's ears. "Nice to see you could make it on time."

Jacy frowned, unsure who she was meeting so discreetly. Her eyebrows raised in disbelief when the other figure stepped into view.

"I wouldn't miss a date with you for anything, baby, you know that," a naked Flair spoke. Neva put her hands on Flair's chest and bent her down to kiss him deep. Jacy's eyes widened again when she saw what was swinging between Flair's legs. Flair's penis was gigantic.

"Did you miss this, sweetheart?" Flair started rubbing it against her leg. Neva looked down and smiled.

"How about we put Big Bob away this time?"

Jacy's brain wasn't connecting all the dots. This time? Big Bob? What the…?

Flair looked up at Neva. "Really? I thought you loved Big Bob."

Neva kissed Flair again. "I do, baby," she reached around and cupped Flair's ass cheeks. "I just want something normal today, instead."

Shrugging, Flair stepped back and did one of those hand movements by his groin and Big Bob disappeared, replaced by a much more average sized phallus. Neva and Flair both looked down at it as Neva took it in her hand and stroked it.

"Better, much better," Neva smiled as she manoeuvred Flair down onto his back. "Remember, it's not always the size of the pen…."

"…it's how you sign the cheque," Flair finished for her.

Neva stripped off her shirt, exposing her 80-inch quadruple W's as she straddled Flair.

"And you, my sexy beast, definitely know how to sign mine." Neva slid down onto Flair.

"Ohhhhhhh," both moaned in unison, and Jacy, confused as can be, backed away as quiet as she could.

"How's the bird watching going?" a voice startled her.

She looked to the right of her and saw The Bam Slicer. "I…uh…I…."

"Or maybe you were picking salal?" Bam chuckled. "Studying the integrity of the cedar boughs?"

He moved closer to Jacy. Jacy stepped away.

"I think you should come with me," The Bam Slicer snarled, and reached for Jacy's arm.

6

Jacy yanked her arm out of The Bam Slicer's grasp. She backed away, not taking her eyes from him.

"No, I don't want to come with you," Jacy said, trying to keep her voice steady. "No offense, of course."

"Maybe you misunderstood me," he took a menacing step closer to her. "When I said…"

Jacy didn't let him finish as she spun and dashed into the bush. Not caring whether she made any noise or not this time, she made it back to the main path quickly.

"Jacy?" A voice from the path made her jump.

"Maise?" Jacy answered and let out a relieved breath at the same time. "Hi, how are you?"

Maise Elantina looked into the dense woods Jacy popped out of. "I'm fine," Maise looked at Jacy, her eyes full of concern. "The question is, how are you?"

"Oh, I'm fine," Jacy said, earning her a what-a-load-of-bullshit look from Maise. Jacy sighed.

"I…" Jacy sighed again. "I was running away from The Bam Slicer because he caught me watching Flair and Neva fucking."

Maise Elantina burst into her infectious laugh. "Was he sporting Big Bob?"

"For a bit, but I don't think Neva wanted it."

"Really?" Maise snorted. "That's surprising. Neva usually wants everything."

"Well, she still wanted to fuck Flair, she just wanted something smaller."

"Yes, I can empathize with a sister on that one," Maise said.

Jacy recalled that Flair and Maise were an item once. "Why were they together, Maise? Aren't they enemies?"

Maise Elantina led Jacy to a bench not far from where they were standing. "Yes, the Skulls and Hats are enemies, but that doesn't mean every single Skull hates every single Hat."

Jacy nodded, though she didn't fully understand that. Maise went on. "As far as the sex goes, that's Flair's 'research', as he calls it. Flair has been wrestling with the mystery of sex since day one here. He grasps your human desires for wealth, success, and power. He doesn't understand how people who have those will risk it all for a blowjob from a stranger. Do you get what I'm saying?"

Jacy nodded. "Flair's not alone in that one. I had a girlfriend in a loving marriage with great kids divorce because of infidelity. It tore their family apart."

Maise Elantina nodded. "It doesn't make sense to us here, either. Flair, though, is adamant he will solve the mystery of it. He thinks if he experiences every kind of sex imaginable, he will have a better understanding of how it all works. On the other hand, Flair loves everything about women. *Especially* fucking them. He likes that most of all."

Maise looked up and saw a swift walking figure coming up the path. "Well, look who we have here. Care to bully the two of us, Bam?"

Jacy whipped her head around, moving closer to Maise. The Bam Slicer saw this and ceased his stride.

"No bullying," Bam wore a chagrined look as he regarded Jacy. "I apologize for scaring you. I was only going to try and explain what you were seeing."

Jacy rolled her eyes. "What I was seeing was pretty self-explanatory."

Bam grunted. "I didn't mean it that way. I meant the 'why' it was happening."

Maise raised her eyebrows. "Why don't you enlighten us both, then?"

The Bam Slicer stared at Maise Elantina for a moment, a curious look inside his hardened eyes. Jacy had a tough time getting a read on how Bam felt about Maise. The Bam Slicer wasn't cowed by anything or anybody, but Jacy sensed he wasn't unafraid of Maise, either.

"See, Flair has this research project that…"

Maise looked at Jacy and they both burst into laughter. Bam watched the two of them in silence.

"Still toeing the party line, eh, Bam?" Maise smiled.

The Bam Slicer shrugged and looked at Jacy. "Whatever. Sorry for scaring you. That wasn't my intention."

"Apology accepted," Jacy said, though she wasn't entirely positive Bam was telling the truth.

"And now that that has been cleared up," Maise and Jacy stood, linking arms together, "Jacy will keep me company on the rest of my stroll."

The Bam Slicer nodded, heading back down the way he came.

"Thanks," Jacy said, after Bam departed.

Maise waved her words of gratitude away.

"Anyways," Jacy went on, "this turned out to be good timing. There's something I was going to come see you about. Can we discuss it now?"

"Of course," Maise Elantina said, and they walked down the path together.

7

Rainy Dissolve entered Maise Elantina's office, just as Jacy, in high spirits, left. Maise seemed happy, too.

"Rainy," Maise greeted her as she closed the door. "I have some good news for us."

Rainy Dissolve sat at her regular chair across the sophisticated desk of Maise Elantina's. As usual, she didn't speak.

"Jacy Morgan has agreed to become a Bone."

Rainy nodded once, a little surprised by Jacy's choice. The council heard about Jacy's meeting with John Peedpant. Rainy did some digging of her own and discovered Jacy's husband and daughter were in his pod. Still, Rainy Dissolve thought Jacy would choose the Hats, but apparently that wasn't the case.

"In time she is going to take her daughter into her pod," Maise Elantina went on. "She is also being offered her husband, and his new wife and son, too."

Rainy looked up sharply at Maise. Maise chuckled. "Jacy's more or less okay with it. It's been nearly 18 Earth years since Jacy died."

Rainy nodded. Maise carried on. "While she is okay with it, she isn't too comfortable having them in her pod, so I have a question for you."

Rainy raised her eyebrows.

"Would you like the three of them in your pod?" Maise asked.

Rainy Dissolve felt the tug of a smile on her face. She would love to add them to her pod.

"I know you were troubled with the loss of three of your pod in that landslide disaster last year. These three are not a replacement of course, but I thought you may be interested in a nice family. They're good people, and Jacy will only allow them to go to someone whom she and I trust."

Maise smiled at Rainy Dissolve. "When I mentioned your name as a possible destination, she was ecstatic. Will you accept?"

Rainy bobbed her head. Maise chuckled.

"Oh, Rainy, how I dream of the day when you speak aloud. You will have so much to say," Maise Elantina grabbed some paperwork on her desk. "You will get them in eight or nine Earth months, maybe even a year. Make your needed preparations."

Maise looked at Rainy Dissolve. "Thank you, Rainy. That will be all."

Rainy Dissolve left the room, happier than she'd been in a long time.

8

Jacy eyed the three people blocking the path. Jacy asked Maise Elantina for a few days to tell certain people face to face about her decision before it was announced. Lita hadn't returned to their room the night before, so Jacy sought Lita to tell her the news.

As she got closer to the trio on the path, Jacy studied the female and two males. She couldn't quite place which group these three belonged to, and that surprised her. She'd become quite adept at that. Jacy slowed.

"It's okay, Jacy," the young man on the left smiled. "We come in peace."

Jacy learned not to take much at face value around this place. She paused, pretending to attempt to recall them, but she secretly searched out any exit points.

"Do you recognize us?" the female in the middle inquired.

Jacy moved closer to them, looking at their faces. There was something familiar about them. The two males were in their late twenties, and very good looking. The female in the middle was of similar age and she was breath taking in her natural beauty. She held both of the males' hands. Jacy narrowed her eyes. Could it be…

"Lucy?" she asked.

Lucy's face split into a massive grin. Jacy's look of surprise grew when she looked at the male on Lucy's right. "Joey?"

Joey smiled and winked at her. Jacy moved on to the man on Lucy's left. "Dickie?"

"Deck the Halls," Dickie sang.

"Jingle Bells," Joey answered.

"Jacy Morgan's tit pit smells," Lucy finished and all four of them broke out laughing. Jacy didn't know what to say when the merriment died down. "What…how…uh…"

"What you see is because of you," Lucy smiled. "We're all grown up again and wanted to thank you."

"Thank me? For what?"

Lucy kissed both Joey and Dickie on the lips before releasing their hands and walking to Jacy. "Do you remember the first time we met at Granny Mandible's house?"

"Was this before or after you three told me my vagina stunk?" Jacy smirked.

Joey winced. "Sorry about that. For what it's worth, I bet your vagina smells like daffodils."

"And petunias," Dickie added.

Jacy stifled a guffaw as she noticed the earnest look on the boys' faces. They were truly apologetic. She bit her lip and looked at Lucy.

"Yes, I do remember," Jacy marveled at the difference between this raven haired beauty and the spiteful little shit she first met. Lucy took hold of one of Jacy's hands.

"Some of your words got me thinking, and when I repeated them to Joey and Dickie, it got these two thinking." Lucy looked at Joey and Dickie with unabashed love.

"Could you come with us?" Dickie asked. "We have something we'd like to show you. We'll explain more along the way."

"If you give me two minutes to check on my pod, I'd be glad to," Jacy said.

"We'll meet you at the fountain in 20 minutes," Lucy said, kissing Jacy's hand before releasing it. She walked back towards Joey and Dickie.

"I'll see you in 20," Jacy nodded. Her curiosity wouldn't let her break this appointment.

9

Neva Tezremsy sighed as she let herself into her perpetually reserved room at Shaky Embraces. Shaky Embraces was for the most part a spa retreat, but Neva used it for her own special reasons. The manager here was a Hat, and she owed Neva more than a few favours. This was one of the paybacks.

Neva's sigh was both resigned and anticipatory. She knew how others felt about secret, sexual rendezvous', but in her view, the issue was murky.

In one eye she could see that even having one secret lover was wrong, and having two was downright slutty. In her other eye, though, she could justify it. She never promised herself to anyone. She was free to do what she wanted as long as she brought no harm to others. That was her motto and she was living that. Was it really that wrong for her to be fucking two different people?

Neva sighed again as she closed the door behind her. She shed her jacket, which was the size of a six-man tent. Her coat engulfed the chair she draped it on.

She moved over to the control panel on the wall. As she fiddled with the lighting knob to get the desired level, she thought back to Jacy catching her and Flair in the middle of it. The Bam Slicer told them when they were finished.

Neva knew she'd have to talk Jacy about it, as the entire episode probably confused the poor girl. Neva would cut her right tit off before betraying Gravigo, but Neva didn't see her and Flair's fling as a betrayal. She never traded secrets, nor gave inside scoops on the Hats. It was just sex between the two of them, and dammit, Flair *was* really good at fucking.

Neva was unsure if Gravigo would regard it through the same lens, though, so she kept her dalliances with Flair quiet. Neva had a couple things not harmful to the Hats that would be helpful to Jacy, so she might try that route to keep her silent on the matter.

This thought reminded Neva of her other purpose here tonight. While she looked forward to the naked activities that would occur, she also had a vital piece of information to share with her companion.

Trading information with the other groups never bothered Neva. Her job was to be the best number two she could be for Gravigo. In her opinion, to be a successful number two, one needed to know as much as their superior. To be a *great* number two, though, one should know *more* than their boss.

It always dismayed Neva that so many number twos on Earth couldn't tell the difference between being a good second-in-command and a boot licker. Neva believed if all number two's stuck together and solved a bunch of issues on their own, the leaders would have more time and space to do just that. Lead.

Of course, loyalty rivalled knowledge as a top quality in a number two, and Neva and her soon to be visitor had that in spades. Nothing would cause either of them to deceive their leaders. The groups always came first, and neither would reveal anything that may harm their respective consortia. Being a number two, though, also opened up an ocean of information that wasn't available for regular rank and file members. Quite often, some intelligence would come up that would be helpful to one group but not harm the one who discovered it.

This is how Neva and the other groups' upper ranks built their relationship. They completely trusted one another. Somewhere along the way Neva and her paramour acted upon their sexual attraction, and trading secrets was no longer the only reason they met. They met at least once a month for these sexy dates.

Memories of their last tryst in this room made Neva blush. She had trouble walking for a week after the last visit. Smiling, Neva played with a dial to find the perfect lighting. She then turned her attention to the varied playlists at her disposal. There were many different genres to choose from. Neva struggled finding the perfect one. Music to perform cunnilingus to? BDSM tunes? Let's fuck hard songs? There were thousands of them.

Neva smiled at the 'Music for the Romantic Hump' title and checked the songs on it. With a perfect blend of smooth soul but with enough playfulness to 'hump' to. Neva gave it a nod of approval when one of her favourite songs, Eric Church's 'Wrecking Ball', sashayed from the speakers. She moved to the mirror to check herself just as a sensuous knock touched the door.

Neva marveled at how her secret lover's simple knock made her knees wobble and warmed her loins. She smiled and opened the door.

"Neva."

"Hey, baby," Neva purred.

Trichina Flame, in all her vamped up sexiness, stepped into the room and into Neva's arms. As the door closed, their lips touched, their tongues danced, and Neva moaned softly into Trichina's mouth.

She would give Trichina the valuable information, but it would wait until later. Much later.

10

"What *is* this place?" Jacy asked, looking around.

"We're in Catalhoyuk," Lucy said. "At one time this was the largest city on Earth."

"Huh?" Jacy was mystified. She'd never profess to be an expert at geography, but she did pretty well at social studies in high school. She'd never heard of Catalhoyuk. Joey, Dickie, and Lucy laughed at Jacy's confused look. Lucy took Jacy's hand. They began to wander slowly. Dickie and Joey, hand in hand, as well, followed.

"Close to 7,500 Earth years ago, Joey, Dickie, and I began to build Catalhoyuk," Lucy explained. "In what you would know today as the country of Turkey, we found an amazing piece of ground. Your archaeologists called it the 'fertile crescent.' It was a splendid place for farming."

Jacy stared at the vast expanse of empty land. "I don't understand what you're telling me. We're on some open plain. Where is this town you're talking about?"

Lucy laughed, looking over her shoulder at Dickie. Dickie kissed Joey, before saying to the other three, "Come on. Follow me." Dickie walked about twenty feet, looking closely at the ground. He then bent over, and pulled up a hatch door. Jacy looked at Lucy, not sure what was going on here. Lucy smiled.

"Let's go see Catalhoyuk," she led Jacy to the hatch and climbed down the ladder into the earth. An uncertain Jacy looked at Dickie.

"It's okay, Jacy. It's safe," he reassured her. Shrugging, Jacy followed, resuming her 'Buy the ticket, take the ride' philosophy.

Lucy lit candles as Jacy reached the bottom of the ladder. Jacy looked around the orange-lit room. On one wall was a plastered bull's head. The opposite one had a leopard painted on it. Jacy wandered the room as Dickie and Joey descended the ladder. Jacy picked up an obsidian mirror and inspected it, when Lucy spoke again.

"You didn't recognize Catalhoyuk as a town, because to you, a town is a very different thing. Your towns have streets or public buildings. Your towns have industrial areas, residential areas, churches, and cemeteries. Am I right?"

Jacy nodded. Dickie picked up the lesson. "Here in our town, Jacy, we had all those same things, but here all those things were in the home. The people of Catalhoyuk stored their food here, they wove wonderful mats, and made intricate jewellery. Along with our excellent farming land, we had streams teeming with fish. At one point we had close to 10,000 people living here."

"And 10,000 people made the largest city on the planet?" Jacy asked, setting the mirror down and picking up a figurine of a female to inspect.

"Yes," Joey spoke. "Remember, this was 7,500 years ago. Your planet didn't have as many humans on it as it does today. Not even close."

"And most of your people of that age were nomadic. They didn't start to settle until they invented farming," Dickie tossed in.

"The size wasn't what made us so proud of Catalhoyuk," Lucy walked over to Jacy. "It was the type of society that was created here. Everyone was equal. There were no rulers, no kings, or priests. We didn't need walls, weapons, or armies. There was no violence of any kind. Every family had ample food, furnishings, and decorated their homes with art and figurines."

Lucy nodded at the piece in Jacy's hands. Jacy placed it down gently. Lucy took her hand as they wandered the apartment sized room.

"Males and females were equal here," Lucy almost glowed as she spoke. "Everyone farmed, hunted, fished, and made things. There was no money, no squabbles. They socialized on the roofs, where we were earlier. They would have blazing hot summers, so most slept there on the hot nights, too."

"So, what happened to this place? It sounds like heaven," Jacy asked. All three fell into a glum silence. Jacy picked up on the mood instantly.

"Um, sorry if that was a bad questi…"

"It's okay, Jacy," Joey looked at her with sad eyes. "It's something we have a hard time discussing, that's all."

"Catalhoyuk was a peaceful Eden for close to 2,000 years," Lucy spoke softly. "When it ended the way it did, Dickie, Joey, and I became lost souls. We could barely function."

Lucy reached out, taking Dickie and Joey's hands in hers.

"Granny Mandible took us in," Dickie said. "She was going through her own troubles at the time, and somehow we came up with the idea of just being children where we didn't have to worry about the big, bad, 'real world.'"

Lucy smiled at Jacy with tears in her eyes. "When you spoke to me, it really opened my eyes what we had become, and I didn't like it. I spoke to these two, and we realized we needed to change. We left Granny's that night and haven't returned."

After a minute's silence, Jacy asked, "Do you think you can build another Catalhoyuk?"

"Not on your present planet," Joey shook his head, dejected.

"The only way it would work is if your planet completely started over," Dickie added.

"Started over?"

"From scratch," Lucy said. "Your people had a chance one time to go down the peaceful path, or the violent path. It's pretty clear which one they chose, and there's no erasing that decision, now."

The four of them remained silent in their thoughts until they climbed the ladder, hugged, and went their separate ways.

11

"Are you kidding me?!" Hammer Coolie asked across the morning campfire.

"That was my first thought," Tagger Merino settled the coffee pot above the flames. He looked over at Karma Twin. "Are you surprised?"

"Not really," she shook her head, looking over at Hammer. "Why are you so surprised? Or are you just disappointed?"

"Fuck that," Hammer waved a dismissing hand. "But yeah, kind of surprised, I guess. I thought Jacy might want to be a free one, not a Bone."

Tagger Merino took his seat on a log. "Well, after the whole Eugene thing, and if she's able to get her daughter into her pod, she probably wants the protection being a Bone provides. Smart choice for her, actually."

"Think she'll get her kid?" Hammer asked.

"Probably. She met with that John Peedpant character," Tagger shrugged. Karma Twin let out a low wolf whistle.

"Mornin' baby," she stood and greeted an approaching Trichina Flame. She kissed her deep on the lips. "I missed you last night."

Trichina ran her hand down Karma Twin's back and ass. "Missed you, too, baby. How'd training with Lita go last night?"

"Probably about the same as your meeting with Neva Tezremsy," Karma smiled, winking at her. "I was late, too, as Lita's new little friend, that Skull, oh, what's her name? Carney, Cooney,

Coney, yeah, that's it. Coney Slut. Lita's been helping her with some training, and the girl just wouldn't leave. When she did, I tried to make short work of Lita, but she's getting good. Really good. Anyways, come on, sit down. We're just discussing Jacy Morgan's choice to become a Bone."

"A logical choice," Trichina said, sitting down beside Karma Twin, holding her hand. She looked at Hammer. "I've got something more important to discuss with you, though." Hammer looked at her.

"I know where Ridded Snot is." There was a split second of stunned silence before all three began throwing questions at a bemused Trichina Flame.

"Whoa, whoa, whoa," she held her hands up. "I have no answers or other information other than he's at the same camp as Rusty Sleeves and all those other losers."

"Re-education Camp 99," Karma Twin said.

Re-education Camps were a mystery to almost everyone, short of the ones who'd been in one. Campers, as they were called, said nothing upon their discharge. Whatever happened in those camps, though, worked very well as very few Campers ended up re-enrolling.

There were only two Re-Education Camps. No one knew why one was called Re-Education Camp 1 and Re-Education Camp 99, and nobody cared. Re-Education Camp 1 was for minor offenders and violators. The length of their stay was predicated by the severity of their transgressions. Re-Education Camp 99, on the other hand, was for last chance violators. Usually their violations were just short of being sentenced to Grass Counting.

Camp 99 also needed one other thing. A sponsor. Because the violations were usually so close to being Grass Counter worthy, it took a sponsor outside of the offender's group to vouch for someone to get a last chance at redemption. That ruled out any Skull as being a sponsor.

"Who would speak up for that idiot?" Tagger Merino asked the question on each of their minds.

"I don't know," Hammer Coolie said, "but we're going to find out."

12

Jacy walked down the sparkling path toward her favourite tea house, The Chirpy Raven. She looked behind her at the following Neva. She returned Neva's smile, and then looked at Gravigo.

"Haven't you heard the saying that three is a crowd? And with her, that makes it almost five or six is a crowd."

Gravigo chuckled. "Don't worry about her. She'll give us our privacy."

"It's fine," Jacy said. "I'm just surprised you brought your bodyguard when all you're doing is having a walk and tea with me."

Gravigo wouldn't bite. "Jacy, you know Neva isn't a bodyguard. She is much more than the sum of her parts."

"More?" Jacy snorted. "She'd be a herd of elephants if she was anything more."

"I heard that," Neva's dainty voice spoke from behind.

Jacy looked back at her. "No offense intended."

"And none was taken," Neva wore a sweet smile.

Jacy started to look away, but turned back to her again. "I've never asked, but how tall are you?"

"337.82 cm."

Jacy tried to do the calculations in her head.

"11 feet, 1 inch," Gravigo spoke under his breath.

"Thanks," Jacy whispered back, a little embarrassed at her shortcomings with the metric system. She looked back at Neva again. "And how much do you weigh?"

"420 kilograms."

Jacy didn't even attempt to do the estimate. She glanced at Gravigo.

"926 pounds," he told her, shaking his head. "You're Canadian. How you don't know your own country's measurement system is a mystery to me."

Jacy ignored the jab. She changed the subject, and her and Gravigo made small talk until they stepped onto the outdoor patio of The Chirpy Raven. Jacy went in and ordered three London Fogs, while Gravigo and Neva grabbed a couple of tables. When Jacy returned, she put two steaming mugs down on the table where Gravigo sat, and delivered one to Neva who was sitting a few tables away.

"Thank you, Jacy," Neva nodded, trying to read Jacy's eyes. Jacy smiled, and returned to Gravigo's table and sat down.

"Thanks for meeting with me, Gravigo."

"Of course, Jacy. What's on your mind?"

Jacy paused, blowing on her tea to cool it down. She rehearsed this in her mind a thousand times this morning, yet still the words felt strange forming on her lips. Finally, she put her mug down and spoke.

"I've decided to join the Bones." Jacy held her breath as she watched Gravigo.

"I guessed that would be your choice," he sighed, after a lengthy pause. "I can't lie and say that I'm happy for myself with this, but I am happy for you, Jacy. You needed to be in a group to reach your full potential."

"Really?" Jacy blew out the held air. "Do you mean that, Gravigo?"

"Yeah," he smiled, "I do. I wish you would've chosen the Hats, of course, but if you want to be in the second best group, that's your prerogative."

Jacy felt immense relief. She took a sip of her tea, glancing over at Neva who pretended to not pay attention to them. Jacy wished she'd never witnessed her and Flair having sex. It was hard to look at Neva now without recalling their naked entanglement.

"There's something else I wanted to talk to you about," she exhaled.

Gravigo nodded and listened.

13

When Jacy returned to their room, she was taken aback to find Lita there.

"Hey," she said as she entered the room, "how did it go today with…" The look on Lita's face stopped Jacy in mid-sentence and shattered her heart.

"Oh baby, come here," Jacy held her arms out. Lita came into her arms like a wounded toddler. Jacy held her tight as Lita sobbed into her shoulder.

"It's okay, hon, it's okay," Jacy soothed.

With all that had been going on, Jacy almost forgot that today was Lita's big idea pitch to Hammer Coolie. Lita had been a Free Agent for a while now, and, minus some rough patches with Serena, she was doing great. She decided this was a good time to tell Hammer about her idea of forming a loose organization of free agents. Lita didn't want it to make it formal like the other three groups, but thought a semi-affiliation would give the free agents a little more juice as a whole.

The entire plan hinged on Hammer Coolie coming on board, though. His participation was paramount.

"It was a stupid idea anyways," Lita sniffled.

"I don't think it was stupid."

Lita offered a wan smile, stepping back from Jacy. She wiped her eyes and looked out the window. "Thanks. Unfortunately, Hammer Coolie thought it was."

"Did he use those exact words?"

Lita let out a heavy sigh and shrugged. "Does it matter? The conclusion was the same either way."

Jacy sat down on one of the wooden chairs and gestured towards the other for Lita to sit. Lita remained standing. Jacy looked at her. "So what did he say?"

"He said that any semblance of hierarchal organization went against the grain of every free agent's heart. He said he had empathy for rookie free agents and their struggles, and he does what he can to help, but…"

Lita shook her head, looking at Jacy with weary eyes. "And he's right, Sugar. We become free agents to be free, not to follow someone like a dog. I just…I…"

Lita's shoulders sagged and her voice splintered. She retrained her focus on something outside the window. "I just don't think I'm strong enough to be a free agent. I'm looking over my shoulder all the goddamned time, I'm worried and suspicious of everyone, whether they're a Hat, a Bone, a Skull, another free agent…"

Lita hung her head. "I'm just getting so worn out working without a safety net, Jace. I'm sorry."

Lita slumped down onto the foot of her bed. Jacy stood to comfort her, but Lita put her hands up. "I envy you, Jacy. I really do. You have whatever 'it' is. Hammer Coolie does, too, and I don't. I just need to accept that."

"I don't believe that," Jacy spoke with a soft voice.

Lita looked at Jacy, the corner of her mouth turning up into a half smirk. "You don't, do you? You honestly believe I have it." Jacy nodded, not breaking eye contact with her until Lita shook her head and looked away.

"You're still so green, Sugar. *So* fucking green. You've done so many incredible things since you got here. You picked yourself up from the whole Eugene thing. You've made your decision about being a Bone. You will have Derian in your pod soon. You've been truly amazing."

Lita turned back to face Jacy. "Please don't take offense to this, Jacy," Lita's voice hardened, "but you don't know jack shit about this place. It's mean, it's dirty…. it's…it's…fuck. They're going to kill Serena."

Lita broke into tears again. Jacy ignored her protests this time and sat down beside her, hugging her close until her tears stopped falling. Lita pulled back from her, but held tight to Jacy's hands.

"Who's going to kill Serena?" Jacy asked, but Lita only shook her head.

"Does it matter?" Lita remained silent for a long time before speaking. "You know what I think about sometimes? A brilliant songwriter. Picture him in his bedroom when he's a teenager and all his buddies are out chasing girls and drinking beer. He stays in that room with an old acoustic guitar his Grandpa probably gave him, and he coaxes out beautiful tunes from it."

Lita looked out the window again. "But then word leaks out, and agents and managers and record companies and lawyers get all their greedy paws on this brilliant songwriter and these incredible songs he has written. The songs are now everywhere, radio, internet, T.V. commercials. Everyone extracts their pound of flesh from this gifted boy. Before you know it, this naïve wunderkind has all that beauty completely sucked out of him and he's left discarded on the side of the road like roadkill."

Lita shook her head. "What if all those greedy pigs had kept their noses from the trough and allowed that boy to bloom when he was ready? Who knows what other magnificent music he may have created?"

Lita returned her gaze to Jacy. "You're that beautiful songwriter right now, Jacy. You're that brilliant tunesmith before the machine chews you up. Promise me you won't come out of the bedroom until you're ready, Jacy. Please."

Jacy was disconcerted from Lita's speech. "I don't know what…"

"Please, Jacy, please," Lita cut her off. "Just promise me you'll stay in the bedroom and write all the songs that you and only you can write. Write all of them before you leave the bedroom, Jacy. Don't come out until you have."

"I'm afraid you've lost me," Jacy admitted. "I'm not entirely sure what you're saying to me."

Lita chuckled. "Of course you don't, Sugar," Lita smiled at her. "That's one of the reasons I love you so much."

Lita placed a gentle kiss on Jacy's cheek and left the room without another word.

14

Jacy went to knock on Fatter Verb's door, but decided against it once she heard the thumping beat behind it. She entered and was blasted by a cacophony of rap music.

"Hello?!" Jacy called out a few times as she made her way down the hallway. Once she turned the corner to the main living area, she was greeted by a vision of Fatter Verb gyrating across the floor, singing at the top of his lungs. Rap had never been Jacy's cup of tea, so she didn't recognize the artist. Somebody was singing about going berserk, though, and Fatter Verb seemed to be following orders. Fatter noticed Jacy and pointed at her, lip-synching the words. Unabashed, he continued his prancing and singing until the song's conclusion. Fatter lowered his hand, the volume of the next song descending with it.

"Well, what do you think?"

"About the dancing or the racket?"

Fatter Verb furrowed his brow, perturbed. "Racket? You don't like Eminem?"

"You *do* like him?" Jacy countered.

"Jesus Christ," Fatter Verb rolled his eyes like an impatient teenager. "He's only one of the top three songwriters of your goddamned generation."

Jacy paused, trying to recollect any information she may have about Eminem. Apparently, it wasn't very much. "Wasn't he always writing about killing his wife and hating homosexuals and stuff?"

"Wow, you humans are so dammed frustrating," Fatter muttered. "Quick! Tell me who Kanye West married."

"Kim Kardashian?" Jacy hesitated before answering as she recalled the path this kind of thing went down when she was in training. "Look, Fatter, I…"

"Exactly," Fatter waved his hands in the air, ignoring her. "How can you know that and not know anything about a brilliant lyricist like Eminem?! Jesus, I was told you knew your music. That theory is now blasted to hell."

Fatter Verb grabbed a drink and took a swallow. Jacy guessed it was Hendrick's gin, tonic, and cucumber slices, Fatter's preferred cocktail. "Weren't you the slightest bit curious about Eminem when you lived on Earth?"

"Not really, I guess," Jacy shrugged her shoulders. "Rap music was never my thing and…."

"Rrrrrrrrrrrrr!!!!!" Fatter Verb manual buzzed her. "Blah blah blah. You humans and your stupid classifications. Look, there is no such thing as rap music, okay? There is no rap. There is also no rock and roll, there's no country, no heavy-metal-psychedelic-acid-jazz-funk-blues, either. There's music, plain and simple. Fuck your fucking labels." Fatter Verb sat down in a chair facing a long blank wall. Jacy did the same.

"Sorry for the outburst," he apologized, "but you goddamned humans can be extremely frustrating. Check out this example."

Fatter pointed his finger at the wall and made some funny movements with it. A few raggedy buildings came into view, followed by a screaming missile which disintegrated the middle one. Chaos erupted on the streets below. Fatter Verb shook his head. "That was a Palestinian hospital destroyed by your friendly Israelis. This is just a microcosm of what goes down on your planet. Do you know how big the Gaza strip even is?"

Jacy shook her head.

"It's about 40 kilometres long. That's shorter than a marathon, for Christ's sake. And how many thousands, mostly Palestinians of course, but how many thousands have died? Even the upper echelon of Israel and Palestine aren't sure anymore."

Fatter took a long swallow from his glass. "You humans, always so gullible when it comes to wars, religion, all that shit. Did you know that the God of Islam and the God of Christianity both followed the teachings of the same man?"

"Pardon me?" Jacy had no idea. She wasn't stupid, but she didn't put many cognizant thoughts into such things back on Earth. Fatter Verb broke into guffaws of laughter.

"Baz had the same dumbass look on his face that you do now!" Fatter Verb slapped his leg. "But yes, both Mohammed and Jesus followed the teachings of Abraham." Fatter shook his head at Jacy's blank look.

"You know Kim Kardashian, but you have no idea who Abraham was? You're as annoying as the rest of your kind," Fatter Verb wiped the image from the wall and drained his glass. "Did it ever occur to you to turn off that squawky box you call television and actually learn something while you were alive?"

Jacy was offended, but, if she were to be honest, she felt slightly stupid as well. "I guess I thought I had more time, that's all."

"Time. Another archaic ritual," Fatter Verb grabbed his glass, stood on wobbly feet, and moved to the counter for a refill.

"Anyways, I doubt you're here for a scolding from a grumpy, old coot," he filled two cups three quarters full with gin, and then added a splash of tonic and cucumber slice to each. He handed one to Jacy before he sat down. "What is it I can do for you?"

"Nothing."

"Nothing?" Fatter looked at her.

"That's right. Nothing," Jacy smiled. "I just wanted to thank you for the introduction to John Peedpant."

"Ah, yes. I take it the visit with him bore some fruit, did it?"

"Not immediate ones, but soon. Thank you."

Fatter sipped his drink. "And how is John doing? It's been a while since I've seen him."

"Good, he asked how you were doing," Jacy lied.

Fatter laughed so hard he choked on his drink. "You're a lousy bull-shitter, Jacy. John hates my guts, and, well, I guess I don't blame him. I'm glad your visit with him was a positive one, though."

He reached over with his glass to clink against Jacy's. She took a small sip of the strong drink and winced.

"Okay, bring me up to speed on this Abraham dude you're pissed off at me for not knowing."

Fatter smiled, and talked for the rest of the afternoon.

15

Maise Elantina spied out John Peedpant sitting at his usual table in his favourite tavern. John was talking with a cute bone Maise liked, Yumsly Rice. Not wanting to disturb him, Maise took an empty stool at the bar and ordered an ice water. She was barely a quarter way through it before she felt a presence behind her.

"Well, that's gratitude for ye. Ye come to my favourite pub and ye don't come and say hi?"

Maise Elantina spun on her stool and faced John Peedpant. "I actually came here strictly to see you, but I didn't want to disturb any chances you may have had with Yumsly Rice."

"Oh," John laughed, "if ye come sit with me, I may get myself a going away screw from 'er. Right now, she doesn't want much to do with an old guy like me, but if she sees me with the gorgeous and famous Maise Elantina? I'll have me the pick of the litter here."

John waved his arm, indicating all the girls in the pub. Maise laughed and stood. "Lead the way to your table, then, my friend. If a simple act of friendship can help your penis have a good time, then I'd be happy to help."

"Jesus, ye are the best. The *best*," John Peedpant led the way to his table, taking the long way so he could stop and introduce Yumsly Rice to his *good* friend, Maise Elantina. When they made it to the table, John smiled at her.

"Thanks," he took a large swig from his beer tankard, glancing in the smiling Yumsly's direction before returning his gaze to Maise. "How are things? You're looking great."

Maise nodded her thanks. "I came by to see how things are setting up for your departure and everything else."

"It's going well," John said. "I'm almost ready to hand over Derian and Beau's family over to Jacy. Is Rainy ready?"

Maise nodded. John took another drink of beer.

"Aye, that's good," he looked almost wistful for a moment. "I'm going to miss them."

He raised his beer and voice in toast. "To good people."

"To good people," many in the bar responded.

"And your side of things are all ready?" Maise Elantina returned her glass to the table.

"Aye," John nodded, smiling. "It seems weird my restless blood returns me home, but the timing is right for me to go back."

Maise refrained from smiling. Jon Peedpant never had a member of his pod be from Scotland, but he embraced the accent and culture of it for so long, he felt it was his home.

"I'm happy for you, John, you truly deserve this," she said, instead.

"And thank ye for pulling the proper strings, Maise," John gestured to her with his beer mug. "I would've had to jump through many more hoops than I did if I didn't have ye helping me."

"Consider it a thank you for the favour you did for us with Beau and Derian," Maise looked around for prying ears before leaning closer to the center of the bar table. "I was also wondering if you could do me a quick favour before you headed over to the Europe building."

"Of course, Maise. What is it?"

"It's nothing dangerous, it's just something I'd rather have done outside of the usual channels."

John Peedpant pretended to zip his lips shut. Maise told him what she needed him to do.

16

"Jacy! Hey, Sug! Wait up!"

Jacy turned around just before she came to a fork in the trail. She smiled when she saw Lita run up. Lita opened her arms as she got closer. Jacy walked into the welcoming arms.

"I'm so sorry for the other day, Sugar. I hope I didn't offend or insult you," Lita clung to Jacy tight. "You're all I've really got up here. Please don't be angry with me."

Jacy enjoyed Lita's embrace for a moment or two before pulling away, still holding onto Lita's elbows. "I'm not angry at you, Lita. I'm a little puzzled, but I'm not upset."

Lita pulled Jacy aside to let two leering Skulls pass. One of them turned around and mentioned something about 'a clam bang.' Lita gave them the middle finger before she locked her brown eyes on Jacy's blue ones.

"Sorry, baby, I was just frustrated with myself for blowing it with Hammer Coolie, that's all. Add that to maybe the teensiest bit of jealousy, and boom! It blew up in my face, and yours, too. I hate myself for allowing that to happen."

"Jealousy? Jealousy of what?"

Lita sighed, drawing Jacy down onto a nearby bench. "Not of what, of whom. And that whom is yoom," Lita playfully poked Jacy in the chest.

"Of me? Why?"

Lita smiled before responding. "It's not a bad jealousy, Sug. It's just that everything's going so good for you and so shitty for me, that's all. You're on your way up, up, up." Lita used her hand going upwards to demonstrate Jacy's trajectory.

"Me, on the other hand?" Lita's extended fingers became flaccid. "Eh, not so much."

Jacy slapped Lita's knee. "Knock that off, Lita. I'm sorry Hammer Coolie didn't like your plan, but you and your pod are doing great."

Lita looked away and sighed. "Again, not so much."

"What do you mean?"

"My pod is doing fine. It's Serena, though. I think I've lost her."

"To who?"

"To what, not who," Lita shook her head. "And the what is crystal meth."

"Oh, baby, I'm sorry," Jacy put her arm around Lita so Lita's head rested on her left shoulder.

"Remember how depressed you were after Eugene was killed?" Lita asked. Jacy nodded. "Even though I'd feel the same sadness you did, I found myself wishing this morning that the same fate would befall Serena."

"Oh, hon." Jacy squeezed Lita closer.

"And that's horrible, right? I mean that's truly horrible, me wishing she would just die. I can't help feeling that way, though. Serena, my sweet, cute Serena, now selling her body and robbing cars and homes for the privilege of poisoning her body. Fuck, Jacy, you wouldn't *believe* what some of those animals do to her."

Lita stood in agitation. "Don't get me wrong, Sug. I was nobody's angel back on Earth, but I did listen when my gut told me enough was enough, that it was time to slow down. People like Serena don't have any fucking idea the gift they have in just being alive and breathing."

Jacy bit her tongue, holding in any clichéd advice. Instead, she simply said, "I'm sorry."

Lita looked at her for a moment, and smiled.

"Thanks," Lita said, sitting back down to hug her. She pulled back and looked at Jacy. "Are we good?"

"Of course," Jacy stood, motioning down one of the forks in the path. "Would you care to join me on the rest of my walk?"

"I'd love to," Lita said, motioning down the other path. "Don't want to do this one?"

"Um," Jacy snickered. "Let's try this one. I didn't have the best of experiences going that way the last time I was out here."

Lita laughed. "Yes, I heard. What's wrong? Big Bob didn't get you wet?"

"Jesus, does everybody know?" Jacy asked.

"This place is one big gossip pit, you should know that by now," Lita laughed and they carried on, enjoying their evening stroll, which was just what Jacy needed. Tomorrow would be a very important day.

17

For all the worrying and second guessing, Derian joined Jacy's pod with a refreshing lack of pomp and circumstance. John Peedpant shook her hand and wished her well, Lita hugged her and marvelled over Derian's beauty before heading to her own pod, and that was it. Jacy sat at the table and watched her 19-year-old daughter watch the movie Bronson on Netflix with one of her best friends, a guy named Loroot Burgeon. Despite the quirky name, Loroot was a nice guy and Derian seemed to be at ease with him.

Since this was her first evening with Derian, Jacy did nothing but observe her daughter. Learning her lesson from the many mistakes made with Eugene, Jacy didn't fret about the horrible health concerns of microwave popcorn or the sugar content in the pop her daughter drank. Jacy kept an eye on her and Loroot as they headed out for a couple of beer at the Sportsman Pub before calling it an evening and going to their respective houses.

Jacy leaned back and smiled as Derian went home, chatted with her dad and Abby, Beau's new wife. Well, not exactly new as they'd been married longer than Beau and Jacy were. Jacy sighed. She liked Abby but shit, she was her husband's wife.

Derian seemed incredibly well adjusted, though, so Abby must be alright. Besides, Derian was Jacy's concern, not Beau and Abby. Jacy looked around the large table of 40-50 gamers, catching Rainy Dissolve's eye. Jacy smiled and nodded. Rainy looked away. Jacy wasn't offended, though. Rainy Dissolve would take good care of the rest of Derian's family, that's all that mattered.

Jacy's life slipped into a wonderful routine of great Game playing, little drama, and lots of time with Derian. Of course, it wasn't all gumdrops and sunshine for Jacy's pod. She lost one nice person in a convenience store robbery gone wrong in Tacoma, Washington and had another die in a horrific work accident near Penticton, B.C.

Jacy picked up others in trades and favours, and overall, her pod grew to 30 members. Gravigo, and Flair stopped by every now and then, reminding Jacy they'd both be happy to have her as part of their respective groups. Jacy thanked them both, told them how much she treasured their friendship and support, but wasn't going to leave the Bones. Maise Elantina was wonderful, checking in on her and Rainy every couple of days.

Jacy's favourite part of this time was the time she spent getting to know her daughter. Derian was a bit of a movie connoisseur, absolutely loathing brain dead blockbusters. She loved the cooking program she was enrolled in at Vancouver Island University, she enjoyed a good party but kept it within acceptable limits, and she had a remarkable group of friends.

In short, Derian was everything Jacy hoped she would be. Beau did an incredible job raising her, and with Abby's assistance in Derian's later childhood years, Derian grew into a marvellous young woman.

Not that she was faultless, though. Jacy had her first drama with Derian about three months in. For one reason or another, Derian began a 'friends with benefits' type of relationship with one of her classmates. This wasn't too big a deal, neither were in a relationship and they used protection, but Jacy began to notice her new 'friend' wanting to take things to a more serious level.

Jacy didn't like this. While this guy was nice enough, he wasn't worthy of Derian in a formal relationship or, Buddha forbid, marriage. Jacy pondered this conundrum for a couple weeks before approaching Lohorn Jive, a table sharing Hat. Jacy invited him for a tea at the Chirpy Raven.

"How's Loroot Burgeon doing?" Jacy asked Lohorn Jive as they sipped their Earl Grey.

"He's doing well. You probably know he's over in Vancouver taking a journalism program at Langara College, right?"

Jacy nodded. "Any thoughts on what he'll do after graduation?"

Lohorn Jive's brow crinkled as he looked at Jacy. "What are you really asking me, Jacy?"

Jacy laughed. "Alright, you got me. Any chance of you trading Loroot to me? I've got some pretty awesome prospects in my pod."

"And what do you want with Loroot?"

"I don't know, I thought that maybe he'd be a good match for someone in my pod, that's all," Jacy acted as casual as she could.

Lohorn supped his tea. "Someone like your daughter Derian?"

Jacy reddened. "Am I that obvious?"

"Kind of," Lohorn chuckled, "but you're not the only one who can see those two would be a jackpot together. Look, Loroot's coming home for the summer break. Let's get those two some alone time together, and if it works out, I'll be amenable to an appropriate trade."

So began the summer Derian Morgan and Loroot Burgeon fell in love. It didn't take too much work on Lohorn Jive's or Jacy's part. A couple nudges here, a few urges there, and before anybody knew it, by mid-August Derian and Loroot were a couple.

When the calendar flipped to December, Jacy traded a great kid named Chester Hayes from Elk Grove, California for Loroot

Burgeon. Both Jacy and Lohorn Jive were happy with the trade, even though both liked the person they gave up.

For the first time since Jacy stepped foot in this place, she was actually happy.

18

BANG! BANG! BANG!

The sonic raps on the front door echoed through the lonely halls and dusty rooms. The sudden aural invasion startled Granny Mandible, causing her to drop the picture she was holding. Granny glanced in the direction of the noise and sighed. With shaking hands, she retrieved the picture she released. Thankfully the glass in the frame didn't break.

Granny Mandible smiled. *Look at them in the picture.* Herself, Gravigo, Flair, Maise Elantina, Fatter Verb, and Tosiri Octavo. They all looked so young, so vital. Five of the six remained. Tosiri Octavo long ago was given the high honour of joining Sir Sullen Slow and Tzarina Rebel Hew as one of the Three Generals.

Granny set the picture back in its normal position. She let her gaze travel the walls and shelves of the musty room, everything chock full of photographs ranging from ages ago to eons ago to decades ago to last year. Ever since the kids left she found herself spending more and more time in this room, studying each picture, struggling to remember the names and facts and dates surrounding each one.

Granny smiled at the thought of the kids. Who knew she would miss them as much as she did? She didn't blame them for leaving. In fact, she would secretly love Jacy forever for giving them the strength to spread their wings and fly. Dickie had stopped by recently to visit, which was nice. It bothered her a little that Lucy and Joey hadn't come, but she knew they would return to see her when they were ready.

BANG! BANG! BANG!

Granny glanced in the direction of the front door again. Whomever was knocking held the key to where and who Granny Mandible would be the next time she saw the kids. Would she be a hero? A Grass Counter? Banished forever? Granny bit her bottom lip with one of her yellowed teeth at the thought. Being a Grass Counter would be horrible, of course, but to be banished would be…would be…would be what?

It'd be life ending, Granny decided. It would be the end of her to never see the kids, the original crew, hell, even Lita and Jacy. Granny chuckled to herself as she shuffled towards the front door, turning out the light after a quick backwards glance at her nostalgia room. Who would've thought Granny Mandible would have those warm feelings for Lita and Jacy?

Granny was a long-time opponent of allowing humans here and becoming players in the Game. It felt unnatural to her. Granny opposed it from the first time with Johnny Bazinski and it continued on to Lita and Jacy when Baz went to the grass.

As things usually go, though, time passed and doubts were never realized. Granny Mandible almost forgot that both girls were human beings. Lita, the fiery little wench, won Granny's respect and approval by the hard way she played the Game. And Jacy; Jacy, she soared miles higher than hers or anyone else's projections or hopes.

Of course, the key word here was 'almost'. As much as Granny endeavoured, she never saw past the fact that they were human, that they were not one of them. It wasn't that Granny disliked humans. Hell no. The exact opposite of that statement was true. She loved human beings more than she could ever express. Her love of humans was the second reason for every wheel she'd set in motion.

The number one reason was for her own people, though. It drove Granny Mandible mad how Gravigo and Flair seemed to forget the real reason they were all here. And every minute they lost sight of that was another minute closer to their people becoming extinct. Christ, even Rainy Dissolve and her not-so-secret crew never lost sight of their real reason for being here. Why…?

BANG! BANG! BANG!

"I hear you, I hear you, keep your panties on," Granny Mandible muttered, stopping in front of a hall mirror to check her appearance. She studied the lines stretching away from her eyes; crows' feet some called them. Granny referred to them as her eagle talons. Her wispy silver hair looked nice this evening, though nothing like the dazzling tresses she wore in her youth. Her bleak, not-quite-broken body was a zillion miles away from her curvaceous, almost muscular body of yesteryear. Granny Mandible straightened the hem of her skirt, and turned from the mirror. She faced the door, and sighed.

"Nothing or all," she whispered, moving towards the door. Once she opened the door, life would either be a bowl of cherries or a sack of maggots.

Nothing or all.

After a final deep breath, Granny Mandible reached for the doorknob and turned the handle.

19

"Wow," Laddie Nines collapsed onto his wet sheets, his body slick with sweat. "So *that's* a rusty trombone."

Sultana Yelp lay down beside the breathless Laddie Nines, slowly running her fingertips over his back. With a silent sigh, Sultana pretended it was Galore's back she was doing this to. She knew each muscle, each scar, every last freckle on Galore's body. Things had been so hectic as of late that she had barely seen Galore, let alone hold him and love him.

Laddie stirred Sultana from her Galore reverie by reaching over for a pack of cigarettes. He took one out and lit it, exhaling a plume of stinky smoke. Sultana slapped him on the ass and hopped out of bed. She walked over to the window and opened it.

"You'd be a lot sexier if you quit that gross habit," she told him, looking out at Granny Mandible's deserted-looking home. "You might even get yourself a steady girl instead of having to jerk off all the time."

"Why do I need a girl for?" Laddie reached into the mini-fridge he used as a night stand and grabbed a cold beer. "I've got you."

"In your fucking dreams, Laddie," Sultana snorted.

"Yeah, yeah, I know," Laddie Nines took a swig of beer. "I've got some news for you, though."

Sultana looked over her shoulder at him.

"That old biddy finally opened the door and accepted a visitor." Laddie used his cigarette to gesture in the direction of Granny Mandible's house.

"Really?" Sultana turned around and faced him. "Who?"

"That crazy old bastard, Fatter Verb."

"When?"

Laddie thought for a moment. "Yesterday. Or maybe the day before."

"Why didn't you tell me sooner?"

"You told me not to contact you, remember?"

Sultana didn't have to hide her reaction to the news from Laddie Nines, as she really didn't have one beyond puzzlement. She had nary a clue what this would mean, but she knew the rest of the council needed to hear this. She returned to Laddie's bed, leaned over, and slowly licked the entire shaft of Laddie's cock. It sprang to attention immediately.

"Keep up the good work, Laddie," Sultana smiled. "Maybe next time I'll let you take a little tour of the Republic of Labia."

Laddie Nines gulped and was stroking himself under the blanket as a chuckling Sultana closed the door. Sultana made her way down the hall to the elevator, and pressed the button. It arrived with a 'ding', and she got on the car with a male and female, both bedecked in black. She nodded hello and noticed no floor number was lit up on the panel. The doors closed and she reached over to push the 'ground floor' button.

As she reached, the male in the elevator seized her wrist and she felt a razor sharp pain in her lower back.

"What the…." was all Sultana Yelp got out before everything went black.

20

It had been awhile since Jacy visited with Baz, so in a rare, calm moment of the Game, she sought him out in the fields. Jacy felt a pang of sadness for Baz when she saw how little he'd moved since the last time she was here. Jacy patiently waited on the sparkling path until Baz made it to an easy number for him to remember. After a couple of minutes, he acknowledged her.

"Well, this is a pleasant surprise," Baz smiled at her. "Please, come sit."

Baz gestured the route Jacy should take to get to him. It didn't take long, as he was only 50 feet or so from the path. Jacy squatted down and hugged Baz, kissing him on the cheek, too. Baz's smile grew wider.

"Now that's a heck of a welcome. You made me forget I'm upset with you for taking so long to come visit me."

"Oh, Baz, I'm so…"

"No, no," Baz waved his hand, "I'm only teasing you. You've got a million more important things to tend to than to visit some degenerate criminal."

"Baz, I am truly sorry. I have no excuse for not seeing a friend for this long," Jacy sought out more words, but none came.

"Oh yes, you do," Baz reached over and patted her knee. "Tell me about your daughter."

A single tear escaped from the corner of Jacy's right eye. "Oh, Baz, she's the most precious, beautiful…. oh, take all the positive adjectives in the world, and that's Derian."

Baz smiled as Jacy regaled him with dozens and dozens of tales of the last four Earth years Jacy experienced with Derian. The lofty peaks, the minimal valleys, the laughter hooted, and the tears shed. To Baz's ears, Derian sounded like a wonderful person who lived a fulfilling life.

Baz reached out and squeezed her knee. "I'm so happy to hear that, Jacy. You've come so far from the scared girl who first came to see me. Look at you, now. How many do you have in your pod, now?"

"88."

"Wow," Baz shook his head in amazement. "I'm so proud of you."

Jacy's eyes welled with tears again. "Thank you, Baz. That means a lot coming from you."

"Well, it's the truth," Baz's face grew serious. "Now, not to be a downer, but are you hearing anything through the grapevine about what's going on?"

Jacy shook her head. "I'm not sure what you mean."

"Well," Baz sighed, "there's been some weird rumours going around. Usually I'm pretty good at separating fact from bullshit, but things seem off kilter somehow."

Jacy furrowed her eyebrows. "Are you hearing things about me? Besides the Game, I've been pretty much keeping to myself and trying to fly under the radar for Derian's sake."

"No, no," Baz shook his head. "Nothing specifically about you. There's just a strange vibe going through this whole place. Promise me you'll watch your back, ok?"

"Of course," Jacy stretched out on an area of grass Baz already counted and stared at the bright, blue sky. "Now, can you tell me some good Baz stories? I would really enjoy hearing them."

Baz acquiesced, and Jacy settled in for the afternoon. She closed her eyes, letting all of her cares melt away to the sound of Baz's voice. She was truly content.

For a little while, anyway.

21

When Sultana Yelp awoke, all was dark. She opened and shut her eyes. She closed them tight before widening them as far as they would go. Nothing. She couldn't see a thing. She knew she was on her back on something hard, but that was it.

Both of Sultana's arms were shackled above her head. She tried to move them, but only had minimal movement. Her legs were tied down, spread apart.

"Hey!!" she yelled. "Hey!"

"Hello," a female voice came from somewhere above her head. Sultana tried to look behind her.

"Who the fuck are you?!" Sultana struggled against her bonds, the metal cuffs digging into her skin. She cried out in pain.

"Ah," the female voice said, sounding happy. "So it did work. We, well, mostly I, but we discovered a way to turn on and off the pleasure and pain receptors against one's will. Splendid. The others will be happy to know of this."

Sultana felt pangs of fear trickle down her spine. She never left her pain or pleasure receptors on unless she was in Galore's presence. Changing one's own receptors was as simple as breathing, but altering someone else's? That was impossible, wasn't it?

"What…what do you want from me?" Sultana cursed herself for sounding fearful.

"Are you scared, Sultana?" the female asked, before answering her own question. "I guess I can understand why. Things aren't looking very good for you at the moment."

Sultana heard the clicking of high highs walking across a pavement floor.

"My name is Jasper Dames," the female said. "I apologize for the blindness. I'm not totally sure yet if it'll wear off or not. If it doesn't, I'll try and figure out an antidote when things slow down a little around here. It's been crazy busy, and they're busting my balls to have everything ready in time."

Blindness? What the fuck? Sultana tried her best to keep her cool but failed. "What do you want from me? I'm just…."

Jasper Dames put her hand on Sultana's cheek and rubbed it gently. Sultana winced at her cold touch.

"There, there, hon," Jasper spoke in a soft voice. "Don't waste your breath. I have no say in this matter. We were just told to bring you in and hold you until they tell us otherwise."

Jasper Dames clicked away. Sultana heard a beeping sound and felt the pressure change when a door whooshed open. "We'll talk later, Sultana. I've got some other chores to complete, so I will go do those while you get reacquainted with a couple of your old friends. See you soon."

Sultana heard muffled voices, and then Jasper's clacking heels receded in the distance and the door closed tight.

"Hello, Sultana." The male's voice made Sultana's skin crawl.

Sultana Yelp hesitated for a few long seconds before responding. "Rusty Sleeves?" "Ah, you do remember me," Rusty's voice moved closer. "Jesus, you are looking good, Sultana. Remember all those times you turned down my advances?"

"I fucked you many times," Sultana said, trying to keep the fear from her voice as the familiar oily stink of him swept into her nostrils.

"Twice. Maybe three times," Rusty Sleeves chuckled. "How about you, Ridded? How many times did you get to fuck her?"

"Never," Ridded Snot spoke from another area of the room.

"Come on," Rusty sounded incredulous. "As high up in the Skulls as you were, and you never had Sultana Yelp yaffle the old yogurt cannon?"

"Not my type," Ridded Snot sounded bored.

Rusty Sleeves? Ridded Snot? What was going on here? Sultana couldn't hide her fear anymore. She began to cry. "Please, you two…"

"Oh, Sultana, just relax," Rusty Sleeves said, moving close enough to her that she could feel his fetid breath upon her face. "A changing of the guard is about to take place. We won't have too long to wait."

Sultana heard the sound of pants hitting the floor seconds before she felt Rusty crawl on top of her. The terror she attempted to evade enveloped her, making her battle with her restraints. Rage bubbled up from her belly, making her choke.

"Now," Rusty's voice was husky, "Ridded Snot and I have been in a re-education camp for a long time. We deserve a little present for our sacrifices, don't you think? What about you, Ridded? What do you say we have some fun with her?"

"You go ahead," Ridded replied, holding up a Nick Hornby book. "I've got some reading to catch up on."

"Suit yourself," Rusty grunted. Sultana felt the spongy head of Rusty's penis force its way inside of her. She gnashed out with her teeth, almost catching Rusty's cheek. Rusty laughed.

Sultana began to scream as Rusty punched her in the face and fucked her. Two hours later, when her voice was a croaking whisper, her face bruised and bloody, and her vagina a beaten mess, she continued to scream in her head.

22

Jacy tried her best to hide her shock when she stepped into the hallway and noticed Neva Tezremsy waiting by her and Lita's door. Jacy thought about turning around and bolting in the other direction when Neva called out to her.

"I come in peace," Neva's melodious voice carried down the corridor. "I just want a minute of your time."

Jacy calmed her breathing and attempted to act normal. She just left Lita, who was having another Serena crisis, so Jacy was on her own here.

"Okay," she told Neva, careful to keep out of arm's reach from the behemoth. "What can I do for you?"

Neva looked around, and then spoke as softly as she could. "I want to thank you for not telling Gravigo about Flair and me."

"You're welcome," Jacy learned long ago that when it came to accepting someone's appreciation or apology, the shortest response was always the best.

"Why didn't you tell Gravigo?" Neva asked.

"I don't know. What you do is none of my business, I guess," Jacy shrugged.

"Okay," Neva nodded. "I want you to know that there is nothing sinister going on here. I would never betray Gravigo. I just like fucking Flair, that's all."

"Why?"

Neva shrugged again. "I don't know why I keep it secret from Grav..."

"No," Jacy cut in. "Why are you fucking Flair?"

"Oh," Neva laughed. Even Neva's laugh was like a song. "Pure curiosity, I guess. Flair is pretty inventive in that area."

Jacy held her hands about a foot and a half apart. "That's not inventive, that's painful."

Neva giggled. "Gawd, he is *so* fascinated with that thing. Are most males on Earth that fascinated with the size of their dinks?"

"Pretty much all of them."

Neva shook her head in wonder. "Anyways, I thank you for your discretion again. Do you have a couple minutes? I'd like to show you something."

Jacy paused, considering Neva's request. Neva had been nothing but cordial with her after their initial meeting, yet Jacy still felt uneasy around her.

"Um..."

"Come on, I won't bite, I promise. There's something I feel you deserve to know, though, and showing you is easier than telling."

"I'm not going to see Flair's big penis again, am I?" Jacy smiled.

"No," Neva laughed. "Come on, it's not far."

Jacy shrugged and followed Neva. Neva was right, as they didn't go too far. They stood at the door of a Simulation Room. Each section of living quarters had one, but Jacy had yet to use it. Neva punched a sequence of buttons on a panel beside the door. When she finished she opened the door, gesturing for Jacy to follow her through.

"I usually only use these rooms when I'm feeling especially homesick, but today I want to give you a glimpse of Gravigo's homeland."

"Gravigo's? Do you have a different homeland?" Jacy asked, not entering the room yet.

"Oh, yes," Neva laughed a delicate laugh. "I come from a very different place than Gravigo."

"I thought most came from Gravigo's planet," Jacy peered through the doorway but didn't enter.

"Most do, but not all."

"Who else doesn't?"

"You, for one," Neva smiled.

Jacy laughed. "Fair enough. Why aren't you showing me your homeland, though?"

"Why? Would you like to see it?" Neva looked surprised.

"Yes, I would," Jacy smiled at her. "What is your homeland like?"

Neva took a deep breath and emitted it slowly, her face a mixture of happiness and despair. Neva's voice became a whisper. "My fatherland is beautiful. Sometimes I miss it so much my teeth hurt. Some of my people, though, they…"

Neva's voice trailed off. Jacy put her hand on Neva's thick forearm, sensing the sensitivity of the subject. Neva looked away, embarrassed.

"Sorry," she said.

Neva took another large breath. "I'd love to show you my fatherland, but that will have to wait for another time. Today, I need to show you this."

Neva waved her arm out towards the murky room. Jacy entered. A low fog settled close to the ground, making it impossible to see anything shorter than two feet. Faceless, formless beings moved seamlessly through the greenish glow emanating from the fog.

"Are these Gravigo's people?"

"Yes," Neva nodded. "What you are seeing are their vehicles."

"Vehicles?" Jacy looked confused. "As in cars or trucks?"

"No," Neva shook her head. "More like your human bodies as vehicles."

Jacy pondered this as Neva explained. "Back on Earth, would you say you, the real Jacy, was her thoughts, her soul, her.... her *essence*, or would the real Jacy be just arms and legs and tits and skin?"

"I.... hmm...I was just me," Jacy furrowed her brow as she watched the simulated people of Gravigo's world.

"Meaning you were much more than your physical body?"

"Well, yeah, I guess so," Jacy looked at Neva, "but if I didn't have my physical body, like my heart and brain and lungs and stuff, then the real me didn't exist, either."

"Fair point," Neva moved farther into the fog. Jacy followed. "Human beings have a much stronger connection between their essential self and their physical self. My people are very similar."

Neva waved an arm towards the replicated life forms.

"Gravigo's people don't need that same connection. They outgrew that necessity millions of Earth years ago," Neva shook her head. "Sorry, I should say they *thought* they outgrew that connection years ago. They thought there were many things they no longer needed. That's one of the reasons their physical being is so bland to look at. Their insides, though, their true, essential selves, are amazing."

"What do they look like?" Jacy was curious.

"What their essence looks like doesn't matter," Neva shrugged. "It's not even quantifiable, anyways. What would a human being's soul look like?"

Jacy shrugged. Neva continued on. "What matters is what their essence is, and their essence is absolutely brilliant. I mean, look at this place. Not just this simulation room, but this whole place they created. It's pretty incredible, is it not?"

Jacy agreed. "Okay, so let's say I'm picking up what you're laying down. Why did you want to bring me here?"

"I brought you here to help you understand the real reason why we're here, and to also help you understand that you may be in trouble."

"Me?" Jacy looked shocked.

"You, or someone in your pod, or your whole pod, or…." Neva shrugged her massive shoulders. "See, Jacy, Gravigo's people didn't create all this just to play some game. They created this to save their race."

"What?" Jacy looked at the fabricated people again.

"With all the amazing advances Gravigo's people made, they lost something essential to their survival. They learned to alter time, they no longer needed to nourish their bodies, and so on and so on. Basically, they evolved into a higher power."

Neva stopped wandering. Jacy came to a halt beside her.

"Once they accomplished this, they thought they were omniscient and would live forever. Unfortunately, they were wrong."

"Wrong about what?"

"About all the important stuff. They weren't able to live forever, but with all of their advances they were able to live through ages and ages. Eventually, they lost the ability to procreate. They didn't realize this until they discovered they couldn't live forever, so by then, it was too late."

Jacy looked at Neva, horrified. "Gravigo's people are going extinct?"

"Yes," Neva stretched the word out. "That is the true reason they are here. They are hoping your people can teach them things they have long forgotten. Number one is the ability to reproduce, of course, but other important things, too. Humans have already re-taught them some of these things, such as the joy music causes and the importance of love and companionship, but they have yet to regain their ability to reproduce."

"Why us? Why humans? Aren't there other life forms in the universe they can learn from?" Jacy's head spun from all Neva told her.

"Of course there are, and they are observing them, too, but humans are widely believed to be the best chance to teach them what they need to know. See, the basic building blocks of life are the same for *all* life forms. It is only the slightest genetic alteration that makes one life form a human, and a different life form a frog, for example…"

"Okay…."

"…so Gravigo's people feel human beings are an early version of them, and they might be right. I don't have all the answers," Neva sighed. "I know this is a lot to take in Jacy, and I'll explain more when I can. I fear we've run out of time, though. There's growing rumblings about you. Are you involved in anything big right now?"

"Is Derian being a part of my pod considered big?"

"Well, yes," Neva smiled, "but that isn't the noise we are hearing. Besides, she still has that safety clause attached to her, so she's fine. It's something else."

Jacy cringed at that last statement. Jacy knew Derian had less than six earth months left of that clause. She did her best to be incognito and hope everyone else would forget about Derian. Jacy thought about the rest of her pod. They were all doing well, but there was nothing major going on with any of them. Jacy shook her head again at Neva.

"Just keep your head up and stay on your toes, okay?" Neva's eyes bore into Jacy's. "Some of us are hearing bits and pieces about something big going down soon."

Neva approached Jacy, gesturing if she could hug her. Jacy didn't know how to disagree with her, so she let herself be enveloped by Neva's cavernous hug, her face being eye level with Neva's belly button.

"I'll let you know more when I hear it, I promise," Neva said, as they turned to leave the simulation room. "You should pop by and see Gravigo, too. He misses you."

"I'll do that," Jacy said, watching Neva depart. That was a horse shit lie. She wasn't going to see Gravigo any time soon. She wouldn't leave her table again. Derian already had to live her life without a mother. Jacy would be damned if something else horrible happened to her.

Jacy returned to her table in a fighting mood. Nobody was going to harm her daughter. *Nobody.*

23

Galore hated this building and didn't like the person he was there to talk to, but he had no choice. Sultana Yelp was missing. Something wasn't right.

Pacing up and down the hallway, and seconds away from barging into the room, a cute, pixie cut redhead slipped from the room, wearing nothing but a pair of high heels. Galore ignored her and stepped inside the door before the latch closed.

Laddie Nines was lying on his back, blowing smoke rings at the roof. "What the…"

Galore put a hand up to shut him up. Laddie Nines wasn't afraid, but something in the little man's demeanor and sinewy movements kept him quiet. Galore snuck to the window, pulled back part of the window shade and looked out. Satisfied, he came over to the bedside.

"I know my woman has been sucking your cock," Galore stated, "but I'm not here for that."

"Okay," Laddie Nines began to get out of bed. Galore shot over in a flash and had his foot on his throat before Laddie could even blink.

"Stay right where you fucking are," Galore spat through gritted teeth. "We don't have much time."

"Time for what?" a wide-eyed Laddie stared at Galore. Galore took his foot from Laddie's throat and stood back. Laddie Nines moved back against his headboard.

"Time for a chat," Galore said. "When did you last see Sultana?"

"Look, dude, I..." Before Laddie knew it, Galore's heel was back on Laddie's throat. Laddie struggled, but Galore pressed his heel down harder, causing Laddie Nines to cough.

"I don't have fucking time for this," Galore hissed. "I'm not a jealous lover, okay? I just need to know where she is." Galore loosened his step on Laddie's throat and did a backwards flip off of his bed. He stood at the foot of it, staring at Laddie Nines.

"I don't know," Laddie sounded scared. "She was here three nights ago. No, four. Four nights ago."

"I know she was here getting information from you about the house across the street," Galore pressed on. "What did you tell her?"
"Aw, come on, dude, she made me promise not to tell. Don't ruin this for..."

All Galore did was tilt his head.

"Okay, okay," Laddie put his hands up to protect himself. "She wanted to know who was coming and going from that old lady's place. Nobody had been there for a while, then Fatter Verb came by and I told her about it. That's it, okay?"

Galore nodded, a split second before the apartment door blew open. Four armed males, all in black, burst in and looked around. All they saw was a trembling Laddie Nines.

"Where did he go?" one of them barked.

"I don't know, dude, he was standing right there a second ago and...."

Before he could finish speaking, the mattress flew up and a naked Laddie Nines soared through the air into the goons. In a streaking flash, Galore leapt feet first through the window, following the shattering glass down to the street below.

24

Jacy returned to her table after taking a quick break from a long stretch of playing, and knew something was up. When she left ten minutes before, everything seemed normal, but now there were subtle differences. The air crackled with electricity. As she entered the Gaming Area, a foreign yet recognizable feeling churned around inside her belly.

Jacy almost laughed at the irony of it. Was she was having a gut feeling? How uncanny was that? And this was no half-assed gut feeling, either. No, this was a full on, Mike Tyson in his prime punch to the pancreas. Jacy would follow this gut feeling through hell if need be.

Her first surprise of the evening was Agent Ninny Mop and one of his troops waiting for her at the entrance to her normal playing area.

"Miss Jacy," Agent Ninny Mop greeted her pleasantly. "I need to ask you to follow us."

"Not tonight, I'm afraid," Jacy apologized. "I've got to get to my table right…"

"We're here to take you to your new table," Agent Ninny Mop interrupted her, looking at her with pride. "You are being moved to the top table."

Jacy looked from Ninny to his partner, Cereal Jenny, to see if this was a ruse. She knew Agent Ninny Mop wasn't the sort to joke about official business, but really? The top table?.

"Okay…. I guess…." Jacy said as Agent Ninny Mop gestured the way she should go. Jacy followed Cereal Jenny. Agent Ninny Mop fell in behind Jacy.

"Congratulations," Cereal Jenny called over her shoulder. "This is a big honour."

Jacy nodded, but didn't feel honoured at all. Her gut feeling hammered her harder than ever. Tonight was Jacy's twenty fifth birthday and her and Loroot's second anniversary. The end of Derian's 25 years of safety falls on the same evening as her promotion to the highest level of the Gaming Area? It was too much of a coincidence for Jacy.

The good thing about whatever was going on was that Jacy felt unstoppable. She had no idea where this bone crushing confidence came from, but she had it times twelve tonight. She could pick out the single trumpet line in Sublime's 'Ball and Chain', blazing at wall shimmering volume yet hard to hear over the din of voices. Jacy had never seen the place so packed.

Jacy thought of the lonely corner table she began at with Eugene. From there to here was quite the leap. "Nobody puts baby in the corner," an amused Jacy repeated a horrible line from one of her favourite movies of all time. Jacy realized she had no Johnny Castle to come rescue her, but she was fine with that. She had Maise Elantina and the rest of the Bones at her back, if she needed any help. The way she felt tonight, though, she didn't need anyone.

When they arrived at Jacy's new, much larger playing table, all the Bones and Hats stood and applauded. The Skulls at the table did their best to ignore her. Jacy nodded appreciatively, but wasted no time getting down to business.

Namely, who was that strange woman lurking in the parking lot of the restaurant where Derian and Loroot were exiting?

25

"Okay," Rainy Dissolve rapped the side of her chair with her knuckles once Cruder Stiletto stepped into the circular room and closed the door. "All of us except for Sultana Yelp are here. Has anybody seen or heard from…"

"That's what I'd like to know," Galore stepped from the wall that camouflaged him. All the ladies stood, astonished. No male had ever set foot in this sacred room. Rainy Dissolve put her hands up towards the other tense women, staring a hole in Galore.

"How dare you enter this..."

"Fuck your stupid rules, Rainy. I just want Sultana. Something's wrong."

Trichina Flame, who stood at least 2 feet taller than Galore, looked as if she may strike. Galore looked at her and shook his head.

"Please don't, Trichina," Galore's voice was quiet, yet firm. "I like you. I like all of all you. I apologize for intruding here, but you all know me. I wouldn't do this if it wasn't important."

Trichina remained tense for a few long seconds before relaxing. She nodded at Galore and sat down.

"We haven't seen her either, Galore," Karma Twin said. "We haven't heard a single thing."

"That's why we're meeting today," Cruder Stiletto spoke. "We need to figure out what our next step is."

"Have you talked to Laddie Nines yet?" Galore asked.

"Not yet," Rainy Dissolve answered. "Karma Twin stopped by this morning to talk to him, but it seems he's vanished. The room was a mess, the bed was overturned, the window was…."

"Broken, I know, I was there," Galore shook his head. "I talked to him in the middle of the night. He hasn't seen her, either. The last time he saw her he told her about Fatter Verb visiting Granny Mandible, and that was it."

"I thought Granny Mandible wasn't accepting visitors anymore," Trichina Flame said. "What does this…"

Galore looked at all four women, scared shitless. Galore was *so* different than his meek appearance showed. He was stronger than steel and tougher than leather, but tonight he looked like a scared, confused child.

"Please tell me what's going on here, ladies. One minute I'm asking Laddie Nines where Sultana is, the next minute four thugs dressed in black barge into his room looking for me. What is going..."

"Four guys in black?" Cruder Stilleto spoke up.

"Why do you ask that, Cruder..." Rainy asked before she was interrupted. A slot in the wall opened, and a voice spoke through it.

"Sorry to disrupt your meeting but I was told this is an emergency. Rainy Dissolve is to contact Maise Elantina on her secure channel, immediately."

The slot closed, and a puzzled Rainy Dissolve went to a console on the wall and proceeded to communicate with Maise Elantina. The other four began whispering, talking about what they should do next. Rainy Dissolve hurried by them.

"I've got an emergency," she told them as she reached for the doorknob. "Please make a plan on what to do about Sultana and keep me posted."

Rainy Dissolve rushed out the door.

26

Alarms bell rang louder for Jacy when she caught the unnoticed interloper. *Who the hell is that? And why does she look familiar?* Jacy raised a slow hand, careful not to overwhelm Derian. In Jacy's eyes, there was a colossal difference in being paranoid and being prepared.

Derian looked in the direction where Jacy last saw the woman lurking in the shadows, but she was no longer there. Jacy scanned the rest of the area and came up empty, too. The trespasser was gone.

Jacy breathed easier, questioning herself if there even was an intruder. Flashbacks of her overprotectiveness with Eugene flickered through her memory bank. Was this a distant echo of those times, magnified because now she was protecting her own daughter?

Derian wrapped her arms around herself as if she were cold, but due to the evening's warmth, Jacy knew it wasn't a temperature chill. Derian looked back at the restaurant where Loroot finished his chat.

"Call me tomorrow," Loroot shook his colleague's hand and made his way towards Derian.

Jacy's breathing steadied and slackened. She stood, stretching her legs. As she did this, she scanned the humongous playing table. There had to be close to sixty people, either playing or encircling it. Some were jovial, some contemplative. She knew and recognized most, others she had never seen before.

Gravigo was there, seated in front of Neva, who smiled at Jacy. Jacy nodded back. The Bam Slicer was far to the left of her, but he paid Jacy no attention. Jacy's eyes fell on the two ominous yet empty chairs across from her. She knew in her gut that one of those chairs would be Flair's. She guessed that The Bam Slicer would move to the other one when Flair deigned them all with his presence.

Jacy shrugged. There was nothing she could do about that until Flair showed up. She perused the surrounding area and saw Agent Ninny Mop pretend he was bored. Jacy knew better, though. Agent Ninny Mop never missed a thing.

Jacy was surprised when her eyes fell on Hammer Coolie staring at her, at the next closest table. Jacy half smiled. Damn, he was handsome. Hammer raised his water bottle towards her, nodded, and went back to his Game.

Jacy returned her attention to Derian and Loroot. They had their arms around each other as they walked to their Murano. Derian's arm slid down her husband's back and caressed his ass cheek.

"I can't wait for my birthday present when we get home," Derian grinned.

Loroot chuckled, bending in to give her neck a kiss. Jacy rolled her eyes. Apparently she would have another night of closing her eyes and plugging her ears to her daughter and son-in-law.

"Well, we have to make sure you reach 25 in style, don't we?" Loroot murmured. Both of them laughed and held each other closer. Despite her own uncomfortableness around this area of Derian's life, Jacy was happy her daughter had a partner she was so connected with. Their active sex life enhanced an already special relationship.

"I love you, Roots," Derian used her pet name for him.

"I love you, too, my lovely wife."

Leaving them to their romantic talk, Jacy did a final scan of the nearly empty parking lot. Still nothing. Maybe it was her over-active imagination taking over again. Jacy was going to have to work on that.

"Ah, shit," Loroot stopped walking. "My jacket."

"Good thing you're pretty," Derian teased him. "Go get it, I'll wait here."

The hairs on Jacy's neck moved. They didn't stand up, which would've made her frantic, but there was just enough movement for her to sit up straighter. Jacy no longer cared if she was being over protective or not. Her hands floated, and Loroot picked up on it right away.

"Forget it," he started to head for the car. "I'll be in for lunch tomorrow or the next. I'll grab it then."

Atta boy, Rootsie.

Derian had other ideas, though. "Don't be silly. Go back and get it while we're here."

Jacy's hand gesticulations sped a little, making Loroot indecisive as he looked back towards the restaurant.

"Come with me," he finally said. "I don't want you out here by yourself."

Good boy, Loroot, Jacy smiled, her hands returning to stillness. Derian's laugh, though, set them into action once again.

"You're worried about me being alone in *this* neighborhood?" Derian chuckled again. "What, some rich person's labra-doodle is going to escape from its doggy chateau and nip me?"

Loroot shared in the amusement, but Jacy wasn't feeling jocular at all. She studied the parking lot and found it empty of people. Loroot raised his key fob and pressed a button. The Murano's doors unlocked and the lights flashed. They were about a dozen parking spaces away from it.

"Okay, but wait in the car, okay?"

"Roots…"

"Just humour me, please?"

"Okay," Derian moved towards the car before spinning around and walking backwards. "Only because it'll give me a chance to remove my panties so we can play on the drive home."

Loroot's eyes widened. "I'll be right back." He rushed off towards the restaurant, making Derian laugh.

A wavered shadow caught Jacy's eye. What was *that*? She checked the area again but still came up blank. Jacy moved her hands faster. She didn't know exactly what was going on, but she didn't think it was her imagination anymore. Derian was seven parking places away from the Murano when a voice spoke. Jacy's blood ran cold.

"Hello, Jacy." Jacy looked up to see Flair sitting across from her. The Bam Slicer hadn't joined him yet, but Jacy knew he'd be by his boss' side soon enough. Jacy swallowed. Here we go.

Game on.

27

"I don't know the exact details yet, Rainy. I just know Beau is in trouble," Maise Elantina and the silent, shuffling Rainy Dissolve rushed to Rainy's table.

It was a busy day in the Gaming Area, and you could sense the charge in the air.

"It's a fucking zoo here, today," Maise Elantina went on. "I need to get to my pod and check on them and Jacy."

Maise smiled at Rainy's puzzled look. "She was moved to the big table earlier."

Maise looked at the buzzing crowd. "I don't know what's happening today, but something big is going down. Have you figured out what it is?"

Rainy Dissolve shook her head. Rainy was still trying to wrap her brain around what Maise told her seconds earlier.

Beau was in trouble.

The noise was deafening, but Rainy Dissolve tuned it out as best she could. They bumped and jostled other Gamers on their route to Rainy's table. Just then Jinnion Crust grabbed Maise Elantina's shoulder.

"Maise! It's Jacy! Her and Flair are about to go head to head! That must be what's going down today!"

"Shit," Maise muttered, looking at Rainy. Rainy made a shooing motion, and signed that she would protect Beau. Maise hugged her and whispered in her ear. "Please don't forget what I asked of you a long time ago."

Rainy Dissolve nodded. She would do anything Maise Elantina asked of her. Jinnion looked long and lovingly at Rainy Dissolve as Maise changed course and headed for Jacy's table. Rainy looked at him and gave him a small smile. A large grin busted out on Jinnion Crust's face.

"I'll come with you," he yelled over the roar.

Rainy moved on, still not quite believing something was going to happen to Beau. Today was his first day out of the 25 safe years he and Derian had been entitled to, for Christ's sake. Why, Rainy bet that...

Rainy's brow furrowed when she saw Trichina at her table. What was going...

"Hurry!" Trichina waved her to an open chair across from her. Rainy blasted into action mode. In the blink of an eye Rainy sat and took stock of the situation. Four Skulls were across the table, all paying Beau close attention. Rainy checked on him.

Beau had just left a Van Heusen store where he'd purchased a couple of new shirts. Rainy tried to size the circumstances up, but felt a step behind it all.

"Excuse me, sir?" A salesclerk from Van Heusen came outside.

Beau turned around to look at Trichina Flame's girl. Rainy heard one of the Skulls swear.

"Yes?"

Rainy began to move her hands up and down, gently nudging Beau towards the salesclerk. She had no idea what the Skulls were up to, but she sensed their agitation at Trichina's interruption. Beau walked towards Triche's girl and stepped back into the store.

Seconds later a car rammed into one of the stone pillars out front where Beau stood moments before. A drug-addled female with scabs all over her face staggered out of the car.

"Fucking hell," one of the Skulls punched the table and left. The other three followed, swearing at both Trichina and Rainy as they departed.

With Beau safe and sound, Rainy smiled at Trichina, standing to go to her. Trichina rose, too, walking towards each other. Just then Rainy waded into a crush of Gamers. She came to a complete standstill. The first thing she noticed was the ten or twelve people pressed up against her all wore black. As this registered in her brain, she noticed another body pressed up against hers. Trichina?

"Rainy? What's going on here?" Trichina looked as confused as Rainy. Who were all these people in black and what....

Rainy Dissolve felt her stomach drop. She looked over at Jinnion, who stood apart from the pack. Jinnion stared sadly at her for a moment, before he dropped his head and walked away. Rainy didn't understand. What was going on here? Why...?

She watched Trichina Flame's eyes roll towards the back of her head. Trichina would've collapsed but the crowd of black figures held her up. What....

Rainy heard a voice she knew well speak into her ear.

"Rainy Dissolve! This is indeed a pleasure!" Rainy heard Ridded Snot speak, just before she felt a sharp pain in her lower back and everything went dark.

28

Jacy steadied her frantic hand dance. She was relieved to see Derian pick up her pace slightly. Jacy did a quick check on the parking lot. The woman was gone again.

Jacy looked up at Flair who was leaning back in his chair, smiling that crooked smile of his. Jacy leaned back in a similar fashion. "What's up, Flair? Come by for some lessons?"

Jacy's comment caused a few laughs, even one from a Skull who received a rough slap across the head courtesy of The Bam Slicer. Bam rose and walked over to Flair. Just as The Bam Slicer went to sit down in the adjoining chair, though, Flair gave him the subtlest of head shakes. The Bam Slicer looked befuddled, but returned to his original seat without a word.

Jacy kept her face neutral. What was *that* all about?

"Why, Jacy," Flair planted an innocent look upon his face. "I'm almost insulted. Can't a friend just drop by and say hello if he's in the neighborhood?"

A wicked smile creased Flair's face. "Especially if said neighborhood is in the slums?" All the Skulls burst into hoots of laughter and whistles, except for The Bam Slicer. He was looking above Jacy's head. Jacy tossed a quick glance behind her.

Maise Elantina stood there. She smiled at Jacy, put a hand on her shoulder, and patted it in encouragement. Maise leaned down and whispered into Jacy's ear.

"Stay cool, Jace. You can do this." Maise's breath was warm on her ear.

Jacy returned her attention to Derian. Her senses were on high alert now. She heard the crushing chords of Rage Against the Machine's 'Guerilla Radio' blasting loud. She felt the excitement and tension rise at the table. And her gut, oh, her gut…

"My apologies, *old* friend," Jacy slobbered her voice with mock sincerity. "I didn't realize this was a social call."

Flair leaned to his left and spoke to a Skull a few chairs away from him. Jacy paid them no heed as something caught her eye two cars away on the other side of the Murano. Derian made it to the front passenger side when Jacy got her first good look at the strange woman. Jacy studied her, scouring her memory pool as to why she looked somewhat familiar. Jacy had seen her before, but where?

"Jacy…" Flair spoke, but Jacy held up a finger for him to wait. She studied the skinny, unkempt woman as she approached Derian from the rear of the Murano.

"Excuse me, do you have a light?" That voice. Jacy heard that voice before. It wasn't exactly how she recalled it, it sounded more tired and worn, now. Hearing the voice did push the memory closer to the forefront, though. This puzzle, this convoluted fucking puzzle was starting to have the last few pieces….

"Sorry, I don't smoke," Derian said.

…fall into place. The pieces were connecting, but weren't registering swift enough for Jacy's liking. Her own gut feeling ploughed into her like a jackhammer.

"Do you have a couple bucks to spare, then?" The increasingly familiar woman was now by the rear passenger door. Jacy mentally washed her, fixing her greasy hair, wiping the grime from her skin, straightening her clothes…

"Let me check," Derian opened her purse and looked into it.

The final piece clicked into place and completed itself. Jacy realized who this woman was, although Jacy had never known her as a woman. She knew her when she was an innocent, clean cut, teenaged girl who changed her mind when her Guns N Roses loving crush talked himself over to help her babysit.

Serena.

It was fucking Serena!

Blood poured like an avalanche through Jacy's veins, her brain screaming for her hands to do something, *anything!* Flair timed his words perfectly with Zach de la Rocha's lyrics that blared at an ear bleeding level.

"Fuck it. Cut the cord," he snarled.

Jacy looked up at the figure taking the seat beside Flair.

"Lights out," Lita growled as Serena plunged a knife deep into Jacy's baby girl.

29

Jacy bounced back from the table, stumbling to keep her balance.

What the fuck just happened here?! A curdling scream wailed from within. With dumb eyes, Jacy watched Serena grab Derian's purse and dash off into the dark. Jacy watched Derian, her Derian, her baby daughter, for fuck's sake, clutch her punctured stomach and slide down the Murano's side to the unforgiving pavement. Jacy's eyes rose from her dying angel to the devil now sitting across from her.

Lita.

She wasn't Lita, though, at least not the Lita that Jacy knew and loved. This new Lita was decked out in head to toe leather-fetish wear and enough whorish makeup to sink a battleship. Flair draped his arm around her. He whispered something to her, never taking his eyes from Jacy, and licked Lita's ear with his snake-like tongue. Lita wore a grotesque smile. Jacy wanted to ask her 'why', but didn't. Nor would she ever.

Jacy looked down at Derian. Blood spilled from the fingers she pushed against her wound. Jacy noticed Loroot exit the restaurant with his jacket in hand. Jacy instinctively moved her hands, causing Loroot to frown and move faster towards the car.

Jacy caught Maise Elantina frantically giving orders in her peripheral vision, but didn't really care. She continued to stare at Loroot and Derian, her hands moving slowly. Through the chaotic mess in her brain, Jacy heard Lita chuckle.

"Fuck you, Lita," Jacy spoke in a gentle voice that betrayed the words she uttered. She didn't take her eyes from Derian as she urged Loroot to hurry. Jacy could tell Flair was staring at her.

"Fuck you, Flair," she used the same monotone expression.

Come on, Rootsie, come on....

Jacy sensed someone standing by her side, surprised to see The Bam Slicer standing there. Even stranger to her was what looked like sympathy in his raging eyes.

"Fuck you, Bam," Jacy's voice remained even. She watched as Loroot discovered Derian. He barrelled through the parking lot, yelling Derian's name.

"Miss Jacy?" Agent Ninny Mop stood on the other side of her.

"Fuck you, Agent Ninny Mop," Jacy watched Loroot frantically dial 911. Agent Ninny Mop moved away. Jacy could now see Gravigo and Neva where Ninny just vacated. Jacy knew there was no more she could do with gut feelings and such. She placed her hands on the table, watching the action unfold below.

"Fuck you, Neva," Jacy kept her expressionless tone as she watched Loroot pull open Derian's jacket and yank up her shirt. He sobbed when he saw the wound. Jacy did the same.

Oh Buddha, oh God, oh fuck....

"Jacy..." Gravigo's voice seemed a trillion miles away.

...*blood, so much blood. Too much fucking blood*... Jacy felt her heart shatter. She made no attempt to contain the pieces.

"Fuck you, Gravigo," Jacy didn't take her eyes from her daughter. Her *dying* daughter. Jacy noticed Gravigo stiffen at her words, but she wasn't quite done with him yet. She turned her head towards him and looked as deep into his eyes as she could.

"And fuck your game, too." With that poetic conclusion, Jacy stood tall and broke the biggest rule of the Game.

She entered it.

30

When Jacy Morgan disappeared into the middle of the table, the entire room quieted to a hush. The only sound Hammer Coolie heard was a chair scraping back, and someone sitting down. He looked at the visitor, and while she looked somewhat familiar, Hammer couldn't place her. She sure was a natural beauty, though. Hammer looked at a confused Maise Elantina. The whole room felt frozen, until Flair broke the silence.

"Well, *that* was pretty interesting."

Hammer contemplated back on this later, and still didn't understand his reaction. He liked Jacy, sure, but he liked a lot of people. In this case, though, he looked over at Flair, stepped onto a chair with his left foot, onto the adjoining table with his right, and launched himself into a flying tackle, catching Flair square in the chest.

The wind gushed out of Flair as he and Hammer hit the ground. Hammer smashed him with three rapid punches before Lita yanked Hammer up and kneed him in the face, knocking him onto his back.

Then all hell broke loose.

31

Jacy didn't have any master plan when it came to entering the Game. She had no clue what she was supposed to do or where she would end up. Would she end up back on Earth? And if so, where would she be? The parking lot with her baby girl? The hospital? Russia? All Jacy's gut reaction told her to do was to do was dive into the table.

Her queries were answered soon enough, though.

"Ugh," Jacy landed belly first on cruel ground. She looked up, spitting sand from her mouth. She furrowed her brow at the cliff in front of her.

What the…

Jacy stood, brushing the sunburned silt from her clothes. She squinted up at the cliff, realization dawning on her. As she hobbled in a haphazard circle, Jacy recognized the countless lines of people streaming across the blood-red plains. The sky was still brighter than blue, the air as fragrant as an angel's rose, and the warmth just as welcoming as it was the day she first arrived in this crazy place.

Jacy completed her circle and refocused her attention on the cliff. Had Derian already been here? Had she been absorbed into one of the numerous lines, like Dougie, the shaggy haired boy with the awesome Dropkick Murphy's t-shirt?

Just then the staircase appeared at her feet. Jacy didn't think. She dashed up the stairs as fast as she could. Up, up, up, higher, higher, higher.

Jacy hadn't made it halfway when she looked up and saw an elegant female making her way down the stairs. The lady looked dreamy with her pallid bathrobe fluttering in the genial breeze as she took in her new surroundings. Jacy stopped for a moment, wondering if she'd entered this place with such grace and panache. She doubted it. Jacy's musings washed away, though, when she understood what was happening.

The stairs were disappearing.

32

Hammer hit the floor with a thud, his nose exploding in a spray of blood. Lita tended Flair, trying to get him to his feet. Hammer struggled to his. He didn't want to fight Lita, but he would if he had to. He made a step towards her.

Just then, he felt a familiar hand on his shoulder, and Hammer knew he wouldn't have to fight Lita.

"Let's do this for real, Lita," Karma Twin challenged her, beckoning Lita to come to her with an open right hand. Lita didn't look like she wanted to partake.

"You chicken, bitch?" Karma asked.

Flair was standing now, blood leaking from his mouth. He stepped in front of Lita. "Fuck you, Karma, I'll take you…"

Hammer lowered his shoulder and blasted Flair's kidneys with a perfect shoulder tackle. Hammer and Flair crashed into the wall, wrestling and punching. Lita went after Karma Twin, but it wasn't really close. Karma locked her in a rear chin lock and would've broken her neck if Coney Slut didn't hit Karma with a leaping drop kick to the back of the head. Karma flew forwards, crashing into the floor.

Karma stood on unreliable knees, shaking the cobwebs from her head. Coney Slut's eyes widened, as a kick like that would incapacitate the biggest and strongest of men. Coney fled the scene.

Another burly Skull wasn't going to let Karma off so easily, though. Shakiest Homa, a mountain of a man, glared at Karma Twin.

"I'll fight you…" he started before Neva Tezremsy shattered a chair across the back of his head. Shakiest Homa dropped to the floor. Karma Twin nodded thanks to Neva, who already moved on to another Skull.

Karma Twin turned back to Lita, but she scurried off with a bleeding, limping Flair. Hammer watched them retreat before smiling at Karma Twin. She winked at him.

They both turned to the table, eyes wide at the sight greeting them. The brawl was no longer contained to just their vicinity. Fights erupted across the entire main Gaming area. Agent Ninny Mop and his deputies tried their best to restore order, but their attempts proved fruitless.

Karma nodded at the lone player still playing the Game at Jacy's table. It was the raven haired beauty Hammer thought he recognized earlier. Someone else noticed her, too. Unmoral Brogan, a muscle filled Skull, grabbed the girl by her hair and lifted her from her seat. The girl squealed. Hammer and Karma pounced.

Hammer smashed Unmoral in the face with his fist while Karma jammed her foot on the outside of his right knee. They heard a snap as Unmoral crumpled to the ground, releasing his steel grip on the girl. The girl scrambled to her feet, clambering back to her chair. Hammer Coolie and Karma Twin shielded her so she could sit down.

"Who are you?!" Karma Twin called above the noise.

"I'm Lucy," the girl answered. "I'm trying to save Jacy's daughter."

33

Jacy raced up the stairs, imploring the majestic lady to stop her descent.

"Stop! Please! Stop!" Jacy's pleas went unheeded. She was now within fifteen steps of the lady, but at least two hundred of the stairs had vanished. Jacy's shoulders sagged.

"Ma'am?" Jacy's word jolted the lady from her reverie, but she continued to descend, causing more and more stairs to dissolve.

"Darling," the lady beamed as she made it within three steps of Jacy. "What *is* this most incredible place?"

The lady reached her hand out and Jacy took it. They were now on similar steps scanning the horizon. "This is the most picturesque place I've ever seen, and believe me, darling, I've seen some pretty places." The lady smiled and stepped from the stair causing Jacy to scramble down to keep even with her. The lady stopped again, giving Jacy a chance to swipe through the air behind them where the stair once was.

Sure enough, nothing. Jacy sighed, as the lady looked at Jacy with a confused look.

"Is…is…is this heaven?" The lady's voice sounded almost child-like in its innocence and wonder. Jacy chuckled, recalling when she asked Gravigo those very same words.

Jacy shook her head. What was she doing? She wasn't a tour guide. She was making a last ditch effort to save her daughter's life.

With a glance back to the top of the cliff, Jacy sighed and realized she'd have to wait for the next person to come along. She led the lady down the remaining stairs. Part of Jacy wanted to tell the lady the Allah forsaken hellhole this place really was, but stopped, realizing the lady wasn't going to the same place Jacy went.

"This place," Jacy squeezed the lady's hand tight, "is even *better* than heaven."

Jacy was showered by the most grateful look she ever received. Their feet touched the sand at the bottom of the no longer existing staircase. Jacy gestured the lady to move on towards the lines of people.

"Are you coming?" the lady asked.

"Not this time," Jacy shook her head.

The lady curtsied, and moved on. Jacy didn't watch her for long. She drew a line in the sand where the last of the stairs had been moments before. She paced off four large paces from it, crouched into a racing stance, and waited for the steps to reappear.

34

As the fracas raged around them, Hammer Coolie, Karma Twin, and Lucy looked down at the scene below.

"Dickie was keeping an eye on things here as we heard things were going to be crazy today," Lucy said. She looked around her. "Crazy's a pretty good word for it, too."

They watched a man in his fifties slow down his car, then stop. He rolled down his passenger window and called to Loroot. "Is everything okay?"

"Please help," Loroot sobbed. The man hopped from his car and ran over to Derian and Loroot.

"This is Henry, better known as Hank. He's a doctor," Lucy told them. "One of the best in Baltimore."

"What's he doing in Canada?" Karma Twin asked.

"On vacation. He actually just came from an escort's place. My doctor friend here has a pretty massive foot fetish."

Hammer Coolie raised his eyebrows at this.

"Don't judge him on that," Lucy chuckled. "Hank's a good guy, and a really fine doctor. Dickie couldn't get one of his subjects here in time. He's got a first responder in his pod, but she's miles away. He called me because he knew I had someone in the city. I nudged my guy to take this route back to his hotel in hopes he'd see Derian."

"Can he save her?" Hammer asked.

"I don't know," Lucy watched. "Let's hope and see."

Hammer watched Hank take charge of Derian's care. Hammer looked closer at Lucy, trying to figure out who this strange, gorgeous girl was. He snapped his fingers. "You're one of those brats that used to hang out at Granny Mandible's house, aren't you?"

"Guilty as charged," Lucy smiled, not taking her eyes from the drama below. "I'm all grown up now, though."

"You three were pretty annoying," Hammer smirked.

"We never made up rhymes about you, Hammer Coolie," Lucy looked at him with dazzling, hazel eyes. "I wouldn't let them. I had a secret crush on you."

Karma Twin sensed rather than heard a Skull approach them. She hit him with a spinning elbow that knocked him cold. Lucy looked impressed. Hammer fake applauded her. Karma remembered something Sultana Yelp told the council recently about Granny Mandible.

"Do you still see Granny Mandible?" Karma asked.

Guilt clouded Lucy's eyes.

"No," she sighed. "When Jacy got us thinking about things, we just left. We felt it easier for everyone if we did it that way. How is Granny doing?"

"We don't know," Hammer shrugged his shoulders.

"What?" Lucy spun her head at him. "Why not?"

"She's not taking any visitors. She hasn't for the last while."

"Granny Mandible isn't taking visitors?" Lucy looked alarmed.

Karma Twin recalled something Galore just told them. "Actually, she did see someone just the other day."

Lucy and Hammer Coolie both looked at her. "Who?" They asked at the same time.

"Fatter Verb."

Lucy's face went white as she stood from the table. Her knees wobbled a bit, so Hammer reached out and steadied her.

"Are you okay?" he asked.

Lucy shook her head, half talking to herself, half to them. "No, no, no, I'm not okay, shit, none of us are okay…. Dickie and Joey…holy fuck…. Jesus Christ…We have…we have…we have to…"

Hammer grabbed Lucy by the shoulders, squaring his face with hers. "Calm down, Lucy, get it together. What is going on here?"

Lucy steeled herself, and then looked dead into Hammer's eyes. "This whole Jacy thing has been a ruse to hide what is *really* going on. We have to get out of here. Now."

"What about Jacy's daughter?" Karma Twin pointed at the table. "We can't…"

"I've done all I can do, now," Lucy looked towards the table. "Hank's training will have to suffice from here. We have to go."

She returned her attention to Hammer Coolie. "Do you know where Bluff 70 is?"

Hammer nodded.

"Get there now. Both of you. Tell trusted ones along the way, but *only* trusted ones, okay? You won't have time to go searching for people. Do you hear me?"

"Yes, but…"

"Questions later! Move!"

The chaotic noise of the brawl was shattered by the deafening 'BONG' of a gong. Lucy's eyes widened in horror.

"It may already be too late!" she screamed before dashing away.

Hammer Coolie and Karma Twin stared at each other during the pause between the first and second peal of the gong. By the time the second gong started, they were gone.

35

Jacy's attention was diverted by a faint reverberating sound off in the distance. She looked off to the horizon, feeling nauseous all of a sudden. The feeling passed in a moment and Jacy refocused her attention back on the line she drew earlier just in time.

The stairs were back.

Jacy sprinted as hard as she could while wailing like a banshee at the same time in hopes the next descendant would stop in their tracks. She had no idea if this Usain Bolt/Yoko Ono act would help or not, but when one is at the bottom of the barrel of ideas, well, one is at the bottom of the barrel. As her legs pumped like oil derricks, she snuck a quick peek and was disheartened to see the early sixties gentleman in jogging pants and ball cap sight-seeing as he bumbled down the stairs. He paid Jacy no attention whatsoever.

"Shit, shit, shit!" Jacy bore down harder, beginning to sense the futility in it all. The view mesmerized the newcomers, who absentmindedly made the steps disappear. This exercise was impossible.

The gentleman was 30 steps away before he finally noticed her and stopped. "You okay, Miss?"

"Yeah….no….no…. yeah…." a heaving Jacy waved her hand in disgust at all of it. She improved in this attempt, but was still too far from the top. "Couldn't you hear me yelling at you to stop?"

"Not at first," he shook his mange of shaggy hair partially contained by a Seattle Sounders hat. "I'm pretty awed by this whole place. I just noticed you now. What are you attempting to do?"

"I'm trying to stop…stop…" Jacy sighed. "I'm trying to get up there and meet someone before it's too late."

The man looked up the way he had come. His eyes widened. He looked at Jacy with a puzzled look on his face. "Where did the stairs go?"

"They disappear the moment you step from them."

"Interesting," the man looked at the vast air expanse between them and the top of the cliff. There had to be at least 500 feet between the two. "I can see how disappearing stairs may toss a kink in your plans."

"A *major* kink," Jacy ascended the remaining steps so she was even with the man. "This is hopeless."

"Is there another way up there?" the man asked.

"I don't know," Jacy shrugged. "I suppose I'll have to look, but I doubt I have enough time." Jacy continued to stare at the cliff top. The man, however, studied the cliff face.

"How are your rock climbing abilities?" he asked.

"My what?"

"Your rock climbing skills," he pointed to the cliff face. "Look." Jacy followed his finger to a jagged edge that jutted from the face about four or five feet out from the face of stone.

"If you can leap and successfully hold onto that crag, you may be able to scale the rest of the way to the top."

Jacy scanned the remaining cliff face and did notice nooks and crannies and various possible footholds. But Jesus Buddha, they were a far way from the top. Adding to her conundrum was Jacy's realization that somehow her pain receptors were turned on.

"Wow, I don't know," she stared upwards at the top of the cliff.

"Is the person you're going to meet important?" The man looked at Jacy. Jacy merely raised her eyebrows at him.

"You can do it, then," he gave her a firm nod before looking back at the precipice.

Jacy took a concentrated breath. She wasn't about to turn back now. "Can you stay right where you are?"

"Of course," the man shuffled towards the side of the final step to give Jacy enough room for launching. Jacy nodded her thanks and moved down ten or twelve steps to get a good run at it.

"Not so far," the man said.

"I need a good run at it, though," Jacy argued.

"That's too far down, though. You won't be at your optimum speed when you reach here. Try the sixth one down from me." The man pointed at the stair.

Jacy mounted four or five more stairs, unsure if the man knew what he was talking about. "This one?"

"One more."

Jacy followed his orders, looking at the top stair. "Doesn't seem like much room. Are you sure about this?"

"I coached some track at Washington State University," the man shrugged.

Jacy smiled at her good fortune. "Really? Long jump?"

"Nope. Javelin."

"Shit."

"You pick up stuff here and there, though," the man shrugged again. "You can do this jump, as the jump doesn't really matter. It's the landing that is the important step here. You need to hold that crag."

Jacy nodded. She knew how crucial her landing was. She steadied herself, taking a deep breath. She stared a hole in the top stair. Not wanting to give nay-saying doubts too long a chance to settle into her brain, Jacy bolted.

"YYYYAAAAAAHHHHHH!!!!" She howled like a screaming eagle as she thrust her legs as hard as they would go. She hit the top stair perfectly and launched herself at the cliff wall, praying her landing would be as sweet as her take-off.

"Oof!" the crag smashed into Jacy's guts.

"Hang on!!" the javelin coach hollered.

Letting go was the absolute last thing Jacy was going to do. Unfortunately, she wasn't given much of a choice. After scrabbling fingers scratched through the dust for a better hold, the crag broke from the cliff face. Both Jacy and the chunk of rock plummeted towards the ground.

36

It was both straightforward and difficult to tell what was going on. Between the crashing bongs, the scrambling people, and the utter cacophony of the place, there was but one, simple answer.

This wasn't good. It wasn't good at all. Hammer stopped as he watched two figures in black drag a crying Bone by her long hair along the fountain's cobble stoned ground.

"Hey..." He started to step in, but Karma Twin yanked him back.

"No fucking time! Move, move, move!"

Karma was off again, Hammer quick on her heels. While the gonging broke the brawl up inside the main Gaming area, it had a more riotous effect out here. People battling, scampering, shrieking. There was no rhyme or rhythm to anything.

Karma blasted a Hat in the face with a running right hook to help clear their way. Hammer leapt over the falling Hat. They pressed on.

"This way!" Karma cut a sharp 60-degree angle to their left. Hammer didn't question her. He could barely see through the dusty quilt of scared and bloodied faces they weaved through. He looked over Karma's left shoulder and could see the direction they ran in.

"Wrong way!" he yelled. "The other way is faster!"

"Keep following!" Karma didn't look back. Hammer gritted his teeth and remained in her wake.

The crowd began to thin somewhat, but there were still stampeding people everywhere. Hammer heard Karma swear and make a rapid 90 degree cut to their right.

"Wait here!" Before Hammer Coolie could say a word, Karma rushed towards a diminutive figure on his hands and knees, bleeding and exhausted. Stalking towards him were three people, clad in head to toe black. Karma Twin stepped on the beaten person's back and leapt. She nailed the outside attackers with expert kicks to their respective chins. The middle one was taken ass over tea kettle by her crotch. By the time he regained his footing, Karma nailed him between the eyes with a perfect punch. He crumpled to the ground like a rag doll.

Karma sensed the fourth one a moment too late. Hammer was there, though. With an uppercut, a body shot, and a gazelle punch, the last attacker was down.

"Come on," Karma grabbed one of the arms of the beaten man she saved. "Grab his other arm! We need to move!"

Hammer threw the man's other arm around his shoulder. Once they stood with both man's arms around both of their shoulders, Hammer noticed his feet didn't touch the ground. They dangled in the air, about knee height. Hammer glanced at Karma Twin.

"His name's Galore!" She shouted as they began to move. "Long story!"

Hammer felt he could wait for the explanation at a later time. The three of them scampered on, getting closer to their destination. The crowd weakened to almost nothing by the time they reached the woods. They entered the main trail system, and stopped.

"This way, quick," Karma hissed. They turned right and waded in through the brush. "Can you carry him?"

Hammer nodded.

"Good. Keep moving forward, and I'll cover our tracks. I'll tell you when to stop."

"I can walk," Galore protested, bubbles of blood escaping his mouth. Hammer ignored Galore and threw him over his shoulder. They forged on.

After ten minutes or so they came to a small clearing. Karma Twin caught up to them and told them to rest. Hammer tried to place Galore on the ground as gentle as he could, but in reality he dropped him like a sack of potatoes. Karma Twin knelt by Galore's face, wiping blood and dirt from it as best she could.

"Thanks, Karma," Galore mumbled. "I took three of them out before those other four came."

Hammer snorted. Both Galore and Karma Twin looked at him.

"Sorry," he waved his hand. "No offense."

Karma Twin looked at Galore again. "Sultana?"

Galore pursed his lips together and shook his head. "What is going on here, Karma?"

Just then they heard a faint shuddering sound grow louder.

"Is that...." Hammer was about to ask.

"Shit," Karma scrambled through the brush, in the direction of the main building. Hammer and an injured Galore followed her.

"Where are you going?" Hammer Coolie asked.

Karma shushed him. "We're not too far from one of the fields. We should be able to see what's happening. Keep quiet and out of sight, though."

Hammer and Galore followed her orders, wiggling like snakes under branches and logs while clambering like squirrels over others. It didn't take long to get close to the field, where an overhanging Weeping Willow branch afforded them perfect cover. The screeching noise grew louder.

All three sets of eyes grew wide as it came into view.

"Holy fuck," Hammer Coolie spoke for all three.

37

"Wow! That was lucky!"

Jacy's javelin coach looked down at her from the top stair. About twelve feet below him, a dazed Jacy stared at the crag-less cliff face she fell from, trying to mold her thoughts into something coherent. One minute she leapt for the cliff wall, the next she was plummeting to the ground.

Apparently a larger ledge caught her fall, and didn't rupture like the previous one did. Jacy chuckled as she stood, gathering her bearings. It seemed like a gazillion lifetimes ago that she thought a messy haired kid named Dougie may have pulled the old 'cartoon ledge' trick on her.

"Atta girl, that's the spirit," her coach cheered her on.

Jacy waved to him, catching the breath that was knocked from her. Holy shit, she was a long way up. A thought hit her, suddenly.

"Can you wait until I get to the top before heading down the stairs?" she asked her javelin coach. "I think only one person can be on the stairs at a time. Maybe if you wait, you'll slow the progression."

"You bet your ass I'm waiting, Missy. I'm not going anywhere until you get to the top."

Jacy thanked him, looking up the steep face of granite for the best possible route up. With coaxing from her coach on the stairs, she made it to another ledge.

"Okay, Missy, that's a good first step," her coach searched the next section of cliff face. "There's another smaller one to your left, about fifteen feet up. Can you see it?"

Jacy nodded. Her coach pointed out another one to the right. "There's one there, too, do you see it?"

Jacy spotted that one, too. "Can you see which one has a better route from it once I get there?"

"Nope," her coach shook his head, looking at her. "We may have to use a trial and error approach. Your only job is to not fall, okay? You got that?"

Jacy gulped and nodded.

"Let me hear you say it."

Jacy stared at the cliff face. "I will not fall."

"Good," her coach clapped his hands together. "I believe you, and the cliff does, too. Now, let's try the left ridge first."

Jacy and her coach worked like that; trying one route or another, arguing, backtracking, moving up at times, and descending at others. It took some time as it was a lot of three steps forward, two steps back, but finally a sweating, dirty Jacy clung to the wall, less than 10 feet from the top.

A shrill noise in the distance caught her ear. What the hell was *that?* Shaking her head to refocus, Jacy called down to her coach. "Can you see the best way to the top?"

Her coach did his best but couldn't hide his concern. "Shit. We've gone left and right. All we have left is up or down."

"I sure as fuck don't want to go down, jackass," Jacy muttered, squinting up for the next handhold.

"I heard that," her coach complained.

"Sorry," she grunted as she pulled herself eight inches closer to her goal.

"Don't be, I like the spunk," he pointed towards her left foot. "There's a better left foothold about three inches up."

Jacy followed his directions. He was right. Jacy rested, catching her breath. Her chest bled through her shirt in tiny rivulets, her arms scraped and bruised. She would've questioned why she was feeling such physical pain, but she was close, so fucking close....

Another notch for her left hand. A cranny for her right foot. The smallest of fissures for her right hand. Her leg muscles screamed along with the rest of her body as she moved upwards, inch by every skin-scouring inch.

"Jesus, you're almost there," Jacy's coach sounded as shocked. She chanced a peek. She *was* almost there. Finding a place for her left hand, she grasped it. She noticed a nice big fat handhold for her right hand. She snagged that one, pulling herself up higher.

"Goddamn, you're going to..."

Her coach's words hung in the air when her latest handhold breaking free. Jacy shrieked, losing her balance and smashing against the wall. Her left fingers, bloodied and raw, pulled away from the cliff.

"No...." her coach yelled. Just then, with a flash of cascading blond hair, two feminine hands grasped Jacy's left wrist. She heard the girl grunt as she held the full weight of a dangling Jacy.

"Hold on!! For Christ's sake, hold on!!" her coach shouted.

"I will," the girl hollered back. Jacy felt for toeholds with her feet. She found one, which allowed her to take some weight off the poor girl's arms. She heard the girl gasp with relief. Jacy looked up at the tousle of blond hair falling over the edge of the cliff.

Holy shit, is that Derian? Jacy studied the wall for a hold for her right hand.

"To your left! Keep going..." her coach called out.

Jacy found it. She clung to it. She then searched for different toeholds, higher up than where her feet were now.

"Hey!" she called out to her saviour.

"Yeah?" It didn't sound like Derian, but the poor girl was grunting under a lot of physical strain.

"I'm going to get some bend for my knees. Once I do, I'll count to three. Maybe if I push off hard at the same time you pull me with everything you have, I can make it."

"Okay," the female voice wheezed. "I'll do my best."

Now *that* sounds like Derian, Jacy thought. She'd have the toughness and heart to help someone in need. Jacy felt a burst of pride. With her coach's aid, she found the perfect notch for her left leg. She'd prefer using her stronger right one, but this was their best shot.

"Ready?!"

"Yeah! On three, or three then pull?"

"On three. One…"

"You can do it, girls!" Jacy's coach called out.

"Two…"

Jacy bounced her weight down so she was springing.

"THREE!!!" All of them bellowed together.

"Hurff!!" Jacy landed waist high on the cliff's edge. Her legs dangled over the edge. They heard Jacy's coach whoop and cheer. Jacy pulled her legs up, inching forward on her pulsating stomach. She raised her head to greet her daughter.

Jacy's spirits plummeted. Her saviour wasn't Derian.

38

Hammer Coolie, Karma Twin, and Galore returned to the tiny clearing wearing dazed looks. None of them could fathom what they witnessed.

"I…what…Sultana…oh…. she…" Galore looked lost. A wordless Karma Twin sat down, staring at her boots. Hammer looked up at the blue sky through the small opening in the canopy of branches and took a deep breath. Neva Tezremsy once taught him some breathing exercises. He rarely used them, but this was a day for breathing exercises.

Hammer looked at his two companions. Were they the only three people remaining besides whoever committed this atrocity? He had no idea. Karma sensed Hammer staring at her. She looked at him for a moment with vacant eyes before inspecting her boots again.

"You okay?" Hammer looked at the minuscule man to his right. Galore looked as if he may speak, but thought better of it. He gave Hammer a curt nod. Hammer returned it and wandered thirty paces away to gather his thoughts.

Hammer played a simple drum pattern on his blood-stained, denim covered thighs. *Think, think, fucking think.* Hammer knew the three of them couldn't stay here. They were too close to the carnage. Hammer didn't take long to make a decision. He took quick stock of where they were and returned to the other two.

"Okay," Hammer Coolie snapped his fingers, happy to be in control of his thoughts and emotions again. "Listen up, you two, I have a plan."

Both Karma Twin and Galore looked at him, but not much seemed to be registering with either of them. Hammer tried a different approach. "Can you two follow me? Nod if you can."

Galore nodded first. Karma Twin watched both of them with a quizzical look.

"You just need to walk, Karma," Hammer Coolie bent down and took one of her hands. "Just put one foot in front of the other and keep up with us, okay?"

A dull light shone from behind her eyes, and Karma afforded what Hammer guessed was a nod. He looked at Galore who stood on the other side of Karma Twin. They helped Karma to her feet.

"Keep her between us," he told Galore. "Get my attention if I get too far in front, but no voices. We need to be quiet."

Galore concurred and the three started off in a diagonal direction away from the horrors they watched earlier. Hammer Coolie's focus ebbed back the farther they traversed. He didn't have a full plan yet, but he had a faint outline. Hammer hoped by the time they made it to their destination, a broader plan would reveal itself.

Hammer kept two close eyes on their surroundings, periodically checking that Karma Twin and Galore were keeping up. He was pleased to see Galore looking more cognizant. There was no change with Karma Twin, though.

Shrugging, Hammer led on. He only had one place for them to go. Bluff 70. The trouble was, there was no way to take the easiest route there. Not after what they watched earlier. Hammer led them the only other way he knew. Unfortunately, a major roadblock lay ahead.

Shrugging again, Hammer left his concerns to deal with once they got there. Maybe Galore and Karma Twin would be of better assistance by then.

Hammer forged on, wits and senses keen, but his mind was elsewhere. He thought of so many people, friends, enemies, confidantes. Tagger Merrino, Trichina Flame, Maise Elantina, Gravigo, Neva, Rainy Dissolve, hell, Flair and Lita, for that matter. Jacy, too. Every single person in this place. So many names, *so* many names. Did any of them exist anymore?

Hammer tried to shake the chill that crept onto his shoulders. A glimmer of hope came when he knew they were close to a crossroads for their trio. Hammer stopped and turned. He held his fingers an inch apart to his partners and gestured the new direction they were taking. Galore seemed to know where they were going. Karma Twin looked blank.

An eighth of a mile further they emerged on the beach of a hidden lagoon. Fourteen waterfalls fed it, and 62 caves circled it. Hammer went straight to the water and splashed the refreshing liquid into his face. He looked back at the other two. Karma Twin stood there, staring at their surroundings as if this were the first time she'd ever been there. Galore watched Karma Twin with uncertainty. Hammer caught Galore's eye and motioned him over. Galore squatted beside Hammer Coolie, dipping his hands into the water.

"How is she?" Hammer asked.

"Hard to tell," Galore answered. He started to wash himself, then thought better of it and waded in, careful not to splash too much. They still needed to be as quiet as possible.

Hammer followed, but didn't dunk himself. He washed as best he could in waist deep water, before standing, stretching, and heading back to Karma Twin. Galore was already out, seated near her.

"Do you know where we are?" Hammer asked her in a hushed voice.

Karma looked at him for a full minute before giving him a forceful nod. Hammer looked at Galore, who signalled in the affirmative.

"How well do you know these caves?" Hammer asked him.

"As well as you both, I suspect," he shrugged. "I know where each and every one of these 62 caves lead. Once inside them, I could find all the offshoots, too."

Hammer looked surprised. Galore noticed it. "I've been around here a long time, Hammer Coolie. You chose not to notice me."

Hammer took the admonition. He looked at Karma. "How about you? Could you make it to Bluff 70 through one of them?"

"Bluff 70?" Galore furrowed his brow in thought. "There are three caves that could get us there. Why are we going to Bluff 70?"

Hammer gave him an update on what occurred with Lucy. "If you have a better idea on where to go, believe me, I'm all fucking ears," he finished.

Galore absorbed what Hammer told him. "Which route do we take?"

Hammer took a big breath and examined Karma Twin. "I need to know if you're okay before I go on. If you're not, then we'll go to Plan B."

"I'm okay," Karma's voice was a bare wisp.

Hammer raised his eyebrows at her. A small flicker of defiance ignited somewhere deep inside of Karma Twin.

"I'm with you, Hammer. I'm fucking here, alright?"

Hammer leaned in and hugged her. "Glad you rejoined us."

Karma looked away. Hammer returned to his haunches and spoke. "Okay. We have no idea what happened back there, right?"

Karma grunted. Galore stayed quiet. Hammer sighed. "Okay, we know what happened, but we don't know the results, alright? The only thing we're certain of is Lucy told us to get to Bluff 70, and she seemed to have at least some idea what was going on."

Hammer leaned his head back and exhaled towards the treetops. "If everyone back there is gone, we'll need everyone we can to join us. If we all go together, we will miss two of the secret passages."

"You're suggesting we should split up," Galore stated.

"Yes, I am. We'll need to ask any and every one we meet to follow us. Hat, Bone, Skull, free one, it doesn't matter, but stay clear of any of those fuckers in black. Don't tell anybody where we're going, either, because we can't trust anyone. We should be able to tell by their eyes if they're as stunned as we are. If they're shocked, they probably aren't on the bad guys."

"Probably?" Galore raised his eyebrows.

"Do you have something better to go on?" Hammer Coolie stared hard at Galore.

"What if they've already infiltrated the secret passages?" Karma Twin interrupted the stare down.

"Then we lead them away from Bluff 70, which is why we don't speak of where we're going. If all is clear, then head for Bluff 70. If you're followed, lead them away. If all goes right, we'll meet in less than a day."

All three stood. Nobody had a preference for which passage they wanted to take as all three knew these mazes like the back of their hands. Hammer dispersed the directions each would go, taking the most difficult route for himself. The three of them strode into the water. Just before they separated, Hammer spoke one last time.

"Remember, if caught or followed, lead them away from Bluff 70. If someone doesn't show there by tomorrow morning, nobody can go search for the missing one, alright? Swear."

Hammer Coolie put his fist in the middle. Karma Twin reached out and touched hers to Hammer. After a moment's hesitation, Galore did the same. Hammer nodded at them.

"See you tomorrow."

The trio swam off in separate directions.

39

"Wow, that was stupid crazy," the similar aged but very different girl Jacy was hoping for said. "Why are you rock climbing? And why…"

The girl paused, frowning as she looked around. "Wait a minute, where…what…where…" Jacy patted the girl's knee as she stood and went to the edge. Sure enough, her javelin coach was still standing on the stairs.

"Atta girl!" he yelled, waving his hat. "I knew you could do it!"

"Thank you so much for your help!" Jacy called down, waving. "Enjoy the rest of your journey."

"And good luck to you. I hope you find who you are looking for," her coach made his way down the stairs. Jacy watched him until he was at the bottom. The stairs were completely gone. He waved as he backed away from the cliff.

"Wow, how did he get down there?" Jacy didn't realize the girl was now at her side. Jacy started to tell her, but then stopped. Who knew how much she was tossing around the natural order of things just by being here?

"You'll figure it out, hon," Jacy stepped away from the edge and sat down on a rock. She did a quick survey of her wounds. It wasn't too bad, mostly surface scratches, minor cuts, and bruises. The girl continued to take in the view as Jacy wondered what to do next.

A splashing sound from below interrupted her thoughts. The girl looked towards the sound and eyed Jacy. Jacy looked away. The girl shrugged and walked to the half wall where she could see down to the pool. She called down. Jacy heard a male's voice respond.

Shit. That's definitely not Derian. Jacy put her hands on her knees, stared at the ground, and took three deep breaths, one longer than the previous one. She slowly felt her anxiety slow to a gentle rumble.

Jacy looked over at the girl who giggled at something the guy in the pool said. Fuck. What if she missed Derian? Her daughter could be anywhere. Jacy continued to watch the girl.

"Hey, mister, what's your name?"

Jacy couldn't hear the reply.

"Nice to meet you, Stan. Just head to the stairs to your right and come on up. Watch out for the first few stairs, though, they're slippery. I don't want you to slip and break a leg or something."

Jacy's eyebrows furrowed as she watched the girl return to the ledge. Something she said struck a chord on her memory guitar. Stan…. stairs…. slippery…. break…

Jacy's eyes widened. Break! That was it. Her mind whirled in reverse to a conversation her and Baz had about entering the Game.

"I'm going to hold you to your promise that you'll never do something as stupid as enter the Game, Jacy."

"And I won't," Jacy insisted. "We're just talking hypotheticals here, Baz. You think I want to end up a Grass Counter, forever and ever, amen?"

"Well," Baz shook his head. "The trick is to not let them break the surface of the pool. Once they do, they can never go back."

Jacy's eyes widened at the memory. She dashed for the stairs that led to the pool.

40

Karma Twin sat on the mossy rock that was Bluff 70, staring at both caves where Hammer Coolie and Galore would exit when they arrived. Karma and her motley group straggled out of their cavern onto Bluff 70 about an hour ago. The trek was arduous to say the least, but she and twelve others stumbled into the rising sunlight to join Lucy and twenty-three others. Karma glanced over at Lucy and Joey, hugging each other in silence. They waited for their friend Dickie, who had yet to surface.

Karma noticed a few familiar faces when she looked around the bluff. Bait Tambit and Chainsaw Helms, a couple of the more harmless Skulls were picked up by Lucy and Joey's party. Karma Twin herself came across a bleeding Walleyed Disdain and a dazed Lohorn Jive, two Bones she recollected in a vague way.

The only other person of her group that she knew surprised the shit out of her when they came across him. The Bam Slicer, battered and wheezing, lurched upon them from behind less than a quarter way into their journey. Karma gave the lead to Lohorn and went back to talk to Bam.

"What happened?" she asked.

"I have no fucking idea," blood spilled from Bam's broken mouth as he spoke. "One second that fucking Lita shows up on Flair's side, the next the place was a battlefield."

"How'd you escape?"

The Bam Slicer spat a glob of bloody phlegm on the cavern floor. "Pure luck. When I left the Gaming Area I met up with Onerous Dray and Rotten Jaws. By then I realized whatever was happening was way bigger than we could handle. I followed them, almost making it to the bush when we were attacked by a group of people, all in black."

The Bam Slicer shook his head, wiping the blood on his lips with the back of his hand. "They were fucking ferocious. Onerous Dray and Rotten Jaws can hold their own, and I'm pretty tough, but Jesus. I barely made it out of there."

"Where are Onerous Dray and Rotten Jaws?" Karma asked.

"I don't know," The Bam Slicer looked mystified. "I think they might be dead, but how can that be? I…. fuck…. I…."

Karma Twin shook her head at the memory. She looked over at The Bam Slicer, staring off at the valley below.

"People are coming!" someone called out. Karma Twin looked towards the two cave entrances, standing when she saw Galore emerge.

"Galore!" she called out, rushing down towards him. Galore ran to her.

"Sultana?" he wheezed, out of breath. He swore when Karma Twin looked away.

"Trichina Flame?" Karma asked. Galore's look softened before he shook his head. Karma Twin kept silent, struggling to keep her mind together. She came too close being broken earlier, before they split up and entered the caves. She wasn't going to allow that to happen again.

"How many of you made it?" Lucy was now at Karma's side, looking at Galore. Joey searched the newcomers, swearing when he discovered Dickie wasn't among them.

"38, including me," Galore looked back at the people still emerging from the cave. "Some of them are pretty banged up."

"We'll get people to help them," Lucy looked at Joey who nodded, leaving to get help for the wounded. "Good work, Galore. I'm glad you made it. We'll be leaving soon."

"What?" Karma Twin blurted out. "We can't leave. We have to wait for Hammer Coolie."

"Hammer's not here, yet?" Galore looked at Karma Twin. "Damn it."

"Why are we leaving?" Karma ignored his question and looked at Lucy. "Why can't we stay here?"

"Because it's not safe," Lucy sighed. "This was never meant to be our refuge. We picked here so we could make sure we weren't being followed. It won't take long for them to check this place out.

We'll leave clues that we were here so hopefully they'll focus on the surrounding areas. We'll be far away by then, though."

"Where are we going?" Galore asked.

Lucy shook her head. "Nobody except Joey and I know that. We can't afford to let it out. There could be spies within us, even now."

Karma looked at the ragtag bunch of dazed refugees milling about. If there was a spy, they were damn good.

"We will wait as long as we can for Dickie and Hammer Coolie," Lucy said to Jacy.

Karma Twin knew Lucy was right, but her heart still hurt. "He made us promise not to come looking for him if he was late. He said if any of us knew we were being followed to lead them away from Bluff 70." Karma watched the last of Galore's group emerge from the cave.

"That sounds like Hammer," Lucy put her hand on Karma Twin's shoulder and squeezed. "He's a good man. Now, let's tend to the wounded, and hope he arrives before we have to leave."

Karma Twin nodded as Lucy left. Just then a familiar looking figure stepped from the cave. "Jesus, Galore, that's..."

Galore was already on his way to the figure. "I forgot to mention her. She's carrying two of our heavily wounded."

Karma Twin didn't know there would be a time when she was so happy to see Neva Tezremsy. Neva carried two bodies, one flopped over each of her massive shoulders. Neva wore the same bewildered look everyone on Bluff 70 wore. Karma followed Galore who was taking one of the bodies off Neva when she arrived to assist him.

"Karma Twin?" Neva's voice was smashed.

"Hello Neva, I'm glad you made it out," Karma answered. Galore and Karma laid the man down on his back. He was barely breathing. Galore called to some nearby volunteers carrying a crude stretcher, who bee-lined over to them. Karma Twin stood and stepped over the injured man to help Neva with the other person she carried.

"Is Gravigo here?" Neva asked.

"No. I'm sorry."

Neva looked too ruined to cry, but a tear escaped her left eye anyway. It squiggled down her bloodied and dirt smudged face. "What happened back there?"

"I don't know, yet," Karma grabbed the person's dangling right arm. "I have a feeling Lucy may know, though. Let's get this one some help first."

Neva hoisted the woman off her shoulder. She and Karma Twin lowered the wounded woman to the ground. Karma Twin gasped in shock.

"Lita," she whispered, looking down at the disfigured face of her one-time friend and lover.

"I know what she did to Jacy," Neva whispered, "but I couldn't just leave her there. The things those monsters in black were doing to people…I…. I…. I had to do something." Neva's voice trailed off, and the colossal woman shivered. Karma sought out another couple of volunteers with a stretcher. She called them over and they moved Lita onto it.

"Where was Flair?" Karma asked.

"I don't know," Neva answered. "Trichina?"

Karma shook her head and looked away. Neva choked in a sob.

Karma Twin led Neva over to where she was sitting before. She handed Neva a bottle of water. Neva drank and washed her face as best she could. Galore joined them and the trio sat in silence until Joey approached them.

"We have to go," he spoke in a somber tone. "I'm sorry, but it's not safe here. We need to move on."

All three nodded in agreement, stood, and followed Joey. Karma Twin was the last to leave, walking backwards, staring at the entrance Hammer Coolie was supposed to stride out of. That never happened, though. All 73 survivors left Bluff 70.

41

Jacy willed herself not to race down to the pool like a crazed banshee. After blazing past a startled and naked Stan, Jacy made it to the edge of the pool. She stared into the water, wondering what her next move should be.

"Ah," movement below spooked Jacy, but only for a moment as a bunch of dark dread locks came into view. The 30 something year old male broke the surface with a confused look.

"Hey!" Stan called down from above. Jacy scooted over as close to the wall as she could. She didn't want to disrupt what was happening here, and she needed to gather her thoughts on what to do next.

The newest human boosted himself out of the water, and with a curious glance at Jacy, headed up the stairs. Jacy let out a long breath and focussed on the pool again. The next person was a balding man in his fifties.

On and on it went. People broke the surface, exchanged names with their predecessor above, and the chain moved along. Jacy was patient, but her worries were growing that Derian was already gone.

Jacy shook her head and sighed. What a bizarre time and place she was in. Here she was, about to meet her daughter for the first time. And the only reason she was meeting Derian was because Derian was dead. Or nearly dead. What the fuck?

Jacy let out another long breath. To top it all off, she couldn't allow Derian to break the surface of the pool. How was she going to…?

Jacy sensed her rather than heard her. Looking down, through the clear water, Jacy looked at Derian who stared up at her. Jacy's heart ground to a halt as an exquisite smile appeared on Derian's face. Derian moved as if to swim to the surface.

"No!" Jacy spoke aloud. Derian couldn't hear her that way, but she obeyed anyways.

Mom?

Jacy smiled, a tear escaping her eye. She didn't reach up to wipe it away.

Derian, my daughter. My love.

Derian remained motionless, maybe ten feet from the surface of the pool. Another female, roughly the same age as Derian swam from below and stopped beside her. Derian and the girl gawked at each other.

Let her ahead of you, Derian. We have much to talk about.

Derian looked up at Jacy, then back to the girl. Derian nodded, and the smiling girl rose and broke the surface of the pool. Jacy never acknowledged the girl as she passed by. She wouldn't tear her gaze from her daughter.

You can't break the surface of this pool, baby. If you do, you can never go back.

Derian's brow furrowed. *Back? Back to what?*

Jacy smiled at her. Back to Earth. Back to life.

I don't understand.

Jacy paused, taking a deep breath. This could take a while, but knowing that time was a fluid concept here, she knew the time here wouldn't affect Derian's chances of survival back on Earth.

As long as she didn't break the pool's surface, of course.

Jacy started with her death and Derian's birth to this moment, leaving nothing out. Derian listened and stared and stared and listened. She gestured newcomers to pass by, never moving her gaze from her mother. After the story, Derian looked at Jacy with regretful joy.

I've missed you, Mom.

Jacy's breath caught in her throat. More tears fell.

I've missed you, too, hon.

Jacy and Derian observed one another for a long time. Nothing was said in this wordless time, yet everything was said, too. Jacy finally said what she needed to say.

You've got to go back, Derian.

I just met you, Mom. I don't want to go back.

Tears squished from Jacy's eyes. Oh, baby, I know how this must all seem unfair. But you need to go back. Life on earth can never be traded for anything else. Please believe me in that. Go home. Go back to your husband.

Do you like Roots?

Jacy chuckled. I love him, and he loves you.

Derian grinned. Maybe I'll keep him.

You should.

Derian nodded as she waved a little girl through. Derian watched her pass by before looking back at Jacy.

I don't want you to leave me again. I will be broken forever.

I'm not leaving you. This time you are leaving me. And this time, it's…it's… More tears ran down Jacy's cheeks.

This time it's the right thing to do.

Derian looked like a lost little girl.

But…

Jacy put a finger to her lips.

There are no buts.

Jacy knelt, reaching into the water as far as she could reach. Derian arose, her hand reaching for Jacy. Their fingers touched, then intertwined.

Please watch over us, Mom. Take care of us.

Jacy spilled silent tears as she listened to her daughter's whisperings. Derian took Jacy's hand and rubbed it against her cheek. Jacy's quiet tears grew in volume.

I love you, Mommy.

I…. I… Jacy could barely breathe. I love you with everything I have.

Derian looked at Jacy for a long time before letting go of her mom's hand. Derian dove downwards, and Jacy collapsed to the ground. Jacy remained like that until four people dressed in black came and led her away.

Epilogue

4,546, 4,547, 4,548, 4,549…

So is Jacy's new life as a Grass Counter, not quite five thousand blades of grass in. *Life*. That seems a strange word for Jacy.

Life is what her daughter has. Her husband has life, too, though technically he isn't only her husband anymore. He is another person's husband, too.

Jacy's unsure who else has life around here. Some, like Flair and Sultana Yelp are prisoners. Others like Gravigo, Neva Tezremsy, Lita, The Bam Slicer… many others, as well, all gone. Too many unaccounted for; too many bulging the newly constructed prison walls.

4,550. 4,551. 4,552…

Jacy and Baz hear some horrific tales emanating from the demolished Gaming building and strange stories of people dying. The Grand Fountain was destroyed, as well, replaced by a statue of a younger Granny Mandible. Granny returned to her younger years, and also went back to her original name, Mother Atlas. She, Fatter Verb, and Tosiri Octavio run this place, now. Jacy hears awful rumours about Maise Elantina, but, for now, Jacy refuses to believe the innuendo.

Jacy sighs, gawping across the field at the other Grass Counters. Baz estimates barely a quarter of them are left. Some escaped, others were caught, some just plain vanished. Buzzed Rottid is missing. So is Baz's friend, Ugly Earful.

4,553. 4,554. 4,555…

Jacy looks over at her dear friend. Because half of the fields were blown up, Mother Atlas made all Grass Counters start at the beginning again. There is low outrage amongst the Grass Counters about this decision. Jacy guesses that most are just happy just to be alive.

Everything is too new for Jacy to get a grasp on how she feels about what happened the day Derian was almost killed. There are *so* many tales and speculation and conspiracies floating around, that Jacy decides to focus on her new career of Grass Counting until everything shakes itself out. Everything will come out eventually, Jacy is positive of that. The truth always reveals itself. Of course, whether people choose to believe the truth or not is an entirely different set of steak knives, but Jacy has to hold onto something.

The hardest part right now for Jacy is that she doesn't know what is happening with Derian. She knows Derian is still alive, at least. Baz retained a semblance of his pipe of information and managed to discover Derian's fate.

But what did her life look like? What did any human's life look like now?

Jacy sighs and returns her attention to her task at hand.

4,556. 4,557. 4,558…

"So, Jacy," Baz's voice breaks her concentration. "Was everything you did worth it so you could become a Grass Counter for all of eternity?"

Jacy pinches the last piece of grass she counted between her left thumb and fore finger. She studies Baz for a moment. What is she supposed to say to that? What is the true answer to that question? That her daughter's brief time on Earth was or wasn't worth the fact that Jacy would be counting billions of blades of grass, one at a time, for all eternity? Jacy looks out at the endless fields ahead of them before she looks again at Baz.

"Well, Baz," Jacy wears a sad smile. "A good friend of mine once told me that forever is a long time."

Baz nods, chuckling softly. Jacy returns to her counting.

4,559. 4,560. 4,561…

Acknowledgments

This has been such an amazing journey, and I would like to thank some people for their help along the way.

Thanks to my wife Lisa and daughter Liliana for allowing me to pound out words on this laptop. I know it takes too much time away from the two of you, but I do my best to find the right balance. Also a shout out to the rest of the Virtanens and the Rodgers clan, as well. I'm sure you're all bored to tears with my writing tales. Thanks for putting up with me.

Ivy Copp, you have been incredible. Not only for your editing tips and story line advice, but you are an inspiration to me because of your own journey you are on. Codie Good, thanks for your insight, too. (Special gratitude for certain advice of yours that has now become a major story arc in book 2). Nowick Gray and Hyperedits, thank you, thank you, thank you. There was way more to this than I ever imagined, and your helpful hand along the way made an arduous trail much easier.

Last in my thanks but first in my heart, thank you, dear reader. If not for you reading this right now, this story would be just a bunch of fun but goofy characters running around in my head. They are now alive and out there. I hope you enjoyed this one enough to give the rest of the series a shot.

Jeff Virtanen
March 27, 2016

Connect with the Author

Twitter – twitter.com/jlvirtanen

Facebook – facebook.com/jlvirtanen

Email – jlvirtanen@outlook.com